JUST A
TEACHER

JUST A TEACHER

Michael Fillerup and Jim David

Soulstice
STORIES

looking *west* • Flagstaff, AZ

Just a Teacher

ISBN 978-1-7331887-5-3 (paperback)
ISBN 978-1-7331887-6-0 (e-book)
Library of Congress Control Number: 2020907637

Design by Mary Williams
Proofreading by Claudine Taillac
Back cover illustration by Joan McKee

Soulstice Stories
An imprint of Soulstice Publishing, LLC
PO Box 791
Flagstaff, AZ 86002
(928) 814-8943
connect@soulsticepublishing.com
www.soulsticepublishing.com

10 9 8 7 6 5 4 3 2 1

Children are the living messages we send
to a time we will not see.

–Neil Postman

Dear Reader,

At first it was simply fatigue. I was tired of hearing about the abysmal state of public education in America. I was tired of clickbait stories about sleazy teachers sleeping with their students when I knew that for every one of them, there were a hundred thousand other teachers who had stayed up past midnight prepping tomorrow's lesson. I was tired of the way legislators sucked the joy out of teaching with punitive policies and obsession with test scores. And I was tired of self-righteous politicians taking cheap shots at public education to leverage votes. But none of that was new, so I changed the channel and life went on.

Then on April 26, 2018, the mouse roared, the lion roared back, and I got angry. On that day, 40,000 teachers and teacher advocates donned red T-shirts and marched on the Arizona State Capitol. They were protesting low teacher wages and penurious levels of funding for public education. It marked the beginning of a six-day strike during which more than a hundred school districts and charter schools had to shut down because there were no teachers for their students.

While many people voiced support, others were critical or viciously delusional. They called the teachers selfish, self-serving, and inconsiderate. They complained because the strike might complicate upcoming graduation or vacation plans. But the ultimate insult was hurled by a state legislator who accused teachers of using children as hostages to extort more hard-earned tax dollars from the good citizens of the Grand Canyon State. She even urged parents "inconvenienced" by the strike to file lawsuits against their children's teachers.

That's when I quit switching channels and hurled the remote at the TV. Teachers selfish? Teachers using kids as hostages? Teachers inconveniencing parents? Seriously? Now you can say a lot of negative things about teachers. Yes, we whine about rotten pay and lack of resources. We complain about misperceptions surrounding our profession and the lack of respect that come along with them. Some of us punch in at eight, punch out at three, and pick up a paycheck every other Friday when what we really should do is get out of the damn business. But that's not the majority. Not even close. And when a legislator—someone with a sworn duty to protect the public interest—makes a malicious statement about the character and motivation of teachers, I get angry. I throw things like the TV remote. In this case, I decided to write a book instead.

I started writing in anger, with smoke blowing out both nostrils. But halfway through the first chapter, I realized that the last thing the world needed was another rant about overcrowded classrooms, meager pay, plummeting test scores (and excuses for them), crumbling facilities, and the covert (now overt) movement to destroy public education as we know it.

I took a step back and tried to view the whole morass more objectively. It seemed that all the hot-button issues surrounding education could be distilled down to one variable: teachers. A school can have prizewinning programs, a sublime mission statement, a cutting-edge curriculum, and state-of-the-art technology, but that's just fancy packaging if a child gets stuck with a humdrum teacher. Conversely, the curriculum can be prehistoric, the roof can leak, the principal can look like Big Foot, but if a kid has a great teacher, that kid will get a great education. Because when you're a teacher, the classroom is your domain. It's your kingdom, your turf, your home-away-from-home. The rest of the planet can be going to hell in a handbasket—banks can collapse, presidents can resign, the football team can go winless—you'll still control the world inside those four walls. It's all on you. If it's a war zone, that's your fault. If it's feeding time at the zoo, that's your fault. If it's Valium Valley, that's your fault. And if it's that electrifying place your students can't wait to enter every day, pat yourself on the back and keep up the good work, because that's your fault too.

So instead of pontificating about issues, I decided to invite you, dear reader, to walk (and sometimes skip, other times stagger) in the shoes of a public-school teacher, not just for a day or a week but over the course of a career. I wanted to give you a glimpse into the heart, mind, and soul of a teacher. So I decided to tell my story.

I'm a retired educator—twenty-seven years as a teacher and eight years as a teacher trainer. Most of my story takes place in a small mountain town on the fringes of the Navajo Reservation in northern Arizona, but it could be anywhere—New York or New Delhi, Cairo or Copenhagen. Good teaching has no borders. And I tried my best to be a good teacher.

As I began writing, anger gave way to introspection; fury was usurped by humility; revenge by awe. I soon found myself confronting old demons, and the straightforward narrative I'd outlined took multiple detours filled with soul-searching booby traps and ambushes. My memoir became part mystery, part romance, part confessional and, if you read between the lines, part teacher-training manual.

This is my story, yet I feel that it belongs to anyone who teaches. We share similar challenges, frustrations, anxieties, triumphs, failures, and pygmy pay-checks. We have private lives filled with chaos and joy and heartbreak. We have spouses, lovers, meltdowns. We shower communally at the local athletic club, where our students see us buck naked and gasp. We marry and have children of our own, and some of them become rocket scientists and others steal hubcaps. We get sick and we get divorced. We lose our homes and our jobs and our minds and our manners. And we sometimes have to make heart-wrenching decisions that could get us fired or thrown in jail or both.

But there's one constant: regardless of how we're feeling personally, we some-how always get our act together and make it to class (or, minimally, we get a sub). Because regardless of what's going on in our private universe, come eight o'clock Monday morning, our kids will be waiting for us to unlock the door and transform those four ordinary walls into either the Magic Kingdom or the daily House of Horrors. It's all on us. For twenty-seven years, it was all on me: the teacher.

Todd Hunter
March 2020

A DANGEROUS BUSINESS

It's not like *Mr. Holland's Opus*, I'll tell you that. The school nurse or the secretary or some fairy godmother doesn't magically appear in your classroom and whisk you away to an auditorium where—ta da!—an army of former students has secretly gathered to sing your praises. They're parents and grandparents now, and some great-grandparents too; doctors, lawyers, realtors, used car salesmen, a congressman, a best-selling author. They're all on their feet, smiling and applauding as you enter. It's a standing ovation for the one-and-only you!

There's cake, too, and a band, and dancing and gifts—lots of gifts. There are tears and tributes, and for two hours, you're King of the World! As one student after another steps up to the mic to share an amusing anecdote or a life-changing epiphany, all inspired by you, it's almost too much, too sweet, like a triple-dark-chocolate dessert.

At that moment, you're thinking it was all worth it—hectic days herding teenagers in and out of class, rotten pay, and long nights grading papers and prepping lessons, conjuring up creative ways to make the otherwise kill-me-now worlds of math and science more than mandatory hoops for young people to jump through, just to earn a framed sheet of paper and a tassel on a goofy-looking mortarboard. Appreciation. Validation. Vindication. Legacy. Love. Gazing out at the adulating throng, you feel so damn happy you think your heart's going to explode right there on the stage.

*　*　*

Maybe in Hollywood. Maybe for a fortunate few. But for most of us, it goes like this: you grab your valise or book bag or backpack and step quietly through your classroom doorway, pulling the door shut behind you. Then, with a curt tug on the knob and a twist of the key—click!—you're done.

It's a perfunctory act I'd performed thousands of times at the end of a daily ritual that included a morning cup of coffee (black, straight), the Pledge of Allegiance (speaking of perfunctory) followed by a moment of silence, first-period announcements crackling over the intercom, hall passes scribbled out in the frenzied scrawl of a family doctor, hall or lunchroom or parking lot duty, a brown-bag lunch wolfed down in the faculty lounge, and back to class for round two until the final bell at three p.m.

Except today's different. Instead of hot-footing it down the carpeted hall and slipping out the rear exit, I pause for a moment, waiting, although for what, I'm not quite sure. A pat on the back? An announcement over the loudspeaker? Fireworks? A biplane dragging a congratulatory banner across the sky: THANKS FOR EVERYTHING MR HUNTER U R THE BEST!!!? Maybe I'm still secretly hoping that fairy godmother will carry me off to Neverland.

It's the last of the last, so I'm thinking I ought to feel something more than this empty stupor. Thirty-five years and I got a paperweight (a polished chunk of petrified wood purchased at a discount rock shop in Holbrook, Arizona) and a certificate of thanks signed by a superintendent who threw me under the bus when money got tight. From the Arizona State Retirement System, I'll receive a little less than $3,000 a month. Those are the tangibles.

Yesterday, I boxed up my personal belongings and loaded them into my battered, brown-on-beige pickup truck—the animal skins and skeletons, the stuffed javelina my students christened "Wilbur," the antique microscope my father gave me on my twelfth birthday, old college biology and chemistry texts, and cardboard boxes stuffed with lesson plans, pop quizzes, and activity sheets.

The students are gone as well. At the last bell (a soft, sedating, New Age chime), they fled for the summer, putting as much distance as possible between themselves and the massive two-story, gray stone monstrosity they called "The Pen," short for "The Penitentiary," although if it bore any resemblance to a prison, it was a white-collar, country-club model.

I had no gripes about the facility. Though a bit old, it was clean and well-maintained. And unlike those newer, claustrophobic schools that seem to box students in and keep nature out, my classroom had picture windows that compelled my kids to ogle the black storm clouds that mushroomed above the mountains on autumn afternoons. Add a dash of lightning and thunder and it looked and sounded downright apocalyptic, Wagner in the pines. The walls shook and the windows rattled while angry pitchforks skewered the sky. It used to scare the snot out of them. There was nothing quite like it to set the stage for a lesson on tectonic shifts.

Trudging down the narrow stairwell—two abbreviated flights—I feel as if I'm already fading to irrelevance. It's a bizarre sensation, like I'm starring in a slow-motion horror flick in which little patches of me disappear with each step. There goes a finger! And another! The whole damn hand! A foot! An ear! My chest! At this rate, by the time I reach Brubaker's office, there'll be nothing left of me except my classroom keys dangling in thin air.

It's a short walk to the finish line, a hundred yards if that, but today it seems like a thousand miles, or the twinkling of an eye.

The goodbyes are over. Group kudos have been offered to us retirees at half a dozen functions, one of which I attended. The other teachers have left except for Lisa Marguiles, an eternally energetic grandmother, steering a media cart toward the library, and Scott Danbury, the remedial reading teacher, an unsung hero if ever there was one. Danbury is ceremoniously ripping an R.E.M. poster from his classroom door. I'm tempted to slip by unnoticed, but manners get the best of me.

"Have a good summer, Scott!"

Without diverting his attention, Danbury replies, "Hey, you bet! Same to you, man."

I walk on, and my mind begins to drift. Amy used to say I'm about as sentimental as an anvil, but halfway down the hall I pause, close my eyes, and listen to the silence I used to savor early each morning, before the yellow buses rolled up and the pickup trucks and conglomerate clunkers jockeyed into the parking lot, delivering the daily exodus of loud, howling, strutting, guffawing, heartbroken, drug-running, laughing, loitering teenagers. The calm before the storm. Except today the silence is both soothing and spooky, like a graveyard.

Listening more closely, I hear echoes from the nineties, my final full decade in the classroom: early arrivals gathering in packs in the halls and on the floor, flirting at the lockers or finishing up homework; goths strolling the halls like Death's angels in their black trench coats and pale, vampire faces; jocks flexing their muscles in their letterman jackets and valley girls flaunting their budding sexuality; baggers in clown pants and stoners with spiked dog collars and shaved sidewalls.

It's a brief indulgence, forbidding rather than inviting reminiscence. That will come later, during what in June had always promised to be an interminable summer but, come August, seemed a heartbeat, another tick in time. I'm delaying the obvious, knowing that once I invite in one memory, the whole dysfunctional family will follow. I'll become irrationally teary-eyed and may even end up sobbing as I hand Brubaker my keys. And I can't have that—Robert Brubaker getting the last laugh.

Bob Garcia, the custodian, is whistling a big band tune as he wheels his portable trash can into Mary Walker's classroom. The Arizona Diamondbacks game crackles on the transistor radio strapped to the can.

I rap lightly on the door. "*Hasta luego, Roberto! Mucho trabajo, poco dinero!*" I say, expending 75 percent of my Spanish vocabulary.

Bob pokes his head out and flashes me a gritty, mustachioed smile. "*Sí, señor! Mucho trabajo, poco dinero. Claro que sí! Vaya con dios!*"

I'm not sure if Bob remembers that this *adios* is for good.

*   *   *

I continue down the hall, trying to sort out my feelings even as I stiff-arm them. My last day. The end. Done. Finished. Through. *No más.* Unlike many of my retiring colleagues, I'm not going to add my name to the substitute teacher list to keep my foot in the door. Nor am I going to teach nineteen hours a week, the maximum allowed without jeopardizing my pension. However tempting, I'm not going to sit out a year and then return to the classroom to double-dip. No, I'm going to rip the Band-Aid off with one swift, masochistic yank and walk away for good. That's the plan.

But first, I have to get out of the damn building, and today I'm stuck in quicksand.

Moseying on, I begin counting: thirty-five years times 180 days equals 6,360 days equals 47,250 hours equals 2.8 million minutes. Seven thousand students taught. Three hundred and ninety thousand papers graded. One thousand, two hundred and sixty faculty meetings attended. Eighty-nine thousand, four hundred and ninety-one dollars spent out of pocket for classroom supplies.

Trivia. I'm not an accountant, I'm a teacher. And a good one.

Then why am I suddenly being accosted by my own insignificance?

Within the silence, I hear the baritone voice of Joe Garfield, the speech and drama teacher whose impromptu Shakespearean parodies thundered so loudly down the halls that the other English teachers banished him to the science wing. I picture him now, booming like a prophet in the wilderness: "Life is a tale told by an idiot, signifying nothing! Nothing! Nothing!"

Was Mr. Shakespeare via Joe Garfield speaking to me personally, or to my profession generally?

My conscience protests. Say it ain't so, Joe!

Deep down in my bones, I know it ain't—I really do! Then why this mishmash of emotions? What, exactly, am I feeling? Relieved? Liberated? Overwhelmed by the eternal ripples I've created in the great sea of Time: the thousands of youngsters I've taught to be cunning fishermen so they can now fish for themselves? Am I blissfully marinating in every platitude of my profession? Have I touched the future, opened hearts and minds, changed the world? Or that queen bee of clichés: have I made a difference? (Doesn't everyone make a difference, in one way or another? If you rob a bank, you make a difference; if you blow up a bridge, you make a difference. Any act, good or bad, makes a difference. Albert Camus might argue that even doing nothing makes a difference, in the same way that no decision is a decision.)

So now I'm thinking about that chart in the foyer of the elementary school, that more innocent and hopeful sanctuary for young learners. *How are you feeling today?* it asks, displaying an array of cartoon faces with captions: Happy, Sad, Angry, Frustrated, etc. Which face am I feeling right now, frozen halfway between the classroom I just locked up for the last time and Brubaker's interrogation chamber? And which face was I feeling a week ago Saturday when I met Fitz for breakfast at Keri's Cafe? He said I looked distracted and worried about something. Not scared, really, but not quite centered, either. He had a point. There were long lapses in the conversation as I fiddled with the tiny bag of pseudo-sugar, my gaze wandering to and from the front window as tourists and town folk strolled by.

"Are you OK?" Fitz asked.

I cut off a corner of my California Special, stabbed it with my fork, and inserted it into my mouth, chewing slowly and deliberately, as if it were my last meal. I swallowed—finally—then spoke:

"You know, my sister taught in the same elementary school for forty-one years, mostly first grade. The day she turned in her keys, the principal invited her into his office, sat her down, and spent half an hour thanking her for all she'd done for the kids and the school and the community. Then he reached behind his desk and gave her a crystal vase with two dozen roses and a $50 gift card to Olive Garden."

I took three more laborious bites as Fitz waited for a punch line that never arrived.

"And?" he prodded.

"I'll probably get a swift kick in my hindquarters on my way out the door. Brubaker will probably bust open a bottle of champagne after I check out."

"So you want validation—is that what you're saying? You want roses?"

I laughed—a good sign, I think. "No, I don't want roses—not from Brubaker, anyway. You want to know what I'm feeling?"

Fitz placed his cupped hands on the table and said, in his best Frasier Crane imitation, "I'm listening."

I laughed again, but there was no nonsense in my voice when I replied: "I feel like a World War II bomber pilot who just made his final run. I feel like I finished my last mission and barely escaped with my ass."

*   *   *

Twenty yards from Brubaker's office, I slip into the library and briefly chat with Lisa Marguiles, who is fussing with extension cords in the AV room, uncoiling and recoiling them. I ask about her summer plans. She's going on a cruise to the Greek islands with her new husband.

"Lucky number four," she says. "I hope this one lasts longer than number three!"

When I say this is my last day, she looks surprised, even shocked, but not half as much as me. Didn't everyone on the planet know I was riding off into the sunset? And won't every last one of them miss my big, gregarious presence?

Sorry, she says without saying a word. This is just another end-of-the-school-year day for us. We're coming back; you're not.

*   *   *

I trudge on, wondering why I wish I was walking backward. I remind myself these feelings will dissipate—maybe not today or tomorrow, but certainly by late summer, when my former colleagues will be brushing off the dust and dragging themselves to the back-to-school festivities while I loiter at home.

No. Not home. Anywhere but home. Every retired teacher I've spoken to agrees on this one piece of advice: get out of Dodge on opening day and go as far away as you can. Because everyone and everything here will remind you of who you were and where you used to be on Monday morning the third week in August: the sea of yellow wildflowers that seemed to blossom overnight as if to announce summer's end; youth soccer games proliferating on every patch of grass; radio announcements promoting the county fair; bow-hunters in camo gear scoping out the woods; school buses bellowing like big, determined beasts as they make their practice runs around town; moms crowding the aisles at Walmart like frenzied survivalists (except instead of MREs and water purification tablets, they load their carts with spiral notebooks, gel pens, and loose-leaf binders).

And the kids. Children and teenagers are everywhere, at Harkins Theatres and the mall and the ice rink and the ball fields. Leave, my predecessors warned. Go someplace as disconnected from school as you can imagine. Do whatever it takes to numb the pain of no longer being part of that little world that was defined as much by seasons as semesters and pep rallies as report cards.

So, I'll go bow-hunting. Two weeks on the North Kaibab. Have deer permit, will travel. And when nostalgia rears its weepy head, I'll remind myself of the things I absolutely will not miss, like the superintendent's annual Welcome Back Bash, where local dignitaries take self-promoting bows and a flamboyant guest speaker from New York or LA rallies the troops with a General Patton kick-ass speech—booster shots in both arms that always leave the teachers (the grunts, the warriors in the trenches—which begs the question: why is our kinder, gentler profession so rife with war metaphors?) flying high until they receive their first paycheck after a long, dry summer. Because this was the real metaphor for our profession: paycheck as reality check. Every two weeks, it was a sobering reminder of the true market value of a teacher in a bread-and-circus culture, reinforced whenever we read a morning headline like "LeBron James holds out for $300 million."

Monetarily speaking, it's a thankless job, fraught with unexpected dangers. Except you don't get a billy club or a revolver or a bulletproof vest; you don't get a helmet and shoulder pads or a license to kill or even to defend yourself. No, you're not in harm's way on a daily basis—not like a combat soldier or a police officer. It's not the physical violence, although there's always the potential for some lunatic to sneak onto campus and shoot up the place. What you're dealing with, day in and day out, is something more subtle and, in many ways, more dangerous.

*   *   *

Brubaker remains glued to his cushioned swivel chair when I enter the office, his nose buried in a fan of documents, as if he were playing poker with giant cards. I hand him my keys. He nods. No handshake, no smile. Just his grim, grandpa frown. For a moment I think he's on the verge of saying something, so I hesitate, waiting for my red rose moment, but his iron jaw remains locked. I briefly consider throwing the last punch, slinging the final word, but why bother? In another thirty seconds, I'll be gone, and Robert Brubaker will be like the memory of a bad meal at an overpriced restaurant: annoying but insignificant, nothing to lose sleep over.

Apparently, Brubaker's the one who can't resist landing the final blow. My fingers are on the doorknob when he plays his hand: a royal straight flush. "By the way," he says, "they're reopening the Abernathy case."

Against my better judgment, I look back. "Abernathy? That thing's as cold as Antarctica."

"I guess they've found some new evidence—DNA stuff." Brubaker smiles meanly. "Just thought I'd give you a heads up—as a professional courtesy."

"Thanks," I say, "for the professional courtesy."

"You may be hearing from Captain Walters."

I answer with a shrug. "So what's new? Déjà vu all over again."

I twist the knob, saunter through the abandoned foyer, and stride down the hall, smiling as if I've just been set free, but it's all show for an audience of one, Jim Potter, the other custodian, standing with mop and bucket outside the men's room. He waves enthusiastically, and I reciprocate. Still smiling, strutting, I push through the double doors, raising my forearm to fend off a blast of early summer sun.

*   *   *

I try to maintain a confident gait as I stride across the asphalt lot toward my pickup, parked in "my spot," just to the right of a tall ponderosa pine that for the past decade has faithfully cloaked my vehicle in afternoon shade. Once safely inside, I take a long, deep, Amy-inspired yoga breath, followed by two more, but my heart continues pounding like a drumroll as beads of sweat colonize my forehead and armpits. The parking lot is empty except for a handful of cars in the faculty section, including Brubaker's ruby-red Buick. I'm alone. So I close my eyes, and, for the first time in more years than I care to remember, I relive that seemingly innocuous Indian summer morning in October 1977.

I'd been an energetic young science teacher at Ponderosa Junior High School who the previous weekend had run the Grand Canyon from rim to rim and back, all forty-two grueling miles. With eight years' teaching experience under my belt, I was confident in my classroom and well-respected by fellow teachers, young and old. Several had tagged me as a rising young star in the school district, destined someday for administrative glory.

It was a beautiful morning: spotless blue skies, a green-and-gold tapestry shrouding the peaks, the first rays of sun converting the frost on the grassy playing fields to a magical mist. Half an hour before the first bell, the school was empty except for the custodian—a much younger Bob Garcia—tidying up the commons, and a few early-bird teachers and panic-stricken procrastinators copying worksheets on the mimeograph machine in the faculty workroom, inhaling those deliriously dreadful, brain-buzzing fumes.

As I placed study guides and plastic beakers on the rectangular, Formica-coated tables that checkered my classroom, my solitude was interrupted by a voice, soft, apologetic, a whisper: "Mr. Hunter?"

When I turned, my eyes met those of a tall, wraithlike girl with straight, dishwater-blonde hair hanging just below her shoulders. A plain cotton dress spotted with delicate red and blue blossoms drooped to just below her knees. Hands cupped nervously in front of her, she looked timid and fragile, like a dry flower that would crumble on contact.

I smiled, trying to set her at ease. "Hello, Jennifer."

She stared at her shoes—scuffed white sneakers, with tiny holes, like eyes peering through the canvas. She had the waifish look of an orphan in a fairy tale. The Little Match Girl.

"Mr. Hunter, I need to tell you something," she said, then paused. "You have to promise not to tell anyone, OK?"

Until that moment, I'd known her only as a shy girl who never spoke in class unless called upon, and then her answers had been short, telegraphic: yes, no, maybe. She rarely talked to the other kids, at best smiling uncomfortably at their adolescent jokes about sex, drugs, and other forbidden fruits. But her test scores were above average, and her assignments were completed diligently and submitted promptly, so I'd assumed she was paying attention in class.

I knew I had to be careful: if I said no, she might clam up and go elsewhere, nowhere, or do who knows what? If I said yes, I might end up later breaking my promise or going to jail, and in my mind, the former is worse than the latter.

She waited, her big, brown eyes filled with disbelief and dread. No child this age should have eyes like that.

"Well, I don't know if I can do that. It might be something I have to tell."

She looked down.

"Then I won't tell you." She turned to go, but I caught her gently by the arm.

"Wait. Let's compromise, can we do that? You tell me what it is, and then we'll talk about whether or not I have to tell and what we can do about it. Can we do that? Is that fair?"

She nodded tentatively, a wooden head suspended by a string. And then she began walking.

I followed her down the aisle and back into the privacy of the storage area, where we were surrounded by shelves of Erlenmeyer flasks, obsolete microscopes, and the noxious smell of formaldehyde. She turned her back to me and, before I could stop her, reached behind her neck, unbuttoned her dress, and let it drop to her waist.

CALLINGS

Y ou'll be wondering what happened to that girl and, by extension, to me, and I'll get around to that soon enough. But first I have to answer a more fundamental question, one that I've asked myself more than a few times over the years: why did I—why does anyone— choose to teach for a living?

It's not for the money. My first contract, signed in August 1969, was for a walloping $8,000. Thirty-five years later, it was almost eight times that. Not too shabby, if I didn't compare it to the surgeons, attorneys, city managers, police chiefs, and other six-figure folks in town. Or the superintendent of schools, who made three to five times as much as any teacher in my district. I knew about the stingy pay when I signed up—we all did—and we joked about it in public and bitched about it in private. Which brings me back to my initial question—why? The answer is: it depends.

For some teachers, it's not just a job but a calling, often recognized at a young age. Amy's one of those. Her epiphany came at age twelve, while she was helping a seven-year-old towhead sound out syllables in her mother's summer school class: *the-hun-gry-cat-er-pil-lar-by-er-ic-car-le*.

"Yes!" she exclaimed. "Perfect!"

The boy looked up with a jack-o-lantern smile parting the sea of freckles on his cheeks. For young Amy, it was like the scene in *Doctor Zhivago* when Omar Sharif is staring at the ice-crusted window as the Siberian sun first strikes the glass: illumination, inspiration, revelation. At that instant, she knew exactly what she wanted to do for her life's work. She couldn't articulate it back then, but it was the euphoria of mutual achievement, an almost mystical moment when discovery and delight converge, forever binding instructor and pupil. I know that sounds like lofty talk, but good teachers know that feeling, and great teachers feast on it.

I'm going to be a teacher, Amy thought. Just like my mom. I'm going to unlock that magic box that would otherwise remain the humdrum brain in each kid.

She did not think: I'm going to take home skimpy paychecks, just like my mom. I'm going to fret every time I have to buy my own kids new shoes. I'm going to spend sixty hours a week at my job. And then I'm going to read front-page news detailing how I and my fellow teachers are failing our students, our communities, our nation, the world, God, the universe.

None of that crossed her mind. All she saw was the image of that little boy. I want to see that look every day, she decided; I want to feel that joy. I want to take those kids places they've never been—to the Great Wall of China and the Congo and the North Pole; I'm going to take them to Saturn and Mars. I'm going to take them as far down that Yellow Brick Road as their dreams and ambitions will go.

Six years later, as a young freshman in her first education class, when the poodle-permed professor printed on the chalkboard in all caps: WHY DO YOU WANT TO TEACH? Amy's hand shot up.

"I'm going to change the world!" she shouted. "One kid at a time!"

Other teachers are less altruistic. Some are frustrated wannabes whose aborted dreams (or in some cases, unrealistic ones: artist, nuclear physicist, inventor, brain surgeon, rock star, NATO commander, actor) dragged them kicking and screaming into the classroom to put food in the fridge and a roof over their heads. For them, teaching's a temporary gig until they get that life-changing callback or acceptance letter or lottery ticket. At first a private joke, over time it can fester to embarrassment and humiliation, culminating in a grim concession to playwright George Bernard Shaw, who infamously said: "Those who can't, teach."

There are plenty of those, and the smart ones admit the obvious: you can't put in what God left out. But they also realize that maybe survival and serendipity have mysteriously merged, paving the way for an unanticipated option: the opportunity to magnify young minds and inspire newer and bigger dreams; to become not the dream or the dreamer but the dream-maker.

And some fully embrace their new calling—not just to pay bills while pursuing their passion, dividing time and energy between two masters, but clattering full-speed, devil-may-care down the dusty, potholed trail. I'm a teacher now! Not an actor or a writer or a submarine commander or a comedian in waiting. These pursuits have been relegated to hobby-hood.

Unfortunately, other teachers gnash their teeth and grab their biweekly paychecks, grimly ticking off the days until they can retire and start living the life they've put on hold for thirty years. Or worse, some toss their shattered dreams in a bucket and project (directly or indirectly; consciously or unconsciously) their cynicism and failure onto their students, saying, in effect: "If I couldn't do it, neither can you! So stay down where you belong. I'm just being honest here. I'm trying to spare you a lot of heartbreak and unnecessary pain. I'm doing you a favor, so thank me and shut up, kid!"

But those are the pathetic exceptions. Most teachers I've known brought life and love to the job, and they took a fairly straight road to get there: Education major in college with a specialization in elementary, secondary, or special education, followed by a semester of student teaching, leading to a classroom of their own.

*   *   *

My path was less conventional. I was finishing my bachelor's degree in forestry with a minor in math, the former because I loved the outdoors and the latter because I was the son of an engineer who could only communicate with me through the language of numbers. His day-to-day words were usually terse, commanding, and corrective. Part of that was his generation, and part of it was how he was wired. Either way, through numbers he managed to forge a bond with me that I confused for love. By my eighth birthday, I'd mastered basic algebra.

Before I graduated in the spring of 1969, the U.S. Forest Service offered me a job in Albuquerque, New Mexico, to conduct research on trees and do species analysis, a task that, according to one trusted professor, would be a dream come true… if you like being chained to a desk eight hours a day. Although a beautiful river ran through it, Albuquerque was citified desert in my mind and definitely not the place for me, especially after I'd spent four years on a mountain campus where I could step out my back door and take an endless stroll into pine forest. I'd grown accustomed to Camelot winters with plenty of snow to play in but blue skies above, the sun burning so close and bright that in midwinter you could cross-country ski in shorts and a T-shirt. Every fall, the oak and aspen trees caught fire, turning the forest into a tapestry of red, green, and gold; spring brought bitter winds but stunning colors, too, and summer made our mountain town a veritable oasis in a desert state, with cool nights and warm days, and the downright intoxicating scent of sun-toasted pine needles.

Some places just speak to your heart, and when they do, you'd better answer, because it's a lot like falling in love. You can't always explain it and it doesn't happen often, but you know it when you feel it.

My junior year, I was hit with both barrels, first by the slow drip-feed that had permanently addicted me to the town, and then by a lightning bolt that pierced my heart as I was hustling through the student union one afternoon. A willowy young woman stumbled coming down the stairs and face-planted in front of me. After a quick check to assure she was all right—blushing, embarrassed, but no broken bones, no blood or bruises—I knelt down and gathered up her scattered books and papers. Then I looked up at the dainty spray of freckles on her face and a dimpled smile that could have melted a heart of steel, and here came the thunderbolt. When you know, you know. We were married six months later.

Of course, I would gladly have moved to Albuquerque—or Wisconsin or the Gobi Desert or wherever there was a decent job—if forestry had been my passion, but it wasn't. It just fit my love for the outdoors. Also, Amy and I needed jobs, a scarce commodity in our college town. As spring graduation approached, it looked as if we would end up in Albuquerque by default.

Then, two things happened. There was a teacher education conference at the university, and—call it fate, dumb luck, or destiny—Amy persuaded me to attend with her. For the most part, I found the speakers forgettable, but there was a lively panel discussion that included Dale Hanagan, superintendent of the local Ponderosa Unified School District. With bushy red hair and mischievous eyes, he looked like a leprechaun in a three-piece suit.

As we chatted afterward, our conversation shifted from education to bow-hunting. I was recommending a few hot spots in hunting section Six-A when Amy strolled over. Hanagan gave her an overly long and overly friendly look before I introduced her as my wife. He asked if we were looking for teaching positions. Amy said yes, absolutely, and I said, maybe. Not sure why.

He asked my major, then said they needed a math and science teacher at the junior high. Teaching positions at the elementary school were at a premium, he told Amy, and you had to either know somebody or be related to somebody who knew somebody—"I'm just being honest here"—but they did have an ESL teacher spot at Ponderosa Elementary. Neither of us knew what ESL meant until Amy looked it up later— English as a second language—but she was willing to give it a try.

"What the hell!" she said. "I'll do about anything to call this place home! I'll learn basket weaving, belly dancing, bison breeding. I'll start an underground newspaper or open a coffee shop if I have to."

It seemed like a perfect plan: the two of us teaching by day and taking classes at night. The university had just started a master's program in TESL—Teaching English as a Second Language—so Amy could work on that while I pursued a masters in whatever. A stopgap until what? Who knows? We were young and in love and had landed jobs that ran from late August to the end of May. That gave us our summers free, which meant that I could still work the Grand Canyon as a river guide as I had for the past few years. So goodbye, Albuquerque plans.

The only hitch was that I had to take some classes at the university that summer to secure a provisional teaching certificate from the ADE, shorthand for the Arizona Department of Education. I learned quickly that the ADE's bottom line was straightforward and unambiguous: no certificate, no teach.

*   *   *

So that first summer, instead of guiding adventurers down the rapids of the Colorado River, I sat in a classroom listening to lectures about teaching philosophies and methodologies, curriculum and assessment, discipline and child psychology, with some legal matters tossed into the mix. Four classes in ten weeks, or twelve credit hours total. I completed my last class on August 18. The next day, Saturday, Amy and I hiked up the mountain to grab a bite of air. It would be the last time for the next nine months. School started Monday morning.

OPENING DAY

It's the night before my first day, and I can't sleep. I'm sure I'm not alone. Plenty of other teachers are probably tossing and turning as well, and students too. As a kid, I could never doze off the night before the first day of school. But kids just have to show up and warm a seat. I, on the other hand, have to teach. I need to be sharp, alert, and attentive, not nodding off at the chalkboard, an instant target for ridicule and parody. And they can be ruthless, these junior-high kids. I know that from personal experience: my buddies and I demoralized dozens of good teachers during my first stint in public education. So what goes around, comes around? I'd find out soon.

I try to visualize pleasant things—Amy in cutoffs and a halter top, wading through a meadow of wildflowers; a herd of elk at dusk creeping down to sip from the stream near our apartment—but my daily schedule keeps rolling through my mind like a never-ending arrest warrant:

Period 1, Biology 1
Period 2, Algebra 1
Period 3, prep
Period 4A, Seventh Grade Science
Period 4, Lunch
Period 5, Eighth Grade Science
Period 6, Algebra 1

Four preps for a first-year teacher! One more reason to put Melvin Jackson at the top of my shit list.

I got off to a rocky start with my principal. At my initial interview, he made it clear that he was only hiring me at the request, quote-unquote, of the superintendent.

"I guess you two are hunting buddies," he said.

"Not really," I replied, frankly surprised Dale Hanagan had even remembered me, let alone targeted me for the job.

"Well, just don't screw it up," Jackson grumbled.

* * *

I didn't exactly grease his wheels when I publicly challenged him at my first official faculty meeting the week before school started. As he was doling out assignments for the back-to-school potluck, I raised my hand.

"Yes, Mr. Hunter," he said; then to the rest of the faculty: "Mr. Hunter's our new science teacher, for those who haven't met him." Jackson flashed me a chummy smile. Welcome to the family! it exclaimed. Welcome to our school!

"It looks like the ladies are getting all the food assignments," I said. "Does that mean guys just get to show up and eat?" I laughed, signaling it was a joke, although it was and it wasn't: the Women's Movement wouldn't take full flight for another few years, but young females were already speaking out about sexism in the workplace. Amy in particular was raising my antennae about gender inequality.

I quickly learned that Melvin Jackson had two primary expressions: his gap-toothed smile when he was abundantly pleased, and a demonic sneer when he was upset. At that moment, his switch flipped from smile to sneer, and the faculty held its collective breath, waiting for his next move.

In this case, he didn't yell. Like a balloon slowly losing air, his bulging cheeks gradually sagged to bulldog jowls as the demonic sneer eased into his third expression, an unnerving, twisted grin.

"Well, Mr. Hunter," he said, "why don't you help us all out by bringing the main dish!"

I blocked a cough, gagged, and finally managed to stammer: "For everybody?"

Jackson's grin arched into an evil-genius smile. "Why not? Lunch for fifty! How does that sound, everybody? Lunch for fifty on Mr. Hunter!"

There were back pats and applause and a few sympathetic headshakes. "Welcome to the club!" they seemed to be saying, as if this were a tribal initiation ceremony or frat house hazing they'd each suffered in turn. All in good fun, of course.

I smiled too, but inside I was seething. A newlywed, scraping by on a teacher's salary with my first paycheck a week away: how was I going to pull this off? I was waist deep in it, and Jackson knew it. His smile was unambiguous. Message received, Mr. Hunter? Don't ever confront me in public again. Got it?

Somehow I—or rather, *we*—made it work. Amy and her book club friends pitched in, and overnight we concocted a chili and corn bread feast the faculty and staff couldn't stop praising.

But a fine meal wasn't adequate atonement for Melvin Jackson. The day after the feast—two days before school started—he informed me of a minor schedule change. Instead of two sections of Algebra 1 and three sections of Seventh Grade Science—two preps total—he was dropping two sections of Seventh Grade Science from my schedule and replacing them with a section of Eighth Grade Science and a section of Biology 1. And just like that, for no rhyme or reason—other than my principal's petty revenge—my daily preps doubled from two to four.

"Asshole!" I'd muttered, just out of earshot—or so I thought.

"What's that, Mr. Hunter?" Like a heat-seeking missile, Jackson's voice had tracked me halfway down the hall.

"Nothing, sir!" I shouted back.

*   *   *

My sleeplessness tonight isn't due to lack of preparation. I've diligently planned twenty lessons for the week. And I know my stuff—that's not the issue. The problem is I've never really taught before. In summer classes, I gave demo lessons to my classmates, but they were education majors, by temperament a kinder, gentler breed, quick to compliment and reluctant to criticize. My presentations were received with robust applause, but so were everyone else's. When I had them slicing up apples and oranges to demonstrate how to add, subtract, and divide mixed fractions, Dr. Hindman called me a natural.

"You've got a gift!" he said.

I shrugged. "Beginner's luck."

Now I'm hoping it was more than just dumb luck as I wage a silent war with the cheap, oversize wall clock in our bedroom. Framed with a corona of golden petals, normally it adds a cheerful touch to our modest sleeping quarters. The long hand advances one tick each minute, a sound so soft it's inaudible unless you're consciously listening for it—or trying to fall asleep before your first day on the job, in which case each click is like a gunshot or a hammer striking stone, all the worse because I know it's coming, every sixty seconds without fail: Bam! Bam! Bam! Like a slow-motion jackhammer.

I pull the pillow over my head, smashing it against my ears as I experiment with various postures: left side, right side, on my back, on my belly, legs bent, legs straight, legs crossed at the ankles. Counting sheep, counting stars, counting the money I'll never make at this job. Counting students, counting elk, counting the damn ticks on that damn clock.

Meanwhile, Amy—the fretful one, the worrier, the list maker, the midnight hunter who routinely paces the floorboards, stalking sleep as if it's an elusive prey—is lying next to me like a bludgeoned prizefighter, mouth gaping, neck bent, a freight train intermittently thundering through her nostrils. (I've always wondered how a lady like her can produce a sound that belongs to Bigfoot.)

I've tried chamomile tea—Amy's favorite antidote. Strike one. Deep breathing: inhale four beats, hold it seven, exhale eight, repeat three times. Strike two. A hot bath. Strike three. It's now two a.m.—too late to take hard-core sleep aids unless I want to be the walking dead on my first day. So I grab a random book off the shelf and sit in the kitchenette, hoping to find the right concoction of boredom and fatigue to knock me out. But as soon as I break the cover open, I know I'm doomed because, even though Amy's wall clock is imprisoned in the bedroom and completely inaudible now, every sixty seconds I can sense that sadistic minute hand pounding on concrete: Bam! Bam! Bam!

I persevere, determined to read until my eyelids become sandbags and my body melts into my chair... which doesn't happen for another few hours, when the black glaze on the kitchen window fades to dishwater gray. The last thing I remember is the book slipping from my hands as my body drops like an anchor to the bottom of the sea.

*   *   *

In reality it's a little over an hour, but it seems like only half a second before a hook reaches down and rudely yanks me to the surface, spitting and sputtering.

"Rise and shine, sweetheart!" Amy whispers, her hand gently nudging my shoulder. Usually her smiling face first thing in the morning is an angelic call to arms. Not today.

"Looks like you had a rough night."

Nodding, I gaze around the cramped room, trying to get my bearings. My lovely insomniac smiles sympathetically: "Welcome to my world."

Fortunately, she has the coffee pot brewing as I shower, shave, and make myself presentable for opening day: straight-cut beige pants, a short-sleeve plaid shirt, brown dress shoes, and a blue necktie with two diagonal stripes, one white, the other red. A subtly patriotic theme. I'm a professional now, a certified, gainfully employed adult, and I've dressed the part—no Wall Street suit and tie, but I'm not showing up in faded bell-bottoms and huaraches, either. I've chosen a middle ground for this mountain town.

With me riding shotgun, Amy negotiates my battered pickup through a maze of residential side streets to avoid rush-hour traffic on Main Street, eventually pulling into the faculty parking lot. Following a good-luck kiss, she guns the engine and heads off to her gig at the elementary school, while I stand on the curb waving goodbye. On the one hand, I feel like an anxious parent sending his child off to her first day of school; on the other hand, I'm like a nerve-wracked kid battling his own first-day angst.

With as much outward confidence as I can muster, I march a hundred feet down the sidewalk and up the twenty-six steps leading to the triple-glass doors with the large, black, embossed letters overhead: Ponderosa Junior High School. Passing the front office, I wave to the receptionist at the counter. She's finishing off a cigarette before the first wave of students pours through the doors. It's the calm before the storm.

I slip into the faculty lounge and merge with the flurry of teachers, some stuffing Tupperware lunches into the fridge, others checking out the bulletin board or exchanging post-summer hellos and hugs. A grizzly old-timer is pouring a cup of coffee from the communal pot while a middle-aged woman runs blurry, blue-ink copies on the mimeograph machine. A gangly young man who looks even greener than me is waiting his turn, trying to appear patient but betrayed by his fidgeting hands. The woman—obviously a veteran—stops and asks if he'd like to cut in. Wincing, he holds up a single sheet of paper: "Can I do a little quickie?"

The woman smiles slyly. "That depends: how quick's your quickie?"

The young man blushes, and the woman laughs. "Welcome to junior high!" she says, motioning to the machine. "Step right up!"

I wait for an opening in the crowd before sliding my sack lunch into the fridge. Other teachers are withdrawing colorful flyers or sealed envelopes or ribbon-wrapped treats from a row of wooden cubbyholes stacked five high. I scan the rows until I locate my name, but inside I find nothing. Disappointed at the moment, within a week I'll be calling that a rare blessing.

When I arrive at my classroom, Melvin Jackson's standing just inside, eyeballing me like a drill instructor inspecting his new recruit.

"Well, Mr. Hunter," he growls, "other than tucking in your shirt, you look ready to go. Any questions?"

"No, sir," I stammer as I stuff the loose flap inside my pants, wondering how it escaped.

Through my window, I watch the first of fifteen yellow school buses lumber up to the flagpole out front. The pneumatic door pops open, and a spindly seventh grader steps off the bus as if entering a mine field. Clutching a notebook in one hand and a brown-bag lunch in the other, he gazes uncertainly up the concrete steps as a mob of older students elbow past. He lifts his chin, squares his shoulders, and steps boldly forward. It's his first day too.

I glance into the hall where teachers have begun manning their battle stations as more waves of students arrive. Within minutes, the once-tranquil commons area has transformed into a circus maximus of chattering, gesticulating, teasing, joking, gossiping, backbiting, clique-creating, hormone-oozing, energy-ridden adolescents. Then the first bell rings—an obnoxious buzzer like you hear at the end of a basketball game—and the mass exodus commences. Human cattle mosey off to dozens of destinations, one of which is my classroom.

*   *   *

It's mostly been a blur to me so far. Nothing really registers until the second bell rings—the tardy bell—officially kicking off the new school year. After Jackson's inimitable bayou baritone welcomes the troops over the intercom, a shrill girl's voice leads the school in the Pledge of Allegiance, followed by twenty seconds of silence, followed by the same shrill voice reading the daily announcements, this time with the incomprehensible speed of an auctioneer. Then there's a very different silence. No more noise from the intercom; no more noise in the hall. My door is shut. The students are waiting. The classroom is mine. Showtime.

I rise slowly from behind the nicked and scarred hand-me-down desk and stroll across the room to the front of the class. My heart is pounding like a drumroll as I turn to face my audience. This is what I see: twenty-six students ages fourteen or fifteen, sitting in five rows of evenly spaced desk chairs, six chairs to a row. They're a fairly even split between boys and girls, mostly ninth graders—the top of the junior-high food chain—although there are a handful of accelerated eighth graders too.

Some of the girls look as if they still belong in grade school, while others are mature young women. Some wear hot pants or miniskirts; others wear long, flounced skirts or bell-bottom jeans patched with peace signs. A few hide their face in a book, while others—the "glamour girls"—preen as a pack in the center of the room, their scarlet lipstick bright enough to label an emergency exit.

Some of the boys are already shaving or need to, while others are probably still singing soprano. A third dress like preppies, a third like hippies, and a third like cowboys, including two who have plopped down directly in front of me, a smirking, gum-popping, Laurel and Hardy duo who are just daring me to try and teach them anything. Sprinkled around the glamour girls, the football stars lean back with muscled arms folded, basking in the afterglow of mythical summer conquests. Here and there sits a quiet kid in oversize glasses or a pimple-stricken giant trying to appear invisible.

The class is about two-thirds white. Four Navajo students—three boys, one girl—are slouching in the back row, heads down, dark eyes boring holes through their desktops. One of the boys has tied his abundant black hair in a bun, secured at the nape of his neck with white string. Three Latina girls sit center-left, one with an elaborate coif. They're flanked by two Latino boys, a wiry stick-figure and a handsome extra from *West Side Story*.

At first glance, my class looks like a hodge-podge of glowering indifference, accidents waiting to happen, and princes and princesses waiting to be crowned. As I look into their eyes for the first time, one thing is instantly apparent: half of these students not only don't want to be here but also would prefer to be just about anywhere else—digging ditches in the summer heat; watching *The Match Game* on TV; sleeping on a bed of nails; boiling in a cauldron of oil.

I'm new and inexperienced, and I make some brash assumptions. Retrospectively, some will make me shudder, but others will be spot-on. In half of the faces I see joy, hope, dreams, hugs and kisses when they walk out their front door. I see summer vacations, bedtime stories, piano lessons, Boy Scouts, Girl Scouts, 4-H Club, father-son outings, and daddy-daughter dates. In the other half, I see ducking and dodging, hiding and flinching. I see last picked and first kicked, bruises and bandages. I see anger and envy smoldering under the volcano. I hear doors slamming, windows shattering. I hear: Retard. Dipstick. Asshole. I hear NO! And NO YOU CAN'T. Lots and lots of NO.

At that moment, I make the most important decision of my teaching career: I'm going to make the bruised and beaten half of my class as successful as the cheerful, confident half. Somehow, some way, I'm going to make the pelicans fly with the eagles. And I'm just young enough and dumb enough to think I can do it. For fifty-five minutes a day, five days a week, those kids are going to soar with the lords of the sky. And if I can't pull that off, I'm at least going to make damn sure that a No. 2 pencil is the lightest thing they have to lug around each day.

CONNIPTIONS

"**D**ammit all!" My hand slams the table, rattling my coffee mug and stirring up the papers strewn across the laminate surface.

Amy flinches. I glance up long enough to see I've awakened an old ghost and instantly regret it. This is a new side of me, one she doesn't like.

Every night, Amy clears and washes the dishes; I dry and put them away. Then we spread our materials across the little table in the cramped kitchenette—me on one side, Amy on the other—and plan our lessons for the next day. Except there's one notable difference. My side is covered with the tools of academia: tablets of yellow, rule-lined paper; manila folders; a slide rule; graph paper; a textbook heavy enough to stop a dungeon door. Her half is cluttered with sheets of colored construction paper, scissors, three-by-five cards, Scotch tape, Elmer's glue, pipe cleaners, crayons, rubber cement, Silly Putty, Play-Doh, poster board, magazines, Marks-a-Lot in assorted colors. Crafts. Toys. Fluff.

Tonight we start with small talk, sharing amusing anecdotes overheard in the faculty lounge and taking jabs at Nixon for escalating the war he'd pledged to stop. But as the evening wears on and it becomes apparent that it's going to be another one of "those" nights, a storm cloud forms over my head, releasing a soft, steady drizzle of panic that soon morphs into a deluge of imminent gloom, at least on my side of the table. I glance at the wall clock for the tenth time in the past hour, conceding the obvious: once again, I'm not going to finish before midnight. At this rate, I'll be lucky to wrap up by two a.m. Then I'll try to steal a few precious hours of shuteye before (once again) dragging myself through the knothole I euphemistically call "teaching junior-high kids"—that is, if (and that's a big, thorny *if*), after chugging down six cups of Folger's coffee, I can somehow convince my hyper-caffeinated brain to shut down the afterburners long enough to fall asleep.

To compound the issue, after only two months in the saddle, my beautiful young bride has mastered the art of lesson preparation. She fans out her materials and sets to work with a joy I find personally irritating and professionally humiliating. Meanwhile, I crumple another sheet of aborted ideas into a wad and hurl it at the wastepaper basket. It rims out and dribbles impotently across the floor. My chin drops in defeat and I press my fingertips to my temples, as if trying to squeeze a few ounces of inspiration from my hibernating brain. Then I dive deeper into my textbook, searching in vain for some magic strategy that will light a fire under my students or at least keep their eyelids open. Because judging by their expressions, my classroom has become a torture chamber where every day they suffer a slow, ignominious death by boredom.

I remind myself that Amy's task is much easier than mine. She's teaching small groups of kids who speak maybe a dozen words of English. She escorts them from their regular classroom to her "resource room"—a windowless den slightly bigger than a coat closet—where for thirty minutes each day she treats them to a Disneyland of English-language fun and games, sending them back to class with smiles on their faces and gold stars on their handiwork. They're mostly Navajo kids from the massive reservation just beyond the mountain, as well as the children of Mexican migrant workers—seasonal short-timers—and some permanent residents, also from Mexico, whose parents clean rooms at the hotels or clear tables at the restaurants. Three international couples who are either attending or teaching at the university add five more student to the eclectic classroom Amy's nicer colleagues have dubbed "The United Nations." The not-so-nice ones have created some nasty monikers: Brownsville, Wetback Row, the Little Rez, Mixed-Shit City.

Amy was given no textbook or curriculum. Initially a sore spot, it now seems like a blessing in disguise, especially after she tried the canned, drill-and-kill-me-now programs her predecessor left behind. Instead, she creates her own curriculum, day by day, lesson by lesson, based on the needs of her students. It's trial-and-error, on-the-job training that some days flows like honey and other days resembles an Abbott and Costello routine, like the time she tried to teach little Alma Rosa Trujillo the subtle distinctions between personal pronouns:

"My name is Mrs. Hunter. What's your name?"

"My name is Mrs. Hunter."

"No, Alma, *my* name is Mrs. Hunter. What's *your* name?"

"Your name is Alma."

"No, sweetie, *your* name is Alma. *My* name is Mrs. Hunter. What's *your* name?"

"Your name is Mrs. Hunter."

And so on.

The upside to this is, unfettered by a required textbook, Amy can spice up her lessons with songs, games, skits, pantomimes. Fun stuff, and it annoys the hell out of me.

"Is that all your kids do is play all day?" I grouse.

"It's the best way for them to internalize the language."

I raise a skeptical brow: "Internalize?"

She flashes me her sunshine smile: "Just learning the lingo."

"What's that?" I say, pointing to her latest construction-paper creation, an orange circle decorated with small black triangles, strategically placed: one for each eye, one for the nose, a set of six for the gruesome teeth.

"It's a jack-o-lantern. We're making them for our Halloween unit."

"You're kidding."

"Nope. It's the best way for them—"

"Yeah, yeah—to internalize the language. I got it." I flip the page of my jumbo textbook, grumbling self-righteously. "Well, some of us actually have to teach."

*   *   *

I'm envious and she knows it. At nine thirty p.m., she's packing up her materials and applying night cream to her face, while I'm gnashing my teeth as I race the clock to get to bed before the Fenris Wolf swallows the moon. Again.

I've got *five* classes and *four* preps, the only repeat being Algebra 1, which is the easiest to plan. I'd thought my science classes would be easy, too, because there are thousands of hands-on activities, at least in theory. But as a rookie teacher, I can't reach into the bag of tricks my older colleagues have accumulated over the years. I can pick their brains for ideas, and some teachers share generously—Grace Swedelson, the gray-around-the-edges math teacher, almost buried me alive with lesson plans that looked as old as the Dead Sea scrolls. But that was for Algebra 1, one prep.

My lone colleague in the Science Department, John Baxter, is from the "I talk, you shut up and listen" school. Or more accurately, he talks and talks and talks, occasionally scrawling a word on the board, stabbing it with the chalk for emphasis, broken bits of white spraying across the room as he cautions in his booming, doomsday voice: "Pay attention now!" And: "You'd better remember this!" And the ultimate threat: "This is going to be on the test!" When I asked if he had any science activities that might fire up my students' imaginations, he regarded me curiously and then sadly, as if my face were broken and could never be fixed.

It will be another twenty-five years before the internet becomes a household commodity and fifteen more before Pinterest and similar websites transform the most pedestrian teachers into all-star lesson planners. Type in any topic—how to teach set theory; how to teach the food chain; how to teach interstellar navigation—and a magic veil will part, revealing an infinity of mouth-watering activities. Abracadabra! Open sesame! Click! Just like that.

But that's still science fiction in my world. Three months earlier Neil Armstrong may have walked on the moon, but I'm on my own trying to figure out how to get junior-high kids stoked about cellular respiration and plant taxonomy.

So here I am, ten p.m. on Thursday night, glaring at the textbook as if it's a stale fruitcake. BIOLOGICAL SCIENCE CURRICULUM STUDY is printed across the hard, green cover in intimidating letters. It's not a bad text—if you're a Rhodes scholar. It was developed by the National Science Foundation for Ivy League prep schools. Apparently, pre-Harvard kids didn't mind a layout as visually interesting as a dictionary: heavy on print, light on pictures and white space. After several big-name universities gave it rave reviews, "BSCS," as it was called, became the go-to textbook for secondary science instruction. Public schools nationwide jumped on the bandwagon, including Ponderosa Junior High.

Never mind that BSCS was written for high-school juniors and seniors, and the average reading level of my ninth graders is about fifth grade. And never mind that the "essential" vocabulary words I print in neat block letters across the chalkboard everyday—homeostasis, lithosphere, ichthyology, oxidation, etc.—may as well be hieroglyphics from the Valley of the Kings.

* * *

Amy returns from the bathroom, yanks open the fridge, and sighs. "How's it going?"

I answer with a Paleolithic grunt.

"I'll take that as 'Oh, everything's going great! Thanks for asking.'"

"Two down, two to go." I glance up at Amy. "Algebra and bio."

She winces. She knows biology is the real bitch—my gnarly ninth graders. I can fake it with seventh and eighth graders, but those apex predators know better.

"Want some ice cream?" she asks.

I glance at the clock: ten-ten. "Sure."

"One scoop or two?"

"Three—no, make it four."

"Cone or bowl?"

"A bowl. Please."

Moments later she makes a small clearing in the collage of papers and folders covering the table and sets down a bowl with four large scoops of Neapolitan.

"Here. Drown your sorrows in sugar!"

I mumble something that sounds like an underwater belch, but it's the closest thing I've got to a civil "thank you."

She exhales slowly. "I'm sorry. You think you'll finish before midnight?"

"I hope so. That's the plan." I don't look up as I start scribbling notes on a sheet of lined paper. This is how I brainstorm: jot down key concepts I want to teach, convert them into learning objectives, and create activities to teach the concepts. One-two-three. A-B-C. It sounds easy enough, and steps one and two usually are. The activities are the ball-breaker. Worksheets are easy to design but boring as oatmeal, and the stuff rarely sticks. The kids don't internalize it, to borrow Amy's phrase. The trick—the challenge—is creating something that keeps the kids interested *and* teaches the concepts. If you just want to keep them fat, happy, and entertained, let them make root beer floats every day—or paper jack-o-lanterns!

"You look tired," Amy says.

Another caveman grunt. "I'd like to take Melvin Jackson and suck him up a vacuum cleaner. Four preps. What kind of principal does that to a first-year teacher?"

I reopen the BSCS and begin leafing through the pages as if searching for something I know doesn't exist. Her hand settles on my shoulder and slides gently across my back.

I start talking to myself, half-wheezing, half-muttering. I don't want to complain—there's nothing more irritating than a chronic whiner. I want to be positive, upbeat, optimistic; the rock- solid, never-faltering, never-flinching man of the house. But...

"You know, this book's an academic masterpiece! But charts? Diagrams? Activities? Anything—*anything!*—that's one bit kid-friendly?" I slam the cover shut. "The damn thing reads like ether!"

And this is when the calm I have preserved thus far suddenly erupts. The simmering pot boils over, and my hand strikes the table: Bam!

"Dammit all! So-much-damn-time!" Four strikes, four lesson plans, four words.

Amy's hand leaves my shoulder and I can almost feel her presence withdraw from the room. I feel weak and ashamed and alone, knowing I've ripped open an old wound. She's hearing the echo of her father staggering home after a midnight binge, her mother trying to mollify him in the kitchen, trying to not wake the whole household while she, Amy, cowered in her cramped bedroom, hands pressed to her ears, futilely trying to block out the sounds of dishes crashing and flesh striking flesh. Hard, loud, snarling language that could never be retracted, pitched back and forth, a mutual mudslinging until her mother slammed the door or her father passed out on the floor or both.

I set the pencil down and put my hand to my forehead, half hiding my eyes. I've stared down a black bear charging at me full speed on the Mogollon Rim. I've negotiated the lethal rapids of the Colorado River a hundred times. I've run from the South Rim to the North Rim of the Grand Canyon and back in a single day—forty-two ankle-breaking, switch-backing miles—and finished with a limp and a shout and a smile. Only this has brought me to tears: teaching disinterested ninth graders.

I hear Amy's spoon barely tap the porcelain dish as it dips for another scoop.

"I'm sorry," I mutter.

Her hand returns to my shoulder. "It's OK."

I'm surprised and a little afraid of how badly I want that hand—*her* hand—touching me right now. I need it, desperately, but I don't want her to know that. I don't want to appear weak or incompetent or, worst of all, beaten. But that's exactly how I feel: Whipped. Pinned. Crushed. Doomed.

This is 1969 and I'm supposed to be the unflappable, manly breadwinner. There are a whole slew of things I don't want to admit out loud. I thought that because I'm young and athletic and run rivers in the summer and ski triple black diamonds in the winter, I'd instantly connect with teenagers and be anointed Mr. Cool Beyond Belief in their admiring eyes. But maybe teaching is much harder than I anticipated, and I'm not so naturally gifted after all. Maybe I'd rather be chained to that desk in Albuquerque measuring the moisture levels of old growth ponderosa pines by proxy. Maybe my wife is a lot better at this than I am. Maybe—just maybe—I need help, a helluva lot more than I'd realized, and maybe I should swallow my pride and ask for it.

* * *

"It's not just the time," I admit. "I could handle the long hours if I was getting results. But no matter what I do, they just stare at me like I'm a piece of used furniture."

"Maybe you need to scale back," Amy offers again, more gently.

"You mean just show up and be a human squawk box like John Baxter? Mr. Snooze? I don't want to be their daily sleeping pill. That's not why I got into this business."

"Every lesson doesn't have to be a Cecil B. DeMille production."

I glare at my notes, and the scribbled lines begin to blur.

"Can I help?" she asks.

The magic words! My hand drops from my forehead and plops on the table. I look up, half-laughing. "Sure. What do you know about photosynthesis and cellular respiration?"

Amy shrugs. "A little. But you've got the knowledge. You just need some ideas for teaching it, right? Let's see what you've got."

I slide my draft across the table so Amy can scan the traffic jam of words: Carbon Cycle Photosynthesis Cellular Respiration Oxidation-Reduction Reaction Phosphofructokinase RuBisCO Pyruvate Glycolysis Citric Acid Cycle Oxidative Phosphorylation Light Reaction Light Independent Reaction Calcium Cycle Chemical Equations for Respiration and Photosynthesis.

"Well, that's a mouthful all right," she says. "How would you explain all this stuff to my kids?"

"Your kids?"

"You know, kids who don't speak English."

I've never thought of my students this way before, as little adults aspiring to learn a whole new language.

"Pictures," I say. "Lots of pictures. Diagrams. Flow charts. But no damn jack-o-lanterns!"

"No, no jack-o-lanterns. But wouldn't you also simplify the language?"

"They've got to learn the terminology!" I want to pound my fist on the table like some banana-republic dictator, but I check myself. "I won't dumb it down!"

"I didn't say dumb it down. I said simplify it." She sits beside me. "Out of this sumptuous Irish stew of words, which ones do your kids absolutely have to know? What are the meat and potatoes here? I mean, photosynthesis, sure, I get that, but phosphofructo-whatever? That sounds like a subtropical disease."

"Are we getting cute here? Irish stew? Meat and potatoes? Because I'm in no mood for cute."

Amy draws a circle around "photosynthesis" and hands me the pencil.

"Now," she says, "circle one more word or phrase your kids absolutely have to know. Just one."

I circle "cellular respiration." I start to circle "glycolysis" too, but Amy snatches the pencil from my hand.

"I said *one* more," she scolds. "Now ask yourself: what do I want my kids to be able to do that they couldn't do before?"

I jab my pencil at the draft sheet. "That, right there!"

Amy laughs and I take umbrage—the clock's ticking and she's talking me in circles.

"Sweetie, that's just a bunch of verbal goulash. What do you want them to be able to do? Teach them that and don't sweat the rest. Anything else is gravy."

I bury my spoon in my ice cream and leave it there like an abandoned flagpole.

"OK," I say, gathering steam, "I want them to be able to explain the process of photosynthesis and cellular respiration. And explain why it's so damn important."

"Is it so damn important?"

"Hell, yes! If you want to be able to eat and breathe; if you want the life cycle to continue; if you don't want to be dead!" I shake my head in disbelief. "Is photosynthesis important! Come on, Amy."

She tilts back in her chair and assumes her battle position, slender arms crossed over her chest: "Photosynthesis the word," she says coolly, "or photosynthesis the process?"

I throw down the pencil. "Oh, come on! You're splitting hairs! You can't know the process without knowing the word."

"OK, settle down, just asking. But there's your lesson objective! Two of them, actually: Your kids will be able to explain the process of photosynthesis and cellular respiration. That's one."

"What's the other?"

"Explain why photosynthesis and cellular respiration are so damn important. Your ice cream's melting."

*   *   *

For the first time, I'm feeling hopeful. My grand design—to create a classroom so enthralling that the front office would have to establish a lottery to determine which students would be lucky enough to be admitted into my royal presence—had been hijacked by the daily pragmatics of my profession, from attendance and lesson plans to discipline and grading to meetings, meetings, and more meetings. And it's all so new to me. Unlike Amy, I'm not the beneficiary of four years of education classes where they forewarn you about the realities of public schooling. I never taught a semester under the mentorship of an experienced instructor who could show me the ropes and let me experiment on real, live students.

"You're really good at this," I concede.

"I've had a lot of practice. And, hey, that elementary education major's gotta be good for something."

As I ponder this reality, I can feel the hope drain away. I spoon a bit of ice cream as if it's medicine.

"Maybe I picked the wrong profession." I glance at Amy, who's staring at me, neutral, waiting. "I hate going to work. I hate stepping into that classroom. Seeing those faces—the absolute boredom, the apathy… the *contempt*!"

Fishing for sympathy, I've momentarily forgotten that Amy doesn't do self-pity.

"And whose fault is that?"

My spoon drops in the bowl with a clink. "So you're putting this all on me?"

Amy tilts back another ten degrees, her maximum defiance pose. "Who else do you put it on? The kids? They're just being who they are— bratty little teenagers. What did you expect?"

"John Baxter says his job is to teach; it's the kids' responsibility to learn. If they don't learn the material, it's their fault."

"So Baxter's your new role model? If his students aren't learning, how can he be teaching? The two go hand in hand."

"Is this the Gospel According to Amy?"

She leans forward and her hand returns to my forearm, lightly. "What's really the matter?"

I look down at the sprawl of papers and keep my eyes pinned there while I make the confession I've been dreading.

"The other day, one of my kids was screwing off—two kids, actually, Bob Creighton and Will Gillespie—good old Laurel and Hardy. I'd given the class an assignment, and as I'm walking around the room monitoring, I see Bob out of the corner of my eye, mimicking me at the blackboard. He's squinting through slitted eyes and pushing his glasses up off his nose with his middle finger over and over—"

"Kind of like you do."

"Exactly like I do! The kid's a good mimic! But now the other kids are laughing, completely blowing off the assignment, so I tell Bob to knock it off and sit down, please."

"You said please?"

"I think so—maybe not. I was pretty pissed off. Anyway, he starts getting mouthy: 'I'm not doing nothing!' he says. 'Then sit down,' I say, 'and knock it off.'"

"Please?"

"Hell no not please! By then his sidekick's doing the same thing, so I walk over and grab him by the collar and pull his face so close to mine I could've bitten his nose off. 'If you ever do that again' I said—except it was more like a death hiss—'I'll pick you up and throw you out that window! Do you understand me?' His eyes got so big I thought they might crack open and little chicks would leap out, running for their lives. I mean, he was physically shaking. It was pretty scary."

"Sounds like it. Is he all right?"

"That little turd? A minute later he was laughing about it. I'm the one who was terrified." I hold up my thumb and index finger to make a half-inch gap. "I was this close, Amy—this close to heaving that kid right through that wall of plexiglass."

I wait for her response, but she remains mute.

"The class went dead silent after that, every pair of eyes staring at me like I'd shot and killed somebody. No one said another word the rest of the period except for Will Gillespie. He kept trying to laugh it off, but his buddies weren't buying it. Heads down, noses in their books. If I asked a question, they stared at their desks. In this case, silence wasn't golden; it was absolute hell. I couldn't wait for that class to end and the day to end, and now I've got to go back tomorrow and somehow fix the mess I've made, but I can't even write a damn lesson plan!"

I almost lower my fist again but catch myself. Instead, my fingers begin tapping the surface as if I'm playing keyboard. And, thankfully, I laugh.

"How the hell do you fix that?" I say. "Any trust I built with those kids just went down the toilet. Hey—you think this is funny?'

Amy straightens up in her chair and literally wipes the smile off her face. "I've had days like that. Much worse, in fact."

"You? Little Miss Sunshine? Miss Songs and Games and Fun?"

"You know, that's the great thing about teaching," she says. "No matter how badly you screw up today, there's tomorrow. You always get another shot."

"But not a fresh start," I say. "Those ninth graders have memories like an elephant. Unless it's a deadline. Or the photosynthetic process. Then they can't remember their own mailing address."

Amy slips her hand into mine, and I think nothing in my life has ever felt so exquisite. "So what are you going to do about it?"

My shoulders collapse. It's ten forty-five. "I don't know."

*   *   *

Amy reaches for the BSCS text, gathering up the scribbled sheets surrounding it. "Well, let's see if we can breathe some life into dead-as-a-doornail photosynthesis."

As she flips through the pages, her hips begin swaying slightly, as if responding to some primeval inner music. "I feel like a mad scientist," she says. "Like Dr. Frankenstein." She makes her brown eyes bug, thrusts out her hands, and exclaims in a quavering voice: "It's alive! It's alive!"

I'm not amused. I'm also wondering how I was fortunate enough to marry this certified kook.

She slams the book shut and looks at me solemnly. "Todd, you're absolutely right. This book's D.B.A."

"D.B.A.?"

"Dead Before Arrival. Maybe even D.B.B—Dead Before Birth. Or D.B.C.—Dead Before Conception. They should have some kind of birth control pill that automatically aborts even the thought of writing a textbook like this."

"OK, I get the picture. It's a lousy book."

But now she's left me—not physically but mentally: eyes closed, fingertips pressed to her forehead, lips moving as if she were quietly communing with the dead. How much of this is show and how much her actual thinking process I'll never know, but after a minute or two her head pops up and her eyes flip open.

"I've got it!" she says, and I can see the creative juices coursing through her body, from the crown of her Shirley Temple curls to the tips of her pink-painted toes. "You could have them work in small groups. Each group draws a diagram of photosynthesis."

"You mean the process?"

"Yes, the process. Photosynthesis—and what's the other one?"

"Cellular respiration."

"Yes, that. They could explain it like a recipe."

My face sours. "Photosynthesis isn't a recipe."

"I said *like* a recipe. Don't be so literal. Don't be so scientific!"

"I'm a science teacher. I'm supposed to be scientific."

"Or! You could have each group create a song about photosynthesis—in the song they have to include the process, step by step."

My head drops and my hands shroud my face.

"Or, or—stay with me now!—you could have them do a role play."

I look up, aghast. "How do you role-play photosynthesis? This is science, not speech and drama."

Amy shakes her head, tsk-tsking. "You need to spend a day with those little critters at the elementary school. You can role-play anything."

"Photosynthesis?"

"Sure. One student can be the sun, another can be a plant, another can be oxygen…"

"That sounds funky. And pretty damn stupid."

"No, it sounds very junior high." Her body stops swaying. "They love that kind of stuff. Think back to when you were that age—first crush, first real kiss, and all the uncertainty and silliness and fear that go along with it. You're still a kid but you want to be an adult or think you might want to, or maybe you're scared to death of what lies ahead, but it's here like it or not and you're right in the thick of it. The sillier the better, but they have to know about photosynthesis to do the drama. Are you writing this stuff down? I mean, I'm giving you some brilliant ideas here!" She rips a sheet of paper from the tablet and taps it with her finger: "Write!"

I begin scribbling.

"You could have task cards—give each group a specific task, maybe they have to diagram and explain one part of the process. Or how about a Jeopardy game?"

"Jeez-Louise! We're playing Jeopardy now? It would take me two hours to write all those questions." I point to my wristwatch. "We're pushing eleven here."

"No, no, no. You tell your students to write the questions. Give each group a category: Oxidation-Reduction Reactions could be one. Glycolysis could be another. Each group writes down five questions, then you play the game with the entire class."

Amy's eyes look radiant—her entire countenance does. This brainstorming business is a turn-on for her, and, in its own bizarre way, for me as well. I'm actually enjoying the moment.

Another tap on my planning sheet. "Write!" she commands.

"I think for tomorrow, given my time constraints, I'll have them do the role play."

"Or you could do a mock news interview. You could have the reporter—"

"OK, good. Enough. Thank you. Please."

"Yes, I'm just a fountain of ideas." She stands and opens her arms like a Metropolitan Opera star or Moses parting the Red Sea.

"Now look who's the drama queen."

I feel her hands slide up under my arms and across my chest, her lips barely touching the back of my neck as she coos softly in my ear: "Just give your Algebra kids the chapter pre-test and come to bed."

"That's a cop-out."

"Not at eleven fifteen it's not. Besides, consider it an investment." She breathes heavily into my ear. "I will inspire you to even greater heights! I promise."

Her hands withdraw abruptly. She grabs my ice cream bowl and places it in the sink.

"Wait! I'm not done!"

"There's a statute of limitations on ice cream. You've got a pool of goo there."

My eyes follow her blue-jeaned hips as she sashays down the hall, peeling off her T-shirt, twirling it overhead, and flinging it across the hall, where it settles on a lampshade.

"What about more ice cream?" I protest.

"Come hither, my love!" she sings as she disappears into the bedroom. "Let me be thy second helping! Come!"

I push back the chair and rise to my feet. It's been a month since the last time, and as much as I don't want to admit it I've been getting snarlier and gnarlier by the day no thanks to that—maybe not the reason, but a contributing factor, all work and no play and especially no sex making me not just a dull boy but an irascible one.

I shove the textbook aside and clomp down the hallway like a caveman, growling: "What's with all the Shakespeare talk? Come hither? Thy second helping?"

"I'm *wait*-ing!" she sings in her mezzo soprano.

VISIONS

We both oversleep. Last night, in the heat of the moment, I forgot to set the alarm clock, but that didn't matter. The annoying little buzzer could have been a jackhammer and neither of us would have noticed, we were both so out for the count. What can I say without saying too much? It was wild and wicked and we went at it like two hungry animals, at least after the initial kissing and caressing because it had been so damn long and before we knew it, we were trapped in a barrel riding hopelessly over the falls. Nothing like it since a bewitching night in a *palapa* in Puerto Escondido under a full moon with the waves crashing softly and relentlessly as we both broke new ground—honeymoon stuff—holding back until that one monster wave crested and crashed, followed by gentle thunder rolling all the way to shore. I think you get the picture.

Last night was loud too, but who cared? So loud the neighbors rapped on the adjoining wall: not an angry pound, but a gentle hey, you guys are getting carried away or hey, we can hear you're having a good time over there, just don't rub it in, OK? Amy laughed first and loudest; she can be that way, as creative under the covers as she is in lesson planning.

"I miss this," I said a dozen times until she repeated: "Do you miss this? Really? Are you sure?"

For one night, all the bad stuff was forgotten—the late-night prepping, the quarantine faces in my classroom, my after-dinner fits, the table slamming, my pathetic woe-is-me act—evaporated by the soft embrace of the woman I love more than life. As I closed my eyes and sank into a deep, childlike sleep, the last thing I remember thinking was, life is good; not just manageable but happy. I was smiling, and so was she.

Then: "Holy hell!" I jackknife to attention, double-checking the alarm: seven thirty-five. Amy and I throw on the first items of clothing our hands can locate and bolt out the door—coffee-less, breakfast-less, lunch-less—tucking in shirttails and slapping sense onto our faces, the smell of last night lingering slightly on our hands and bodies, but through all the rush and tumble only smiles pass between us. And when Amy drops me off outside the junior high, we share a long, smoldering kiss even as the bell rings, which means I've now got five minutes to get my act together. But at the moment, it doesn't matter—none of it matters, not even Melvin Jackson's glower as I trot up the steps smiling like a circus act, pointing to my neatly tucked-in shirt.

"Good morning, Mr. Jackson!"

"You're late," he grumbles. "And where's your jacket?"

I laugh. "I guess I left it at home! Beautiful day, isn't it?"

And it is: a bright sun already poking its nose over the mountain but frost sparkling like diamonds on the grass and every breath of every tardy student hustling toward the doors registering a white puff of autumn mist. The heat of last night still fuels me as I fly through the entrance, past the office, and down the now-deserted hall to my classroom, where my ninth graders, upon seeing me, immediately shift gears: Chatty conversations cease. Those sitting on their desktops slide down into their seats. Those loitering on the perimeter trudge toward their chairs as if heading to the gallows. All assume their silent posture of boredom and gloom.

"How's everybody this morning?" I ask cheerfully.

Silence. Rolling eyes. A grunt.

Then a baritone voice over the intercom, the almighty Melvin Jackson: "Please stand for the Pledge of Allegiance followed by a moment of silence."

As my students repeat the pledge, I notice something different. Instead of dreading the end of the morning ritual, I'm mentally urging things along: hurry hurry hurry! I need every second of class for this activity, and hopefully the fish will take the bait. If not, it's going to be another fifty-five minutes of torture—forty-five by the time Melvin Jackson finishes reminding us that the seventh graders are selling suckers for their fundraiser and there's a sock hop Friday night at five p.m. in the gym. Then, finally, silence.

"We're going to do something a little different today," I say, but then remember: attendance. If I don't mark my roll sheet and stick it in the envelope outside the door, Betty Castillo the attendance secretary will come roaring down the hall like a momma bear looking for her lost cubs. I do a quick check of the seating chart—a timesaving trick John Baxter deigned to show me.

I note one empty chair, fifth row, third seat down: Karla Walker. I mark the roll sheet, slip it in the outside pocket, pull the door shut, and now it's just me and them.

"OK, we're going to do something different today," I repeat, and I may as well be talking to bags of peat moss. They've heard this before, sooooo many times from sooooo many teachers. I smile, thinking to myself: buckle up, kids! You've got no earthly idea what's coming.

*   *   *

When Amy picks me up that afternoon, I'm standing curbside with my back to the street, a tall, lean figure that from a distance probably looks as if it's been drawn with one bold, swift slash of the pen. It's Friday heading into a three-day weekend, and the school has been abandoned. By three thirty, the buses had hauled off the last students, after which teachers and staff fled the building as if it were on fire. Standing on the corner, I look like the lone survivor of a nuclear holocaust.

As she pulls up, Amy can read catastrophe in my broken body language: this can't be good. She tries to present a cheerful front, leaning toward the passenger seat and calling through the open window in the sexiest voice she can muster at four in the afternoon at the end of a long workweek: "Hi, handsome!"

I turn around, my face an unfinished puzzle: not happy, not sad, not angry, not content, not confused. It probably looks like a stick-figure face, to match my physique from afar: a straight line for a mouth, two dots for eyes surrounded by little black circles for eyeglasses, a triangle for a nose.

"So how'd it go?"

"The play?"

The lilt in my voice must have sparked a moment of hope and optimism: "Yes, the play!"

"Shitty."

She winces, probably anticipating another depressing weekend with her brooding sphinx. And she's probably thinking: maybe he's right; maybe he wasn't cut out to be a teacher after all. Six weeks in the classroom has kicked the joy and humor out of him. For her, teaching is a nonstop, high-speed rush until she crashes at bedtime. For me, it's like the world's worst mind- and mood-altering drug.

"I'm sorry," she says. "Want to talk about it?"

My hands are buried so deeply in my pockets that if I push any harder my pants will drop to my knees. I shrug. "Not much to say. I told them we were going to try something different. When I explained what it was, they told me to go screw myself."

"They did not!"

"Not in those exact words, but that was the gist."

Squinting, Amy lifts her hand to visor off the sun that's just beginning to dip below the pines. "Come on, get in!" she says, but I remain standing on the curb.

"They weren't buying it, Amy. I put them into groups, told them what to do, and nothing—well, not nothing. Some of them had a few choice words I won't repeat."

Amy cuts the engine. "I can't believe they just sat there! What a bunch of deadbeats."

"Yep. Like twenty-six bumps on a log. I could have stood on my head and hula-danced in the nude and they wouldn't have twitched an eyebrow."

Amy slaps her hand over her eyes, shaking her head. "I'm sorry, but that image—it would get us both fired *and* thrown in jail. Did you try some positive reinforcement strategies? Rewards? Incentives?"

I step down off the curb and lean in, elbows propped on the open window. "Other than a naked hula, no. But I threatened them with extra homework. I told them the assignment was worth a ka-zillion points so they'd better get on it. I even threatened to send them to the principal's office, but they passed around a signup sheet to see who got to go first. Anything to get out of that cockeyed assignment!"

"Nothing worked?"

"A play. I should have known—no, I *did* know, Amy, I *did* know. Deep down I knew it wouldn't fly." I step back and made a fake smiley face, swiveling my hips and fluttering my hands as I half talk, half sing: "I'm a happy Sunbeam, la-la-la, and you're the Go-Go Chlorophyll, cha-cha-cha. Ninth graders! What the hell was I thinking?"

"You were trying to light a fire, Todd. There's nothing wrong with that."

I back away from the truck, shaking my finger at her but in fact scolding myself: "That's not how you teach science! Plays, games, entertainment! Science is bigger than that! You don't have to disguise it like dumping sugar into medicine. Science is real. Science is life!"

"But sometimes you have to dangle a carrot—you know, just to get their feet inside the door," Amy counters. "Like you said, they're ninth graders. They're living in No Man's Land—little kids inhabiting almost adult bodies." Her face puckers as if she's just bitten into a raw lemon. "That sounds creepy, like *Night of the Living Dead* but with all teenagers."

I'm only half-listening. I've turned away again, my back to the street and to her, as I gaze through the chain link fence surrounding the green athletic fields that are just beginning their transformation to a crisp, autumn brown. Beyond them stands a wall of ponderosa pine trees that has caged the sun and is casting jagged shadows across the grass and the sidewalk and me. To the left of that wall, I zero in on six large, grayish mounds that could be mistaken for a herd of elephants if I were on safari. I've seen those mounds hundreds of times before but never from this perspective, never as an ass-kicked, crestfallen young teacher who's ready to wave the white flag, praying for a miracle.

* * *

At that instant I feel a chill. The scientist in me says it's just autumn shadows lowering the daytime temperatures. The latent artist in me says it's my muse whispering, and I need to listen.

When I turn back to Amy, my straight-edged lips contort into a smile that vacillates between sinister and simpleton.

"I've got it," I whisper.

"What?"

My smile widens, joyfully, then plummets into doubt. "But if it doesn't work?"

Amy waits: two three four five seconds. "Is there a punchline here?"

"Me," I say. "If this blows up in my face, I'll be the punchline."

"Well, get in! We'd better get home and get to work. You're just lucky you've got three days to prepare."

"Nope. No work. I just need to make one phone call, and then we're going to the North Rim. We're going camping."

"Seriously?"

"Start packing."

JUNK

Tuesday morning, after taking roll to avert the wrath of Betty Castillo, I turn to my students with a salesman's smile, clap my hands, and announce: "Everybody—up! We're going on a field trip!"

I see the usual smirks (Bob Creighton and Will Gillespie), a few smiles (Amanda Stone, future valedictorian), some rolling eyes (Jake Bonner, brooding poet), and a theatrical yawn (Susannah Thompson, freshman cheerleader). Mostly, however, I see bewilderment as the kids remain frozen in their chairs. I clap again—three more times—trying to rouse the troops from the psychological trauma of returning to school following a three-day weekend: a Tuesday masquerading as a Monday.

"Up! Up! Up! Everybody!"

One by one, the kids stand and begin moving toward the door in their stingiest, most I-don't-give-a-damn-about-anything shuffle.

"Follow me!" I call over my shoulder. "No stragglers!"

As my begrudging charges plod past the other classrooms, students sitting obediently at their desks watch with curiosity and envy. We cross the commons area, which only minutes before was a hormonal beehive of activity but now looks like a morgue. Leaning on his push broom, Bob Garcia tracks us with an approving smile.

The kids follow me out the rear exit and down a long, gravel path that slopes to the outer edge of what looks like the aftermath of a massive earthquake: six giant cinder mounds—two rows of three—grotesquely studded with broken slabs of concrete, chunks of cinderblock, and a potpourri of discarded washers, dryers, refrigerators, and television sets. Rusted poles, shafts of PVC pipe, and splintered two-by-fours protrude by the hundreds, like the bones of half-buried victims. Between the mounds, trash: shattered glass, gum wrappers, ancient chairs, shards of mirror, broken bicycles, hubcaps, shredded sofas, and box springs converted into rodent hotels. Weeds and noxious plants sprout in scattered clumps and thick jungles. An eastern breeze carries a foul stench that elicits expressions ranging from disgust to nausea.

"Gross!" several of them mutter, almost in unison.

It's a large area, almost the size of two football fields, and for the students of Ponderosa Junior High School, it's their backyard. Beyond stands a lush forest of aspens and ponderosa pines, and behind those, the iconic peaks angle majestically into the turquoise sky. But when the students look outside their classrooms, instead of exceptional beauty they see this: the unofficial city dump. This is where municipal trucks deposit excess cinders in the winter and where construction crews and residents illegally jettison junk throughout the year. This is where anything that's broken, mangled, worthless, or unwanted finds a home.

* * *

As my students contemplate the city's most prolific eyesore, it's a beautiful October morning with a slight chill in the air and the first dusting of snow on the peaks. A middle-aged man in Levi's, a plaid Pendleton shirt, and work boots is standing in the middle of the junkyard, kicking at a pile of dirt. He's built like a bear—big, round, powerful—and he's wearing a bush hat and a long, droopy mustache that's prematurely gray.

"Who's that old man?" Susannah Thompson whispers.

"What's he doing here?" Bob Creighton says.

I tell the kids to form a semicircle around me and the visitor, who still doesn't appear to notice us.

"Jeezos peezos!" he barks, kicking at a tall but withered plant. He reaches down, grabs it by the stem, and rips it out of the earth. "Jeezos peezos! This is much worse than I remembered! It's really fucked up!"

There are several audible gasps. Amanda Stone's hand flies to her mouth as if in a delayed attempt to vicariously suppress the foul adjective. Bob Creighton and Will Gillespie chortle enthusiastically.

The visitor looks at me, shaking his head, aggrieved: "I mean, Todd, this is really, really fucked up!"

More chuckles and gasps. Amanda's eyes look as big as croquette balls.

I turn to my students. "This is Roger Youngblood. He's a friend of mine, and he works for the U.S. Soil Conservation Service. He may be helping us for a few weeks. We'll see."

Roger chomps down on the wad of tobacco bloating the left side of his mouth and scans the twenty-six students like a crusty old sea captain with a rookie crew. Half of the students are still gaping in disbelief.

"Thanks for stopping by, Roger," I say.

"Let me know what you want to do," he says.

"We'll be in touch." Turning back to my students: "All right, let's go back to class!"

Among the whispers, chuckles, and gasps are expressions of utter confusion. In the silent language of teenagers, they're all screaming, *What the hell's going on here?*

* * *

Back in the classroom, I tell the kids to sit down, and they do. Immediately. It's the first time in six weeks that I've commanded their undivided attention: bug eyes, rabbit ears.

"All right, before we go any further, I need to tell you something about my friend, Mr. Youngblood. He got a little carried away and used some language he probably shouldn't have used. But do you know why he did that?"

In the middle-center row, Susannah Thompson is staring up at me, her mouth ajar.

"Susannah, do you know why?"

"Why what?"

"Why Mr. Youngblood—our visitor—do you know why he used some language he probably shouldn't have?"

"Ah… 'cause he's not Christian?"

"No, Susannah, I've heard plenty of Christians use far worse words than that. How about you, Bob. What do you think?"

Bob Creighton rolls his massive shoulders before letting them drop into an indifferent shrug. "I dunno."

Amanda Stone's hand shoots up.

"Amanda?"

"Well, I could be wrong, but he seemed really upset about the junkyard, the way it looks and smells and everything. And sometimes when people feel really strongly about something, they use bad language. It's like they're so upset they can't describe it in their own words, so they use swear words instead. Kind of."

I smile—my first sincere smile in this classroom. "Yes. He talked that way because he gives a rip about nature and conservation. Do you know what conservation is? What does it mean to conserve something?"

Susannah's baby blues pop open: "Take care of it?"

"Yes. To protect and take care of it. Mr. Youngblood loves the outdoors and he loves the natural world, and he hates seeing all this beauty turned into a junkyard."

I notice Bob has checked out again, sleeping off his three-day weekend in the back row.

"How about you, Mr. Creighton! Do you like your school sitting right next to a dump? Bob?"

Bob's head jerks to attention, compliments of a friendly elbow from his sidekick. "No, Mr. Hunter!"

"Thank you, Mr. Creighton. Good to see you back with us. How are things in the Land of the Dead?"

"What?"

"Well, the last five minutes you've looked like you were dead, so I'm just asking: how are things in the Land of the Dead?"

"Fine, Mr. Hunter."

"Good to hear it! Now here's the other reason Mr. Youngblood used that language: he was talking to you like adults. He was treating you like adults, not like little kids. And he was treating you like adults because this is serious business—adult business." My volume's rising and my kids are riveted; even Jake Bonner is looking at me instead of hiding behind his midnight bangs.

"If any of you want to stop this thing, all you have to do is walk down to Principal Jackson's office and tell him what our visitor said, and he'll end it right here and now. I can promise that." I take a step back and let my words percolate as I scan faces for potential defectors.

"But if you want to be part of this," I say, "it'll be an experience you'll never forget. I can promise you that, too."

Susannah lifts a hand tentatively. "Part of what, Mr. Hunter? What are we going to do?"

I smile. She's just swallowed the bait hook, line, and sinker. "Great question! What *do* you want to do? Right now you've got a junkyard for a backyard. We can either go out there and do something about it, or we can sit in here with our noses in a textbook. So what do you want to do?"

* * *

Silence. Five seconds. Ten. Twenty. Thirty. A short lifetime. Fidgeting. Squirming. Doodling. Eyes up, eyes down. Eyes left, eyes right. Enough.

"OK, let's vote. Show of hands: how many want to do something about it?"

Six hands shoot up and two more rise slowly, as if wounded. The lack of enthusiasm catches me off guard and I start to panic, realizing my brainchild could die in embryo. The kids need a nudge.

I write the number eight on the chalkboard and then snatch the BSCS textbook off my desk and hold it up like a threat.

"OK, and how many want to sit in here for the rest of this semester *and the next* with your nose in this ugly green monster?"

Bob Creighton looks at Will Gillespie, who's shaking his head. Two more hands go up.

"If we're going to do this, we need a commitment. Let's do it again, and you have to vote for one or the other. All those for doing something about it?"

This time all twenty-six hands go up, although some more reluctantly than others.

"Those for sitting in here?"

Silence. A few wandering eyes looking for a last-second alliance, but no takers.

"Going once? Going twice? OK, it's unanimous!"

I've timed it perfectly: the bell rings, the students rise. "I'll see you all tomorrow. And get a good night's sleep. You're going to need it!"

SEEDS

The kids are curious, and that's a good thing. Seated in their desk chairs, they're whispering among themselves, the cumulative effect creating a loud, steady hum that hovers above them like a gray cloud threatening rain. Eavesdropping, I catch snippets, the sum total of which can be reduced to this: what's up with all the rakes and shovels and stuff in the corner? Except that it's rakes, shovels, and one cardboard box on the floor by the door.

The tardy bell has rung, I've taken roll, and now I'm standing in front, arms folded, waiting for the group hum to fade and silence to prevail, which, after another two minutes, it does. Then all eyes turn to me. Bob Creighton speaks for everyone when he tilts his head sideways and opens his mouth, and absolutely nothing comes out.

My turn. "Well, what are you waiting for? Grab a tool and follow me!"

Slipping through the doorway, I give the cardboard box a gentle kick. "And don't forget to grab a pair of gloves on your way out!"

They obey, but slowly and suspiciously. They haven't bought into this, whatever "this" turns out to be. One by one, they step up and select a tool, handling it cautiously, as if it's been booby-trapped. Down the hall and across the deserted commons, rakes and shovels over their shoulders, they trudge along like a ragtag army reluctantly conscripted for war.

At the bottom of the gravel path, Roger Youngblood is waiting in overalls and work boots. His frosted breath looks like cigarette smoke. It's overcast with an autumn nip in the air and storm clouds brewing over the mountain. Most of the kids are wearing sweaters or light jackets. Roger welcomes them in his gravelly baritone and gives them a brief safety lesson: always keep your shovel below your waist; if you lift it above your waist, you could smack somebody. Always work in the same direction as everyone else. Be aware of your surroundings. Don't use the tools like toys or weapons. Don't try to lift more than you're able. Lift with your legs, not your back.

As Roger reviews the rules and regs, Will Gillespie and Bob Creighton are judiciously studying Susannah Thompson's backside, sharing lewd summations of their findings.

I sneak up behind them and whisper: "Now is that how you'd talk about your sister?"

They look surprised and a little embarrassed.

"All right then, knock it off," I tell them. Then I raise my voice to claim the group's attention. "Listen up. The safety rules matter. One injury out here and they'll shut us down."

Susannah turns around, grimacing. "Mr. Hunter, do we *have* to do this?"

I close my eyes, shaking my head. Didn't we cover this ground yesterday? The long, pensive walk down to the junkyard; Roger Youngblood's dramatic and profane performance; the classroom discussion afterward? Didn't we all vote on it? And wasn't the vote unanimous? I hear Amy's voice chiming in: yes, but they're ninth graders, the top of the junior-high food chain but the mental and social equivalent of loopy high-school freshmen. Yesterday may as well have been five years ago. And don't forget, you're a first-year teacher who should know better but doesn't.

"I'm going to say this one time and one time only, so listen up." My eyes lock on Susannah's before panning the group. "No, you don't have to do this—none of you have to do it. You can be out here doing some good and learning about science, or you can go back to class and stare at that green book until the bell rings. It's your choice. Are we clear on that?"

Susannah nods slowly.

I lift my empty hands. "What about the rest of you? Are we clear?"

I see heads shaking, some quite vigorously. When Bob starts to raise his hand in protest, Will smacks it down, hissing: "What are you doing, moron!"

Amanda Stone blurts out: "I want to stay!" Her declaration spawns an enthusiastic chorus of "Me too!"

"OK then, it looks like we stay outside. But if any of you ever ask me that question again, all I'm going to say is two words: broken record. Now let's get to work!"

*   *   *

Roger divides the students into four groups: pickers, scoopers, shovelers, and rakers.

"This is what we're going to do today," he says, "We're going to remove stuff that doesn't belong here. We'll start with the human stuff, the trash. And today we're going to focus on paper products—paper plates, potato-chip bags, old books and magazines, cigarette butts— anything made from paper. Shovelers and rakers, you're going to create piles. Scoopers, scoop the piles into the plastic bags. Pickers, pick stuff up and put it in the plastic bags. Everyone understand? Are we ready? Then let's get after it!"

I quickly discern the kids who are accustomed to manual labor from those who were raised on Captain Kangaroo and Saturday-morning cartoons. The former work swiftly and efficiently, while the latter blister early and take frequent breaks to stretch their backs and check their watches. By the end of the hour, they can all see the fruits of their labors: forty giant garbage bags bloated with trash and stacked five high creating a wall along the south end of the junkyard. No one says it was fun, but I detect a sense of satisfaction and accomplishment, and I try to validate that.

"Hey, good work today! Good work! I want you to look around. Does it look any different?"

Will shrugs. "It don't look no different to me."

"It looks the same," Susannah groans.

"Well, it's a damn big junkyard!" Roger grumbles.

"Mr. Youngblood is right, it's enormous," I concede. "It wasn't created overnight and it's not going to be cleaned up in a day. But how do you eat an elephant? Do you swallow it all in one gulp? No, you eat it one bite at a time. Now look at those bags over there—forty bags of trash. That's a pretty good-size bite out of that elephant. Tomorrow we'll take another bite."

"What if I'm vegetarian?" Jake Bonner quips.

"Then I guess you'll be eating a jungle. That's one bite out of Jake's jungle. Hey—everybody! Good work today!

The students shuffle off, half chatting happily, the other half mumbling uncertainly. Will's twirling an index finger next to his head. Message received: Mr. Hunter's lost his marbles.

The next day, Roger tells the kids to focus on products made of wood; the day after that, items made of metal. He rotates groups so pickers become rakers and shovelers become scoopers and so on.

Thursday we're on our own, so I assign each group a small plot to clean near the south side of the yard. By the end of the period, fifty more bags are stacked five high and the little corner section looks immaculate.

"Take a look at that big bite you've taken!" I say, and they gaze down at the litter-free plot proudly, as if it's their own. It looks like one completed corner of a very large jigsaw puzzle, but at least the project's beginning to make sense.

* * *

On Friday, after my students march down the gravel path with their rakes and shovels, I gather them in a semicircle.

"Look, I know some of you are wondering what's all this got to do with science. Aren't we just picking up trash? You need to trust me. I'm your teacher and we've got some stuff to learn, and we're going to find a way to learn it."

I'm trying to speak with sincerity and optimism, using the collective "we": we've got, we're going to, we can, we will. Half the kids are looking at me, squinting into the sun while the other half stare at the dirt.

"Scientific research is nothing more than looking at something and realizing it's not the same as it used to be, for better or worse. And if it's for the worse, you try to find out what went wrong so you can fix it or make it better. And if it's better, you try to find out why so you can replicate it."

Most of them are looking up now. Susannah is surreptitiously chewing a stick of gum, a violation of school rules. I'm waiting for Bob to ask me what "replicate" means, but he doesn't.

"In medical research, if you see lots of folks dying, you try to find out why. Well, look down into that little ravine."

As if all connected to the same string, my students' eyes rotate left until they're peering down into the trash- and cinder-infested wash.

"We know it didn't always look like that, so what do you think happened?"

Silence. Instead of answering for them, I take Amy's advice and play the good waiter—not the table-serving kind, but someone with the patience to let the students mull over the question and formulate an answer. So I wait: six, seven, eight, nine seconds that seem to crawl along kicking and screaming into infinity. Finally, Amanda speaks:

"The city ran out of space to dump their trash?"

"OK," I say, "there's a start. Every winter when it snows, what do the city trucks dump on the roads?"

Will snaps his fingers as if he just discovered a cure for cancer. "Got it. Cinders!"

"Yes, cinders. And what do the city trucks do with the excess cinders?"

I motion with my head toward the giant mounds swelling from the ravine. "This is not a trick question, folks."

"They dump it here!" Susannah says.

"Bingo! And what about those giant, broken slabs of concrete? Where did they come from?"

Bob shrugs. "More trucks."

"Yes, but where does the concrete come from?"

"Buildings," Daniel Carlyle in the preppie argyle sweater says. "Old buildings, bridges I imagine. Construction sites. Anywhere they use concrete."

"Sure. Or any time they tear up a sidewalk or a driveway and replace it." I sweep my arm out toward the yard. "And what about this other stuff—refrigerators, old sofas, bedsprings, pop cans?"

"People," Amanda says. "Inconsiderate people. Isn't it against the law? To toss your trash here?"

"Maybe," Bob says, "but you gotta throw your trash somewhere. If there's no city dump or nothing."

"But it doesn't have to be *here*," Amanda says. "Not right behind our school!"

Will puts his fists to his eyes and rubs them, blocking false tears. "Boo hoo, Amanda!"

"All right, all right," I say, reining him in. "What about this plant?" I bend down, grab a tall, stubborn plant by the stem and wrench it from the earth. "Who can tell me what plant this is?"

"It's an ugly-ass weed," Bob says. I shoot him knife eyes. "Sorry, Mr. Hunter," he says.

"No, it's a plant," I explain, "but there's something unique about it."

"Is it ragweed?" Amanda asks.

"No, it's not ragweed." I entertain three more guesses, some of them outlandish: sunflower, hazelnut, bottlebrush.

"No this is a common mullein. Do you know what's unique about it?" Twenty-six heads shake solemnly.

"This is an invasive plant. Do you know what that means? Invasive? What does it mean to invade something?"

"You go in and try to take something over," Bob Creighton says.

"Yes. Like mice coming into your house or one country invading another. So an invasive plant is a plant that doesn't belong here, but somehow it got here. And now it's taking over the ecosystem."

"So bad shit?" Will Gillespie says. "I mean, stuff."

"Yes, really bad stuff," I say.

"They're just stupid little plants," Bob says.

"Little but not stupid. They take water and nutrients from the soil and crowd out native plants."

Jimmy Goldtooth mutters something to Dora Smallcanyon, who snickers.

"Jimmy," I say, "would you like to share your insights with the rest of us?"

Jimmy's eyes are nailed to the ground.

"Come on, Jimmy. You're among friends here."

Dora gets Jimmy off the hook: "He says it's like the white man invading Indian land."

I laugh—I can't help it. "Great analogy! And what did the white people do when they invaded? They took the best land, the best water, the best minerals. Kind of like invasive plants." I pause a moment for this to sink in. Some clearly get it, others don't.

"So far we've been doing mostly cleanup. We've taken some of the trash that doesn't belong here and gotten rid of it. Some of this stuff is too heavy for us to move, so we're going to need help. A lot of it we can move ourselves. But I think we want to do more than just clean up around here, don't we?"

I scan their faces. The ones who are looking at me appear suspicious, as if this has been a weeklong, too-good-to-be-true setup for a trap, and now I'm going to spring it on them.

I direct their attention to a wooden storage shed on the south end of the lot, a new addition compliments of Roger Youngblood and U.S. Soil Conservation. "OK, put your rakes and shovels in the shed and let's go back inside for a bit."

*   *   *

Fifteen minutes later, as they settle into their seats, I ask the million-dollar question: "What do you want to do with that junkyard out there? Besides clean it up. Any ideas?"

Bob lifts one massive shoulder, then the other, as if he were Atlas rolling the world from left to right. "I don't know. I thought you said we were back inside now."

"Just for today," I explain. "And occasionally when we need to do some book work or if the weather's bad. But that's your real classroom—out there."

I see smiles again, nods and nudges. No wonder they'd looked so pissed off. They thought this classroom incarceration bit was permanent.

"So what do you want to do with it?"

"I don't know," Will says. "You're the teacher."

"Yes, and I can help. But it's your project."

"What about that Mr. Youngblood guy," Susannah says. "Can he help some more?"

"Oh, he'd love to help! And he has all kinds of resources. But we have to ask. We'll have to write a letter and request help. And before we can write a letter requesting help, we've got to figure out what we want to do."

"We already know what we wanna do," Bob says. "We wanna clean the stupid junkyard."

"We need a plan," Ricky Watson grumbles impatiently. A husky boy with bushy black hair, Ricky lurks in the back row reading Tolkien when he isn't secretly sketching muscle-bound superheroes in his spiral notebook. It's the first time he's offered anything unsolicited in my class.

"Yes," I say. "We need a plan. With details. What do we want to do and how are we going to do it? Step by step. So here's your first assignment. I want you to go home tonight and write up a plan for what we're going to do with that junkyard. I want you to be creative. Think big. Don't just say we'll clean it up. What are we going to do with it after it's clean? Don't worry about the cost or how hard it sounds. Think big and dream bigger!"

Bob's hand goes up. "Mr. Hunter, how many pages does it gotta be?"

"As many as it takes. It doesn't have to be long, but it better be bold and it better not be boring."

A distressed future valedictorian half-raises her hand, withdraws it, then starts to raise it again, sort of.

"Amanda? You have a question?"

"Mr. Hunter, I get that we're going to do this project cleaning up the dump and all that, but are we going to learn anything about real science? I'm on the college track and I want to take AP classes when I'm a junior."

I stare at Amanda a good five seconds before I reply: "Don't worry, Amanda. You're going to get your science—*real* science—and plenty of it."

ROLLER COASTER

At dinner that night I make my first confession. "On the one hand, I've never seen those kids so excited about anything." Amy arches an eyebrow. "Then I guess you haven't taught the unit on sexual reproduction yet."

"OK, never so excited in *my classroom*. Better?"

"Much. What's the other hand? I'm waiting for that shoe to drop."

I smile, shrug, shake my head. "I have no idea where this thing's headed. It's like I'm leading them through the labyrinth with a droopy candle that casts just enough light to see a foot ahead of us."

"You mean you're flying by the seat of your pants?"

"Yes! Trial and error, on-the-job training—it's a leap of faith, and I'm just hoping my parachute will open before Melvin Jackson and the school board get wind of what I'm up to."

Amy leans across the table and kisses me on the lips, soft and lingering, then withdraws abruptly: "Just don't get fired, Buster."

"Since when do you call me Buster?"

"Since right now—Buster!" Her index finger pokes me playfully in the chest, and I return the favor with two swift, flying hands to her thoracic region.

"Watch it, Buster!" she says, trying to squirm free, but I'm a two-armed octopus coiling all over her. She's laughing and so am I. Things have been much better in the house since the launch of my project. Three days camping on the North Rim didn't hurt either.

But I know ninth graders—or I'm learning quickly. It's all about energy and momentum, and I want to keep this locomotive rolling down the tracks. The next day, after taking roll and acknowledging the presence of Roger Youngblood, I hop right to it, dividing the kids into six groups: "All right, listen for your number! Sue, you're a one. Bob, you're a two. Karla, a three." And so on. Then: "All the ones over here, twos over there, threes in the far corner…"

I'm dismayed by how this seemingly simple task translates into a fifteen-minute rendition of the Exodus. (Patience, I remind myself. It's process as much as product. It'll get easier. Baby steps, Todd—for me and them.)

Instructions. Be clear. Precise. Specific.

"I want you each to share your plan with the other members of your group."

Will Gillespie's arm stretches toward the fluorescent lights as if he means to swat them. "What plan?"

"The plan you were supposed to write up for last night's homework," I explain. "And if you didn't do it, you get a zero for the day." I need to send a message now, at the outset—the first of many come-to-Jesus moments during this journey.

"Let's be clear. This isn't *laissez faire* anything-goes *que será será* play-time. You'll have assignments, lots of them, and they'll be graded. You'll have exams too, and quizzes. I'm giving you each a folder and you're going to keep a portfolio of all your work, and at the end of the semester you'll be graded on both the quality and the quantity of your assignments. Do you understand? Mr. Creighton?"

Bob Creighton, who has been yawning throughout my little diatribe, mumbles into his sleeve.

"I'll take that as a yes. How about the rest of you? Do you understand?"

Nods, mumbles, a handful of audible assents.

Susannah Thompson's arm rises like a swan. "Is Mr. Youngblood here to help?"

I glance over at Roger, who's standing by the door like a grim-faced bouncer.

"Mr. Youngblood came to show us a plan his people have put together."

"Why don't we just use that?" Susannah asks, and it's as if someone had shot off a gun. The room goes completely silent. The Navajo kids in the back row look up. Ricky Watson closes his spiral notebook. Amanda Stone stops scribbling her diligent notes. Twenty-six faces are staring at me, waiting for an answer.

"Because this is *your* project, and we want to hear your ideas first."

Bob shrugs. "What's the point if you're just going to use their plan?"

"We're not. We're going to take the best ideas from both plans—yours and theirs—and then we're going to make a single master plan. I want to hear your ideas first because I'll bet you my Ford pickup that a lot of yours will be a helluva lot better than *that* guy's!" I throw my finger like a dart at Roger, who shields his face with his hands.

"Don't shoot the messenger, Todd!" he says.

I'm fired up; this is a big-time teaching moment, and I don't want to blow it. I'm speaking to the next wave of the Now Generation, young teenagers who've been warned by everyone from Jerry Rubin to the Beatles and the Rolling Stones to trust no one over thirty. They've watched adults gun down Robert Kennedy and Dr. Martin Luther King, and their parents have elected a president who preaches law and order but in four years will come within a hair's breadth of impeachment. Their self-righteous elders scoff at anti-war protests as the body count in Vietnam proliferates on the nightly news. I'm holding an "us against the grown-ups" card—play it.

"Don't be intimidated by these guys," I say, as if the room were suddenly filled with conspiring adults. "Yes, they're professionals; yes, they've got some good ideas, but you've got ideas too. And when it comes to creative thinking, you kids don't have to take a back seat to anyone!"

I see nods, some smiles, a little uncertainty, and a sliver of a grin beneath Roger's mustache.

So much for that little detour. Back to the main highway: instructions.

"I want each person to share your plan with your group. Then you can either choose one of those plans or you can make a composite plan."

"Mr. Hunter, what's a composite?"

Will Gillespie. Is he seriously missing a few cards or is he just yanking my chain?

"It's a combination of several plans blended into one."

Will nods. "OK."

"All right then, let's get to work!"

*   *   *

Some groups jump right into it. I can already hear Amanda as she reads her master plan, detailed step by detailed step. Other groups are dead silent—four strangers stuck in an elevator. They need some prodding, so I join their circle.

"Mr. Creighton! Let's see what you've got!"

That's Day One, idea-sharing within the groups. The following day, Roger returns to listen to each group's spokesperson sharing their plan with the class. But first, some rules and guidelines.

"What we're doing here," I explain, "is brainstorming. We're trying to generate all the ideas we possibly can. So I'm going to write down the best ideas from each group—your group plan—and then we're going to choose the best of the best for our master plan."

As I survey the students' faces, I see the full spectrum: confusion (Will Gillespie), indifference (Jake Bonner), unbridled enthusiasm (Amanda Stone), consternation (Daniel Carlyle), and consummate boredom (Bob Creighton).

"There's one cardinal rule about brainstorming: there's no such thing as a bad idea. So no laughing, no teasing, no ridiculing anyone else's idea. Some of the greatest scientific discoveries in history began in absurdity. The Earth is round? The Sun is the center of our solar system? Bah, humbug! Do you understand what I'm saying?"

More nods, mumbles, half-hearted verbal assents.

I stand at the chalkboard with chalk poised as each spokesperson explains the group plan. They are, for the most part, uninspiring, but I print them on the board: clean up the dump (thank you, but that's a given); make it into a park; use it to expand the athletic fields; build an ice-skating rink; plant a garden; plant an apple orchard; convert it into a rodeo ground; make it into a parking lot and charge people to park there.

"Some good ideas," I say when they're done. "You all brought your thinking caps today." I'm trying to disguise my colossal disappointment, especially after my rousing endorsement of the creative fires of youth. I was hoping for something bigger, more imaginative and visionary; a statement to the community and the state and maybe the entire nation about what science education could and should be. Instead, they're going to clean up somebody else's trash and maybe plant a few trees. And none of them—with the exception of Amanda, who oozes exuberance if they announce a sock hop or a raffle over the intercom—seem excited about any of the options. Shrug. Yawn. Whatever. Yesterday's enthusiasm was a footprint in the sand.

I'm ready to concede the floor to Roger to present the U.S. Soil Conservation Service plan when I notice Dora Smallcanyon timidly lifting her hand maybe six inches off her desk, as if it weighed fifty pounds.

"Yes, Dora?"

Unlike Jake Bonner, who glares at his desk to assert his aloof belligerence, Dora Smallcanyon lowers her eyes out of respect: I'm an adult, the teacher.

Her voice is a soft, staccato rain, her sentences flowing even as they strike little speed bumps. "Mr. Hunter, I was just thinking. There's a little stream of water running through that junkyard. Could we make it like a creek or something? Then the animals would come. Plants would grow and all kinds of things like that."

Dora has said more in the last thirty seconds than she will the rest of the school year, but that's OK: fireworks are exploding in my head.

"Thank you, Dora," I say as I turn to the board and print: CREE…

"Or a river!" Will shouts. "With fish and everything!"

"Or a lake!" Susannah says.

A loud, familiar laugh—Bob's—is instantly killed by my withering glare.

"Or a pond," she offers apologetically.

I nod, urging them on. "What about a pond?"

And so the real discussion begins.

"We could build a dam on the south end," Joaquin Sanchez says, "where that road crosses over to the forest."

"We could make an island in the middle," Jimmy Goldtooth says.

"A pond with an island!" Bob crows. "Cool!"

"With fish and ducks and birds and plants," Susannah adds.

Will joins in: "Cattails and trees."

"Water will attract the big animals too," Jimmy says. "Deer, coyotes…"

"Like an animal sanctuary!" Amanda offers.

"OK, a wildlife refuge," I say. "Keep talking!"

But my hand can hardly keep pace with the flow of ideas, some inspired, others preposterous, and some downright tacky.

"A hiking trail—like a nature walk, with plaques to identify the plants and stuff."

"Concession stands!" Bob shouts. "We could sell popcorn and hot dogs."

Boos fill the classroom.

"Hey, I thought we were brainstorming!" Bob says. "There's no such thing as a bad idea. Right, Mr. Hunter?"

I reach up and snatch Bob's thought out of the air, crumble it in my hand, and toss it into the wastepaper basket. The classroom erupts in applause. Playing along, Bob drops his head in mock shame and defeat.

"Not cool, Mr. H! Not cool!" he says, but he can't keep a straight face.

The vibe is so good, so strong, that I don't want the period to end. I glance at the clock: fifteen minutes to the bell. Energy and momentum. Keep the train moving.

"OK," I say, reining them in, "what'll be the purpose of the pond? This wildlife sanctuary?"

"A meditation pond!" Karla Walker in the paisley skirt and peasant blouse suggests.

"No!" Bob objects. "We ain't no California hippy freaks!"

"How about to do what we're doing," Amanda says.

"That don't make no sense at all," Will says.

I point to Amanda. "OK, and what's that? What have we been doing, Amanda?"

She shrugs. "Learning about science. That's what you said the first day of class." It's the brilliant idea I'd been hoping they'd discover on their own, but it needs a bit of shaping.

"So are you talking about creating an outdoor classroom?" I suggest. "To study science in the real world?"

"Instead of that dumb-ass BSCS," Bob impugns. "Bullshit and chicken shit."

"Watch your language, Mr. Creighton. Although I agree with your assessment of the BSCS text."

"Yes!" someone shouts exuberantly, a girl but not Amanda. Others join the choir: yes yes yes yes. Now their eyes are fanatical—in a good way. Even Jake has fingered back his bangs for a better look at the scrawl on the chalkboard.

It's time to cede the stage to Roger, who compliments the kids on their enthusiasm and innovative thinking. He briefly reviews the U.S. Soil Conservation Service's proposal, noting the similarities between it and the students' plan: clean out the trash, dam the stream, and create a pond that can be used as a living science laboratory and wildlife refuge. Nature trails, archeological digs, reforestation projects, all of that and more.

He flashes the students a gritty smile. He's looking forward to working with them, he says. Collaborating with them. It's going to be a great project—great for the school, great for the community, great for the environment. My kids are only half-listening. They're too enamored with their own ideas to recognize that most of them are mirror images of the plan Roger just presented.

I thank him and remind my students that he'll be working closely with them throughout the project. They smile and nod and say good, good, whatever, fine.

The moment Roger exits, my kids begin shouting out more ideas, insisting that I add them to the board, and I do, as quickly as possible because the clock's racing to the end of the period. But I want to reach up and grab the minute hand, freezing time forever. This is the day—the moment of ecstasy—I'd envisioned when I put ink on my first teacher contract three months ago; this is the mystical moment when teacher and students merge as one, when passion, inspiration, and enlightenment dance the inseparable dance, eternally binding instructor and pupil. If I hit the buzzer-beater to win the NBA finals, I couldn't fly any higher than I'm soaring right here, right now, with these kids. Instead of recalcitrant, bored-to-tears teenagers, they're thinkers, creators, problem-solvers, collaborators—they're going to be Scientists, dammit! With a capital *S*! And chomping at the bit to get at it. They're a locomotive plowing through the heretofore dreaded wilderness of science, and nothing's going to stop them. They've got momentum; they've gained the summit and they're barreling full-speed downhill and heaven help the fool who tries to stop them.

I could kiss them all.

* * *

Instead, I give them homework.

"Good work today," I say, noting one minute till the bell, when the magic will vanish and I'll turn back into an oh-so-ordinary pumpkin. "So we have a goal—to create an outdoor science classroom. Now we need a plan."

"I thought we just made a plan?" Bob says.

"We need details; we need specifics. How are we going to do it? Tonight, I want each of you to make a list of everything that needs to be done to make this happen. Brainstorm with yourself. Write down everything you can think of. Then put it in order. What needs to be done first, second, third, fourth, and so on. Understand? Yes, no, maybe so?"

And it's as if I've just cut their collective carotid artery and bled all the energy and enthusiasm out of them. I'm staring at a gallery of shell-shocked soldiers.

"Come on, you can do it! It's brainstorming! No bad ideas, no bad answers—except for you, Mr. Creighton." I laugh because it's just a joke and they should all know that by now, shouldn't they? Apparently not. Mr. Creighton's not laughing. Neither is anyone else. What the hell have I done? As the bell rings, they stand and shuffle quietly out the door, looking as if I've just sent them off to be fed to the lions.

SAUSAGE

Energy and momentum. Peaks and valleys. One minute I've got them floating in the clouds; the next, reality smashes them in the mouth—hey, folks, this means work, and lots of it!—throwing them into a frantic free fall. But that's just growing pangs. They'll catch on; they'll get used to it. I've got a process now, and this is how it works: I give them individual assignments and then they report to their groups; each group shares its best ideas with the class, and the class gleans the best of the best. Everyone participates. Everyone has a voice, a job, a role to play. Everyone's dependent upon everyone else. Everyone will lift, load, and learn.

I split them into new groups to share their individual plans, except now I'm calling them teams, as in Team One, Team Two, Team Three, and so on, because I want them thinking teamwork and collaboration, with a little healthy competition too. But some teams are chattering like magpies, while others look funereal. Bob Creighton wants to know why they can't have a team name. "Team Three sounds so boring!" he groans.

I shrug. "Who says you can't have a name? It's your project."

The other teams want a piece of the action, so they blow half a period drumming up names. The results are a mixed bag: Pink Panthers, Sun Devils, Scowling Skunks (Bob's team), Wildcats, Mountaineers, and Four Cowboys and an Indian.

"Now, everybody share your plan with your group and then create a group plan."

As I bounce from team to team, peppering up the troops, I notice a critical detail missing from every plan.

"Time-out! Before we can do anything with that junkyard, isn't there something we need to find out?"

Silence.

"Mr. Creighton! What would you do if a truckload of kids drove up and started digging up your front yard?"

"I'd give 'em five bucks! Nothing in my front yard but weeds!"

Mass laughter.

"I'd get my daddy's shotgun," Will Gillespie says, "and fill their ass with buckshot!"

Another round of guffaws.

"My point exactly," I say. "What do we need to know before we can do anything else to that property?"

More silence. I try to wait them out, but it's a war I can't win today. I have things to teach, and they can sit there and run out the clock.

Finally, an exasperated voice from the back: "Who owns it," Jake Bonner says. "You've gotta know who owns the stupid land." Arms folded, staring at his desk, his chiseled face half-hidden behind those droopy bangs.

Speed it up, Todd. You're molasses to the bright kids.

"Yes. We need to find out who owns it, and then we need to get permission to use it. Be sure to include that step in your plans."

*   *   *

It's pathetically slow going at first, but by the end of the week each group has drafted a plan and the group's designated spokesperson has presented it for comments and feedback. On Friday, the kids vote for the plan they like the best (Amanda Stone's Wildcats win by a two-to-one margin—no surprise there), but there's an interesting twist. Students can recommend that parts of the other plans be integrated into the main plan. So Bob's Scowling Skunks lobby hard to include some kind of dock that will extend twenty feet out over the pond to be used for extracting samples for scientific analysis and, of course, for fishing.

The process isn't always pretty—in many ways it's like making sausage—but by the end of week two, the kids have drafted a master plan I tape to the chalkboard next to the U.S. Soil Conservation Service proposal so they can compare the two.

Fortunately, there's about 90 percent overlap, so with a bit of tweaking my students merge the two into one super-plan that Susannah Thompson, the duly elected scribe, writes on the board in her elegant cursive. Then Amanda Stone, the class spokesperson, reviews the final plan with the class. What's supposed to be an opportunity for students to offer constructive feedback ends up being a long, dry recitation that gives Will Gillespie and Bob Creighton a green light to catch some extra z's:

THE PONDEROSA JUNIOR HIGH WILDLIFE REFUGE AND OUTDOOR LEARNING CENTER

Goal: To create a wild-life refuge and outdoor learning center for teaching science in authentic contexts.

STAGE 1: AUTHORIZATION & PREPARATION

Goal: To obtain permission to create the outdoor learning center

Develop proposal and presentation

Present proposal to principal and school board

Identify land owners

Present plan to land owners

Identify individuals, agencies, and resources that can assist

Submit written requests to individuals, agencies, and resources

STAGE 2: CLEANUP

Goal: To clean out the junkyard

Obtain necessary tools for cleanup

Identify individuals, businesses, and agencies that can assist

Submit requests (verbally or in writing) for cleanup assistance

Develop systematic cleanup schedule

Clean up! All hands on deck!!!

STAGE 3: FLORA MANAGEMENT

Goal: To remove invasive plants and cultivate/plant native plants

Identify individuals, businesses, and agencies that can assist

Submit requests (verbally or in writing) for flora assistance

Identify native and invasive plants

Remove invasive plants

Cultivate existing native plants

Plant additional native plants

STAGE 4: POND DEVELOPMENT

Goal: To create a pond

Identify individuals, businesses, and agencies that can assist

Submit requests (verbally or in writing) for assistance with construction

Complete landscaping to best accommodate water flow

STAGE 5: NATURE TRAIL

Goal: To develop a nature trail around the pond

Develop a plan for the trail

Identify individuals, businesses, and agencies that can assist

Submit requests (verbally or in writing) for assistance with trail and signs

Build the trail

Research information for the signs
Create the signs

STAGE 6: MAINTENANCE AND EXPANSION
Goal: To maintain the high quality of the pond ecosystem and expand
as needed
Identify maintenance tasks
Create a maintenance schedule
Perform routine maintenance (weeding, planting, etc.)
Create a team to explore options for improvement and expansion
Develop a plan for improvement and expansion

Amanda finishes her review, smiles courteously, and takes her seat.

"We've got a plan," I say. "Let's divide it up and conquer! Pink Panthers, you guys need to find out who owns the land and who we need to talk to, to get permission to use it. Roger Youngblood should be your first phone call. His people at U.S. Soil can help. Wildcats and Sun Devils, develop a proposal we can present to all the permission people. This is a big project, so I'm putting two teams on it. Mountaineers and Four Cowboys and an Indian, same deal. You guys write letters to Roger, asking for help. You're going to write a bunch of other people too. Scowling Skunks, you'll make a list of agencies and organizations we can ask for help. I'm talking about businesses and construction crews. That may sound easy, but you've got to do some research. Find out who the contact person is, his name, address, phone number, all of that. Talk to your parents and get them involved. Maybe they can help with labor or publicity or whatever. Do you all understand what you need to do?"

I've been talking like a racetrack announcer and their expressions show it: a gallery of faces all miming Edvard Munch's "The Scream." I hear Amy catcalling from the peanut gallery: try it again, Todd, and slooowly this time! Remember? Kids who don't hardly speak no science? And a visual wouldn't hurt.

I draw three columns on the board and label them TASK, TEAM RESPONSIBLE, and DEADLINE. Then I repeat the instructions—slooowly—filling in the columns as I go.

"How's that?" I ask. "How about nod if you understand."

Half the heads bob slightly: the other half are statues. Fine. Close enough for government work (and junior high).

I clap my hands, trying to revive their now defunct enthusiasm. "Let's get after it!"

No one moves. I wait. And wait. And wait. But today they are, quite literally, saved by the bell. And so am I.

*   *   *

I trudge home that night wondering when word will finally leak out about this oddball science teacher who teaches everything but science. And every day, I return to work expecting to see Melvin Jackson standing outside my classroom waving a pink slip in my face.

Amy tells me to hang in there. "Those kids may surprise you," she says. "Give them a chance."

And, once again, Amy's right. A week later, Amanda Stone's Wildcats and Jake Bonner's Sun Devils present me with a detailed, ten-page proposal, a one-page executive summary, and an outline for a ten-minute oral presentation that includes Dora Smallcanyon's stunning watercolor rendition of the completed pond (Stage 5). Joaquin Sanchez's Mountaineers and Jimmy Goldtooth's Four Cowboys and an Indian have written fifteen letters requesting various types of assistance and have already received positive responses from five of them. Bob Creighton's Scowling Skunks present me with a list of thirty local businesses that verbally pledged support, including two local construction companies that have agreed to haul away the broken slabs of concrete and other heavy-duty junk. (Later, at open house, I'll meet Bob's father, the owner of one of those companies.) And Susannah Thompson proudly hands me a schedule of upcoming presentations to key stakeholders, including the school board a week from Tuesday, the city council (because the city owns the property; thank you, Pink Panthers) the following Wednesday, and Principal Jackson this afternoon.

"We hope you're ready to go, Mr. Hunter," Susannah says, flashing her brightest Miss America smile.

HIGH NOON

A t first I think he's having one of his lousy, rotten, miserable days, and I should reschedule. Or maybe he's just being irascible Melvin Jackson, slouching in his leather swivel chair, bulldog jowls scrunched up against his palm, bloodshot eyes glaring at me like chlorinated cue balls. When I hand him Susannah Thompson's one-page executive summary, he grunts. When I direct his attention to Dora Smallcanyon's watercolor visual and two posters summarizing the six-stage project in bold bullet points, he tilts his head back and yawns. And the more I talk, the lower his frown droops, until I think Bob Garcia the custodian will have to scoop it off the floor. By the time I finish my pitch, my enthusiastic voice has faded to an apologetic whisper as the air hisses out of my balloon.

"Well, I guess that's it," I say, bracing myself for the inevitable thumbs-down.

But Jackson's floor-bound frown is magically resurrected as a gap-toothed smile: "I love it!" he says, pounding the desk three times. "I love it! I love it! I love it!"

My eyes brighten, but then his mouth drops again.

"What's wrong?"

"Next time, let the students give the presentation." He makes a fist and upper-cuts the air. "More clout when they present to the city council."

"Don't we have to go to the school board first?"

"Don't worry about those assholes. If I like it, they'll like it. Now go on, get the hell out of here! You've got work to do!"

*   *   *

Jackson's correct about the school board. With Amanda Stone and Jake Bonner copresenting, four of the five board members vote in favor, with one abstention, Shirley Horton, the mayor's wife. Of course, there wasn't much suspense. After Amanda's opening line ("We would like to propose to the governing board an innovative, experiential approach to teaching biology in an authentic, real-life context while integrating multiple disciplines that will result in a symbiotic benefit to the students, the school, and the community…"), she could have sold them Brussels sprouts for ninety bucks a pound and they would have agreed. But school board members are all educators or former educators. The city council's a different animal.

Although all five members are white, they're an eclectic mix of professions and opinions that can generally be distilled down to one of two perspectives: pro-growth/pro-business or anti-growth/pro-environment.

A decorated World War II hero, Major Gordon McDowell is a local developer and staunch Republican who keeps a tight fist on the city's purse strings while at the same time seeding local businesses. He wants to know why the hell the federal government has hijacked all the surrounding forest land, "economically strangling our little city."

Renae Heller is a realtor who wears skirts that show off her tennis-honed calves. Those distracted by her figure underestimate her prowess as a businesswoman, a mistake she exploits liberally.

Phyllis Rasmussen popped out of an 1880s time capsule: long skirts and granny glasses. She's an anti-growth granola who pedals her Schwinn one-speed three miles to council meetings. Yes, in the snow.

A handsome, barrel-chested Captain America, Don Ostanovich is the wild card. As owner of the local ski resort, he wants tourism to flourish, but he needs to protect his primary investment as well: the forest. He's pro-growth to a point.

On the surface, Dennis Hancock is the strait-laced, affable fellow you'd let chaperone your wife on a weekend trip to Las Vegas. But beneath the surface lurks a schemer. Philosophically speaking, Dennis is neither pro-growth nor anti-growth. His decisions and opinions are driven entirely by politics and, more specifically, whatever will position him best in a mayoral run.

This is the benevolent buzz saw my students don't realize awaits them as they settle into the padded theater chairs in the city council chambers. I'd briefly considered coaching them with a scouting report on each councilman's positions and proclivities, but then I decided, What the hell? It's the fall of 1969. The Beatles have recently released their masterpiece album, *Abbey Road*. On college campuses, young students in glorified rags, sandals, and tie-dyed headbands are protesting the Vietnam War, racial discrimination, environmental pollution, the obsessive materialism of their parents. And while we live in a small town in the mountains where cultural trends lag five years behind the mainstream, my students watch the news on TV. They see GIs plodding through jungles. They see police in riot gear beating black men and women with nightsticks. They see young people just a few years older than they are squaring off with the National Guard. And they listen to the radio. They buy records. They go to movies. Images of Woodstock are fresh in their heads. Nationwide, the seeds of rebellion have been planted and the flowers are blooming. My kids are ready for this. Let them carry the day.

*   *   *

The meeting begins with the usual business—Pledge of Allegiance, approval of the agenda, and comments from the audience. Fortunately, tonight's agenda is low profile, with no hot-button topics to attract the masses. Still, with twenty-three of my students present plus many of their parents, it's a standing-room-only crowd. A reporter from the local paper is sitting off to the side, which bodes well for us: it will be harder for the city council to play Scrooge to a group of well-intentioned junior-high kids, especially on a slow news day when it might earn a front-page headline.

Council chair Dennis Hancock asks the audience how many are here for item five on the agenda, "Proposed Outdoor Classroom," and all but five hands go up.

"Then in the interests of these young citizens who have school tomorrow," Hancock says, "I move that item five be moved to front of the agenda. Do I have a second?"

A smiling Phyllis Rasmussen seconds the motion, which passes.

And with that, Hancock calls Amanda Stone and Jake Bonner forward. Amanda has dressed the part: a dark skirt with a white blouse, her brunette hair in a Jackie Kennedy flip. Professional yet warm, charming. She stands ramrod straight, as if addressing the United Nations. Jake, on the other hand, saunters up in baggy bell-bottoms and a paisley shirt with the tail hanging loose, black bangs almost covering one eye. His posture says, You're really lucky I'm here tonight because I've got a million important things I could be doing right now.

Amanda approaches the podium and squares off with the five council members seated behind the dais, each with a nameplate and a microphone sticking up like a metal weed. Smiling, she says, "First and foremost, I want to thank you, the members of the city council, for the many hours of dedicated service you give to this community. And I want to thank you for giving us the time to present our proposal tonight."

Perfect. Grease the wheels first. Most definitely coached by her father, the dean of the College of Business Administration at the university.

"What if I told you about a project that would allow students to learn about science the way real scientists do—not in a stuffy classroom but in the field, getting their hands and feet dirty, digging, measuring, calculating, hypothesizing, analyzing, theorizing"—Amanda pauses, not to look at the notes she doesn't have, but for dramatic effect—"while at the same time cleaning up an embarrassing eyesore in our community and transforming it into a place of peace and beauty, a veritable refuge for the flora and fauna of our town."

I try not to over-smile at this Oscar-worthy performance. The reporter is earnestly scribbling in her notepad. A good sign.

"And would you, the city council, support such a project? Please ponder this as my colleague, Jake Bonner, elaborates on this innovative, experiential approach to teaching science while beautifying the community."

Amanda has loaded the bases for Jake, who saunters up to the podium. He may not have dressed to impress, but his presentation is clear, concise, persuasive. As Dora Smallcanyon holds up her watercolor rendition and Bob Creighton and Will Gillespie display the other two posters, Jake explains each stage of the project. When he describes how we'll make a V-shaped island in the middle of the pond with the wedge end facing southwest, Don Ostanovich asks: "Why does that matter? To have the wedge end facing that way?"

Jake doesn't miss a beat. "So in the winter, when the wind blows over the top of the V, the water's calm there, and ice won't be able to form inside it."

Don Ostanovich and the other council members are impressed. So am I. How the hell does Jake Bonner know about wind direction and ice formation in a lake that doesn't exist yet? We're still picking up trash out there.

When Jake finishes, his classmates respond with thunderous applause. Several parents leap to their feet, clapping. Hancock waits a full two minutes before pounding his gavel to restore order.

* * *

The kids aren't through. Bob walks up to the podium, hitches up his pants, and leans into the mic: "It's like a new method so we can learn science in a realistic way," he says. "More realistic than the stuff that's written in an ugly green book that we can't hardly understand." Bob gazes at the council members as if facing a firing squad. "Well, that's all I have to say, I guess. Thank you." Bowing awkwardly, he returns to his seat amid enthusiastic cheers.

Next, Susannah Thompson strolls up to the front. The southern California transplant is playing up her beach girl image, casually brushing her platinum hair away from her eyes. "We can learn about these things—science things, you know—out there, outside, in nature, and then we can go back to the biology book and see how it all connects."

More applause for Susannah as she heads back. Then she abruptly stops and returns to the microphone. "You know, I just want to say—"

But Gordon McDowell interrupts in his gravelly, commander's voice. "I think you've said enough already, young lady."

Without thinking, I blurt out: "You didn't let her finish!" The chamber goes dead silent. McDowell the war hero is a member of multiple do-gooder community clubs and committees, so well-known and highly esteemed he doesn't have to campaign for his seat. And I have just publicly pooped in his mess kit.

In my defense, I'm young and brash and new to this game of small-town politics. In my mind, there's a right and a wrong way to do things, and what he's done—cutting off my student while she still has the floor—is wrong. I'm also naïve. I don't know which side of my bread is being buttered, by whom or for how long. I'm a principled fool with a touch of the papa bear: I don't care if McDowell single-handedly planted the Stars and Stripes on Iwo Jima—no one talks to my kids like that.

"She's not finished," I repeat. Then: "Go on, Susannah."

Susannah looks down at the floor, then up at the council members, shooting them a demure smile that could have calmed a maelstrom. "I just want to say, I'm from L.A. and there's lots of cool stuff in L.A. They've got the ocean and Disneyland and Hollywood, but their schools don't have anything like this. I mean where you can walk out your back door and learn all about nature and science. What we're trying to do—I mean, this is so much better than Disneyland. And I hope you can see that. Because I see it. All of us here—" Susannah turns a half circle so her back's to the council and she's facing her classmates and their parents and me: "We can all see it. We can all see that pond." Turning back around: "I hope you can too. Thanks for your time."

The crowd erupts: applause from the adults, hoots and hollers from the kids. This is followed by three more testimonials (Bob Creighton, Jimmy Goldtooth, and Daniel Carlyle, each stoking a similar response).

Meanwhile, my whole body's tingling with a pride and joy I've never felt quite like this before. The closest thing was probably my senior year of high school, when ten thousand spectators cheered as I stepped onto the victory stand after placing first in the pole vault at the state track and field finals at Sun Devil Stadium. Except that was all about me. This is about them—me *and* them—and the exhilaration I experienced back then is a whisper compared to what I'm feeling now.

*   *   *

Dennis Hancock thanks the presenters and all those who have come out to support them. Then he turns to the others for comments and questions. Now that the applause has faded and their smiles have settled, they've got plenty, especially after Hancock reminds them that the proposal, if approved, will mean granting rights to the school district to clean up and develop the property in question as an outdoor classroom and wildlife refuge. "Currently, that property falls under the jurisdiction of Parks and Recreation," he says.

Phyllis Rasmussen can barely suppress her excitement: "Oh, yes! Yes! I absolutely vote for this wonderful project!" She presses her palms together as if thanking God for the city's good fortune. "And I just want to say, kudos to these wonderful young people for a magnificent presentation!"

There's one vote. We need three.

Renae Heller wants to know what will happen when we lose our city dump? "We've got to put that trash somewhere. We can't just toss it in the woods."

Don Ostanovich wants to know why we need to create an outdoor classroom when the city is surrounded by a million acres of national forest?

This is where I step up to the podium. I introduce myself and pay tribute to the students who have worked so hard to put this presentation together, reminding the council that these young people worked with the U.S. Soil Conservation Service to conceive the idea and draw up the plans, and so on.

"Yes, we're surrounded by a million acres of national forest, but these kids would have to travel ten minutes by bus to get there. That doesn't sound so bad until you consider that each period is only fifty-five minutes long. If you figure twenty minutes round-trip for transportation plus the time spent getting students on and off the bus, to and from the classroom, by the time you factor in all that you've got maybe ten, fifteen minutes of actual instruction time.

"But with the proposed project, these kids can walk outside and be working and learning in less than five minutes. That's not to mention the ownership factor: the students will be more invested in their learning if it's theirs and not some hobgoblin who wrote a textbook in New Jersey. Of course, they won't own the land, but they'll have skin in the game. They'll own it in the same sense that we all own this town—it's the place we live, so we want to take care of it and make it beautiful and not trash it up with graffiti and broken beer bottles. The pond will be something they helped create and they can take pride in that and be stewards over it."

Phyllis Rasmussen quietly applauds, but Renae Heller isn't so sure. "What about the safety factor?" she asks. "If you build a pond right behind the junior high, won't kids drown? Unless you hire a full-time lifeguard…"

"We'll have to put up warning signs," I say, "as a precaution. But the pond won't be more than four feet deep in any one spot."

"You can control that?" Don Ostanovich asks. "The depth of the pond?"

"Sure we can. Once we build the dam, we'll pretty much be controlling the flow of water in and out of the pond."

The gravelly voice of Gordon McDowell interrupts: "Dam? What dam?"

"Damn," I whisper to myself, because this is the one part of the plan I'd hoped would go unnoticed. It's exactly the excuse McDowell and Heller need to torpedo the project.

"We'll need to build a small dam on the south end of the pond," I explain. "That's to catch and control the water."

"How small?" McDowell asks.

"Nine, maybe ten feet high."

"Maybe?"

"Nine feet," I confirm. "Max."

McDowell reverts to military mode: his bullet eyes narrowed, his eagle's beak sharpened. "And where will it be located?"

"Like I said, on the south end of the pond."

"Can you be more specific, please?"

I try to speak with authority and conviction: "It'll be built where Colter Drive crosses the ravine."

McDowell's mouth opens wide enough to swallow the room. "You want to close a city street?"

"No, we'd build the dam right in front of the street. Alongside it. You'll have a street with a dam."

Renae Heller is rolling her eyes and Don Ostanovich, who I thought was leaning in our favor, stares at his notes. Even Phyllis Rasmussen looks as if someone's just delivered a stinky pizza.

McDowell drops his pencil and crosses his arms like the great chief making a historic pronouncement: "Well, that does it for me! I think it's quite obvious that, however well intentioned, this is a bad idea—not just a bad idea but a *very* bad idea. You can sit down, young man."

I start to speak, but McDowell aims his finger at me like a pistol: "You don't have the floor!"

*   *   *

All I can do now is sit and listen and hope they call on me for clarification. And pray against all odds that good-hearted Phyllis Rasmussen will somehow persuade her fellow council members that this is a wise idea.

"I want to applaud the students for their hard work," Renae Heller says, "but I do have concerns about public safety. And the city will lose its dumping ground, for lack of a better word."

Don Ostanovich also compliments the students but shares Heller's concerns. "And the potential road closure," he says. "That's a real red flag for me."

Then McDowell unloads: "Not only will this project cost the city a junkyard and a road closure, it'll create a public nuisance. What if we build this pond and someone dies? Who's liable for that? And have you thought about how this will affect the Fourth of July powwow? I think you're all aware of how much revenue that event brings into the city."

Of course. Every summer, the city sponsors an Independence Day powwow and rodeo that includes a week's worth of cultural events, attracting tourists from all over the country. On the north end of the junkyard, between rows of cinder cones, was a large field of dirt and gravel where families from the neighboring Navajo and Hopi reservations set up camp for the week. And without them, goodbye powwow, goodbye cultural events, and goodbye a whole lot of money. No wonder McDowell was lobbying so hard against the pond.

"These kids have the entire national forest to study the outdoors," McDowell said. "This is Parks and Rec property and it should stay that way. I motion that the request be denied."

But before Dennis Hancock can ask for a second, Phyllis Rasmussen saves the day.

"I think," she says, "before we go any further, maybe we should hear from some of our adult constituents."

Adult constituents. Parents. Voting citizens.

So they come forward: Bob Creighton's father and Susannah Thompson's mother and both of Will Gillespie's parents.

"My boy's never shown one iota of interest whatsoever in school let alone in science," Mr. Creighton says, "but now that's all he ever talks about! I can't shut him up about that damn pond, and I'd call that a step in the right direction, wouldn't you?"

"Whatever else are you going to do with that ugly piece of land besides dump more junk in it?" Mrs. Thompson says. "These kids just want to make something beautiful out of a dirty dump! What's the big deal?"

"I'll tell you one thing," Mr. Gillespie says, "there's a council election coming up in May, and I for one won't vote for anyone who hasn't got the chops to go to bat for these kids! And I know a lot of other folks in town who feel likewise!"

As more parents step up to the podium to solicit support, the council members can see the writing on the wall. They can also see the young reporter flipping another page for more frantically scribbled notes. To dodge a nasty headline—CITY COUNCIL REJECTS STUDENT PROPOSAL or CITY COUNCIL BACKS JUNKYARD OVER STUDENTS—they vote three-to-two to table the issue until the Pond Committee can provide more information. Specifically, the council members ask the committee to address: safety concerns and liability; environmental impact, including the displacement and replacement of soil; a more detailed plan for revegetation; a plan for the use of heavy equipment; a plan for long-term sustainability. The laundry list of specifics is mostly generated by the two council members who voted against Phyllis Rasmussen's motion to table the request until a future meeting: Renae Heller and Gordon McDowell. No surprise there. Maybe they're thinking—or at least hoping—that the list will seem so overwhelming that the students will throw up their hands in despair and say, "What the hell! Let's go party!"

Not these kids. Looking around as we leave, I see that my students have just tasted their first bite of fighting City Hall, and they're yearning for more.

From my perspective, the meeting is a triumph. Yes, I pissed off Gordon McDowell and have been added to his blacklist, and that will come back to haunt me more than once. But by postponing the vote, the city council has granted us the gift of time. Questions that would have put a dunce cap on my head as I hemmed and hawed and invented bogus answers at the podium can now be thoroughly researched, and my students can't wait.

*   *   *

"We'll show those assholes!" a blustery Bob Creighton crows in the parking lot.

They want another shot. In their young minds, it's Us vs. Them, Good Guys vs. Bad Guys, Right vs. Wrong, Young vs. Old, David vs. Goliath.

So I turn them loose: more phone calls, more letters, more guest speakers describing how their agencies can help. It will take two more meetings before the city council finally votes, but by then we'll have amassed hundreds of supporters: students from the junior and senior high schools; parents; community members; professors from the university. We'll have representatives from the U.S. Forest Service, Arizona Game and Fish, the U.S. Geological Survey, and the Museum of Northern Arizona. Roger Youngblood will promote the benefits of the project for students, the community, and the environment. A prominent county Health Department official will testify on our behalf regarding public safety and the pond. Representatives from the National Guard and the city's maintenance office will offer their support with heavy equipment and labor.

In the end, the forces in favor of our project will be too politically overwhelming to rebut, in spite of the backroom machinations. Because unbeknownst to me at the time, there are deep political and historical currents working against us. The mayor, Tom Horton, who sat there like a stuffed toad throughout the three council meetings, chairs the Fourth of July Powwow Committee and his wife, Shirley, is a member of the school board, which explains her tepid response to the pond proposal: no, she didn't vote against the request, but she wasn't all jumpy-Lou-hullabaloo about it either. And there's Gordon McDowell, another member of the Powwow Committee, as is Dale Hanagan, the school superintendent. So we're fighting an invisible, three-headed monster blindfolded, which is probably just as well: in this case, ignorance isn't necessarily bliss, but it does allow me to sleep at night.

Ultimately, the only item that matters is the final vote, which occurs almost three months after that first meeting. Predictably, it's three-to-two, with Dennis Hancock, Phyllis Rasmussen, and Don Ostanovich voting in favor and Renae Heller and Gordon McDowell voting against. The triumphant shout voiced by the winners echoes from the chambers of City Hall all the way across the railroad tracks.

"Congratulations," a smiling Phyllis Rasmussen says, "Godspeed!"

Moments before I'm swarmed by a congratulatory mob of students and parents, the grating Gordon McDowell strolls past and whispers for my benefit alone: "You're going to lose your job—I hope you know that!"

CATCHING FIRE

Over the next thirty-five years, I will teach more than seven thousand students and remember the majority of them, but I will not forget a single name or face from that first class, the one that started the Pond Project. This is where I'll cut my teeth; this is where I'll learn the difference between teaching and blabbing. This is where I'll learn about inspiration, motivation, leadership, and vision. And this is where I'll learn that to teach is first and foremost to love.

It won't be easy. Yes, we received the approval and begrudging blessing of the city council and school board, but in the aftermath of political triumph comes the reality of work. Labor, and lots of it. Walk the talk. Put up or shut up. Pick your cliché. And they are, after all, ninth graders, fourteen- and fifteen-year-old kids posing as quasi-adults. So I have to keep it all fresh, interesting, relevant. On good weather days we go outside for cleanup work—raking, shoveling, hauling, gathering. I give them a specific task or area to clean so that when class ends, they can see a little progress. Success. Little bites that will devour the elephant over time.

"Today we're going to gather all the little flip lids from pop cans. Look for flip lids!"

Some days I make it a game, other days a friendly competition.

"Today we're targeting Styrofoam. Pick up anything you see made of Styrofoam. Let's see which team can find the most!"

On bad weather days—snow, rain, extreme cold, or wind—we do indoor work: identifying what types of vegetation to plant and where; calculating how steep the banks will be and the dimensions for the V-shaped island. I give lectures too, but always with a direct link to the project.

"What kinds of animals are going to live in and around our pond?"

"Fish!" says Will Gillespie.

"What kind of fish? Are we going to have sharks and marlins? Why not?"

"That's crazy! They live in the ocean!"

"Yes, they live in the ocean—they're saltwater fish. So we need freshwater fish, but what kind? Looks like we'd better talk about habitat. Look in your books on page two forty-four…"

Any reference to the BSCS text elicits death groans, but at least I'm not ponderously plowing through it chapter by chapter. I'm hopscotching according to the topic of the day, which is determined by our progress outside. So now, even in the tiny, soporific print of the BSCS text, the word "habitat" makes sense to my kids because they can connect it to the pond. The same goes for life zones, succession ecology, symbiosis, survival plants, regeneration, mitosis, host cells, indicators, melanism, pathogens, metabolic water, virulent phage, and prokaryotic. It's a rat's maze for me, the teacher, especially knowing that at some point this crazy quilt-work has to mesh into a cohesive curriculum. That's the academic way of saying I'd better make damn sure my kids have learned the state standards for biology.

* * *

So there are risks, academically and otherwise. One day, Bob Creighton tries to play Hercules lifting a boulder and trips over his own shadow instead, sustaining a gash in his lower leg that requires a trip to the emergency room and eight stitches. After Will Gillespie's mom calls and reams me out because her son tore a brand-new pair of Levi's while clearing dead brush, I go to Goodwill and buy a few dozen pairs of cheap shoes and shirts and pants for students to wear so they won't ruin their school clothes. The more fashion-conscious kids bring their own work outfits, but now I've got plenty on hand for those who don't. No excuses. No one's going to say, I can't because I don't want to get my clothes dirty. Or my hands or my face. And people pitch in. The local Safeway donates sanitary wipes for quick cleanup at the end of the period. I do everything I can to reduce risks and eliminate excuses. And after four weeks, heading into Thanksgiving, it all seems to be working.

Then one morning as I'm helping students pull an old chaise lounge out of the wash, Bob Creighton sidles up to me like he's exchanging top-secret info in a spy movie.

"Mr. Hunter," he whispers, "I think you'd better check this out." He motions toward the two porta-potties that the city has graciously placed at the south end of the junkyard.

I saunter over, not overly concerned because by now I've seen about everything imaginable—except for this: standing behind the two outhouses, seven of my girls are staring at a stooped, scruffy, bearded man in a plaid shirt who has dropped his drawers, treating the young ladies to a full frontal view. Some girls are gasping and others are giggling.

I call the cops and the old guy's whisked away in a squad car, but when Melvin Jackson gets wind of it, he hauls me into his office and reads me the riot act.

"Did you know you could get fired for this? You and me both?"

"Why? I didn't know some pervert was exposing himself behind the outhouse!"

Jackson's bloodhound eyes are bulging. His fist pounds the desk. "That doesn't matter! You're the teacher! You're responsible for every damn thing that happens to every damn one of those kids regardless of the circumstances or your personal stupidity! If a kid throws a rock and knocks out another kid's eye, you're not supervising closely enough. If a kid cuts off his finger with a handsaw, you didn't provide adequate training. If a kid sticks a barrel up his mouth and pulls the trigger, you didn't recognize and respond appropriately to the warning signs! Have you got a dick for brains? Think next time, Hunter, or I'm shutting you down!"

Point taken. Lesson learned. It's a dangerous business, and it would be so much easier to play it safe, to sit in class and read a book.

As my feet pound down the deserted hallway back to my classroom, I shout aloud, catching the unsuspecting ear of Bob Garcia, who's sweeping up in the commons: "Screw all that!"

Bob looks up and we briefly make eye contact before I pound on, muttering to myself. You roll the dice. You take the leap. And accidents happen, stuff happens, shit happens. You want to learn science? The name of the game's risk, experiment, trial and error; it's plunging headfirst into the unknown. Well, we're plunging, dammit!

* * *

Surprisingly, there's a domino effect.

When Judy Macnamara, the ninth-grade English teacher, catches Jimmy Goldtooth working clandestinely on a letter during silent reading time, instead of castigating him, she seizes the moment and devotes the next three days of instruction to the art of formal letter-writing. At week's end, she tasks each student with writing a proper request to some agency or organization in town. So kids like Jimmy who are also in my biology class get to double-dip. And the other students are so jazzed —

real people, adults, are reading and responding to their words—that Macnamara corners me in the faculty lounge to see if we can go into cahoots, mixing science with English.

In time, Tony Carpenter, the social studies teacher, approaches me about sneaking local history into my lessons (did the kids know, for instance, that tiny trickle of water was once a river the native people and, later, the first white settlers used as their primary water source?). Fred Erickson, the ninth-grade math teacher, bends my ear about the plethora (yes, his word) of opportunities to integrate arithmetic into the project (for example, calculating soil ratios and water flow rates). As a fellow math teacher, I'm quite capable of incorporating numbers and formulas into the daily pond tasks. Still, I can't resist the resurrected gusto of my bifocaled and suspendered colleague who a week ago had one foot in the grave and the other in a retirement home, so I welcome him aboard.

Meanwhile, the Pond Project presses forward. Volunteers from the city maintenance crew donate time, labor, and materials to help remove the most cumbersome junk—cars and refrigerators, slabs of cracked concrete, woodstoves, washing machines, dilapidated pianos, abandoned travel trailers. Bob Creighton's father (owner of Creighton Construction) sends his heavy equipment crew to help remove the heavy stuff as well.

*　*　*

Approaching the Christmas holidays, Melvin Jackson calls me into his office to inform me, once again, that I'm the single biggest pain in his big black ass (his words), this time because all the eighth-grade parents are hounding him to reserve a seat for their kids in my classroom next fall. He's smiling when he says it because teachers and parents are also commenting on the new vibe in the school—energy, enthusiasm, and fewer discipline problems.

"My students act like they actually want to be in school," Macnamara enthuses at a faculty meeting. "It's almost spooky."

But not everyone's thrilled.

"This is creating a real morale problem," Swedelson snipes.

Baxter gruffly agrees. "Do you know how hard it is to get my students settled down and focused when they're looking out the window wondering why they can't be horsing around like Hunter's kids."

The faculty has divided into two camps: those who are piggybacking on the Pond Project (Judy Macnamara, Tony Carpenter, Fred Erickson, etc.) and those who view it as a superfluous, time-wasting diversion

(Grace Swedelson, John Baxter, etc.). Open war hasn't erupted, but tension and tempers are on the rise, mostly in the faculty lounge before school and during lunchtime. For the time being, I'm avoiding the lounge and eating lunch in my classroom with a small group of social outcasts who seek asylum from the controlled chaos of the commons. While most parents have given me an exuberant two thumbs up, some are unimpressed and a few are downright hostile, most notably Daniel Carlyle's father. He confronts me at the winter open house while I'm explaining the Pond Project to a roomful of parents.

"You're a first-year teacher, aren't you Mr. Hunter?" He's wearing wire-rimmed glasses, a sweater-vest, and a gray goatee.

"Yes, I am."

He chuckles softly. "Can I just say that your youth and inexperience are showing."

"Excuse me?"

This time he doesn't mince words: "Well, it's pretty obvious you don't know what you're doing."

He says this with a smile, but he may as well have whacked me with a crowbar. I take a step back, composing myself, then return his phony smile. "Look, this really isn't the time or the place…"

"You're not following the curriculum," Dr. Carlyle says. "These kids are going outside every day and playing in the dirt. That's all they're doing."

I maintain eye contact, but peripherally I can see smiles on the faces of several parents slowly drooping. Damage control. Fast.

"Mr. Carlyle—"

"It's Doctor."

"Sorry—*Doctor* Carlyle—but if you're not happy with what I'm doing, you need to talk to the principal." I want to leave it at that, especially since he's already begun to free his wiry body from the desk chair so he can make a fuming exit for Melvin Jackson's office.

"This is supposed to be a biology class," he says. "Not Camp Kumbaya."

"With all due respect, there's a lot more to science than just reading books and taking tests," I say.

"You don't need to lecture me about science, young man." Carlyle shakes his finger at me like a stick. "I'm a professor. You're just a damn teacher."

I remind myself, keep cool, Todd. Remember Amy's yoga tips: inhale-two-three-four, exhale-two-three-four. Remember the counsel from Melvin Jackson about parent-teacher confrontations. Yes, yes, and yes.

Inside I'm seething, but I manage to smile with gritted teeth. "Like I said, you should discuss this with the principal."

"I sure as hell will," Carlyle says as he stomps out the door.

*   *   *

Carlyle's public outburst turns sympathy in my favor, at least for the moment, as the other parents rally to my defense, offering encouragement and support. But I'm furious when I arrive home and unload on Amy:

"That arrogant sonuvabitch! In his mind I'm teaching in the minor leagues because I don't have the brains to teach in the majors. That's what *he* thinks, anyway. Which is laughable because some of those university profs are horrendously bad teachers—monotone droners who'd be chewed up and spit out by a classroom of middle schoolers."

"You're still hurting, aren't you?" Amy says.

"I'm twenty-two years old and I'm trying to do something good for those kids." I yank open the fridge, grab a bottle of orange juice, and begin guzzling.

"Would you like a glass?" Amy asks.

I shake my head.

"Isn't Dr. Carlyle just trying to look after the best interests of his son?"

I lower the bottle and run a forearm across my mouth. "He's a pompous asshole!"

"Are you maybe feeling a little defensive? Wondering what happens if this whole experiment backfires?"

"No."

"Are you scared?"

I turn away and stick the bottle back in the fridge. "I said, no."

Amy sneaks up behind me and slips her arms around my shoulders and whispers in my ear: "Of course not."

SCARLET LETTERS

Actually, I'm terrified. And defensive. Does Dr. Carlyle have a point? I've been busting my tail trying to build a bridge between the pond and that behemoth BSCS text, assuming all along that my students are learning the stuff—in teacher-speak, internalizing the concepts through the participatory process, to wit: a simplified explanation digested from the textbook followed by hands-on application and dual reinforcement in the field and in the classroom. *Voilà!*

Although some of my students have performed admirably—and some magnificently (Amanda Stone, Jake Bonner, Jimmy Goldtooth, Ricky Watson)—on their first major exam, others (Will Gillespie, Bob Creighton, Dora Smallcanyon, Susannah Thompson, Alex Hickman, Marsha Hodge) may as well have been shooting pool in a bar the past three months. Exhibit A is their grades, in no particular order: F, F, F, F, F, and F.

When I try to tutor them individually at lunch and after school, I realize that there's a lot of truth to the adage: you can't put in what God left out. For some, it's simply lack of basic gray matter. Others just don't do well on traditional tests: multiple choice, fill in the blank, true/false. Either way, the ugly truth is that no matter how long and how hard I work with certain kids, they're never going to get it—not at the same level as Amanda or Jake. Even worse, they're not going to pass my test unless I water it down with a fire hose, in which case, what's the point? And with my curve-based grading system—10 percent earn an A, 20 percent a B, 40 percent a C, 20 percent a D, and 10 percent fail—they're doomed.

This is my dilemma as I write report cards at the end of the first semester: good kids earning horrible grades. Yet they're so eager and enthusiastic. If a student whines about cleanup, Will Gillespie smacks him with a verbal reprimand: "Hey, get with the program, dipstick! We've got work to do!" Dora Smallcanyon made the watercolor rendition of the pond that was a major selling point for the city council. That has to be worth something. And then there's Marsha Hodge, banished by genetics to the far corner of the commons during lunchtime: a childlike brain in a gargantuan body. But she gives every ounce of what she's got. Every assignment's submitted on time, painstakingly scrawled in an awkward, oversize kindergarten script. What do I do with her? What's the point of the pond, the projects, all the hands-on hoopla if in the end the kid gets an F anyway?

*   *   *

Grading—student evaluation—becomes a nightly topic at my postprandial skull sessions with Amy.

"So what are you going to do, give them all A's?" Amy asks.

"No, I can't do that. It wouldn't be fair to the kids who've worked their asses off to do superior work. What's the motivation if I give everyone an A for just showing up?"

"How do you know they worked their asses off?" Amy counters. "Maybe they're just naturally smart."

"Am I grading on knowledge or effort?"

"Or both? By the way, what are you going to do about Maria Teresa Santiago-Gonzalez?"

I'm silent for half a minute. "I have no idea."

"Well, think fast. Semester report cards are due next week."

The light bulb comes on the next day as I observe Joaquin Sanchez explaining the difference between a phylum and a kingdom to Maria. Necessity being the mother of invention, at midsemester I'd paired Joaquin, a U.S.-born boy who speaks English at school and Spanish at home, with Maria, a new student from Chihuahua, Mexico, who spoke three words of English. At the time she'd seemed gratefully relieved because, with the aid of Joaquin's translations, now she could understand most of what the tall, rangy gringo at the chalkboard was yammering about. It didn't hurt that her interpreter looks like a young Rudy Valentino.

Amy puts a defiant hand on her hip that means, Tread lightly on my ESL kids. "What did you decide? Are you going to flunk her just because she doesn't speak English?"

"No, I can't do that."

"Then how are you going to grade her, if you want to be fair to Amanda Stone and the rest of your geniuses?"

"What do you do with *your* kids? They're all over the map, aren't they?"

"I grade them on three things: progress—how much have they learned; effort—how hard have they tried; and attendance—how often are they here."

This makes sense to me. There's measurable criteria, so I'm not grading on hunches and emotions. It seems criminal to flunk Maria just because she can't speak English, but if I can make concessions for her, why not for the kids who were dealt fewer cards at birth as well? And who says I have to use a grading system based on the bell curve, where only the top 10 percent earn an A? Who says I have to base my grading on term papers and exams? And who says every kid has to be tested solo?

I think back to my first day on the job, when I mentally sorted those twenty-six kids into haves and have-nots. As I recall my private pledge to help the pelicans soar with the eagles, I slap my head because it's so damn obvious. Why not pair the high fliers with the waddlers and strugglers and misfits.

Not all of the brainiacs will buy into it, I know that. The stuck-up princes and princesses whose biggest concern is how many days until their next European river cruise will turn up their noses and cry, "Ewww, cooties!" At the other extreme, some of the strugglers seem determined to learn absolutely nothing. For some, the wounds are so deep and the distrust so toxic they seem destined to self-destruct. If I give them a match and a stick of dynamite, they'll put it in their mouth and light it just to get me fired.

*　*　*

Marty Housman's like that, slinking into class in baggy jeans and a frayed shirt, his dishwater-blond hair hanging to his shoulders. Ragged tennis shoes and no socks, slouching so low in his chair that he's growing a second butt. If I ask him a question, he'll smart-ass the answer, daring me to throw him out of class.

"Marty, if you don't do the work," I warn, "I'll have to give you an F."

A shrug. A grunt. Sometimes a nasty little epithet: "No skin off my ass." Or: "Do it!"

That kind I try to group with like minds and quarantine them so they don't infect the others. Fortunately, I only have a handful this year, evenly dispersed through five classes. So Marty sits by himself watching his classmates work, doing and saying nothing. These are the terms of our confidential armistice. In exchange for his silence, he can remain in my class and he will earn an F and he will laugh about it.

Then there's Ricky Watson, with his bushy eyebrows and thick, round glasses reminiscent of Groucho Marx. The girls aren't lining up for autographs, but he's quick-witted and blessed with a photographic memory. He never has to study or crack a book except to let his brain snap a picture of it. Or unless it's science fiction—Robert Heinlein's *Stranger in a Strange Land*, Arthur C. Clarke's *2001: A Space Odyssey* or anything by Ray Bradbury.

The first week of class, I'd challenged my students to memorize the periodic table of elements and promised three movie tickets to the first person to do it. The next morning, Ricky raised his hand.

"Mr. Hunter, I'm ready," he said.

"Ready for what?" I asked because I'd forgotten all about my challenge. It was a joke; I may as well have asked them to fetch the Golden Fleece or hunt down the Holy Grail.

"The periodic table of elements?" he said.

I laughed. "OK, Ricky, have at it."

"One. H. Hydrogen. Two. H-e. Helium. Three. L-i. Lithium. Four. B-e. Beryllium. Five. B. Boron…"

I was an instant believer. I was also out three movie tickets. But I soon discovered that Ricky's gifts weren't limited to memorizing facts and figures.

"Who can explain the process of glycolysis?" I asked, scanning the rows of eight a.m. faces glazed over from last night's too-late TV. "Ricky?"

He looked down at his desk and feigned invisibility because he didn't want to stand out; the jocks already called him Groucho the Gaucho and make fake farts whenever he answered a question. The class guffawed, especially Susannah Thompson and the other once-and-future cheerleaders, and I could see Ricky's head droop and his colossal body slump as if he were a human scoop of ice cream melting before my eyes.

But he's one of my eagles, maybe my highest flier of all with the exception of Amanda Stone. I need him. So I meet with him one-on-one and share my plan.

"What do you think?"

He looks surprised that I'm confiding in him, and flattered. He nods. "Yes. It's a good idea."

"You're on board?"

He shrugs his burly shoulders. "Sure."

I want to hug him. "Thanks, Ricky." I give his back a manly pat instead. "Thank you."

*   *   *

I meet with the others individually too. First, the other eagles: Amanda Stone, Jake Bonner, Jimmy Goldtooth, Joaquin Sanchez, and Daniel Carlyle (who begrudgingly agrees when I suggest he include this on his college admission application under extracurricular activities). Then my pelicans: Will Gillespie, Dora Smallcanyon, Bob Creighton, Susannah Thompson, Marsha Hodge.

My meeting with Marsha almost leaves me in tears. I'm holding a copy of her latest quiz. She looks like a giant in a fairy tale as she sits with shoulders fallen, resigned to her fate.

"Marsha—" I say but she cuts me off.

"I know, I know. I got an F again."

"Marsha, you're all done taking tests by yourself."

She looks up, puzzled; her nose crinkles, rearranging the freckles on her face.

"From now on, you're going to take the tests with the smartest kid in here, and you're going to earn a C for this class."

"Really?"

"Yes, really. You've got to be a good student and complete all your assignments, and I'll give you some additional things to do like watering the plants and feeding the fish in the aquarium, but you'll get a C. And you have to promise me you won't take Biology 2, OK?"

She nods solemnly. Then: "Who's my partner?"

"Amanda," I say, and Marsha's eyes grow bigger than her face.

"I never got a C in science before," she says. "I never got a C in nothing."

"Well, you're going to get one now."

"Amanda Stone," she gasps, as if her new partner were a movie star.

I do the same with the other pelicans—Will, Dora, Susannah, and Bob—extracting a promise from each that they won't enroll in another biology class. Is it right? Is it wrong? Is it helping or hurting them? Only time will tell, and I'm willing to roll the dice.

*   *   *

I pair Ricky with Will and Daniel with Alex Hickman, another quiet, unassuming ghost, trapped in the chatty crossfire of Sabrina Cunningham and Joyce Kosinski, the campus go-go girls. I team Jake with Dora, and Jimmy with Susannah. Joaquin continues to tutor Maria.

Next, I introduce group testing, which means the eagles can explain each question to the pelicans, talking them through each option, jointly discarding the wrong answers before settling on the correct one and then explaining why. No more guessing here.

And the test questions aren't easy. I'm not lobbing softballs so the slow kids can hit home runs.

> Make a diagram of a food web in which the northwestern Washington barn owl is positioned at the highest trophic level. Make your diagram as comprehensive as possible. Use dotted lines to indicate uncertain relationships. Pictures of organisms that are part of the barn owl's food are included on the attached poster.

Is it right, this team approach? Are Will and Alex and Marsha and Dora and Susannah and Maria learning anything besides how to pretend they know what the hell they're doing until someone feeds them the answer? What happens in the real world, when Will has a job with a real boss and real deadlines and expectations and performance evaluations and pink slips, and there's no Ricky to slip him the answer? Then what?

But is the answer to let him stammer and stutter and at the end of eighteen weeks to stamp a red F on his forehead? I'm not talking about the Marty Housmans who refuse to lift a pencil or anything else except their middle finger. Will tries; Alex tries. Maria labors over that green textbook that in her mind signifies absolutely *nada*. Do extra-credit projects and reports and never missing class and answering questions whenever called upon even if the answers are embarrassingly wrong count for something? Not just in my class but in life? Even after I ask Alex to explain how sedimentary rocks are formed and he clears his throat and closes his eyes and takes a deep breath as if he's standing on the cliffs of Acapulco summoning the courage for a death-defying dive into the Pacific.

"Sedimentawy wocks—"

And the class—the expected portion, in any case—explodes with laughter and mimicry: "Wock? Wock? Who's going to wock? I'll wock yow wock!"

I swiftly calm the storm: "That's enough of that!" But they nickname him Elmer anyway, for Elmer Fudd, and Saggy Socks because he wears a cheap brand with flaccid elastic that let his socks droop down over his sneakers.

"Go on, Alex," I prod, and he takes another deep breath, glancing left, right, left, to see if more bullets are about to fly.

"Sedimentawy wocks aw fowmed in layus like you see in the Gwand Canyon."

A surprisingly tough kid who powers through even as Bob kicks the side of his chair every time he mispronounces a miserable R. I love Alex for that grit and persistence. "Good job, Alex! Excellent!" No way in hell am I going to fail that kid.

So I devise a new grading system, one based upon multiple measures instead of traditional fill-in-the-blank, multiple choice, true/false tests that emphasize memorization and regurgitation over comprehension and real-world application and leave way too much to chance, not to mention the fact that even some of my brightest kids freeze in the clutch or overthink the questions and bomb out.

And what about effort and attitude and how much you help the guy or girl sitting next to you? Isn't that part of it, too? Establishing a community of learners? Not grading on a cutthroat curve where 10 percent are statistically guaranteed to fail. From now on, I tell my kids, 40 percent of your grade will be project-based. This will include write-ups on the Pond Project and a daily journal recording the work you've done, people you've contacted or worked with, and additional work you've done outside the classroom. You may know facts and figures, but so what if you can't apply them? Another 40 percent will be information-based: tests, quizzes, lecture notes, pamphlets, and other resources you've created. Another 10 percent will be based on your attitude and behavior: how effectively do you work with your peers on the project; are you sharing the project with your parents and getting feedback from them for at least thirty minutes twice a week? Are you helping your neighbor? Are you participating in class? Are you toxic or inspiring? A help or a hurt? What are you bringing to class each day? Insight, energy, humor, inquiry? Or anger? Hate? Sabotage? Backstabbing?

* * *

But that's not the real world, my colleague John Baxter scowls.

Oh, yes it is. A multiple-choice test isn't the real world. Pulling a quick answer out of your brain isn't the real world. But working as a team to solve a complex problem is. Getting along with your teammates is. Personality clashes. Egos. Somehow negotiating the human food chain to get the job done. And you've got to be there! Attendance is part of it. And finish on time; you have to meet deadlines. Otherwise the rocket ship never gets built and the Russians beat you to the damn moon! Life's not a multiple-choice test, and I've tried to reinvent my class to reflect that.

"And what about the other 10 percent?" Susannah asks.

I smile. "Teacher discretion."

Bob wants to know what I mean by it.

"I grade you based upon how much I think you've learned and how much you've contributed to this class. Have you tried hard, do you help your classmates, are you taking the things you've learned here and using them to make this a better community? Because that's what this is really all about—making each of you a better person so you can go out and make the world a better place."

Bob rolls his eyes. "Whatever you say, Mr. Hunter, just as long as we can keep going outside and working on that pond."

But I need something more objective than my gut feeling about a kid for that other 10 percent—or 20 percent, if you add in attitude. They leave too much room for personal biases, and I've got them. I'm an underdog kind of guy, having been one myself growing up. The Daniel Carlyles and Susannah Thompsons who are born with a homecoming crown on their head have always grated me, and anyone who picks on the Marsha Hodges of the world deserves a special place in hell. I like to think I know the difference between a sincere "Good morning, Mr. Hunter!" and good, old-fashioned sucking up, but I'm as susceptible as the next guy to flattery and fake niceness. It's blundering human nature.

So I develop an attitude survey, a simple self-evaluation that separates the self-aware students from those who are about as introspective as a grasshopper. At the end of the semester, I also have them write me a letter expressing their feelings about the class—good, bad, or ugly.

*　　*　　*

Most of my students like the new grading system: light on book-based tests, heavy on real-world application and socialization. With the exception of Marty Housman, no one gets lower than a C on their semester report card. However, Daniel isn't happy, and neither is his father, who lets me have it with both barrels at a parent-teacher conference.

"Can you explain why an A student's getting a C-minus grade?"

"He's not an A student," I say.

"Not according to these!" Dr. Carlyle holds up a stack of his son's tests and assignments, rattling them fiercely.

"Well, for starters, he's plagiarized half his work, he's not a team player, and his attitude stinks. Tell me how that's an A student?"

"You grade my boy's knowledge of biology," Carlyle fumes, "not his socialization skills! You leave that to me!"

"Then I give you an F-minus," I say.

In two seconds Carlyle's face gets so red I think it might explode. "Do you know who you're talking to, young man?"

"Yes, I do," I say. "And here's why I give you an F-minus. If you say to someone, 'Hey, let's go play poker tonight!' and he says, 'No, I've gotta go to church,' what he really means is, 'I don't wanna play poker with you because you're a dick!' Kids don't learn that on their own, Dr. Carlyle. They learn it at home."

Carlyle storms out of my classroom—no surprise there. And it's no surprise that Daniel is transferred out of my biology class and into John Baxter's the next morning. Fair enough.

*　　*　　*

On the upside, I won't see or hear about Dr. Carlyle again until one afternoon seven years later, when I'll meet his ex-wife, Cindy, a detective for the city police department. She will come to my classroom to ask me a few questions about one of my students, specifically: where the hell is she?

But that's many miles down the road. For now, I'm flying high with no intention of letting anyone or anything shoot me down.

COLOR BLIND

As a sophomore in high school, I ran the forty-yard dash in 4.6 seconds and was the fastest, shiftiest tailback on the roster, but I mostly sat on the bench watching the coach's Frankenstein-footed son carry the ball (and our team) to a humiliating two-win season. When I complained to my father, he hitched up his jeans like he always did before tackling an unpleasant task and said, "Yep. I'm afraid Coach O'Connor is blinded by love for his son."

Ever since, I've been obsessed with fairness. And when I signed my first teaching contract, I vowed to treat all students equally. Skin color wouldn't matter; I would play no favorites.

Yet in my first day on the job, it would have been impossible not to notice the two pockets of color amid the sea of white in my first-period biology class. Five Latinos, including Joaquin Sanchez and the always-smiling Maria Gonzalez, were huddled together in the middle rows, chattering away in Spanish. In the back sat four Navajo: Dora Smallcanyon, who usually wore her raven hair long and loose like a cape that would have made Zorro envious, two boys with military crew cuts (Henry Benally and Tommy Tsinijinnie), and Jimmy Goldtooth. None of them spoke unless spoken to, and even then, their responses were telegraphic, as if they were being charged for each word.

After three weeks of school, I noticed a pattern. Every Monday and Friday, Dora, Tommy, and Jimmy were absent, and it was killing their grades. Friday was test day and Monday was the due date for major assignments. Makeup tests were not allowed, and late papers received a 25 percent point-deduction each day. Tough rules, but I was preparing them for the cruel world of high school and beyond.

I finally took Jimmy aside and asked, What's the deal? Jimmy stared down at his sneakers and explained that the Navajo kids lived in the Indian dorm in town. They went home on weekends. Their parents picked them up early Friday and brought them back late Monday.

News to me! I had no idea there was a dormitory in town for these kids, or that they left town every weekend with their parents, or that they lived anywhere from a hundred to two hundred miles away.

"OK, what about Henry Benally?" I challenged. "He's never missed a Monday or a Friday."

"He's local," Jimmy said.

*   *   *

No way could I stop those kids from going home on weekends, so I had to find an alternative. For starters, no more tests or quizzes on Mondays or Fridays. And no more Monday deadlines. I also created makeup packets they could complete during lunch hour or after school.

That same afternoon, I visited the dorm. Kyle Farnsworth, the director, gave me a tour. A few deep breaths from full retirement, Farnsworth looked like a relic from a Southwest curio shop: bolo tie, cowboy shirt with fake pearl buttons, snakeskin cowboy boots. As he showed me around, he complained about funding and broken promises and how the federal government doesn't give a rip about these kids.

The three cinderblock buildings—one for the boys, another for the girls, and a third that served as a multipurpose room for meals, sports, and social activities—supported his case. Built in the early fifties, they were penal in appearance, minus the barbed-wire fencing. The interior of each dorm featured multiple rows of bunkbeds with a shoulder's width between. Communal showers, very military.

But Farnsworth was all right. When I asked if I could arrange some after-school tutoring on-site, his washed-out blue eyes lit up: "Love to!" And when I pitched the idea to Melvin Jackson, he grumbled in his put-upon way, but the next morning I found a note in my box stating that complimentary tutoring services at the dorm would commence next week: Monday through Friday from four to six p.m.

*   *   *

I'd met a few Navajo while studying at the university and seen quite a few around town—especially on weekends, when families from the reservations pile into the beds of their pickup trucks and make the pilgrimage to the big city to load up on groceries, eat at a restaurant, and see a movie. But back then, I only knew a bit about their history and culture. For instance: their homeland is the high, red deserts of northern Arizona, which are scorching in the summer and bitter cold in the winter. Many either live in cracker-box government housing or in hogans, one-room, octagonal dwellings that may or may not have a dirt floor and more often than not lack electricity or running water. Most likely, their families own some sheep and goats and horses and raise a modest garden that produces corn, melons, beans, and squash. And the women weave some of the most beautiful, intricate rugs on the planet.

I don't realize just how superficial my understanding of the Navajo people is until one day in mid-October, when Jimmy sheepishly approaches me after class.

"I'm sorry, Mr. Hunter, but I have to go home for two weeks. My family's having a sing."

I'm not happy. "Two weeks? It's the middle of the semester! Look, I'm all for music and all of that, but—two weeks! To sing?"

Jimmy's head drops so hard I wonder if he'll ever lift it up again.

During lunch, I confer with Darryl Johnson, the ninth-grade counselor, who passes the buck: "Go talk to Priscilla," he says, never lifting his eyes from his *Golf* magazine.

"Priscilla?"

"Priscilla Manygoats, the Indian ed counselor."

"We've got a special counselor for Indian kids?"

"It's one of those token, federally funded positions. Your hard-earned tax dollars at work."

I hunt down Priscilla, a dark-eyed woman with straight, black hair that could rival Rapunzel's in length and beauty. When I explain my dilemma, she smiles.

"First year?"

I lower my head. "It's that obvious?"

"Hey, at least you're asking questions. Most people don't even try to understand. They just keep doing what they've always been doing, thinking what they've always been thinking. Have a seat."

I settle into the cushioned chair near her desk. It's a windowless office, but gracefully decorated: a sandpainting on one wall, a Ganado Red rug covering most of another. A dozen framed family photos—two boys and three girls at various ages; a pensive man wearing a velveteen tunic and a turquoise necklace—crowd one end of her desk.

Priscilla explains that in the Navajo culture, if you become ill—physically, mentally, or otherwise—it's because you're out of harmony with the universe.

"We call it *hózhó*," she says. "There's no good word for it in English—peace, beauty, harmony, happiness, balance. All of that together. So sometimes you'll hear the phrase 'go in beauty' or 'walk in beauty.' That's what it really means—*hózhó.*"

According to Priscilla, the cause of illness can be something you did or something done to you, recently or years ago. She says that a few years ago, she broke out in a terrible rash and nothing fixed it. She tried dermatologists, specialists, the works. Finally she resorted to the old ways and went to her uncle, a medicine man. Actually, he was more like a diagnostician. He was a crystal-gazer, meaning he could look into a special crystal and identify an ailment's cause. The uncle told her that, when she was a little girl, she threw a stick at a snake—a taboo in Navajo culture—and that's why she broke out in the rash.

"Twenty years later?"

Priscilla smiles, lighting up the perfect bone structure of her face. "Yes. There's no expiration date on breaking a taboo. So I had a healing ceremony—we call it a sing."

"Oh! It's not some kind of choral presentation. I thought maybe Jimmy's family was the Navajo version of the Von Trapp family singers or something."

"No," Priscilla laughs.

Ceremonies last from one to nine days, depending on the sickness, with a four-day incubation period afterward in which the patient is severely limited in what they can do and where they can go. During the ceremony, the medicine man sings sacred chants all night long. Sometimes there's ceremonial dancing as well. If the medicine man— the singer—repeats all the chants perfectly every night, then harmony's restored and the patient's healed.

"It worked for me!" Priscilla says.

"Why does Jimmy have to go for two weeks when his cousin's the one who's sick?"

"It's a family affair. Everyone goes. It's an insult not to. And everyone benefits, not just the patient."

I don't know that there's science behind it, but I'm trying to respect the belief, or at least understand it. It's a quantum leap for me, and she can tell.

"I know this is hard to understand—for white people. You think they're superstitions. But try and take a step back. Crawl out of your skin and put on mine for a minute. Are you Christian?"

This puts me on my heels, hemming and hawing. My mother is Lutheran, my father was Episcopalian, neither of them particularly devout.

"Yes?"

"Well, you believe a guy was nailed to a cross, his dead body was thrown in a tomb, and three days later he rose from the dead. What's the science behind that? One man's religion is another man's superstition. By the way, the tutoring program at the Indian dorm? My program pays for that. Thanks for getting the ball rolling. Every little bit helps."

I return to my classroom and assemble two weeks' worth of makeup packets for Jimmy.

*　*　*

After that, things flow smoothly, more or less, except now I'm beginning to see the world and my bucolic little community through a slightly different lens. The railroad tracks that were the town's umbilical cord during its infancy now divide the community in half. Whites mostly live in north town, Blacks, Hispanics, and Indians live in south town. There are two Catholic churches; one for the whites (large, elegant), the other for Hispanics (smaller, plainer). Up until two years ago, black children attended a separate elementary school. There are no signs in restaurants, hotels, or businesses denying entry to any particular race, but everyone knows that blacks drink at the Imperial, Hispanics at El Rancho Grande, and whites at the Sacred Peaks Hotel. Indians buy their liquor at the drive-through and imbibe at one of the city parks. And, of course, there is the annual Fourth of July powwow, when natives from the four directions converge on the town to buy and sell and raise a little hell—just enough to justify the revenue they generate from the hordes of tourists who flock to watch them.

I begin to question the value of this yearly exploitation in the name of cultural preservation. And I notice things I'd overlooked before. At a downtown clothing store, when a Navajo woman tries to purchase a blouse and jeans with her credit card, the woman at the register demands half a dozen forms of identification. The Navajo woman finally rolls her shoulders and departs. When I put a new pair of pants on the counter and hand the clerk my Visa card, she smiles, runs it through her machine, and hands me a slip of paper. "Sign here, please."

I think it's not right or fair, and I wish I'd said something, but it all happened so quickly and subtly. It's one more drop in my bucket that, in time, will fill to overflowing. For now, I take note and make private pledges: not in my classroom, not if I can help it. And I move on, because good things are happening. The Pond Project's moving forward, and my kids are excited. Every day they grab rakes and shovels and plastic garbage bags and march out to take another bite out of the elephant.

Then shortly after Thanksgiving break, a monster storm drops a foot of snow on our mountain town, forcing us indoors for a week, which (in contrast to the freedom of the pond) feels like a jail sentence. And as the snow finally melts, another storm reburies the town and banishes us to the classroom until that glorious Friday afternoon in mid-December when a universal shout of joy goes up from students and teachers alike as we're turned loose for the long-awaited winter break.

For the kids, it's an extended vacation—two weeks of fun and games. Christmas for most, Chanukah for some, respite for all. For teachers, it's a mental and physical oasis in the middle of a harried year. For me and Amy, the first week is consumed by Christmas shopping and gift-wrapping and card-writing and decorating the blue spruce we chopped and hauled down from the mountain. My father's long gone and my mother lives in Florida—too far and costly to travel to on our meager wages—so we pay a short visit to Amy's mother in Anaheim, hoping her estranged husband won't crash the party.

For first-year teachers, in addition to sleeping in, winter break is also a chance to play catch-up: papers to grade, lessons to plan, events to calendar, and units to organize. It's an opportunity, at midyear, to reflect on where you've been and where you're going; to make minor adjustments or major overhauls. In my case, it's my classroom that's in desperate need of a makeover, at least according to Amy.

"What have you done?" she gasps. It's the first time she's seen my room since the start of school, and she's unimpressed. Appalled, actually. "Or maybe I should say, what *haven't* you done? This place looks like a morgue!"

One poster—The periodic table of elements in black on yellow—gives a dash of color to the south wall. Otherwise, my classroom is a blank slate.

My excuse, of course, is the Pond Project.

"My classroom is the forest," I rhapsodize, "not this sterile, oversize hospital room with desk chairs."

Amy arches an eyebrow, her way of gently putting a boot to my butt.

"Winter's upon you," she says. "You're probably going to be indoors a lot more than outdoors for a while. Bring in a few things to stimulate their brains—or at least get them seat cushions so they'll be more comfy when they doze off. No wonder they'd rather pull weeds than sit in this place. This looks like an interrogation chamber. Cruel and unusual punishment, Todd. It's against the law, you know."

"OK! I get the message."

So the second half of winter break, I bring items from home to jazz up my classroom, mostly animal skins (elk, bear, mountain lion, deer), skulls (mouse, squirrel, horse), skeletons (chipmunk, bobcat), and one stuffed javelina.

"Better," Amy says. "But now it looks like a taxidermist's shop."

So I add an antique brass Bausch and Lomb microscope, a gilt pocket barometer, antique microscope slides, and an old weather station with a rain gauge.

"Nice conversation pieces," Amy says.

I plaster the walls with posters featuring The Life Zones, The Water Cycle, The Creation of the Grand Canyon, Our Solar System. For a finishing touch, I bring an aquarium with tropical fish and a terrarium ruled by a two-foot garter snake.

Amy folds her arms and smiles. "I like it."

"Really?"

"No, I love it!" Before I can digest the compliment, she spins around like a little girl, the ruffled hem of her peasant dress lifting off the floor as her arms loop around my waist. And instantly, the little girl grows up, drawing me in tight, her lips attacking mine with a primal urgency I'll later attribute to two things: the preponderance of feral accoutrements surrounding us, and a growing desperation to create life. Dr. Bailey has no medical explanations and little advice other than to relax and keep trying. "Maybe a change of venue will do the trick," he'd said.

Well, maybe. As her lips go after my throat, I can feel her teeth gently biting the flesh. And as she begins tearing at the buttons on my shirt, ripping the top two from the Pendleton fabric, I realize this is no New Year's Eve joke: her wild side has been unleashed. Her urgency fills me more with sadness than desire (although not so much that I'm unable to enjoy the moment).

As far as I know, there's no one else in the building, and it will be three decades before security cameras and metal detectors become standard fare in public schools. We're all alone with no primary or secondary witnesses. So in the early afternoon of the last day of the year, the two of us live out every teacher's secret fantasy or worst nightmare: we strip each other down and make love in a classroom. Twice.

*   *   *

Returning from break, my students are even more impressed than Amy with my renovated classroom—most of them, anyway. A few keep a cautious distance from the new additions, but the majority want to feed the fish, fondle the skeletons, and smooth their fingers along the soft, furry pelts draping the counters and decorating the walls. They have stare-downs with the garter snake and mock conversations with the javelina they christen "Wilbur."

Amy was right: the embellishments add pizazz to my classroom, and it's a good thing, because the El Niño winter produces an endless chain of Pacific storms that enjoy unleashing the tail end of their wrath in the form of snow on the Arizona mountains. So there will be no outdoor work until late March, but in the meantime I keep it interesting indoors, prodding my students to prepare all things necessary for the Pond Project so they'll be ready when the weather clears.

Everything is going well—no conflicts, no drama—until one day around mid-February, when Jimmy Goldtooth comes to class with his face red and swollen. It looks as if someone's clubbed him with a baseball bat.

"Who did this to you?"

Jimmy shrugs. "Nobody."

"Are you sure?"

"Yeah."

"All right, go to the nurse."

"I already been. Been to the clinic too. The doctor gave me some pills."

"Probably an antibiotic. Are you taking them?"

Jimmy nods.

"Well, make sure you do."

Next day, Jimmy looks worse. His face is a red balloon that gets fatter every day. Whatever Jimmy has seems to be spreading, because Tommy Tsinijinnie's face is red and bloated too. And Henry Benally has been absent for a week, and Dora Smallcanyon checked out early yesterday complaining of nausea. I start putting two and two together and—bingo!—it's just the Navajo kids, and they've been avoiding that terrarium like the plague.

That afternoon, I schedule a meeting with Priscilla Manygoats.

"What's in the terrarium?" she asks.

"Not much. Just a garter snake."

Priscilla gasps. I may as well have said I was performing ritual human sacrifices.

"What's wrong?"

"That's *bahadzid!*" she says. "Taboo. Big time."

"You're telling me these kids—all four of them—are sick because I've got a garter snake in my class?"

Priscilla sighs. "Yes. Big time."

I'm a scientist, and to me this supernatural explanation—or rather, non-explanation—is an absurd superstition hearkening back to the Dark Ages. And yet... when I gaze into Priscilla's brown eyes, it's like looking into the past and the future at the same time. Instead of fear and hocus-pocus, I see a woman baring her soul; I see sincerity and a faint glimmer of hope that somehow, I'll be able to see this through her eyes instead of mine.

"What do we need to do? Besides get rid of the snake."

"We'll need to get a *hatathli*—a medicine man—to do a ceremony. Kind of like a cleansing ceremony."

"To make it all good—restore peace and harmony and all that—what's the word?"

She smiles, impressed. "Yes. *Hózhó.*"

"So where do we get a medicine man? And is this a one-day, a five-day, or a thirty-day ceremony?"

Now she's laughing. "This is a small one. We should do it after school when everyone's gone. We don't want the attention. It's very serious, and you know how kids can be."

"Parents too."

Priscilla nods. "Yes. The less publicity, the better. I'll talk to the four students privately and tell them what we're going to do, and I can get the medicine man."

"Just like that?"

"My uncle—he's a *hatathli.*"

"Should we tell Mr. Jackson?"

"We can—Mel won't object—but we don't need to."

"Keep it low profile."

"Yes."

"So what *can* I put in that terrarium?"

Priscilla shrugs. "A lizard?"

"A lizard's OK but not a snake?"

"Yes. And no owls."

"I don't have owls. Wait: what's wrong with owls?"

"It's a bad omen."

"How bad?"

Priscilla waits a good five seconds before answering. "Death," she says.

That Friday, long after the students, faculty, and staff have vacated the school, Priscilla opens a back door to the building and leads her uncle to my classroom, where he performs a purification ceremony. I wait outside, out of respect.

On Monday morning, my classroom looks unchanged except for three things: the absence of the garter snake, the appearance of a chameleon in the terrarium, and four Navajo students, all present and all looking normal again.

*   *   *

Back in October, when I first started the Pond Project and divided my class into teams, I intentionally split up the four Navajo kids, hoping a change of scenery, however subtle, might loosen their lips. I was dead wrong, except in the case of Jimmy, who quietly emerged as the leader of "Four Cowboys and an Indian." In fact, he coined the team name. He's not only smart, but kind and funny too, and Susannah Thompson took note. She liked to play the ditzy blonde with him. I'm not sure if she has a genuine crush or if it's just a teenage tease, testing the racial waters.

Whatever the dynamic, the combination seems to work, the five of them (Jimmy, Susannah, Will Gillespie, Ricky Watson, and Marty Housman) master-minding some of the most creative aspects of the Pond Project, including the archeological dig, the outdoor amphitheater, and the nature trail. When they huddle, these mismatched misfits transform into a garrulous band of joyful creativity. Ricky gives life and order to their brainstorming sessions via sketches and diagrams, while Will contributes nonstop streams of sometimes ludicrous and other times brilliant ideas with the reckless fervor of a mad scientist. Hard-boiled Marty adds a pensive if sometimes cynical filter to the process. Meanwhile, there's Susannah, laughing and teasing and giving Jimmy an occasional punch in the shoulder.

I don't think much of it—they're just kids, after all. Ninth graders horsing around in biology. When Susannah bombs her first tests, I think pairing her up with a highflier like Jimmy—already on the same team, already friends—is a natural fit. At first, it works like magic. With Jimmy's help, Susannah's test scores climb from the lower dregs to the upper 10 percent. She's smiling; she's happy. One day she twirls into the room and out of the blue exclaims, "Mr. Hunter, I love this class!" The next day while they're sitting together reviewing for the unit exam, I notice Susannah's hand brush across Jimmy's forearm. His facial response is a blend of exhilaration and terror that swirls around for a confusing moment before settling, as his eyes lock with hers, into a look of hopeless, hapless teenage love.

This doesn't sit well with the boys in jeans and cowboy boots, especially Bob Creighton, who breaks horses for his grandfather in the summer and arms and noses on the football field in the fall. He'll have something to say about Susannah's teammate, although not on my watch. He'll settle that score a year later with a cheap-shot tackle during a meaningless flag-football game in tenth-grade P.E. class that will land Jimmy in the emergency room with a destroyed ACL and an aborted cross country career that might have earned him a college scholarship.

Susannah's parents, however, act more swiftly, submitting a written request that their daughter be transferred to another team. Immediately. I respond in kind: "Susannah is doing exceptionally well with her current team and I see no reason to make a change at this time."

The Thompsons follow up with a phone call demanding a meeting after school, a regular showdown at the OK Corral, featuring me, Corbin Thompson (a real-estate mogul who owns half the town), his wife, Sheila (a fortyish twin of her daughter), and, of course, Melvin Jackson in administrative white shirt, checkered red tie, and sports coat.

Sitting across from Jackson's desk, Corbin and Sheila Thompson try to tactfully justify the need for their daughter to switch study teams as Jackson tilts back in his swivel chair, listening with crossed arms and bloodshot eyes.

"So let me make sure I understand," he drawls. "You want Susannah on a different team because?"

During the squirming, fill-in-the-blank silence, the Thompsons exchange glances before Corbin finally says, "We think she needs to be more challenged."

"We wanted her in the honors program," Sheila adds.

Jackson pretends to scan the contents of a student folder that in fact contains old promotional flyers for the annual Christmas basketball tournament. "Evidently, she's partnering with one of the brightest youngsters in class," he says. "Isn't that right, Mr. Hunter?"

I'm sitting to the left of Jackson's desk, chin propped in one hand, glaring across the room as if trying to dissolve Corbin and Sheila with my eyes. I don't even acknowledge them with a grunt, just a slow, lethal nod. Everyone knows the agenda here.

"Yes, but she needs a little more, you know, umpf!" Corbin says, punching the air.

"Her grades have actually improved," Jackson notes. "Her total points have doubled since she started working with Jimmy."

"We know," Corbin says. "But we still think it would be better if…"

"If?" Jackson's satyr eyes narrow as he waits for the man to fill in another awkward blank, knowing eventually he or his wife will slip. Sometimes it takes an hour; this time, less than two minutes.

"We think she'd do better with someone more her kind," Sheila blurts out.

A gooey smile forms on Jackson's face. "More her kind?" Jackson says. "Tell me, what's Susannah's kind?"

Now it's squirm time. While there are plenty of parents who would have no qualms about expressing their feelings in straight, simple, candid, ugly prose, as in, "We don't want our daughter working with a filthy Indian!" the Thompsons pride themselves on being educated, enlightened, open-minded, progressive, and, up until that moment, privileged.

"Her temperament," Corbin interjects.

"How would you describe Susannah's temperament?" Jackson asks. He's truly enjoying this racial striptease.

"She's very lively," Sheila says. "Outgoing."

"And fun," Corbin adds. "She loves to laugh."

"Jimmy Goldtooth's one of the funniest kids in school. And one of the brightest. Isn't that right, Mr. Hunter?"

Another nod. I've kept a lid on it so far and am determined to stay the course, although I'd like to reach over and knock Corbin and Sheila's heads together. But lift that lid now and who knows what vindictive lava might start flowing from my mouth.

Prior to the meeting, Principal Jackson had whispered three brief pieces of advice: "Keep your cool. Don't say anything. Let me handle this." Now, he closes his bogus folder. "I think we'll leave Susannah right where she is. She seems to be *thriving* in her present situation. Wouldn't you agree, Mr. Hunter?"

A third and final nod. Thriving. Yes. Absolutely.

Sheila Thompson's high heels clatter across the linoleum floor as she and her husband storm out, issuing the usual threats: The superintendent's going to hear about this! We're going to speak to our attorney! We'll enroll Susannah in another school (at the time, Ponderosa Junior High's the only game in town). We'll call the governor! We'll call Superman, the Green Lantern, the Rolling Stones, dammit! We'll have you fired! Both of you!

As their quarreling voices fade down the hall ("I told you *you* should have—"; "No, I told *you!*" "No, *you!*"), Jackson flashes his inimitable smile. "Well, I guess that takes care of that."

"You think so?" I'm new to this game: threats, retribution, revenge; attorneys, governors, Superman.

"What you're doing out there is good for kids, and that's all I give a damn about. Keep doing it. Let me handle this other shit."

We've come a long way since the day Melvin assigned me four preps. He's definitely an ally now, and I'd almost call Melvin Jackson a friend.

KUDOS

E arly one morning in mid-May, I wake up in a panic: the school year—my first as a full-time teacher—is almost over! What should be cause for skyrockets and sweet hallelujahs instead leaves me despondent. Where's the time gone? What cunning thief came in the dark of night and heartlessly stole this, the happiest year of my life?

As I lie in bed reflecting, the previous nine months flash by like a dream dappled with bits of nightmare. What had seemed like a daily death sentence in August and September has magically morphed into purpose, passion, and joy. The students who at the beginning of the school year were a pack of teenaged strangers killing me piecemeal with apathy and indifference have blossomed into enthusiastic, inquisitive young scientists. They've become far more than my obligatory charges or even my students. They're my children now, and I marvel at how beautifully they've collaborated to make a pond out of a pipe dream.

There's still plenty of work—no question about that. But they've put all the puzzle pieces seamlessly together. Bob Creighton's team contacted three construction companies that donated time and equipment, including a D9N-Cat to remove the bulkier trash and then smooth and sculpt the earth to the specifications of the plan. Jimmy Goldtooth's team worked with the local nursery to get free vegetation and in-service training on how to plant and care for it. And Joaquin Sanchez's team arranged for guest presenters to lecture in class and demonstrate in the field.

Meanwhile, teams led by Amanda Stone and Jake Bonner worked together to create a catalog of potential pond-related projects: pond and island development, wildlife habitat improvement, ecosystem plantings, an anti-litter campaign, an outdoor amphitheater, a trail system, rock house reconstruction, a weather station, soil monolith preparation, and a geology wall.

All the kids picked up trash, removed the invasive stuff and replaced it with native plants and shrubs—a herculean task, but somehow they did it. And every student has turned in a portfolio folder bloated with class notes, observations, daily logs, reports, exams and quizzes, and a self-evaluation. Documentation. Proof of what they've learned during the year, not just for their benefit and their parents' but to silence the naysayers who've accused me of wasting taxpayer dollars to provide glorified (and often messy and dirty) childcare camouflaged as science education. My kids know better, and they've got those portfolios to prove it. And I've got their personal letters to me.

The majority are positive. In fact, only Marty Housman (scribbling in his angry teenager's cursive) calls me a narcissistic, controlling son of a bitch and my class a pathetic waste of time.

Some letters are short and to the point:

> Dear Mr. Hunter,
> I had fun in your class this year. Have a great summer.
> Bye,
> *Sabrina Cunningham*

Some are barely readable:

> Mr. Todd Hunter
> I've loved being in your class it puts me in a good mode and I Relly hope you next year your my faviart teacher and favforite hour.
> *Marsha Hodge*

Others are complimentary:

> Mr. Hunter,
> I want to thank you for your patience, caring, and understanding with me this year. You are the greatest person I know! I love you to death and I'm gonna miss ya! Stay as sweet and cool as you are and I promise that I will visit you next year. Thank you for everything you have done for me.
> Love always,
> *Amanda Stone*

Some are confessional:

> Dear Mr. Hunter.
> Hello! How are you? I'm fine. I bet your pretty tired of reading these projects and letters huh? Well I'll try to make this as interesting as possible. This class has changed me because of how I made it. It wasn't very interesting at first because I didn't participate in anything. As the

year went by I started getting acquainted with some of my classmates. As it got warmer we started going outside for our class time. I enjoyed digging those trees and picking up trash, I'm going to miss this class and the teacher that ran it! What I'm really trying to get to, Mr. Hunter is thank you for making this class a cool one! Keep it up in the future because you are really a good teacher.
Always me,
Dora Smallcanyon

And there are a few smart alecks:

Dear Mr. Hunter,
You're making us do all this but your really not reading it unless you put a smiley face.
Bob Creighton

To which I add a note: "Never fear. I read every word." ☺

* * *

The portfolios are good, the letters are fine, but they need something more.

So on the last day of school, after taking roll, I tell them I've got a surprise. Will Gillespie wants to know if it's food. Jake Bonner wants to know if it's money.

"Sorry, Jake; sorry, Will. But I think this is better than food or money." I douse the florescent overhead lights and switch on a Kodak Carousel to project the first of two dozen slides onto a freestanding screen with a conspicuous tear in the lower right-hand corner. There are no artsy graphics or dreamy background music, just plain, full-color still shots that change with the sound of a prolonged click each time I advance a frame. My commentary is succinct.

Slide one features a giant wasteland of junk: conglomerate mounds of soil, gravel, and cinders studded with broken blocks of concrete, smashed bottles, rusty appliances, and vandalized furniture. Litter and diapers speckle the ground like giant bird-droppings. A gloomy gray sky prevails.

"Man, that looks like an earthquake or something," Bob says.

I say, simply, "October first."

Click.

Slide two reveals a long shot of the same junk heap minus the bird droppings and concrete slabs. A few patches of earth, raked clean and leveled, look like fresh skin grafts on an otherwise craggy face.

"November 20. The week before Thanksgiving."

Click.

Slide three looks like a winter wonderland, with snow-frocked ponderosa pines and skeletal aspens flanking a sparkling meadow. The giant elephant mounds and other major obtrusions are gone. The field looks like a vast canvas waiting to be painted.

"Oooh! Pretty!" Susannah says.

"January 10," I say.

Click.

In slide four, a D9N-Cat squats in the middle of a large field of red earth that looks as smooth as a freshly dragged baseball infield. Several young people are working the grounds with rakes and shovels. Others are planting trees and shrubs.

"Hey, that's me!" Marsha says.

"Look at that handsome dude with the shovel!" Will crows.

"March 22."

Click.

In slide five, the smooth, red field has been shaped and sculptured into a large, shallow basin. Around the rim, banks slope down to the field. A V-shaped island protrudes from the center with the wedge side facing windward. Small trees and shrubs dot the perimeter and the shoreline.

"May 15," I say and immediately click to a slide of the entire class posing in three rows, like a team photo.

Bob stands up and claps once, twice, three times before he's joined by Jenifer, Jake, and Amanda, and soon the entire class—except for Marty— is on its feet, applauding.

After three minutes of this, I say, "Let's take a walk," and my students follow me out below the red EXIT sign and down the familiar gravel path to the former junkyard that is now their handiwork. Without direction, the students gather around me in a semicircle.

"This is the "after" picture," I say, motioning to the field. "I want you to take a good, long look at it because this is what you guys did this year."

I could lecture them about the project's educational goals—hammer it home so they fully understand the connection between what they've done with the pond and what they learned in the classroom. But they've seen it in print—in hieroglyphic academic-speak—all year. *The scientific goals*: to show the great diversity of life—plants and animals—on any given land or water area; to teach students how to identify common plants and animals and to explain their relationship to man; to show the interrelationships between plants, animals, soil, and water; to analyze the cyclical nature of living things and the close relationship of the cycles to weather. *The sociocultural goals*: to develop *esprit de corps* through joint participation in outdoor projects; to enhance awareness of the importance of natural-resource conservation and the basic techniques involved in environmental studies; to acquire the rudiments of outdoor manners and conduct; to develop an understanding and appreciation of natural beauty; to realize that food comes from soil and water, not the supermarket; lumber comes from forests, not the lumber yard; paper comes from trees, not the stationery store. And even *the recreational goal*: to provide healthy and productive forms of exercise and outdoor activity.

These are the written goals we showed to the city council and school board, parents and Melvin Jackson and the U.S. Department of Education. These were the academic justifications for devoting so much time and energy to, in essence, building a pond in the backyard. And they're all legitimate, all true, not just some smoke job to placate the powers that be so we could horse around outdoors for an hour a day. This is science, pure and simple. Let John Baxter fret and fume and break his chalk-stick on the board bleating about academic rigor. His poor kids spent the year memorizing every silly characteristic of every silly animal in every silly phylum, while mine were outside doing science. No apologies to anyone for that.

Yes, I could harangue all day about the whys and the whats, but this is their moment, and I'm going to let them savor it (and it's a gorgeous mountain-high moment, too, with the morning sun hanging like a trophy over the peaks and the pine trees an electric green and summer just waiting in the wings to possess us). They know what they've done and they know what they've learned—far more than I can list on a curriculum.

"But we didn't finish," Will says a little sadly. "We didn't eat the elephant."

His words pass through the ranks like a lightning bolt, and the cheerful smiles instantly turn dour.

"No," I say, "you didn't eat the whole elephant, but you sure as hell dressed it and cooked it and ate a good portion of it. And now it's all ready for the next group of kids!"

The frowns lift slightly, but they need more.

"Remember the plan. Stage one, stage two, stage three… You guys have already done the first three stages!"

"But there's no pond," Susannah says.

"There will be," I say. "There'll be a pond, and a whole lot more."
I see smiles, nods, even a few tears.
"Come back a year from now and you'll see. This is your project. This is your pond. You did this. All of you."

* * *

They take it with them, not just in their heads but in their hearts. Two of them (Joaquin Sanchez and Karla Walker) will become attorneys and a third (Amanda Stone) will earn a doctorate in biochemistry before distinguishing herself as a best-selling writer of historical romance novels. Jake Bonner will scale the academic ranks as a literature professor and part-time screenwriter. Her junior year, Dora Smallcanyon will get pregnant, drop out of school, and return to her family at Kinlichee, but after raising three children, she'll get her GED and then a bachelor's degree in education before landing a full-time position teaching fifth grade in her hometown. Will Gillespie will conquer his academic phobias and attain a doctor of dentistry degree at the University of Southern California, and Susannah Thompson will seize the moment and eventually become CEO of one of the nation's premier health-club franchises. When he's not wheeling and dealing in real estate, Ricky Watson will be seen doing stand-up comedy at Indian casinos and night clubs.

They won't all have happy endings. Marty Housman will get caught in an eternal loop, bouncing around from jail time to menial job to jail time to menial job. Shortly after winter break her junior year, Maria Gonzalez and her family will be deported and never return—at least not to my knowledge.

The romance between Jimmy Goldtooth and Susannah Thompson will heat up for the next three years. Jimmy will be voted Homecoming King and Susannah Homecoming Queen, and for a while it will look like a fairy tale come true. Then, the summer after graduation, they'll have a falling out. The rumors will be all over the map. Susannah got pregnant and had an abortion. Susannah met another guy. Jimmy met another girl. Susannah's father hired some thug to threaten Jimmy's family. Whatever the reason, Susannah will go east to school while Jimmy stays local. Halfway through his senior year, he will inexplicably quit college and return to Black Mesa... and pretty much fall off my radar.

The biggest heartbreaker is Bob Creighton, who will drop out of high school his senior year to join the Marines. He will fill one of the last body bags shipped home from Vietnam.

As I look at them now, all squinting into the sun—Susannah in her mini-skirt, Amanda with her light-up-the-night smile, Jake's guarded eyes, Bob in his way-too-tight muscle shirt, Dora with the raven hair, the Hollywood-handsome Joaquin, and all the rest—they suddenly look so young to me, kids, my little children launching out into the raucous world of high school. I want to gather them all in my arms and warn them about what lies ahead. I want to somehow shelter them from the pain that lurks within the joy, waiting to ambush them. I feel like weeping, but it's not the time or the place. No. It's *their* time and *their* place. I want to say goodbye, but not really.

They seem to be taking this much better than me. They're smiling, laughing, pointing to various locations on the field as if watching themselves (or ghosts of themselves) on a replay. Beaming, positively beaming with pride. They've taken science by the horns and used it to do adult work, and they know it. They feel it. It's theirs.

Soak it in, kids. Soak it in.

HARD KNOCKS

Playing river guide in the Grand Canyon may sound exciting and romantic, but it's far more work than play, and for the most part you're kowtowing to spoiled adult brats who can afford to shell out five or six grand for a seven-day whitewater cruise on fat rafts we called "boats" through a towering corridor of majestic, red rock desert. There are exceptions, but most clients are accustomed to getting what they want when they want it, and your task (in addition to keeping them safe and un-sunburned) is to make sure they get it—*pronto*! Plus there are always a few loudmouths, people out to prove something on the river that they can't prove back home. However, the wages are good, the tips generous, and the scenery breathtaking—pastel-colored sedimentary layers stacked to the sun. And nothing beats the adrenal rush of negotiating class-four rapids.

If there's one highlight on the river that summer, it's Claire Van Dyke. She's a loner in her mid-forties who doesn't mix easily with the other clients on my boat. During the day, as we cruise down the Colorado River, she sits in back in a long-sleeve shirt, floppy straw hat shielding her face from the menacing sun as she swats at mosquitoes and bugs (even if there are none). She doesn't like getting wet, which leaves me wondering why she chose a river trip as her summer adventure.

After we beach each night and finish dinner, the passengers and boatmen all gather around a Coleman lantern and swap stories for a few hours before turning in to bed. (Real campfires are prohibited in the Grand Canyon—hence the lantern substitute.) One night about halfway through the trip, as the raconteurs begin trading tales, I slip into the darkness to find a private place to relieve myself. I've gone about thirty yards when I notice Claire's silhouette. She's perched on a boulder shaped like an ottoman.

"Are you OK?" I ask.

Her head jerks around and snags my flashlight's beam just long enough to expose the tear tracks staining her cheeks.

"It's me," I say. "Todd Hunter."

She stands up, wiping her face with her hands. "Oh, hi! I was just …"

Her rear end plunks back down on the boulder. "Oh, shit! I was just crying my eyes out."

"Is there anything I can do to help?"

She laughs—a big guffaw. "Sure! Find me a new life! That's why I came on this trip. Fresh start, all that crap."

I usually don't fraternize with clients—it was rule number one when I was hired—but this seems more in line with rule number two: ensure that every passenger has a positive river experience. More importantly, it's simply the right thing to do.

For the next hour, I sit on the sandstone ottoman and listen to Claire's story, which is far more interesting than the usual barrage of mostly fictional campfire tales. Claire and I have a few things in common. She teaches, at an elementary school in a small town in northern Montana. Her father, like mine, was a civil engineer. She was born in southern California but grew up in Arizona. She has no children.

She's also recovering from a divorce, after a twenty-four-year marriage.

"He dumped me!" she says. "For a younger, newer model. That's why I'm on this trip. I got a little cash from the settlement, so I thought, What the hell? Who cares? Why not?"

At first, she sounds more hurt than angry. Then her tone heats up: "He never wanted kids, you know? I love kids—he knew that. He kept making excuses and putting it off—it's not the right time, there's not enough money, the moon's too high in the damn sky! Any excuse in the book. Now it's too late. I can't believe how incredibly stupid I was! I wasted my life on that asshole!"

She looks up, shaking her head. "I'm sorry. You don't need to hear all about my messy life."

I try to console her. "I know it seems like the end of the world right now, but things will get better. It will work out."

"You really think so?"

"Sure," I said. "You've got a whole life ahead of you. Don't let that jerk ruin it." I'm twenty-three years old and still a wet-behind-the-ears newlywed. I have no idea the depth of pain she's suffering right now, although my turn will come.

Then I do something I'd never done to a client on the river. I put my arm around Claire's shoulder. She reaches up, grasps my hand, and holds it for several moments.

"Thanks for listening to my soap opera," she says.

"Claire, you say you don't have any kids, but I'd say you've got hundreds of them. You're a teacher. Our whole life is about kids—teaching, nurturing, mentoring. And I'll bet you're a damn good one!"

She looks up again, smiling and sniffling. "I am!" she says. "I'm a damn good teacher!"

* * *

I don't want to take credit for Claire's transformation—I'm sure her "alone time" on the rock had far more to do with that than my pep talk—but for the duration of the trip, she wears nothing but a one-piece swimsuit and a life jacket and sits in the front of the boat howling like a cowboy on a brahma bull as we roller-coaster down the rapids. At the end of our journey, she wraps her arms around me and says, "Thank you, Todd! This trip has changed my life!" She hands me an envelope with a substantial tip and her name, address, and phone number printed on one side of a blank business card. On the other side she's written: *If I can ever do anything for you, call me! Seriously!* Then in all caps: *I MEAN IT!! EVER!!*

I smile and pocket the business card along with five twenty-dollar bills, not thinking too much about her kind note. On the river, clients come and go; acquaintances are quickly forgotten and seldom morph into genuine friendships. I assume Claire Van Dyke will fall into the former category, although I'll think about her often over the years, and every time I will smile.

* * *

After eight trips in eight weeks without a break, I'm ready to call it a summer and sleep in my own bed with my young bride, to shower, shave, and don the shirt and tie and semi-dress shoes of my profession so I can try, once again, to light a fire in the hearts and minds of the hundred and fifty adolescents enrolled in my classes.

The word is out about the Pond Project, and all spring and through the summer parents badgered Principal Jackson to get their kids into my biology class. The demand was so high that he assigned me all five sections of biology and raised the enrollment cap per class from twenty-six to a seam-bursting thirty. He also moved me into the special lab classroom, which has two large sinks with running water; an emergency eye rinse station; a storage closet filled with microscopes, test tubes, and other materials; and, instead of desk chairs lined up in neat rows, thirty stools arranged around six Formica tables with individual power outlets and gas faucets for conducting more in-depth experiments. In short, I get the one bona fide science classroom in the building, which means John Baxter inherits my old room, which means now there's even less love lost between us.

As I straighten my tie in the bathroom mirror, humming an old Beach Boys song, an eavesdropping Amy leans against the doorframe and says, "Well, look at you. What a difference a year makes!"

*   *   *

Yes, what a difference. A year ago, I was a young impostor, feigning confidence when in fact I was staggering one step ahead of my students. It was strictly on-the-job training, with plenty of trial and error. This year I know exactly what I'm going to do and how I'm going to do it. I've got a teaching philosophy, a plan, a process, a methodology. And I've got the pond. This year I'm confident, maybe even a little cocky. But already I'm hearing my father's voice catcalling from the peanut gallery: "Don't get too damn big for your britches!" His favorite epithet every time I experienced one iota of success. Overcompensation had become my antidote.

As a first-year teacher I'd done remarkably well—even Jackson agreed, at least in writing, showering praise on my annual performance evaluation. But this year I'm determined to be even better. And discipline is the watchword on campus. Apparently, last year's feel-good vibes from the Pond Project have already been forgotten.

"We've gotta crack down on these kids," Jackson exclaimed at the year's first faculty meeting. "We've gotta let them know who's in charge."

He reminded us that last year a few things got out of hand: a massive food fight in the cafeteria the day before Halloween; three student sit-down strikes in the commons, one to protest the school dress code, another to decry the Vietnam War, and the third for who knows what? The kids were getting mouthier and more disrespectful. Hairstyles were lengthening on the boys and hemlines were rising on the girls. Feeding off the "law and order" frenzy of the Nixon administration, in a midsummer survey, parents had cited discipline as the top priority for the 1970–1971 school year.

Reflecting on my own classroom, I admit that at times I'd been lax in the discipline department, although incidents of misbehavior plummeted once I started the Pond Project. And this has become a central tenet of my teaching philosophy: keep students eagerly engaged in meaningful instruction, and classroom discipline will be a non-issue. Still, I want to be a team player. If discipline is this year's clarion call, then I'll join the parade. Onward and upward!

But in less than a week I'm reminded, in humbling fashion, that I'm still a rookie with a lot to learn.

On a Wednesday at noon, I step outside to do lunch duty by the south parking lot, a favorite hangout for young smokers, ditchers, and mischief-makers. Aside from the idle vehicles of faculty and staff, the lot's vacant—as it should be—except for one boy. He's hanging over the edge of a trash can, his upper half hidden inside, his Levied legs sticking out the top, like a rodeo clown diving into a barrel to escape a marauding bull. I smile to myself as I beeline to catch the troublemaker red-handed. Ten feet away, I bellow like a drill instructor "Hey! What are you doing in there?!"

The boy pops out of the barrel like a legs-first jack-in-the box. I recognize him instantly: the short, coarse black hair; the patched jeans; the rangy arms: Johnny Davis.

He's clutching a cellophane bag in one hand and a smashed and half-eaten peanut-butter-and-jelly sandwich in the other. Bits of strawberry jelly speckle his lips like drops of blood. He holds out the remains of the sandwich like an offering and squeals guiltily: "Nobody else wanted it!"

*   *   *

That afternoon, I learn how to get free lunch tickets. After school, I drive to the trailer park south of the railroad tracks, where the topless bar and the student hostels and the smoke shop and the Goodwill depot coexist. Walking through the dirt yard scattered with kids' toys and past a Ford sedan rotting on cinderblocks, I knock on the door of what looks like an oversize plywood box. Sheets of plastic have been stapled over the windows to keep the warm air in or judgmental eyes out, or maybe both. The dead vines climbing the south wall look like gruesome fractures.

I knock several times before the door cracks open and a bloodshot eye appears.

"Is Mrs. Davis here?" I ask.

"That's me," says a voice as deep as if dredged from the bottom of a well.

"I'm Todd Hunter," I say. "I teach at the junior high."

She continues staring, waiting.

"May I come in for a moment?"

The door opens slowly. I step inside and smile at a round woman in a flimsy summer dress with multiple stains on the front: medals of motherhood. An infant is crushed against her side, and a crying toddler clings to her leg like a bear cub hugging a tree. Three other toddlers are playing in the corner while four grade-school kids watch cartoons on a black-and-white TV with a coat hanger for an antenna. I feel as if I've just walked in on Mother Goose.

I'm surrounded by runny noses and dirty hands. I have no idea how many of these children are hers and how many she's watching to earn pocket change. A swampish smell pervades the room, and the scent of rancid butter. Cheerios polka-dot the dirt-brown carpet like animal droppings.

The woman smiles and I notice two rows of immaculate teeth except for an absent incisor. Her high cheekbones glisten.

Taking a breath, I explain the school's free lunch program. I hand her a form and she thanks me, nodding as she scans the application, which she's holding upside down.

"Is it just for Jonathan?" she asks.

"No, all of your school-age kids. Breakfast and lunch."

Her eyes widen.

"I can help you fill them out."

One of the toddlers squeals. I turn to look just as the offended lowers a wooden block on the head of the offender. Self-defense?

Mrs. Davis smiles. "That would be real good."

Sitting on a rickety aluminum chair at the vinyl table discolored with coffee and who-knows-what other stains, I print the information she provides.

"How many children?"

"Five," she says.

"What's your annual income?"

"Oh, maybe a thousand dollars."

I try not to wince.

"When can they start getting lunch?" she asks.

"Johnny's starting tomorrow. I promise you that. And the others— give me another day. You've got... what? Two kids in elementary?"

"Two there, two at home with me still, and Johnny."

"One more day for elementary. I've got to talk to some people."

"Thank you," she says.

"No, thank *you*," I say, although I'm not sure what for: a lesson in gratitude and humility and not making assumptions; a glimpse into the bigger, more worrisome world beyond the safe walls of my classroom; a reminder of what a teacher can offer hundreds of children like Johnny: opportunity, options, escape, transformation.

* * *

This is the first of hundreds of home visits I'll make over the next thirty-four years. From this day on, I'll never again be able to separate home from institution, student from parent and provider.

Three months later, I volunteer to help serve Thanksgiving dinner at the soup kitchen. As I stand in the serving line dishing out mashed potatoes and gravy, I notice five of my biology students waiting patiently in a line that snakes down a long hallway and out the front door. Joining them are young mothers in tank tops clutching the hands of stick-thin toddlers, old men with gnarly beards and canes and a Parkinson's quiver, middle-aged men and women with broken smiles. The smell of urine is strong, and the smell of despair even stronger.

I signal for a backup to relieve me while I speak with the supervisor, a Wagnerian woman with a net over her beehive hair.

"I can't serve those kids," I explain. "I'm their science teacher."

She rounds them up and puts them to work beside me in the serving line, and the five of us josh and joke as peers until everyone in the long line has been fed. Then we serve each other and sit down together in the crowded hall with the scarred cafeteria tables to joyfully break bread.

QUIJOTE

Year two isn't all hard knocks—at least not with the pond, where I've got people from the U.S. Soil Conservation Service and the U.S. Forest Service coming in weekly to give lectures and outdoor demonstrations. Meanwhile, my kids are tackling several of the twenty-two projects Amanda, Jake, and their cohort created the previous year. These aren't Mickey Mouse projects you can slap-dash finish in an afternoon. Each one includes a stated purpose, a description, a timeline for completion, a list of people who can provide technical assistance, and general instructions. For instance:

PROJECT NUMBER 4: ECOSYSTEM PLANTINGS

PURPOSE

Plantings will be made on the site to:
Maintain or improve the soil resource base.
Demonstrate the plant community concept.
Beautify the area.
Attract various species of wildlife.
Provide a learning experience for the planning, selection, planting, and care of native plants.
Demonstrate proper site selection for native plants.

DESCRIPTION

Plantings will be made in units as shown on the plan maps and installed on a yearly basis until all areas are planted.
Special units of plantings include:
+Native Grassland type
+Pinyon-Juniper type
+Ponderosa Pine–Oak type
+Mixed Conifer type
+Aspen type
+Wetland and Riparian types

On-site investigation will be carried out to fit the ecosystems into the best available sites.

Plant lists will be developed for each vegetative type.

Sources for plant materials will be developed.

Proper planting techniques and timing will be carried out.

TIMING

The plantings will be made from April through July. The bare-root and containerized stock will be planted from April into May. The grassland type will be established in July. The timing on the aspen and grassland areas depends on when these areas receive the needed topsoil.

Plantings will be made on a yearly basis until the ecosystems are established.

TECHNICAL ASSISTANCE

Needed technical assistance will be supplied by the U.S. Soil Conservation Service and the Forestry Division of the State Land Department.

HOW DONE

Students will plant the needed plant materials according to the planting plan. The U.S. Forest Service and the Forestry Division of the State Land Department Youth Conservation Corps programs will assist in the summer planting projects. County natural resource conservation experts will assist by providing the large pinyon pines and junipers and the necessary equipment to dig them. The city will dig the necessary larger holes at the planting site.

Each student is assigned to a team, and each team gets a specific project. Teams are responsible for completing everything on the project worksheet. This includes the onerous task of calling local businesses for donations of labor and materials. As a result, forty-five tons of topsoil are dumped on-site by local construction companies, and my kids rake and shovel every ounce of it into a six- to twelve-inch layer across twenty acres of land. They also plant twenty-three different trees and shrubs and sixteen different grasses. They build rock piles, brush piles, nest boxes, nesting islands, spawning beds, and bat roosts, all to lure local wildlife back to this new and improved neighborhood. They re-seed denuded areas for protection against the elements while leaving other areas bare to study the long-term effects of erosion. They analyze soil samples, weather patterns, and wildlife activity. They each keep a portfolio of everything they do, and I read every word of every single one.

*   *   *

My year-two kids make phenomenal progress in many areas, but their crowning achievement is completing the small but effective dam at the south end of the site.

It's only nine feet high, three feet thick, and one hundred feet long, and it bulwarks a paved, one-lane street that will serve as a bridge between one side of the pond and the other. It requires 1,800 cubic feet of concrete and forty man-hours of adult labor volunteered by parents and other community members. And, most impressively, it's completed by the first week of October. From that time forward, the trickle of water that once looked like a tiny fracture in the middle of a junkyard begins accumulating at the base of the dam. It gradually grows into a puddle and then into a pool, and, by the end of the school year, it's a pond so big it looks more like a small lake.

The last day of class, I lead my year-two kids down the gravel path to a sandy swath of earth that has been transformed into a pocket-size beachfront blooming with shrubs and flowers. I point to the pond and repeat the ritual I initiated with my first class: "You guys did this—you and the class before you. Don't ever forget that!"

All of them smile and a few dab their eyes, including me, because I know that for some of them this moment will be the highlight of their lives.

*   *   *

By year three, "The Pond Project" is a familiar phrase around town. My students no longer need to solicit help from teachers, local businesses, or agencies because they're coming to us, offering time and resources. The Arizona Game and Fish Department regularly stocks the pond with trout, bass, sunfish, and catfish. Two professors from the archeology department at the university volunteer to help the students create a mock "archeology dig" featuring replicas of Navajo and Hopi artifacts. Dr. Pomeroy from the university biology department helps my students design informational placards for the various trees, shrubs, and grasses that appear along the nature trail. Roy Harrington, the P.E. teacher, suggests adding ten fitness stations along the trail—pull-ups, sit-ups, standing broad jump, straddle hop, rope climb, etc.—for circuit training. His students draw up plans, obtain materials, and provide labor. With assistance from the county and the local historical society, a century-old pioneer cabin that's been rotting on the mountain is transported, log by log, to the pond, where it's reassembled and converted into a "living classroom." A local welder whose nephew is in my class builds a large outdoor grill near the pond's sandy beach. Once completed, every Friday the school will provide a free lunch of barbeque beef to all comers—students, teachers, parents, passersby. Local supermarkets donate the food, and Melvin Jackson personally mans the grill. Dr. Gereaux from the university history department assists my students as they research and write a history of the pond ecosystem dating back to the 1800s. Joanna Engelhardt, the flighty speech and drama teacher, teams up with Andy Pfeiffer, the taciturn, no-nonsense woodshop instructor, to build an outdoor amphitheater on the pond's north shore. His students also build a fishing dock… where Joanna and Andy will exchange wedding vows in mid-May. Meanwhile, my kids stay more than busy building, researching, analyzing, monitoring, hypothesizing.

The awards follow, and the accolades too: District Teacher of the Year, State Teacher of the Year, and more. I'm featured in the local paper and *The Arizona Republic*, and I even earn a mention in *Time* magazine and *The Harvard Educational Review*.

* * *

At the start of my fourth year, I appear to be at the proverbial top of my game. I'm revered by my students, esteemed and envied by my peers, and hated by the curmudgeonly John Baxters of the world. If I step on toes or cross the line, Melvin Jackson looks the other way. I've put him and his school on the map, and he knows it. To an outsider looking in, I'm invulnerable. I can do what I want and say what I want.

For instance, one day a crew of city employees shows up to chop down some old-growth trees around the pond. I get wind of it and rush my students outside with instructions to mark every tree with spray paint, knowing that marked trees won't be cut. The city workers pitch a fit to Jackson, who comes charging down the gravel path:

"Hunter! What the hell do you think you're doing! Get those students back to class!"

"We're conducting an experiment," I holler across the pond. "This is field-based research."

"You get over here!"

Ignoring his order, I stroll across the wooden bridge to the island, where I begin recording fake observations on my clipboard.

Jackson calls for reinforcements. A half hour later, Ray Yarvitz, the assistant superintendent of maintenance and operations, rolls up in his school station wagon. The ex-Marine officer's in no mood for schoolboy pranks.

"Hunter!" he bellows across the water. "You get out of there or I'll throw you out!"

I yell back: "If you come across that bridge, I'm throwing you in the pond!"

"I'm coming after you!"

"Well, unless you're Jesus Christ, you'd better plan on getting wet!"

"I'm not Jesus Christ," Yarvitz says, "but I'm an assistant superintendent!"

"Then you're going to sink!"

Later that afternoon, I drive over to the district administration center to make peace with Yarvitz, not because I have to but just because. When I step into his office, he thrusts out his hand.

"I made a mistake," he says. "Those assholes had no right to cut down those trees. I'm sorry."

I'm touched, frankly. Yarvitz is a by-the-book guy, an ex-military hard-nose with a short fuse, but he's fair, he's honest, and he can admit when he's wrong.

"Don't let all this stuff go to your head," he cautions.

But he's a year too late. I'm the one walking on water now. To the new teachers, I'm "that guy," the one they want to emulate; the one who broke the mold. To the veteran teachers, I'm a source of inspiration or perspiration—the former to teachers who are constantly trying to reach beyond their grasp, the latter to deadbeats who are stuck in neutral, coasting to the finish line. To students, I'm the great liberator, freeing them from textbook bondage and boring, butt-in-chair education. They wave to me in the hallways, at the supermarket, at the movie theater, at the mall. "Hey, Mr. Hunter!" "How's it going, Mr. H!" "We love you, Mr. Hunter!" I smile and wave back, by all indicators enjoying my celebrity. Sauntering down the hallway during the congested passing periods, I almost seem to float above the crowd. But once I lock up my classroom and leave the school grounds—once I remove the Superman cape and the magic blue underwear and take a good hard look into the Quijote mirror—I am despondent, lonely, and miserable.

HEARTBREAK

It should be one of the happiest events of my life, and it certainly starts out that way: the first-class flight to Washington, D.C., three nights at the Watergate Hotel, a two-day tour of the nation's capital, including most of the major monuments and a full day at the Smithsonian, all in the company of the forty-nine other honorees, each representing their respective states; each having done something extraordinary to inspire the embryonic young scientists in their classrooms.

At least this is what the keynote speaker, a goateed, professorial-looking fellow in a black tuxedo tells us and the hordes of dignitaries who have packed the hotel ballroom to sit through this annual awards banquet in exchange for a four-course gourmet meal (Caesar salad, New England clam chowder, filet mignon with au gratin garlic mashed potatoes, and chocolate mousse for dessert). Alternately blocking a cough and dabbing a handkerchief at his nose, Dr. Horace Mayfield still manages to speak eloquently of recent advances in science, especially in outer space exploration, but also here on Earth where hot-button issues like overpopulation, pollution, poverty, and world hunger are screaming for solutions.

"Never before has science been so vital to the survival of our planet," he says, "and you—all fifty of you, the teachers of today—are grooming the scientists of tomorrow. Without you, there is no progress, no innovation, no imagination, no hope, no future."

The ballroom explodes with applause. It's an emotional time and a pivotal moment for the nation. Nixon is finishing up his first term in the White House as the body count grows in Vietnam. The country is weary of a war it can't win, and the president is looking for a graceful exit. Racial violence has escalated in the Deep South. Women are demonstrating for equal rights in New York and Los Angeles. A few months earlier, Mark Spitz won seven gold medals at the Summer Olympics in Munich, but the U.S. basketball team lost the gold medal to the Soviet Union for the first time, and Black September Palestinian terrorists shot and killed eleven Israeli athletes and coaches and a West German police officer. On the upside, American astronauts have landed on the moon not once but five times, with another mission planned for next year. And for another couple months, the word "Watergate" will mean nothing more than a swank hotel in downtown Washington.

The cheering gradually subsides and Dr. Mayfield once again thanks the U.S. Department of Education and the National Science Foundation for so generously hosting tonight's event, slipping in a plug for additional funding for both entities before looping back to us, the teachers, the true stars of the show and the reason we've all gathered here tonight, so with no further ado…

A silver-haired woman in a lavender gown and a stout man in a black tux position themselves on either side of the podium. Alternating turns, they call out the winner from each state, and the recipient stands to bask in the glory of a five-second ovation:

"From the state of Alabama, Mrs. Daphne Randolph, Applegate Middle School."

"From the state of Alaska, Mr. Ralph Henderson, Yukon High School."

And forty-eight more, the applause getting a bit softer with each name.

After they announce the science teacher of the year for the wonderful state of Wyoming, there's a prolonged silence as the woman in lavender cozies up to the microphone.

"And now," she says, "the moment we've all been waiting for. On behalf of the United States Department of Education and the National Science Foundation, I'm honored to present the award for the National Science Teacher of the Year." There's a dramatic pause as she slowly tears open the envelope, removes a slip of paper, and reads: "From the Grand Canyon State of Arizona, Mr. Todd Hunter, Ponderosa Junior High School!"

*   *   *

This is what I remember: thunderous applause, so loud that for a moment I think the walls are shaking and the ka-zillion crystal prisms clinging to the rows of giant chandeliers will break loose and rain down like a hailstorm; my legs turning to mush as I rise; the woman sitting next to me, Miss Lupe Hernandez from Austin, Texas, smiling as she reaches over to touch my forearm—and the unexpected electric jolt that follows. One by one, people stand: first up, Mr. Jerry Bartholomew from

San Dimas, California, who has worn bell-bottom jeans to the black-tie event, then Miss Hernandez, then four others and five others and a dozen others until the entire congregation is standing, clapping as I make my long, awkward, wobbly-legged hike to the podium, weaving around the dinner tables, flashbulbs partially blinding me as I shake hands with a coterie of big shots who have suddenly appeared on stage and whose faces I won't remember except for the woman in lavender, who hands me a walnut plaque with a brass plate that bears my name, and the dead-fish handshake of the plump penguin as he steers me toward the mic, and the applause that seems to last for an hour although it's more like thirty seconds, and in its silent aftermath, the soft but annoying clatter of dishes and silverware as the busboys began clearing the dinnerware prematurely.

And then it's my turn to speak, jelly legs and all.

First, I butter my bread, thanking the people, agencies, and organizations that have made this evening possible. I thank my wife, Amy, who couldn't attend due to a health issue but without whose love and support I wouldn't be standing here tonight. I thank my principal, Melvin Jackson, who was supportive from the get-go, and my superintendent, Dale Hanagan (omitting the part about how at best he was a neutral observer who took *ex post facto* bows on my behalf and at worst was an impediment, conspiring with city council cronies to sabotage my project—but that's a story for later on). I remind the other forty-nine teachers that there are no losers here tonight; they're all winners or else they wouldn't be here. In other words, I say all the right things. I have to ad lib, because I hadn't expected this.

"You know, this award isn't mine. It belongs to every teacher in this room, and it belongs to every teacher in this country—all of us—every teacher who suits up, whether you're feeling sick or well, happy or sad, inspired or humdrum nothing—you suit up and show up and you try to make a difference in the lives of our kids. Everyone here tries to make science more than an eat-your-peas ordeal kids have to endure to get their name on a diploma. We try to make science part of who they are. We try to spark inside them the curiosity and the intellect to not just ask the hard questions but to take the right steps—scientific steps—to find the right answers. Not just the ability to hypothesize and experiment, but the courage as well. Not just the knowledge to put a man in outer space or invent a time machine, but the moral fiber to do it for the right reasons. Not to destroy the planet but to save it; not to blow up buildings but to build bridges between people and communities and nations."

I don't know where the words are coming from—I'm saying things I've felt but have never written down, and I'm afraid that if I keep going my tongue might slip into the murky morass of politics—stop this damn war, for starters. And from there, who knows what? I've got a captive audience and the adrenaline's surging through my veins like champagne from a fire hose. Quit while you're ahead, Todd. Remember the Broadway axiom: always leave them wanting more. Or my laconic father's favorite platitude whenever I'd go off on a verbal wingding: "Don't cut the chicken's head off twice." Whatever that meant.

I hold the plaque above my head: "This isn't mine—it's ours! It's for all of us—and for our students!"

Another deafening round of applause, followed by back pats and handshakes as I slalom back to my table. I'm the hero of the hour, and before the night's over I'll shake two hundred more hands and pose for two dozen photos. When the ballroom finally clears, we—Lupe Hernandez from Austin, Texas; Jerry Bartholomew from San Dimas, California; Sam Washburn from Des Moines, Iowa; and me—all agree that the evening's still young and we're in Washington, D.C. on a Friday night and how often do a bunch of underpaid schoolteachers have an opportunity like this? So Lupe recommends a night club just down the street where we all have a few drinks and talk and laugh, not wanting this perfect evening to end.

*   *   *

But eventually it does, and I'm just a little drunk when I trudge into my hotel room at two thirty a.m.—alone, although Miss Lupe Hernandez might have joined me if I'd given the slightest inkling of interest. On entering, the first thing I notice is the red light on the phone blinking like a beating heart.

"Oh, shit."

Because Amy and I have an understanding: long-distance phone calls, especially from a hotel room, cost a small fortune, so we never ever call unless it's a life-or-death emergency. Anything else can wait: good news, bad news, neutral news.

I plop down on the bed, replaying in my head our parting conversation as I remember it, knowing Amy's recollection will be radically different.

"It's not that big a deal," I'd said. "I don't have to go—I'll still get the thousand dollars."

"I'm fine," she'd insisted. She was sitting on the queen bed, propped up by half a dozen pillows, her hand caressing her volleyball belly. "Dr. Bailey says everything's looking great."

"Then come with me."

Silence. That should have been the red flag.

"That's it," I'd said. "If you don't go, then I don't go."

"Go!" she'd insisted. "It's a once-in-a-lifetime. And it's only four days."

"You're sure?"

"Are you kidding? You worked your ass off for this. You earned it."

"*We* earned it."

"Oh, don't give me that humble pie nonsense. *You* earned it. Now go!"

I could have pushed back harder, but deep down I was aching to go. Surely she'd sensed this—of course she had, but that didn't matter now. The whole damn conversation was moot. Even the end bit.

"Look!" she'd said. "Look me in the eyes."

I did: two beautiful brown disks with my puppy-dog face imprinted on them in miniature.

"I want you to go," she'd whispered. "Please."

So I did.

*   *   *

I check my watch and calculate the time difference—eleven forty-five Arizona time—then dial the front desk and ask the operator to put the call through. Listening to the soft, rhythmic rings, I pray for the impossible on the other end: good news—in fact, news so good that she'd broken our protocol. But just before the fifth ring, she answers and any lingering hope is dashed.

"Hello?" Her voice is faint, hollow, dead.

"Everything all right?"

The static within her silence sounds like ocean. Her voice is buried in the depths of the sea.

"Amy? Are you OK?"

"No."

"What's the—" But I already know. "I'm sorry, sweetheart. I'm so sorry."

I don't ask for details and she doesn't offer any. I ask innocuous questions, assuming she will talk when she wants to talk. Or not.

"Are you at home?"

"Yes."

"In bed?"

"No."

"Are you alone? Is someone with you?"

"No."

Arriving home the following afternoon, I'm greeted by a long-haired, long-legged zombie in a peasant dress. Dark half-moons droop beneath eyes that look like holes. Her mouth is a small, expressionless slit, her usually robust lips pale and chapped. When I reach for her, she pivots away.

"Amy?"

When I wrap my arms around her, it's like hugging a fencepost.

FAITH

After her first miscarriage, Amy said it was like a giant corkscrew in her gut that kept turning tighter and tighter until it felt as if every inch of every cord in her intestines were contorting into a Gordian knot that would eventually burst and all the noodly goop and blood would spill out of her onto the floor and that would be the end of it and her, too: lights out, game over. But in the end, it was much ado about nothing. All that pain and agony to expel a slimy impostor, an unrecognizable alien so small we chose not to give it a name.

Three months in the making, and Dr. Bailey reassuring her that it was fairly common with a first pregnancy, not to fret over it, of course you're sad and disappointed but you're young and healthy and there's no apparent reason—no physical reason—why you shouldn't be able to bear enough youngsters ("little hellions" is how he phrased it) to field a football team if you want. Patting her naked knee: "Just you wait. One day you'll be in here begging me to do something to *stop* all those kidlets from coming." That had made her laugh. That had made her feel better, optimistic, hopeful. And things had returned to normal quickly: teaching, camping, hiking, lovemaking.

Two years later, another miscarriage. Dr. Bailey was more guarded that time, and so was Amy. Still, he'd looked for silver lining. She'd made it four months this time, that's improvement, that's good. Third time's a charm, right?

Clasping her hand in the emergency room, I'd added my two cents: "We can try again."

To which she'd pulled her hand away: "Easy for you to say! It's not your body that's going through the meat grinder."

Up to that point I thought I'd been patient, long-suffering, supportive. Not pointing the finger or playing the blame game, not stating the obvious: you've been able to get pregnant twice, so please don't blame me for this. I'm sure as hell not blaming you. Don't you get it? I want kids too, you know. I want kids like all the other young families on the block. They started out like us and now they have two, three, four kids, a houseful and a half, and we've got a calico cat. You're not the only one who's suffering. You're not the only one who's lost a child. I'm hurting too; I'm sad; I'm all of that and a whole lot more, but I can't go moping and pining about it. I'm supposed to hold the roof up right now. Especially now.

Until then I'd kept a lid on it: we're in this together, husband and wife, the yolk and egg in one shell. But as I gazed at her lying listlessly in the hospital bed—cheeks shellacked with tears, her dainty ski-slope nose red from weeping—I could almost hear her heart cracking.

"I'm sorry," she whispered, and I re-clasped her hand, squeezing firmly. I bent down and kissed her on the forehead.

"It'll be OK," I said.

She nodded, sniffling. "I know."

*　*　*

And it was again, at least for a while: teaching, hiking, camping, lovemaking. But her longing soon turned into obsession. Whenever she saw a young family with a child, especially an infant, her body seized up like a giant cramp and a hollow, agonizing nausea returned. At the mall when a towhead toddled out of J.C. Penney's on Charlie Chaplin legs, his young mother chasing after him, she wanted to snatch the boy up and call him hers: "Finders keepers!" She smiled at mothers pushing strollers around the neighborhood, but it was like chewing gravel.

At book club, she bit her tongue until it bled when the mothers (three-fourths of the group) bitched about their kids: the lack of privacy, the constant demands, how their sex lives had been stashed in the icebox and they couldn't go to the bathroom without an audience. You want motherhood? Take it! You can have mine any time. Teacher, attorney, doctor, accountant—humor yourself with any label you want. Once you add the *M* word to your resume, you are first and foremost and forever after, the Mom. M-O-M. Mercy On Me. Take my advice: you've got a good thing going; don't muck it up with kids.

But she knew this was all prattle and posturing—call it maternal venting; they were draining the well so they could replenish it, and maybe throwing a consolation bone to the non-mothers in the group. Because these moms adored their children. For every poopy diaper, there were a dozen hugs and kisses and Kodak moments. Finger-painting portraits of the one-and-only you, handcrafted with artless and unpremeditated love by the one-and-only them, with four crudely scrawled words: "I love you mommy."

It gouged, this baby-world that surrounded her while simultaneously rejecting her, as if a ten-foot wall had been constructed around its border: NO TRESPASSING. You can look but you can't touch. But you can participate vicariously, to a point. So she did, five days a week, teaching kids as young as five—when they were still big-bodied babies dipping their toes in the water—on up to the twelve-year-olds who were beginning to feel the roller-coaster rush of hormones, still cute but now cunning and mischievous too, vulnerable and optimistic mostly, still capable of being cured with a mother's (or a teacher's) hug.

Yes, but she wanted one of her own to nurse and coddle and put to bed every night; to feel the perfect softness that is the gift of newborns. The smell of new life, hope, perfection for a season. To hold that precious part of us and call it ours. Son. Daughter. To feed them with milk manufactured in her body; to caress them, sing them to sleep, kiss their pains and make them magically disappear; to wait, breathlessly, for their first awkward step, their first ecstatic word.

She became philosophical. Her first miscarriage was life: shit happens. Her second, at least in her mind, was punishment. This is what she got for dishonoring her parents and breaking their hearts; for leaving home like a thief in the night without a note or word of explanation; for ignoring God all these years.

*   *   *

Growing up, she had been a sometime Lutheran, attending Sunday services with her parents and siblings on Christmas, Easter, and two or three other times during the year. She knew the basics: faith, repentance, baptism. Her parents usually said grace at meals and she was expected to be honest and respectful and to follow the Golden Rule, but all that went out the window when her father staggered home late one night and plowed his fist into her mother's face, giving a whole new meaning to the Sunday school axiom, turn the other cheek.

That night she'd knelt by her bed as sirens screamed in the streets and begged God to please make her father disappear, meaning: never come back, and leave us the hell alone.

She had crawled into bed, skeptical but hopeful. When she woke up the next morning and heard him whistling a big-band tune in the bathroom, her heart sank and her ten-year-old brain concluded the obvious: either God is a fairy tale, or the Good Lord doesn't give a waffle about us. From that point on, any religious worship was perfunctory on her part, to appease her mother and avoid her father's wrath. But once she left home for college and was living on her own (albeit in a basement apartment shared with three equally broke roommates), religion was relegated to her personal file of bad and inconvenient memories.

I, on the other hand, was raised by a God-fearing Methodist mother and an agnostic father, the two philosophies neutralizing one another in my formative mind, eventually shaping me into a sometimes skeptical believer. I prayed when it was expedient. I believed within reason. In my mind, God wasn't obligated to clean up my messes, but I certainly appreciated it when He did.

Somehow Amy connected the dots between her two miscarriages and her failure to petition God for help. She grew repentant; she grew Biblical.

"I'm barren by design," she murmured. "God has sewn up my womb."

One Sunday morning she boldly announced: "We need to go to church!" Which caught me off guard but only a little. Dr. Bailey had insisted there was nothing medically amiss. No good reason this should have happened again. Diet, exercise, bed rest, vitamins. How about a mandrake root? If it was out of our hands, then why not put it in God's? What did we have to lose other than a couple hours every Sunday?

"Sure," I said. "Which one?"

We tried Lutheran because it was the one she remembered from her childhood and when we met privately with the minister he spoke words of comfort and reassurance, not hellfire and damnation. He spoke of God's infinite love for His children and His eternal design, how life is like a mosaic or an Impressionist painting. Close up, through mortal eyes, it can appear like nothing more than a chaotic blur of clashing colors, but if we step back and look through God's eternal lens, it makes perfect sense within the greater context of eternity.

"I can't tell you why your baby was called home at such a tender age," he said, "but I do know this: God sent that little child to the mother who was best prepared to love him under whatever circumstances, however tragic, and you've proven that here today."

Amy wept.

So we started attending church on Sundays and Bible study Wednesday nights, and there were socials and service projects too. We made new friends and we prayed together morning and night and said grace before every meal and early in the spring of 1972, when Dr. Bailey confirmed that Amy was indeed pregnant for the third time, we were grateful but cautious. Although Dr. Bailey insisted there was no need for special precautions, this time we took no chances: leisurely walks but no strenuous hiking, especially on rocky or uneven terrain; no volleyball or other sports that might precipitate a collision or a fall; no evening glass of wine—no alcohol, period; limit sugar and fatty foods; during the winter months, steer clear of snow and ice (if in doubt, wear crampons); keep feet elevated whenever possible; and last but not least, no sexual intercourse. (I contested this one but in the end relented with a compromise to explore other creative methods for physical bonding.)

By mid-May, when she'd passed the two-month mark, we began talking about it obliquely. She was kneeling at the toilet a dozen times a day, retching as she offered up her latest meal, but she never complained: this is a gift, she said, and I'm not returning it. By Independence Day— the four-month mark, and a clean bill of health from Dr. Bailey—we started looking at cribs and talking about names: Ann Carol if it was a girl; Thomas if it was a boy. Amy was showing well then. At school she wore loose, colorful *mu mu* dresses that downplayed the drama growing in her belly, but at home she loved to stand sideways in the mirror, naked, smoothing her hand over the miracle bulge in her midsection. She loved the tautness and sleekness of it, and the way her navel had taken on a life of its own, protruding like a little nose in the making. She marveled at the new abundance of her breasts, swelling like ripe fruit, tender to the touch. Cupping her hands under the soft, pendulous weight of motherhood, she imagined the baby sucking voraciously on those magnified nipples, and she smiled.

By summer's end we'd painted and decorated the spare bedroom as much as possible without knowing the sex of our new addition and set up the crib there. And shortly before the start of the new school year, I answered a phone call from the state Department of Education congratulating me on being selected as Arizona Science Teacher of the Year. A month later, I received a written invitation to the banquet in Washington, D.C., where the National Science Teacher of the Year would be awarded to one of the fifty statewide honorees.

"Oh, you have to go!" she'd said. "You have to!"

At the time, it had seemed like the perfect culmination to what she had called the best summer of her life.

FURY

God shoulders her first wave of anger because He's everywhere all the time and almighty, which means He has yea or nay power. He could have prevented this. He could have kept her little baby's heart beating, but He either: (1) chose not to, which means He's cruel and uncaring or (2) isn't the big shot can-do-anything He's cracked up to be, which reduces Him to a feel-good notion on par with the Tooth Fairy. Plus there's easy access. She can curse and scream at Him pretty much twenty-four/seven: in the shower, in the kitchen, walking around the block, on the toilet, in bed, whenever or wherever. When Jill Simmons from church stops by bearing casseroles covered with tinfoil, she doesn't answer the door. Jill knocks three times and leaves the Corningware container on the doormat. "Jesus loves you!" she says.

Well, I don't love Him, Amy mumbles. I don't love anyone.

*   *   *

I take the second wave because I'm close and convenient and an easy target: while she was being dragged through hell at home, I was gallivanting around Washington, D.C., with my fellow science divas. While I was yukking it up with strangers, she was giving birth to a corpse.

Any efforts to replay the scenario—my futile pleas to remain home with her, her insistence that I bask in my well-earned accolades—incite a revisionist indictment of a cold, self-serving husband who abandoned his pregnant wife at her most dire time of need.

For the first few weeks I give her wide berth. I go to work while she sulks around the house in a terrycloth bathrobe or an old summer dress, doping herself on TV game shows. At night she pieces together jigsaw puzzles on a TV tray. Suggestions to go out to dinner or a movie are politely and mechanically declined. I do the shopping and the cleaning and the cooking of meals, which she nibbles at experimentally and unenthusiastically. She goes to bed early and sleeps in late.

By the end of the second week, she burns her tenth and final day of sick leave, which means now she'll be docked pay. Fortunately, there are only three weeks until the winter break, which will give her another two weeks to recuperate before returning to work in January, so we won't be hit too hard financially. But the situation at home is deteriorating by the day. Whenever I try to start a conversation, she looks away and says she doesn't want to talk about it, "it" meaning anything.

There are fights, mostly verbal but once, in the kitchen, as I'm preparing to fix dinner—opening and closing drawers, digging into the freezer, removing condiments from the fridge—she grabs me by the shoulder and slaps me across the face—whack! whack! whack!—left cheek, right cheek, left cheek.

"Listen to me when I'm talking to you!" she wails. "Listen to me! You never listen!"

Hyperbole reigns in our house. Every day, it seems, she makes some reference to my absence at her darkest hour. She casts blame as if it's bird seed.

Annoying habits become epic transgressions. For instance, the way I never rinse out my coffee mug, leaving a nasty brown ring around the bottom. Do you know how freaking hard it is to clean that out once it's dried there? Do you? I mean, is it so impossibly hard to just rinse out the damn mug? (And she demonstrates with strident, step-by-step directions tailored for an imbecile: "You take the mug like this… put it under the tap like this… turn the water on like so… fill the mug until it's about one-third… then empty it out and—ta da! No ring whatsoever, see? Now is that so damn hard?")

I'm patient and penitent at first, nodding and acquiescing: yes, yes, you're right, I should definitely rinse it out. But over time they grow old, these daily tongue-lashings, and my overblown apologies morph into a robotic sarcasm: "Yes-I-will-do-bet-ter. How very inconsiderate of me. A complete lack of respect for anyone. I should be chained to a refrigerator and tossed into the sea."

"Oh, you think you're so damn funny! I'll show you funny!" She pounds into the bedroom, returning moments later with a folded blanket and a pillow which she hurls off the porch and onto the gravel driveway. "There! Now *that's* funny! Ha! Ha!"

"What the hell's wrong with you?"

"What's wrong with *me*? That's the pot calling the kettle black! Nothing's wrong with me! I'm happy! Can't you see that?" Her lips bend into a grisly smile. She stomps back into the bedroom, slams the door, and shouts: "Hip-hip-hurray! Happy!" She remains there in a brooding silence until morning.

*   *   *

I sleep on the sofa in the living area, or try to. Sleep has evaded her. Late into the night I can hear her footsteps pacing the creaky floorboards or the steady rush of water as she fills the bathtub, hoping a warm-water dip might induce sleep. She begins popping valerian pills from the health food store, and then tries over-the-counter remedies—Tylenol PM and Nyquil. If she does manage to fall asleep, it's usually on the verge of dawn, so in real time it seems but a deep, dark, luxurious instant before her alarm clock rudely awakens her from the dead. She soon graduates to the heavy-hitters—habit-forming prescription drugs that knock her out for the night but leave her as groggy as a drunken pirate.

Each morning, she gropes for the phone and calls in sick again. This is OK at first: she's a pullout teacher, which means she takes kids out of their regular class, so she doesn't have to have a sub. Her kids can just stay where they are. The other teachers know her story and her situation. Her principal says, "Don't worry about a thing, Amy. Take all the time you need." It's a generous thing for Patty Shoemaker to say, but then one week becomes two, which becomes three, and soon a month has passed and Amy's still in bed with the curtains closed and the TV on, curled up under the covers like a cave woman nursing a fire in the dark.

Principal Shoemaker calls the house but Amy doesn't answer, so she contacts me at the junior high. I assure her Amy will be ready to return after Christmas break, if she can hold on that long.

"Of course," Shoemaker says. "Tell your sweet bride we just want her to get well."

"I'll do that," I say, but when I do, my sweet bride hisses at me like the Bride of Frankenstein.

I finally persuade her to see Dr. Bailey, who runs test after test but finds nothing physically amiss other than the fact she no longer has ovaries or a uterus and will never be able to give birth again. (This was the other piece of bad news: in addition to losing the baby, the substitute doctor had also performed an emergency hysterectomy.)

"I can see why you've hit rock bottom," Dr. Bailey says. "Lack of appetite, lack of ambition, radical mood swings…"

He suggests a shrink—professional counseling is how he phrased it—but to her, psychotherapy's still a taboo pseudoscience for lunatics and she's not a lunatic—she's not! Or the D-word! She's not that either. A touch of melancholy maybe. Postpartum blues perhaps. It's common, Dr. Bailey concedes, but this case seems extreme. He gives her a recommendation, which she stuffs into her purse and ignores.

* * *

Home becomes Hell. Every time I step inside, I'm either entering a graveyard or submitting to the Spanish Inquisition; dead, brooding silence or in-my-face interrogations. My classroom becomes my refuge. I'm tired of grieving over this double loss: a child and a wife. She doesn't want to talk about adoption or God or work or Nixon's impeachment or the Vietnam War or getting another cat or a dog or a parrot.

Fine. I've got work to do. Students to teach. Roger Youngblood from the U.S. Soil Conservation Service is meeting me at the pond Monday to discuss the next round of soil deposits. On Tuesday, Gary Bradford from the U.S. Forest Service is slated to lecture on invasive plants. The mayor's coming Wednesday to present a special award to my students for their latest beautification program. We're starting phase six of the Pond Project. This spring, three professors from the university are assisting students with the expansion of the archeological dig. Visiting teachers from Italy, Mexico, and Ireland are coming to witness our work firsthand. And as National Science Teacher of the Year, I'm obliged to hit the banquet circuit. The feds pay for my transportation, lodging, and sustenance, with a modest honorarium too, but it's time away from my classes and from home (which, right now, seems a blessing).

And I have the outdoors. Hunting trips with Fitz, even when I don't have a tag. Archery-deer in late August, rifle-deer in the fall, javelina, turkey, elk, antelope. Year-round almost. Anything to escape the house's gloom, although there's always hell to pay when I return, mostly in the form of cold-shouldering silence. So there's no escape, really. I carry it with me even into the wilderness—anger, frustration, and guilt, the triple alliance. But I don't notice because I'm not me anymore. That's what Fitz said on our last outing.

After three cold, windy days stalking deer up and down ravines on the North Kaibab, just before sundown Fitz bagged a six-point muley. We spent the next two hours hauling it to Fitz's pickup, the deer dangling by its lashed-together legs from a pole, each of us shouldering one end, like Nubian slaves toting home the king's latest kill.

It was dark and cold when we arrived at the wildlife check-in station near Jacob Lake Inn. The uniformed ranger stepped out of his heated office, perturbed that we'd already deposited the buck onto the concrete slab under the ramada. I motioned toward a big, steel bar with a chain hanging from it and asked: "Can we string him up and skin him here?"

The ranger raised his chipmunk nose, sniffing the cold November air. "We have no facility for that," he said. He removed a tape measure from his pocket, dropped to one knee, and attended to his business, stretching the tape between the buck's two biggest antler tips.

Fitz and I were tired and hungry and I was pissed off at the world, spoiling for a fight. I stepped out from under the dimly lit awning and into the starry night, muttering just loud enough for the ranger to hear: "This guy's nothing but a pissy bureaucrat."

I glared back at the ranger, who pretended to ignore me. Fitz said something to him, probably apologizing for his hunting buddy's irascible behavior. I knew I should just shut the hell up, but I couldn't stop myself.

"No, I don't want to skin it here," I growled. "I want to get as far away from this asshole as possible!"

Fitz and I drove home in silence—three-and-a-half grueling hours' worth.

*   *   *

I'm like that now, perpetually on edge except in my classroom, where I somehow maintain a cheerful, gung-ho optimism. But my marriage is hanging by a thread. One bark, one boo, one dumb breadcrumb will snap it.

Then I see a ray of hope in the form of an insert in the weekend paper advertising homes for sale in the exclusive Mountain View Estates. The ad prompts a phone call that will eventually lead to the purchase of our proverbial dream house, thanks to a cycle of circumstances in our favor: a bank foreclosure, an unexpected windfall in the form of Amy's grandfather's will that leaves her $10,000, and a sluggish housing market that creates just enough desperation to make an otherwise shrewd negotiator sell low. As a result, we are able to buy a luxury home that two schoolteachers have no business buying, not with a combined monthly salary of $1,544 after taxes.

It's a spacious two-story with a cedar exterior nestled in a mini-forest of quaking aspens and ponderosa pines. I like the two-car garage with an adjoining shop for storing the outdoor toys I've been accumulating: kayak, cross-country skis, downhill skis, backpack, sleeping bags, boots for hiking, biking, and hunting. Amy loves the malpais rock fireplace and the great room with the vaulted, tongue-and-groove ceiling that suggests posh ski lodges in Aspen and Sun Valley. But more than anything, she loves the view! The instant you step through the front door, your eyes zoom across the great room to a wall-size picture of a snow-capped peak that seems to hover above the forest like a distant Shangri-la, except it's not oil on canvas but the real thing, and it appears so close that your first impulse is to reach out and touch it.

"It's gorgeous!" she says—shouts, actually, employing an adjective I've never heard from her lips and smiling a smile that's been AWOL for months. That's the deal-breaker for me, the joy on her face, the return of her smile that means hope. A new house, a new leaf, a fresh start. Maybe that's all she needs—*we* need—a change of venue. Box up the previous life, the fights, the gloomy Tuesdays that stretch to Saturday, the insomniac nights and weeks of brooding silence and withdrawal. The petty accusations and careless words that are first barbs, then daggers, then double-bladed broadswords dipped in poison. Maybe this is the answer. Not the house itself: Amy doesn't crave fancy, doesn't yearn to rub elbows with the doctors and lawyers and the country club crowd. In fact, we both hate golf but will have to pay the mandatory fee because it's part of the homeowners association package. The golf comes with the clubhouse and the groomed walking trails, none of which she needs, but she loves the house. There's no hiding that.

All of this is spinning through my head while the realtor—Ronnie (short for Veronica) Bird—guides us from room to room, highlighting the upgrades and conveniences: the avocado-green refrigerator that could store enough food to feed a Scout troop; the sunroom where Amy can pedal her stationary bike while day dawns over the mountain; the massive kitchen with an island in the center and oak cabinets and a tile floor; the master bathroom with oil-rubbed bronze fixtures and tile work with Byzantine motifs. There's something almost decadent about it, Roman excess colliding with frontier chic, but Amy is pirouetting from one room to the next, like a Disney princess at the royal ball. I've never seen her like this—utterly enchanted, breathlessly happy. Or maybe it's just been so long ago I've forgotten.

It's far more house than we need—3,600 square feet, with five bedrooms, four bathrooms—what will we possibly do with all that space except maybe have kids, which is completely off the table, at least for now. And it will be a stretch financially. We'll be house poor. Ronnie Bird's trying to allay my fears. If we can put $10,000 down and secure a thirty-year mortgage, she can try to negotiate a lower monthly payment with a hefty balloon bill the final three or four years. By then we should be making considerably more money.

I laugh, reminding Ronnie that we're both teachers and that "considerably more" means not a whole helluva lot. I also don't like balloon payments. Or down payments. Or monthly payments. Up until now we've always saved up and paid cash for everything.

"Welcome to the real world," Ronnie quips.

I do some quick math in my head and determine we can make the monthly payments, but barely. We'll have to tighten our belts. No more adventurous splurges. No more spring-break vacations. A sack lunch to work, but I've been doing that anyway. I'll have to get a better-paying summer job—both of us will. I can maybe work the fire crew for the U.S. Forest Service. Good money, but it's ankle-breaking work, grueling on the joints, all that hiking and lugging equipment over killer terrain. I'll get in shape though; that's a plus.

No way am I teaching summer school. Peanut pay to force-feed math to mostly obstinate kids who didn't get it and didn't care the first time around and now want to be anywhere on God's green Earth but in a classroom. Probation kids. Last-chance kids. Besides, I need those ten weeks to refill the well for the fall semester. I've seen what happens to the summer-school crew. With no break, they drag their battered souls to the back-to-school barbeque, where everyone else is showing off suntans and swapping vacation tales, Energizer Bunnies starting their engines. Meanwhile, the summer-school teachers have the haggard look of shipwrecked sailors.

How much is that smile worth? How much is my marriage worth? How do I put a price tag on that? I suggest—and Ronnie vehemently concurs—that it would be a great investment. The house is a steal, we all agree. And in this town—a mountain town where, once the secret leaks out, every person with money or means in the city of Phoenix will be buying a second home to escape summer's inferno—housing prices are going to skyrocket. "Through the roof!" Ronnie prophesies, jabbing her index finger in the air. "Through the roof!" And she's right—we'll be making money in our sleep.

"I've been in this business a long time," Ronnie says. "An offer like this only comes around once. And don't forget this…"

But as Ronnie grips the cord to draw back the master-bedroom drapes, I beat her to the punch.

"We'll take it," I say.

Ronnie looks startled, even a trifle disappointed, her hand still tugging lightly at the cord that with one swift yank would have brought us both to our knees and closed the sale: signed, sealed, delivered, done!

Ronnie smiles coyly and says, "Well, then, I guess you don't really need to see…"

She pulls the cord down slowly, the curtain splitting in the middle and retreating toward either extreme, inch by inch exposing a picture-postcard view of the snow-shrouded peaks.

"I said we'll take it," I repeat.

Ronnie smiles. "Make an offer."

Amy stares at me with a mixture of shock and consternation. We can't afford this! her eyes scream. Yet at the same time they're pleading for a rabbit to leap out of the porkpie cap I'm holding in my hand. She's digesting it cautiously, as if this is one of my irritating teases to get her hopes up only to pull the rug out. But when I say it a third time—"We'll take it!"—her face brightens like a little girl's: I've just delivered her yearned-for but never truly expected dream-come-true birthday present.

"Oh, Todd!" she whispers, and she wraps her arms around my shoulders and kisses me on the lips, deeply, sincerely, like our perfect honeymoon moment on the shores of Puerto Escondido: half the sun burning in the sky and the other half buried in the sea, Amy sitting on my lap under the palapa sipping a margarita. I'd thought we could never be happier, yet somehow, at this moment, we are.

Worth it, I'm thinking. Worth every damn nickel. Worth every damn red cent.

And the two of us are happy again, for a while; six months, to be exact.

DEAD END

It's right after the archery-elk hunt that I broach the idea of a separation. "Maybe we need a short break from each other?"

Amy's not working—in fact, she hasn't been for almost two years. She never returned after Christmas break. Principal Shoemaker bit her lip until it bled before hiring a long-term substitute. Amy's contract wasn't renewed for the fall. One year led to two, and here we are.

"A break?" she says. "What kind of break?"

"A separation. You could stay here. I'll find someplace else."

She turns her head, sniffling softly. It's the first time I remember her shedding tears unrelated to the baby. But she doesn't fight it. She doesn't object.

These things are always a two-way street, I know that, and I shoulder my share of blame. I'm no saint. I've reminded her I'm the only one bringing home the bacon these days, so, yes, I do have a superior say when it comes to family finances, and if I want to buy a new pair of downhill skis, I don't have to ask her permission, not under the present circumstances; not when I'm making all the money and sleeping in the guest room. By the way, if I want to buy a new couch or a new house or a new car or a new anything, what's it to you? It's *my* money.

And, yes, I'm something of a social butterfly at school and around town, the smiling Mr. Nice Guy Big Shot Science Teacher of the Universe, slapping backs and shaking hands, putting on the show, but what am I supposed to do? Trudge around wearing a hair shirt? We lost three potential children. I get it. I get it I get it I get it. And I'm damn sorry I wasn't there for the last one. I should have said no, I'm not going. I'd just as soon toss that damn plaque in the trash, for all the grief it's caused. But I'm not H.G. Wells: I don't have a time machine. If I did, I'd turn back the clock. But if I'd been there to hold your hand and wipe your brow and dab your tears and force-feed you Cheetos, would the outcome have been different? Other than you not having a convenient scapegoat to kick every morning before breakfast?

"When?" is all she says.

"I'll move out tomorrow."

* * *

Her life may be on hold, but mine isn't. So following another gourmet meal from a can that I eat but she doesn't, I don shorts, sneakers, and a T-shirt and head off to the junior high for a friendly volleyball game. Amy's sitting on the sofa, having her nightly stare down with the TV.

"I'll be back in about two hours," I say.

She nods.

During warm-ups, Judy Macnamara's husband leaps high on the other side of the net and spikes a lazy setup into my unassuming face, splitting my eyeglasses at the bridge. No apology, no excuses, not even a polite, "You OK?"

I'm in no mood for cheap shots, especially from a rangy ringer from the university, but I hold my peace for now. As he struts back to mid-court amid the high fives and attaboys of his teammates, I calmly gather up the two halves of my glasses and rejoin them with adhesive tape. Then I reassume my position on the front line.

It's midway through the first game when Stan Macnamara and I finally face off at the net. We exchange neither looks nor words; in fact, Stan seems to have forgotten the glass-breaking incident altogether. I'm an insignificant stranger whose team will soon be crushed.

Fitz serves a hard, low-arcing ball that barely clears the net. A man at mid-court digs the ball, and a woman pops it high with her fingertips, a perfect set. Stan crouches low and launches himself upward to execute his signature kill shot. But the only kill tonight will be delivered clandestinely, from the other side of the net, for as Stan leaps up, I step forward and thrust an upward fist into his family jewels.

It happens so quickly that everyone knows something's transpired but they're not sure what. Stan, of course, doubles over, his body slamming against the wooden floor. Two teammates rush over and carry him to the sidelines, where he remains, hunched over like a hell-beaten-out-of-him prizefighter, for the rest of the night. No one says a word to me about it, but my opponents are careful not to serve the ball in my direction, and even my teammates maintain a cautious distance for the rest of the night.

There's one more little detail worth noting—something that neither the players nor the spectators heard, only Stan as he was falling to the floor, just before impact, when I whispered, "Now you don't have to pay for my glasses."

* * *

When I arrive home just after nine p.m., Amy's watching *I Dream of Jeannie*.

"I'm back," I announce, detouring into the kitchen to pour a cold glass of orange juice.

I hear Amy talking, but not to me. As I step toward the living area, it appears that she's speaking to the scantily dressed blonde in harem pants on the TV screen.

"He was a boy," she says. "A beautiful little boy."

I stop and modulate my breath: soft, slow exhalations. I don't want to make any sound that might break the spell—a footfall, a slurping tongue, the clink of ice cubes against glass. I listen as she tells her story to the smiling stooge who's replaced the shapely genii on the TV screen: two days after I left, late afternoon Arizona time, she'd felt a terrible pain in her abdomen—similar to the two miscarriages but much more intense. It felt like some sadist had shoved a knife in her gut and every two minutes on the money twisted the blade for laughs. Contractions, she thought, but it was six weeks early. Food poisoning? Or her appendix maybe, except the pain was drilling dead center in her gut.

Jill from church drove her to the emergency room, where she had to sit in the cramped waiting area with squealing kids and a ghost-eyed old man and a surly-looking teenager with his arm in a makeshift sling while the doctor attended to more urgent cases. She couldn't fathom anything more urgent than this power drill boring through her innards. Jill did her best to lobby on Amy's behalf, but the receptionist just said: "We'll call you when it's your turn." And the second time, more tersely: "Wait your turn!"

Amy had always prided herself in being tough, not a whiner. Halfway up Mount Humphreys she'd sprained her ankle, but she didn't say a word until she was standing victoriously on the summit of Arizona's tallest peak.

When the next contraction struck like a bomb detonating in her belly, she let out a scream that turned the head of the wounded teenager, zipped the lips of the screaming child, and woke the octogenarian Lazarus from his standing sleep. Most important, it caught the eye of the receptionist, who lowered her bifocals and said, "Miss? Come here, please."

With Jill at her side, Amy half-limped, half-waddled to the counter. Two minutes later, she was in bed in a curtained cubicle, where a nurse inserted an IV and a young stranger who looked like he ought to rush home and scrub up for the junior prom was telling her to spread her legs so he could have a look inside.

She would have preferred her actual doctor, Dr. Bailey, someone who had to shave in the morning, who had nursed her along all this way assuring her everything was fine, just fine, no worries: strong heartbeat, strong this, healthy that; strong enough and healthy enough for him to pack up the family—the pretty wife and the four adorable kids and the boat and the golden retriever and the ice chest—and head off to Lake Pleasant for the weekend. And now look at her—look! Look at this! Look at him, this young kid with Clearasil and a stethoscope, preparing to insert his latexed hand in her vagina. Quite frankly, she was in so much pain at the moment, he could have been Donald Duck or Dick Nixon and who gives a damn, just do what you need to do and do it fast!

She'd wanted to deliver the baby naturally, of course—no fish knife up the gut for her, but oh my god she knew it was going to be painful awful, the jaws of hell cracking her open from the inside and everything else her mother had said (OK, Mom, I get the picture: it really hurts) but nothing like this.

She glanced at the clock on the wall: 2:20. Add three hours for eastern time, 5:20. The awards banquet would start in less than an hour. Well, I sure hope you enjoy it. I hope you enjoy every ounce of filet mignon or chicken cordon bleu or whatever it is they feed the winners while I'm lying here being split in two like an apple by my very own once and future son or daughter.

Todd, where the hell are you!

And she couldn't remember if she said it or screamed it or just imagined it (or thought it), but it didn't matter because the doctor's peach fuzz cheeks were looking flushed, his forehead rippled: and then the nurse squirted a glob of cold, clear jelly on her medicine-ball belly and the doctor inserted the rubber tips of the stethoscope into his ears and placed the stainless steel chest piece on the glob of jelly and began listening for evidence of life.

"What's the matter?" she'd asked. "Is something wrong?"

The nurse put her hand on her forearm and spoke in the soft, soothing tones of a professional dealing with a crisis.

"It's all right," she said. "Just relax. Everything's going to be all right."

Which meant hell had hit the handbasket.

And then Dr. Training Pants was saying some hopeless conglomeration of technical and lay mumbo jumbo that bottom-lined into two words: Caesarian section.

Now she was being rolled down the hall and into another room, the nurse injecting something into her IV—something strong, painkillers or a knockout drug that went to work before she could ask clarifying questions, because that's what good teachers teach their students to do, ask clarifying questions.

She remembered the overhead lights and the masked trio gazing down at her like three banditos disguised in angelic clothing come to steal her baby. And when her eyes opened who knows how many minutes or hours later, she was right: they had stolen him (it was a boy, they confirmed, a son). A stillborn preemie. Profuse apologies from Dr. Training Pants and sympathetic eyes from the two nurses and a sincere and comforting hand on her forearm.

Not your fault, Dr. Training Pants reassured her. There's nothing you could have done.

A son, D.O.A. Actually, D.B.A.: Dead Before Arrival. Maybe a day or two, Dr. Training Pants said.

She looked at the clock: 4:52. Dinner done. Awards awarded. Todd?

"Can I see him?" Amy asked.

Dr. Training Pants winced. "I don't think that's a good idea."

She felt so tired, groggy, loopy, the light so bright, the walls bending.

"Let me see him," she said, and when they hesitated, she hissed: "Now!"

The nurse brought a blanketed bundle and set it gently in her arms. Amy slowly drew back the fabric and sobbed. The first one had hardly been anything and the second had been a bloody turd of tissue, but this one was a little boy with arms and legs and toes and fingers and eyes to see and lips to speak. A little boy. Our little baby boy.

I want to die, she thought. Here. Now.

*   *   *

Amy switches off the TV. I edge quietly toward the sofa until I'm standing right behind her.

"Amy, I'm sorry. I'm sorry I wasn't there with you. I'm sorry about what happened."

I've said this a thousand times before, but this time it's different; this time it's coming from a deeper, darker, and far more anguished place in my heart. I see tears shellacking her cheeks.

"Me too," she says.

When my hand touches her shoulder, she reaches back and clasps it briefly, then lets go. I bend down to kiss the top of her head, but she dips away.

"No," she says. "Please."

The next morning when I load my belongings into my pickup, she remains in her bedroom. And when I gently rev the engine to signal my departure, she doesn't come out to say goodbye.

ICONOCLASTS

"Why are you so damn fearless?" he asks. He's young, with a three-day stubble peppering his chin and upper lip. A rich college kid on summer break. "I mean—man!—aren't you afraid of anything?"

We're sitting around the campfire on a sandy beach deep in the Grand Canyon at the end of a long, violent, and nearly fatal day.

The young man and fifteen others have paid good money for their twelve-day float in rubber rafts so bloated and shockproof that, when they hit whitewater, their vessels glide glibly over a progression of gently rolling hills, like a kiddie roller coaster at an amusement park. By contrast, I've been soloing for the past five days in a streamlined, fiberglass kayak, shooting through narrow apertures with William Tell precision, then plunging like a human spear into the abyss, lost, gone, buried beneath the churning white madness—three, four, five seconds; a little lifetime it seems—until my helmeted head pops up like a cork, followed by the rest of me, Houdini magically sprung from a trap.

The first time they witness this from their fat rafts, the tourists cheer wildly, waving ball caps, straw hats, and beach towels. But I have no time for bows or photo ops. I'm working my paddle like a knight fending off a family of pissed-off dragons—left side, right side, left side, right side—utterly focused in the moment as I try to find within the frothing white chaos a oneness with the water. Not conquest or domination, which seem almost laughable, but the far more elusive grail of harmony. It's like breaking a wild horse, or a whole runaway herd of them, all thrashing and bucking and resisting until, at last and quite suddenly, calm waters, a satin-smooth, blue-green peace.

For a short stretch at least, and then it's World War III all over again, with another daredevil plunge, Orpheus descending into a split-second Hell and hoping for deliverance, but this time a mighty jolt heaves my body from the waist up forward while grabbing my sleek craft from behind, pinning me between a pair of sandstone boulders that, until this moment, have been cleaving the water (gallons, seas, oceans of it) into an endlessly replicating double-saber-toothed pattern with far more precision and consistency than any manmade machine.

I've broken that pattern by my presence, which partially dams up the aperture, disturbing an eons-old motif. Now I'm paying for the transgression: water pours over me like a punishment, stealing my air, stealing my breath, hammering my backside and burying my last hopes and aspirations, pounding me harder and harder until I'm wedged too deeply for escape and too tightly for rescue.

But I fight back. Blinded by the crashing whiteness, invisible to the rafters who only moments before were singing my praises but now are shaking their heads or crossing themselves, I flex my core muscles, grip my paddle at my side, and lean forward to rest my forehead against the blue fiberglass deck. I wait, holding my breath, hanging on to hope and giving the water time to do its work. I'd scream but it's a waste of strength and energy and besides, no one but God could hear me in this thunderous mess. Then—the angels in my head swooping down to usher me off to that better place no one in their right mind wants to go— I'm upright! Upright and breathing air—authentic air! Sucking, gasping, heaving, but breathing. The sun showers down like gold dust, so bright and so exquisitely warm because only now do I realize how violently I'm shivering, my hands and legs seizing up from the adrenaline and the shock and the cold.

Four hours later, belly full, blood thawed, shoulders rested, I'm sitting by the fire with the tourists, answering the young man's question.

"Why are you so damn fearless?"

I stare at the blanched stick of driftwood in my hands, testing it until it snaps.

"I'm not," I say. "I just don't care."

He's only twenty, a boy still by life's standards. Part of his CEO father's family entourage.

"But why?" he asks.

I reach down the front of my sweat-stained T-shirt and withdraw a gold band fastened to a silver chain that circles my neck: "My wife."

He looks down, penitent for having reopened this wound. "How long?" he asks.

I toss the broken sticks into the fire and watch the flames lick them like a dog licks a bone. "Ten months," I say. "And fourteen days."

* * *

This is how I measure time now—not "Before Christ" or "Before Common Era" or "Anno Domini," but by the number of months and days before or since I scribbled my name—hastily, sloppily, as fast as I could just to get the whole damn thing over with—on the sheet of paper that officially terminated my marriage. Hence, B.D. (Before Divorce) and A.D. (After Divorce).

During those ten months and fourteen days, by mutual agreement, Amy and I sold the Dream House and split the profits fifty-fifty. With my share, I purchased an acre of forest at the foot of the mountain, where I will eventually build a log home with a peak view. In the meantime, I'm living in a one-bedroom trailer on the east side of town. Half the cracker-box homes showcase a rusted jalopy in the front yard. There's a lot of yelling and screaming on Saturday nights, mostly in Spanish. For three hundred dollars a month more, I could have moved into a bigger place in a quieter neighborhood, but I'm trying to save money for a new house, a dream house all my own. I'm also doing penance.

Amy has taken her half of the money and moved to parts unknown—at least to me—to start a new life. Over the past ten-and-a-half months, the gut-wrenching pain I suffered the day I signed the papers has gradually diminished. I still sense Amy's phantom presence, but I no longer feel the huge chasm in my bed at night or the profound loneliness when I wake up in the morning. Tsegi has a lot to do with that.

I found him shivering outside the Cameron Trading Post near the southwest border of the Navajo Reservation. A part-husky, part-whatever pup, he was taking refuge from a vicious winter snowstorm that covered him with a frosty white coat although he was curled up under an awning. It was late and the post was closed for the night. Returning from a weather-aborted hunting trip on the North Rim, I'd stopped to gas up, not to rescue animals in distress. But the little guy looked so cold, desperate, and lonely.

"Join the club, buddy," I said.

He looked up at me with yearning blue eyes, his white, vulpine face bordered by a black band that made him look like a masked bandit. His flaccid ears would grow erect when his hormones kicked in. A good hunting dog maybe?

No. I didn't want—and certainly didn't need—a dog. One more mouth to feed. House training. Dog smell on everything. Dog slobber. Vet bills. He's cute and cuddly now, but give him six months and he'll be a full-grown, furry ball of trouble, one more hassle to accommodate whenever I wanted to go hunting or biking or anything overnight or longer.

"No!" I snapped, shaking a finger at him. "No!"

He tilted his head slightly, lower ear dangling, eyes pathetic yet cunning.

"And don't look at me like that!"

I stomped off to the gas pump. As I lifted the nozzle, my little friend hopscotched toward me via the trail of indentations my boots had stamped in the snow.

"Oh, hell's bells!" I scooped him up, his warm tongue licking my hand as if it were a popsicle.

In spite of my prophesied hassles—all of which came to pass, in one form or another—the dog has become my daily delight, greeting me enthusiastically first thing in the morning, waiting faithfully at the window for my return each night, so desperately grateful for the slightest favors or affections—a pat on the head, a "good boy, Tsegi!" or a glorious bowl of tasty brown nuggets. If I surprise him with a bacon treat or a belly rub, he gazes at me with unfaltering love, allegiance, and ecstasy.

He does all the cute and annoying things puppies do—making mincemeat of my socks and sneaking onto and then into my bed at night. But he's surprisingly obedient and trainable, someone to keep me company other than National Public Radio in the morning and the TV at night. He's one of the three bright spots during an otherwise dark time.

The second is my students and the Pond Project. The third is a chance to witness the ultimate fruits of my labors as a teacher.

*   *   *

For their Honors English project their senior year at the local university, Amanda Stone and Jake Bonner teamed up to lead a crusade. Every summer, our mountain town hosted a Fourth of July powwow and rodeo. Thousands of Hopi and Navajo would converge for a wild week of parades, fireworks, dances, celebrations, and the indiscrete and unchecked consumption of alcohol. It was a boon to local merchants, as tourists flocked from all quarters to snap photos of "real-live Indians," who were given free rein to sing and dance and raise hell for a week. But at the end of each day, the inebriated ones were rounded up and trucked over to the city dump—present home of the Pond Project—to be bathed en masse with firehoses, compliments of the local fire department.

Other Hopi and Navajo came to the field voluntarily, to camp out and cook, avoiding the tourist-priced hotels. It was a good time, until it wasn't. A good time until the whiskey ran low and the tourists packed up, and then it was time for the Native Americans to pack up too and get the hell out. And if they didn't, things could get complicated; things could get ugly. And that ugly part was the focus of Jake and Amanda's senior project.

First, they recruited ten other students, who took hundreds of photos revealing the dark side of the annual event. Jake and Amanda wrote a five-page exposé with photos and sent it to the local newspaper. They also created a narrated slideshow for the city council. Prior to the meeting, they put up posters and distributed flyers throughout the community advertising the event. They sent personal invitations to friends, family members, and local VIPs. The night of the meeting, the council chambers were packed with students, parents, community activists, university professors, and a conspicuous delegation from Native Americans for Community Action, many wearing traditional Navajo or Hopi attire.

When Jake and Amanda stood before the five council members, Major Gordon McDowell immediately recognized the duo from their Pond Project presentation. Smelling a rat, he vehemently objected. However, the presentation was already on the approved agenda, cleverly disguised by Jake and Amanda with the laudatory title: "The Fourth of July Powwow: A Tribute to our Local Heritage."

Amanda, who looked very much the professional in her red dress suit, began by thanking the council and mayor for this wonderful opportunity to showcase one of the hallmarks of our community. Jake Bonner—holey blue jeans, sandals, a ponytail halfway down his back—called for the lights to be dimmed and started the slideshow, focusing on the good: smiling dignitaries in cowboy hats and bolo ties waving to cheering crowds as their Cadillac convertibles cruised down Main Street; Navajo, Hopi, and members of other tribes, in full regalia, marching or riding on horseback or standing on flatbed floats drawn by pickup trucks; dancers performing in the town square; bucking broncos and twisting bulls trying to throw their riders; rodeo clowns diving into barrels; smiling kids eating snow cones and cotton candy; the street festooned in red, white, and blue; fireworks lighting up the night. Even Gordon McDowell was smiling by the end of this segment.

Then Amanda took the microphone. "The Fourth of July, a great time for everyone," she said. "Or maybe not."

The audience gasped as damning image after image appeared on the giant screen: young men sleeping in alleys and storefronts; an old man with a two-toothed grin passed out in the gutter while tourists took his picture; hundreds of Native American families camped in tents, lean-tos, and makeshift shelters, the trash piled a foot high, the smoke from multiple campfires congesting the air, the stench of feces not visible on film but presupposed by the absence of porta-potties and the swarms of flies swirling about; more trash, giant mounds of it; the police tossing drunken Native Americans into the back of a van like dead bodies and then dumping them in the dirt field behind the pond; the fire trucks rolling in and the firemen plying their hoses as bodies spring to life like zombies awakened; a close-up of an old Navajo woman being hosed, screaming as if she were on fire; another Navajo woman in velveteen throwing up into a trash barrel.

Halfway through the presentation, McDowell stomped out of the room. The mayor dipped his head, looking for a corner to slither into. The reporter from the local paper scribbled madly to keep up with the narrative.

Amanda turned toward the four remaining council members and said calmly, "As they say, one picture is worth a thousand words, so I'll be brief. To our esteemed members of the city council, you've seen the pictures—some good, some bad, and some very ugly. So we ask you, is the Fourth of July powwow a badge of honor for our community, or a mark of shame? We say the latter, and we say end it now!"

Every single person who was not the mayor or a city council member sprang to their feet as applause shook the chambers. Five minutes passed before it simmered enough for the mayor to thank the two young guests for their presentation, assuring them their proposal would be given full consideration. The crowd booed. They wanted action now. The mayor said the presentation was a non-action item—"I'm afraid our hands are tied for the time being." This chicken response earned him another round of boos. But it didn't matter. Delay or no delay, the damage had been done.

The reporter cornered Jake and Amanda, who they handed him the expanded version of their original exposé, with additional photos. They followed up with three more public presentations, one at the university, another at the local theater, and a final one to the Chamber of Commerce. They recruited university kids to hit the streets with petitions to terminate the powwow. Within two weeks, they collected over six thousand signatures.

*   *   *

To keep the story hot, Jake and Amanda released additional tidbits to the newspaper. In one, they mentioned the Pond Project and how every summer the students' work was partially undermined by the annual trash-fest euphemistically called the powwow. They called it "a mockery of the great traditions of our Native American cultures." They recruited Jimmy Goldtooth, also a senior at the university, who spoke about the tragedy of alcohol and suicide among the Navajo. "My people, our culture, it's more than dances and colorful costumes. We try to walk in beauty, but there's nothing beautiful about what's going on in those damn pictures."

When Gordon McDowell read the comments about the Pond Project in the newspaper, he immediately assumed I was the ringleader behind this circus. The next afternoon, after my students were gone and the buses had left, he paid me a visit, shaking his gnarly finger in my face: "Who do you think you are, causing all this trouble? I've lived in this town since the 1920s. Through the Great Depression! Through a world war! You just showed up here yesterday!"

But the old Silver Star war hero had caught me at the wrong time in the wrong place. His question should have been: "What makes you so damn fearless?"

I glared beyond his finger and into his milky blue eyes. "Yes, and isn't it too damn bad that it took a wet-behind-the-ears punk like me and a couple of college kids to rid this city of a cancer you personally created?"

*   *   *

In the end, there was just too much momentum, righteous indignation, and public outrage. Gordon McDowell, Dale Hanagan, and the other Powwow Committee members dressed up in their white hats, bolo ties, and white sport coats and formally declared that, due to changing priorities, the Fourth of July powwow would be discontinued. News spread quickly, with hugs, kisses, high fives, and generous rounds of legal and illegal drinking.

For me, it was a moment of pride and validation. Two students—two kids—brought a group of stuffy autocrats to their knees and a town to its senses. This was the true essence of education. Not reading, writing, and 'rithmetic. Not regurgitating facts and figures. Not parroting your parents or your pastor or your teacher. It's what Paulo Friere meant by "praxis": "reflection and action upon the world to transform it." What's the point of acquiring knowledge and skills if you don't use them to make the world a better place? Reflection alone is just navel-gazing. Action without purpose is simply hell-raising. But put those two together—reflection and action—in the hearts and minds of some courageous young people, and magic happens. And miracles.

ENOUGH

So life is… better. Improving. Even good at times. Not perfect, but whose is? Good enough for now. The school year's off to a great start. In addition to taking on the usual pond-related projects, my latest crop of students is also building a rock drainage and a nature walk—this is year nine, and every year, a few new projects move forward. And I couldn't have handpicked a better group of kids. They're excited, enthusiastic, and hardworking.

As a former National Science Teacher of the Year, I carry both prestige and clout. Melvin Jackson gives me a long leash, and even my most outspoken critics concede that the Pond Project has been an unprecedented success. Through all my domestic turmoil, school has been my anchor and my antidote. But that's all about to change.

On this Monday morning in October, I'm gimping around like an old man as I place study guides on the lab tables. Running across the Grand Canyon and back in one day isn't how most people choose to celebrate their thirtieth birthday, but I did, and now I'm suffering the consequences. Every muscle from my waist down feels as if it's on fire, and every joint is hardening like concrete, scoffing at Advil, Bengay, and other over-the-counter attempts to reduce the wrath of payback for my hubris and stupidity.

But it's a beautiful day: generous sun, blue sky, fall colors burning on the mountain. I can't help but smile.

"Mr. Hunter?"

I turn and see her standing waif-like by my desk: the loose, cotton dress with the floral print; the long, dishwater-blonde hair with the straight-cut bangs; the holey white sneakers; the vulnerable doe eyes. Skinny arms that could snap like toothpicks are crossed over her chest, hugging her ribs. She almost seems to be shivering, although the thermostat is set at a comfortable seventy degrees.

"Hello, Jennifer."

Her voice—soft, barely audible, apologetic. "Mr. Hunter, I need to tell you something," she says, then pauses. "You have to promise not to tell anyone, OK?"

"Well, Jennifer, I don't know if I can do that. It might be something I have to tell."

She glares at me—not meanly but pensively. Frail on the outside but iron within. "Then I won't tell you." She means business. She turns to go.

"Wait! Let's compromise, can we do that? You tell me what it is, and then I'll talk about whether I have to tell and what we can do about it. Can we do that?"

The rest is a bad dream. I follow her into the storage room, where my shoulders barely squeeze between the shelves on either side and the smell of formaldehyde is strong enough to sedate an elephant. She turns her back to me and drops her dress to the waist. Stitches, fresh ones, crisscross her bony, freckled back like barbed wire or a chaotic string of railroad crossings. Her ribs and shoulder blades jut out like a refugee's.

I try to keep my cool, but I can feel the anger boiling in my skull, swelling my cheeks and forehead.

"My father told the people at the hospital I fell down the stairs," she says. "If I tell anyone, he'll kill me. He said so."

The girl lifts the fallen half of her dress to cover herself before turning to face me. "This is the sixth time, and now he's going to kill me." She says this matter-of-factly, without teenage histrionics, as if announcing that her father was taking her to the dentist at noon.

I'm doing my best to control my absolute rage, but it's times like this I wish hunting season were extended to certain *Homo sapiens*. What kind of human beats his own child like that? What kind of father?

*   *   *

Legally I'm obligated to tell the school counselor. That would be Darryl Johnson, a letter-of-the-law, cover-your-ass-above-all-things guy. Ten years from retirement, he will walk on eggshells right to the finish line of a long, innocuous career in public education. The beanbag chairs in the corner of his office create an illusion of laid-back confidentiality. But Johnson had revealed his true colors the day after the Dunaway boy, a misunderstood misfit, committed suicide.

"Well, it doesn't surprise me," he'd quipped coldly. "Knowing his parents, knowing him."

Three years ago, the nation passed the Child Abuse Prevention and Treatment Act, establishing baseline standards for reporting and dealing with issues like this, but nothing's been institutionalized yet, and it will be another several years before Child Protective Services can ride to the rescue in cases like this. For now, parents are still the masters of their children's fates. So I can call the cops, who will interview the father, who will repeat his lie. Then when Jennifer returns home from school, daddy will administer thrashing number seven, possibly Jennifer's last.

Johnson will toe the line. He'll reach for the phone without discussion, pressing the digits resolutely, convinced he's right legally, morally, ethically, educationally. If I object, his eyebrows will arch like tortured caterpillars, followed by a self-righteous harrumph and a cross-examination with his eyes, the silent threat: no no no. If you do do do, I will will will have to to to report you you you...

"Do you have anywhere you can go?"

Jennifer shakes her head.

"Any friends you can stay with?"

A double-shake.

Now what? I can't take her home—under no circumstances can a fourteen-year-old girl spend the night in the trailer of her divorced male teacher.

"When does your father get home?"

A shrug. "It depends."

"Usually—what time usually?"

"Between five and six, I guess."

"OK, this is what I want you to do. Come here after school, all right?"

She nods obediently and starts to go, but I stop her.

"Wait, Jennifer. On second thought, I want you to go home. Do you have your own room?"

She nods.

"Do you ride the bus?"

A nod.

"Take the bus home and go to your room and shut the door. Can you lock the door? Does it have a lock?"

She shakes her head.

"Then just go to your room, shut the door, and wait. Can you wait about two hours?"

"Yes."

"Just wait there and don't come out—no matter what you hear or think you hear, stay put. Can you do that?"

"Yes."

"It looks like the bell's about to ring, so go on to first period."

She's frozen.

I put my hand on her shoulder, very lightly, like a butterfly. "Have we got a plan?" I smile; she doesn't. Following a slow, cautious nod, she exits.

* * *

After school ends and the buses depart and Melvin Jackson finally stops droning on at our weekly faculty meeting, I drive ten miles south of town before veering off the paved highway and onto a washboard dirt road that snakes deep into the ponderosa pine forest. Five miles later, I'm greeted by a splintered, wooden sign hanging by two rusted hooks from a threshold of log beams: INDIAN SPRINGS VILLAGE. In another fifty yards, my pickup rolls into an erratically zoned maze of hodge-podge dwellings: battered, single-wide trailers barricaded behind walls of hastily stacked firewood are flanked by board-and-batten craftsman homes and elegant A-frame cabins. The roads are dirt, the driveways gravel, the streets named after various Native tribes: Choctaw, Mohawk, Navajo, Hopi, Shoshone, Seminole, Cheyenne, Cherokee, Comanche, Sioux. The dwellings are numbered arbitrarily—504, 615, 549, 322, 13— as if the developer had intentionally created a refuge for those who don't want to be found.

I drive around for half an hour before finally intersecting with Cherokee Trail. Heads or tails. I turn left and cruise along until I arrive at a trailer with tires holding down the roof. A section of skirting has been ripped out along the trailer's edge, making it look like a yellow smile with a missing tooth. A German shepherd chained to a stake is gnawing an elk leg. Wooden steps lead up to a mudroom enclosed by a transparent storm door brutally bandaged with duct tape. Plain blue curtains seal off the windows, and a column of blue smoke rises from a stovepipe.

I verify the number penciled on my notepad—611 Cherokee Trail— with the number spray-painted in red on a large boulder squatting by the driveway. Then I park three houses down the road, check my watch (4:52), crack open my latest read (*A River Running West*, by John Wesley Powell), and wait.

At five-forty, as the tree shadows merge with evening twilight, an old, blue pickup grinds down the rutty road and swerves past the spray-painted boulder. I climb out of my truck, quickly sizing up my adversary as I double-time up the road. From a distance, he looks formidable: broad shoulders and narrow cowboy hips, dirt-stained jeans and heavy work boots. A trucker's cap and a bushy beard. A large man who walks with a ponderous but powerful gait. I can see the silhouette of a gun rack in the rear windshield of the cab. He's reaching into the back, hopefully not to grab a weapon.

"Excuse me," I say, but not loud enough. I try again, with gusto. "Excuse me!"

He pulls his giant frame out of the cab and a metal lunch pail along with it. He looks even larger up close, a good six-foot-six. The dog is on its feet, the chain jangling as it hustles over to its master, teeth bared, snarling, slowly working up to a one-more-step-and-I'll-bite-your-ass-off bark.

"Are you Mr. Abernathy?"

Two things are immediately obvious: he doesn't like strangers and he doesn't like answering questions.

"Jennifer's dad?" I extend my open hand. "I'm Todd Hunter, Jennifer's science teacher."

He glares at my palm as if I'm offering him a poison apple.

"Is Jen giving you trouble?"

"No, no—not at all. She's a very good student."

I'd thought—hoped?—that this would be a classic case of a household bully venting his frustrations on a defenseless kid, and that judging by Jennifer's genetics, he would be a spindly adversary I could easily intimidate. Instead I get a full-fledged Goliath with a fierce and loyal dog.

"What do you need? I paid her fees when she registered in August."

"No, it's not that."

"Then what is it?" His voice seems to rumble up from the center of the Earth. His lunch pail looks like a sardine tin in his gargantuan hands.

Sensing danger, the dog unleashes a barrage of vicious barks and then lunges at me, its chain pulling taut.

"Cody!" Goliath bellows. "Stay!"

The dog's chain goes slack as he slinks back, casting wolf eyes at me.

"So what do you want?"

There's no easy way to say this and no point in beating around the bush. I quickly survey my surroundings. The clapboard house across the street looks like an abandoned barn. The grandiose A-frame to its left, obviously a vacation home, has been locked up and prematurely winterized; at the double-wide trailer on the right, the inside lights are off and there are no vehicles in the driveway. The sun is gone, and night is quickly shading in the jagged gaps between the houses and the pine trees. Jennifer, I assume, is safely ensconced in her room. There are no witnesses in sight, certainly none within earshot.

"What the hell do you want?" Goliath says, his voice miming a volcano on the verge. "Are you some kind of freaking deaf-mute or something?"

"Mr. Abernathy," I say, "I just want you to know that Jennifer's a really good student. She's a good girl."

Goliath's massive shoulders settle a bit, and his voice softens. "Good to know. Anything else?"

I can feel the courage draining out of me, threatening to dribble down my leg. Then I picture Jennifer cowering in her room, the nasty railroad tracks crisscrossing her back, her lifeless blue eyes as she had calmly foretold her future: "He's going to kill me."

"Just one more thing," I say. "I collect Winchesters—lever-action repeaters."

"I'm familiar with the Winchester models."

"Well, I've got six of them."

"You looking to buy or sell?"

"Neither."

"Then what's that to me?"

"Nothing, really," I say. "Just that if you ever lay a hand on Jennifer again, I'm going to come over here with one of those Winchesters and blow your fucking head off."

Done. I didn't yell, I didn't scream, I didn't squeal. I said it calmly and directly, as if explaining a proof to a geometry class.

Goliath scoffs. "Is that supposed to be some kind of a threat?"

"No, no threat. Just a simple statement of fact. You touch that kid and I'll blow your brains out."

I know he's guilty because he doesn't budge for a good fifteen seconds before he finally says, "Get your ass off my property before I blow *your* fucking head off!"

The dog barks and lunges again.

I stand my ground. "I hope I don't have to, but if I need to, I will. That's up to you."

Goliath smashes the lunch pail against his thigh; the lid pops open and a thermos spills out. "Get the hell out of here!" he bellows.

A light pops on inside the trailer. Jennifer.

I back up fifteen paces before turning my back on him and marching toward my pickup, all the time wondering if an arrow or an axe or Bowie knife is going to strike between my shoulder blades.

* * *

Jennifer doesn't come to school the next day or the next. I check in the office with Betty Castillo, who says she called in sick.

"Jennifer called?"

"No, her dad."

It's the Friday before a three-day weekend, which gives Jennifer a total of four days to recover from whatever illness Goliath invented. When she doesn't show up again on Tuesday, I'm angry—and a little desperate. I consider taking the matter to Darryl Johnson, but I know he'll follow the book. Besides, I don't want to introduce any new characters into this soap opera. Instead, I ask Darryl one question: "How many days of school can a student miss before you call the cops?"

"That depends," Johnson replies. He's wearing a tidy tie and sweater-vest ensemble that gives the impression of an English butler.

"Ten days without parent notification," he adds.

"And with it?"

"Indefinitely. We usually like to see a doctor's note if it's more than two weeks, though. Why do you ask?"

"Nothing. Just for future reference."

Johnson gives me a suspicious, sideways look, as if I'm the prime suspect in a mystery spoof of his own making.

"What?"

Johnson's bushy eyebrows jump. "I hope you're not getting into any mischief, Mr. Hunter."

"Me? Mischief? Never."

"Well, be careful. We can't afford to lose you."

I half-laugh, flattered and very surprised. "Darryl, I didn't know you cared!"

"Hunter, you're a pain in the ass but a damn good teacher. Just don't get a big head about it, and don't be stupid."

*   *   *

It's three more days before Jennifer shows up at school. She enters my classroom third hour on Friday morning with her eyes glued to the floor. When I greet her with a cheerful, "Good morning, Jennifer!" she doesn't look up.

It's an indoor day, and I make a point of not calling on her during class. Just before the bell rings, I ask her to stay behind. She looks up, startled, her angular face even thinner than before. Cadaverous is the word.

"I just need to talk to you about some makeup work," I say. Lie.

As the other students do their usual Wild West stampede out the door, Jennifer slowly gathers up her book and notebook, clasping them against her chest as if protecting it, and approaches my desk, head down. I notice shadowy bruises on her cheeks and under the left eye seeping through a futilely applied layer of makeup.

"He did it again, didn't he?"

She shakes her head, but the tears are already flowing.

* * *

I've done a little research. Each school year, the Life Glow company makes a small fortune by taking photographs of every student in the district. Parents get one photo for free, but the big money's in selling them packets of variously sized prints of their progeny. As a courtesy to the schools, Life Glow also provides the school with a complimentary, wallet-size photo of each student. These photos appear in school yearbooks as well as in each student's cumulative folder, which presents a kind of visual history from age five until they graduate from high school.

So during one of my visits to the front office, when the staff was short-handed, I slipped into the records room and pulled Jennifer Abernathy's cumulative folder from the file cabinet. Nothing illegal or unethical—I am, after all, her teacher—but I didn't want to arouse suspicion. I studied the progression of Jennifer's portraits from year to year: the wide-eyed kindergartener with missing front teeth; the giggling third grader; the gangly, smiling seventh grader. The ninth grader looked as if a vampire had sucked the life out of her.

I closed my eyes to hold back tears. How the hell does this happen? In two years, how does she go from a healthy, happy kid to *this*? From life and joy to zombie-hood?

I dug deeper. From Darryl Johnson's report in Jennifer's folder and some strategically guided chitchat with Judy Macnamara, Jennifer's English teacher, I pieced together a tragic tale. When Jennifer was in sixth grade, her father was killed in a rollover accident on I-17. No seat belt laws in those days.

Jennifer's mother married a year later, settling for this Goliath, who did foundation work but was trying to start his own company instead of getting the scraps from hourly labor. He got off to a good start, but Jennifer's mother contracted ovarian cancer and the money from the business was diverted to treatments that ended up being a lot of pain for a lot of money for the same ultimate result. That was midway through eighth grade, and it had been hell on Earth for Jennifer ever since.

Somehow, some way, everything was her fault—the father's death, the mother's death, the failed treatments, the doomed business—and Goliath made good and sure she knew it and would never forget it.

The sad backstory had given me some insight and even a little empathy for the poor son of a bitch, but beating the hell out of a fourteen-year-old—physically and emotionally—was a deal breaker.

*   *   *

"Jennifer," I whisper. "Look me in the eyes, please?"

She lifts her blue eyes slowly, but any lingering tint of sky or sea or youth or joy is gone.

"You don't need to be afraid. That man is never going to touch you again. Do you understand? Jennifer?"

She nods, but barely.

"Good." I scribble a note excusing Jennifer for being late to her fourth-period class. "Take this. And then come to my classroom after school today. OK? Can you do that?"

Another ambiguous nod.

"Yes?"

"Yes," she whispers.

"Good. Don't get on the bus. Come straight here. And don't tell anybody anything. OK?"

"Yes," she says but she's crying.

I have no idea what I'm going to do and about three hours to figure it out.

INQUISITION

I look up from the desk where I'm entering second-quarter grades and squint at the two figures standing just inside the doorway: a bald, rotund man with a bushy mustache and a tall brunette in a black pantsuit. They appear a little blurry in the afternoon light. I remind myself to get my eye prescription updated and to clean my lenses.

"That's me."

The man steps forward, holding up a small rectangle with a miniature silver shield in the middle. A damn badge.

"Detective Gruber, Ponderosa P.D.," he says. "This is my partner, Detective Carlyle."

The woman nods, all business. Her mouth is an emotionless slit, betraying nothing. She looks vaguely familiar, but I can't put a name to her face. I close the grade book and pull my hands down under the desk, an instinctive reaction that, on second thought, must look stupidly suspicious. I quickly place my hands back on the desk, obediently cupped together, and smile. "Can I help you?"

"We've just got a few questions," Gruber says.

"Sure. Would you like to sit down?"

An hour later, Gruber's still firing questions at me while Carlyle's observing, her no-nonsense expression unchanged. She could be posing for a portrait or sleeping with her eyes open during Gruber's droning, broken-record interrogation.

"The last time you saw Jennifer was October 28—is that correct? Sorry, but I just want to make sure we've got the timeline right."

"Yes—for the fourth time."

"Isn't that a little strange? That you remember the exact date?"

"I remember it because it's right here!" I open the spiral-bound grade book and thumb through to my third-period class. I drag my finger to the top of a column on the left side, where I've hand-printed the name of each student, in alphabetical order, last name first in all CAPS, followed by the first name in lowercase. To the right of the box is a grid that's divided into eighteen weeks, with each week furthered subdivided into five small squares, one for each day, Monday through Friday.

I put my finger under the first name, which happens to be ABERNATHY, Jennifer. "If a student's here," I explain, "I mark an X in the box. If he's absent, I mark a zero. If he's tardy, I write a T." I slide my finger across a long row of X's that abruptly stops about a quarter of the way across the grid. "If you go to the tenth week of school, Friday, October 28, you can see that's where Jennifer's X's stop. After that, it's all zeroes."

Gruber taps his forefinger to the grid. "It looks like she had some zeroes before the twenty-eighth. How many—five, six, seven? What was going on there?"

"I checked with the office, and they said Jennifer's father called her in sick."

"They? You mean Mrs. Castillo?"

"Yes, Betty—Mrs. Castillo." I look directly into the dark pools that are Gruber's eyes, trying to appear calm and affable without being too ingratiating. I've been anticipating this interview, and I'm not wholly unprepared.

For starters, I consulted my cousin, a special agent for the FBI, who gave me a crash course over the phone in law-enforcement interrogation techniques.

"If they're just trying to get information, tell them the truth and be done with it. They'll know. But if you think they're fishing around for something and you may be a suspect, it's a different ballgame. Look them in the eye when you talk; try to avoid obvious incriminating behaviors like twitching, licking your lips, fiddling with your clothes or keys. It's OK to show emotion—in fact, you should—but don't overdo it. No soap-opera stuff."

"When have I ever?" I'd said, eliciting a laugh before he went on.

"Be as brief as possible. Remember, they're trying to trick you into confessing. They want to tire you out until you either break down or contradict yourself or lose your cool. Whatever you do, don't sweat! And if at any time you think there might be reasonable suspicion that you're guilty, just say the four magic words: 'I want my attorney.' That'll really piss them off. It's the last thing they want to hear, and it'll shut them up, fast. Hey, why do you want to know all this? Are you in trouble?"

My turn to laugh. "No! This is all preventative. I'm a junior-high teacher. Every day's a ticking time bomb with those kids. You just never know."

No, you really don't, and now here I am.

*   *   *

"Did you ever visit Jennifer's home?" Gruber asks.

I pause a bit too long this time. His eyebrows arch suspiciously. His partner leans forward. I recognize her now: Cindy Carlyle, the ex-wife of the stuffy professor who had rescued his wunderkind son, Daniel, from my "do nothing" (dad's words) ninth-grade biology class my first year on the job. The question is: does she remember *me*?

"Mr. Hunter?"

"Yes," I say at last.

"Yes you went to Jennifer's home?"

I nod.

"And when was that?"

"I don't remember exactly."

Gruber makes a notation in his spiral notepad and flips over the page. He's made himself quite at home in the velour sofa chair one of my parents donated last spring. Carlyle is perched on a lab stool, legs crossed snugly at the knees, top foot beating time to a lazy tune. Her face remains tense, but her lower body's losing interest.

"Do you make a habit of visiting your students at home?" Gruber asks.

"Not a habit, no."

"Do you have some type of criteria then? After such-and-such, you make a home visit?"

"No, I don't have a set policy—nothing like that."

"Then why did you decide to visit Jennifer's home in particular?"

"I don't know," I say. "As a teacher, sometimes you just have a gut feeling about things—" Idiot! Leave your feelings out of it! Facts, man! Stick to facts! One other piece of advice from my cousin. I can see the smile growing under Gruber's mustache.

"A gut feeling about what? Did you think she was in some kind of danger?"

Careful here. If I say yes, they'll want to know why I didn't alert the counselor or the principal or the police. I've got to maintain a credible distance. "No, nothing like that. I just get a feeling about certain kids. Jennifer was always very quiet in class, almost invisible. Good student— always finished her assignments on time, always aced the exams. Suddenly, something's different. I just wanted to find out what was going on."

Gruber intermittently taps the eraser tip of his pencil against his upper teeth. "Did you talk to Jennifer when you visited her home?"

"No."

"Why not?"

"Her father was there, so I talked to him directly. He'd just gotten home from work. I talked to him in the driveway."

"What did you say to him?"

"I told him I was Jennifer's teacher. I wanted to know how she was doing and if I could help."

Gruber vigorously scribbles in his notepad. Carlyle does the same.

"Did you say anything else?"

"Not that I remember."

Gruber flips back several pages in his notes. "Did you tell Mr. Abernathy that—and I'm quoting here—you were going to blow his fucking head off?"

This is where I try to look comically confused. Nothing over-the-top. I laugh, lightly. "What?"

Gruber closes his eyes and sighs as if he's just finished a long race. My cousin warned me about this: beware the "gotcha" moment. The entire interview is designed to lead you through a meandering maze of oft-repeated questions that are nothing more than diversions to catch you in a contradiction or a lie.

"Did you tell Mr. Abernathy you were going to blow his—"

"No!" My blue eyes bore into his brown counterparts. "Absolutely not," I say. Lie.

Now what? I've got no idea how much Mr. Abernathy-Blabbermouth has said or how many incriminating tidbits he's tossed into the mix. It's my turn to go fishing.

"Why would I say something like that to the parent of one of my best students?"

"I don't know," Gruber says. "You tell me."

"Did Mr. Abernathy say why I said that—allegedly? There has to be some context." I need to pivot here and change the narrative, fast. "I mean, he seemed really upset that night."

"What do you mean, upset?"

"Irritable, angry, pissed off at the world. He basically told me to mind my own effing business—excuse my French—and to get off his effing property. Look, if anyone was going to get their head blown off that night, it was me!"

Gruber leans back in the sofa chair, digesting my words like a walrus after a big, fatty meal.

"Any news about Jennifer?" I ask. The story had made the front page of the local paper for several days running: "Junior-High Student

Mysteriously Disappears!" The rumors have run the gamut from a routine runaway to kidnapping and foul play. The father's a prime suspect, and so, apparently, am I.

"And that's the last time you saw her? October 28?"

"Yes—for the fifth time. I swear it."

Gruber's eyes linger on me for several more moments, waiting for me to waver or break.

I don't.

"Mr. Hunter, are you willing to take a polygraph test?"

"No," I say. I want to add, "Go screw a mountain goat!" but don't. My cousin was adamant about lie-detector tests: "Never ever take one! They'll say you can prove your innocence, but it's a lie. For one thing, the results are inadmissible in court. So it's a no-win for you. If you pass, it doesn't matter, and if you don't, they've got you by the balls—scared, vulnerable, desperate to cut a deal. Because the real purpose of those tests is to weasel a confession out of you. They'll try to wear you down until you're so tired, hungry, and miserable you'll do or say anything to get out of there. Bottom line: if they say lie detector test, tell them to go screw a mountain goat."

*   *   *

"Well, all right," Gruber sighs. As he rises from the pillowy sofa chair, I feel the tension that has been twisting my body into a massive knot slowly relent. I stand up to show them the door, but Carlyle remains seated.

"Mr. Hunter," she says almost coyly, "did you ever remove Jennifer's dress?"

This time there's no forethought or strategic planning. My mouth drops open and one word plops out: "What?"

"Did you ever remove Jennifer's dress?"

"No! No way, no how! No!"

Carlyle uncrosses her legs and flips through her notepad. "We have a witness who claims that on October 19, she saw you remove Jennifer's dress."

"No! No no no! Who said that?"

"I can't disclose that, but it was a student. She said she saw you and Jennifer in the storage room." Carlyle aims her pencil at the partially closed door at the back of the room. "Is that it? The storage room?"

I nod.

"According to the witness, you were taking Jennifer's dress off in the storage room. When you saw her—the witness—you stopped."

"That's a damn lie."

"You're single, aren't you, Mr. Hunter?" Carlyle asks.

"Divorced. Why?"

"You're living alone?"

"Yes."

"Are you currently in a relationship?"

"What's that got to do with any of this? That's none of your damn business!"

Carlyle looks up from her notepad just long enough to lock eyes, then looks back down. "We'll see about that. Are you currently in a relationship?"

As a matter of fact, things had been heating up between me and Priscilla Manygoats, the Navajo counselor—nothing too serious yet: dinner, a movie, a hike in the Sedona red rocks.

"I've been dating someone, yes."

"How old is she?"

"I don't know—late twenties, early thirties."

"What's her name?"

"Why do you need to know that?"

"We may want to talk to her."

"What the hell for?"

Carlyle lowers her notepad, looks at me, and smiles. "Information."

"What kind of information? What are you trying to imply here?"

Carlyle's shaking her head, literally tsk-tsking. "I'll be frank with you, Mr. Hunter, this doesn't look good."

"What do you mean it doesn't look good? What's that supposed to mean?"

Gruber checks back in, shaking his head. "Sexual misconduct with a minor. You could get twenty years for this. I suggest you start cooperating."

My voice clogs, then shifts to a frightened falsetto. "What are you talking about? I have been cooperating!" I can feel the blood in my head plunging to my feet. The floor begins tilting and my legs turn to mush. I grab my desk to steady myself.

"Are you all right, Mr. Hunter?" Gruber extends a helping hand, but I brush it aside.

This is when I'm supposed to say the magic words—I want my attorney—but for some inexplicable reason, I don't.

HELL

s it turns out, I don't need a lawyer—at least not yet. I haven't been officially charged with anything.

"Just gathering information," Gruber had said, but the teasing little smirk beneath his bushy mustache suggested otherwise.

Over the next two years, I'll be interviewed four more times by Gruber and Carlyle. Five articles chronicling the strange and sudden disappearance of Jennifer Abernathy will appear in the local paper, all ending with the ominous rider "the investigation continues." All five articles will cite Grace Swedelson, Jennifer's sixth-period teacher, as the last adult to see her, but two of the stories will also mention my name. A special feature story on safety in the local schools will highlight the Jennifer Abernathy case to portray Ponderosa Junior High as a low-security, predator's playground.

The school board will drag me, Grace Swedelson, and Jennifer's four other teachers in for a two-hour, closed-session interview during which the six of us will be grilled about how appropriately we followed (or didn't) the district's safety procedures and protocols.

A week later, the newspaper will print an exclusive interview with Jennifer's father, in which he'll describe in detail my visit to his home, calling it "disturbing" and "highly suspicious."

This will trigger another closed session with the school board, but this time I'm alone on the hot seat. The president of the governing board will make it clear that this is not a criminal investigation, but the board does have some questions about my visit to the Abernathy home. They also want to know about the allegations that I undressed Jennifer in my storage closet.

So once again, when asked, "Did you say to Mr. Abernathy, quote, I'll blow your fucking head off?" I will lie. And this, as much as anything, will torment me, because if I have one redeeming virtue, it's honesty. I've always prided myself on telling the truth. But over the next two years I will lie, and I will lie often. And I will get very good at it. Whether it's to the cops or the school board or the press or a stranger on the street, I will deny ever threatening Mr. Abernathy, and I will insist that I have no idea where Jennifer Abernathy is, that the last time I saw her was October 28 in my third-period class, and I will say this without blinking or twitching or licking my lips. I will say it so often and so well that even I will almost believe it.

*   *   *

The price will be heavy. I will pray for Jennifer daily, fearing the worst, hoping for the best, and lying to everyone. In the beginning, I'll feel as if each lie is a little hole being punched in my soul and, over time, if I keep this up, I'll be one big hole with no soul left. I'll try to compensate by being 100 percent honest in all other things. But this won't work because I'll have to do so much pretending, which is another form of lying. I'll pretend I'm unfazed, happy, innocent. I'll pretend I'm the same good old Mr. Hunter.

But I'm living on pins and needles. Just the thought of the possible consequences is like a water torture drip-drip-dripping on me every second of every day. I'm so consumed with worry that I can't eat, sleep, or teach—not like I used to. If a student asks a question—"Mr. Hunter, when are we going to finish building the fitness stations?"—it's a coin toss whether I'll answer with a cheerful "Pretty soon!" or my eyes will glaze over as my thoughts stumble through a jungle of worry. When the latter happens, a smart aleck will slink up to snap his fingers under my nose, like a hypnotist breaking a trance. My head will jerk back as I gaze around as if I've just awakened from the dead. The class will laugh, briefly. "Are you OK, Mr. Hunter?" the smart aleck will ask, genuinely concerned.

I try to laugh it off, but there's no humor left in the tank. Or fun or patience or goodwill. That drained out with the four follow-up interviews and the closed-door sessions with the school board. I still haven't been formally charged, but I know what's at stake. If I tell the truth, I'll immediately be fired and, shortly after, carted off to prison. Good luck ever landing a teaching job in Arizona or any other state. All my altruistic rationalizations—I was trying to do the right thing; I was trying to save a girl's life; somebody had to do something before Mr. Badass killed his daughter, and believe you me he would have—would be eviscerated in a court of law. Easily.

Why didn't you report it to the school counselor? (Because he's an

172 | *Just a Teacher*

incompetent, ass-kissing bureaucrat who'd probably ask the dad's permission to file a police report.) Why didn't you report it to the police? (Because they'd interview the dad, fall for his persecuted, single-father-doing-his-best-to-raise-his-kid routine, and call it good.) Why didn't you tell the principal? (What could he do? Tell the police—and the police had been told before. Nothing was happening—that's the whole damn point! Someone had to do something, and I did. So shoot me!)

The problem is, they just might. Worst-case scenario, they could try me for murder. That's what the psycho father wants: "Where's my daughter? What the hell did you do to her?" He's threatened to file a civil suit even if the police don't nail me with criminal charges.

*　　*　　*

My fellow teachers don't know the details, but they've read the newspaper and lapped up the gossip. I'm getting the stink eye from John Baxter, Grace Swedelson, and others who are quietly reveling in my colossal screwup.

"Pride goeth before the fall!" Swedelson says.

"He's always played it loosey-goosey," Baxter says. "Always bending the rules. Bend something enough and it's going to break! I knew it would catch up to him eventually. It always does. If you stick your neck out enough times, eventually somebody's going to chop it off! It's too bad. The kid had real potential."

The kid. Some of the old-timers used to call me "The Sundance Kid" for my swashbuckling verve in and out of the classroom. Not no more.

I'm radioactive now. Parent requests for my biology class have dwindled to a loyal handful. I'm down to one section of biology with other science and math classes for filler. Priscilla Manygoats tactfully avoids me.

Maybe Baxter's right. Play it safe. Play it easy. Open the textbook, teach the damn lesson, and grade those easy-to-grade multiple choice/true-false/fill-in-the-blank tests. Keep my nose clean and the students quiet, get a paycheck, and go home. And sleep like a baby at night, which is far more than I'm doing right now. Once I hit the mattress and close my eyes, my brain takes off like a jackrabbit fleeing a pack of wolves. No tricky symbolism here: I'm the jackrabbit and the wolves are all the ugly nouns chasing after me; termination, incarceration, reputation kaput. Sex offender. Kidnapper. Murderer. I'll never teach again, anywhere.

I try all the remedies to induce sleep, from the lightweights (chamomile tea, valerian root, melatonin), which don't make a dent, to the heavy hitters (benzodiazepines, doxepine, eszopiclone). My students keep a cautious distance, expressions vacillating between fear and pity. Their parents, friends, and older siblings had praised me from the ramparts. "The best class you'll ever take in your life! The best science teacher—the best anything teacher ever!"

I'm a monumental disappointment, and I know it.

* * *

I try to ignore the alarm clock on my nightstand as the blood-red digits commence their dreaded nightly countdown to dawn—12:35 a.m., 12:36, 12:37, 12:38, 12:39, 12:40. Every minute the numbers change, and every change is a needle in my neck. I'm walking in Amy's moccasins, pacing the shag carpet, futilely stalking sleep as Tsegi watches curiously from the floor mat masquerading as his bed. When the phone rings, I jump. Who the hell's calling at half-past midnight? I wait, counting the rings: six, seven, eight, nine, ten. Silence. Only then do I realize I've been holding my breath.

I lie down on the sofa, close my eyes, and try again. Multiple stress points have formed an alliance and taken up residence in my gut, tying my intestines into knots that either plug me up for days or flush food through me so fast I'm sprinting for the toilet on the quarter hour. My belly's painfully distended, swollen to bursting. I feel as if I'm gestating quintuplets. Food tastes fecal. I go days drinking only fluids because any kind of solids will release the demons in my gut—cramps, nausea, constipation, diarrhea. My muscles shrink and my flesh begins to vanish. I try Pepto-Bismol, laxatives, Milk of Magnesia. Nothing works. Doctors subject me to a barrage of painful and humiliating tests, many of which require preparations that are worse than my symptoms, always with the same result: there's nothing functionally wrong with me. One doctor finally gives it a name: "IBS—Irritable Bowel Syndrome. It's a catchphrase for what happens when all hell breaks loose in your gut and we can't figure out why. Are you maybe under a lot of stress?"

I grow leaner, weaker, and more exhausted by the day. Yet somehow, every morning at eight a.m. I'm standing at the door of my classroom producing my best semblance of a smile, welcoming my students and wishing them a good day. I'm going through the motions and I know it, but I suit up, plod through the day, and then come home and collapse on the sofa, too drained to take Tsegi for a walk, thinking that tonight, surely, I'll be able to fall asleep. But then the phone rings or there's a knock at the door or a shout in the street or a dog barking or the neighbor's kid squealing or my own heart beating—it doesn't take much—and I'm up pacing the planks again.

Except tonight *is* different. Tonight, I'm in a windowless cubicle watching a stranger in a bathrobe sipping coffee with Amy in my breakfast nook while Tsegi lounges nearby, happily thumping his tail. I can't see the stranger's face, but he has a thick head of silver hair, very suave, very debonair, and he's reaching across the table to take Amy's hand, gently squeezing it. Together they gaze out a picture window, but I'm on the other side of a river now that divides the building in two—half house, half cubicle, the two separated by a large wall of glass. I yell, but nothing comes out. I pound the glass, but it's like punching rubber. I turn around and see that I'm only one among a tribe of men in white boxer shorts and wife-beater shirts. There's a toilet in the corner, vacant, with a large TV screen directly overhead. The men are watching a football game, yelling and screaming at the referee.

I look across the river where the stranger is pouring Amy a glass of liquor—champagne, it looks like. They tap the crystal glasses together. Amy smiles. I shout her name, and the other men mock me, chanting: "*A*-me! *A*-me! *A*-me!" I wake up soaked with sweat, panting as I try to get my bearings, then grateful—so grateful—when I realize I'm lying on my sofa and not floundering in that godforsaken cell. A black-and-white movie is playing on TV, casting a ghoulish light on the floor. Tsegi rises from his mat, slinks over, and gazes up at me with blue eyes that look cold but sympathetic. He puts his paw on my hand. I slide my other hand over Tsegi's paw and give it an encouraging pat. But I'm afraid to go back to sleep now, fearing a rerun of that awful dream, or, even worse, a sequel.

I look at the clock: one forty-seven. Sometimes when this happens, I go for a run, hoping to tire my body to submission. Tonight's different. Tonight, it's about escape. Cold, clear, and mostly quiet except for the distant whisper of a passing car or the plaintive moan of a freight train rolling through the heart of town. It's mid-January, and the festive ornaments of the holidays have been removed from the streets and neighborhoods. It's been thirteen months since those detectives first strolled into my classroom to ruin my life, and still no end in sight. Cramps again, a power drill boring through my belly. Tsegi wants to join me, but not this time.

As I trot toward the park, my sneakers clapping rhythmically against the pavement, the naked aspens look like vertical cracks in the night sky. I cut across the soccer field, dodging patches of snow, and head up the narrow road switch-backing to the observatory. A ski cap on my head and puffy black gloves on my hands, double-layered in sweats, I look like a leaner version of Rocky Balboa huffing and puffing up the hill. In my weakened state, the road seems much longer and steeper. Each stride takes a gruesome bite out of my thighs and squeezes the life from my lungs.

I press on, slowly, stubbornly, lifting one pathetic foot in front of the other until, a hundred yards from the summit, I stop at an overlook. Bent double, hands on my knees, I gasp as I gaze down at the city lights, a galaxy of dim little dots waiting to be connected. I see the golden arches of McDonald's and the bell tower of the university and the domed athletic stadium bulging above campus like a giant mushroom. Overhead, the glittering heavens, countless angels keeping vigil over the peaks. I look down at the geometric neighborhoods where parents and children sleep soundly. I ache with envy. To sleep again; to escape this hellish everything for a few hours. Or forever.

I'm not serious, of course. And yet I climb atop the short, stout rock wall separating the road from the ledge that plunges three hundred feet to a river of blacktop. One step forward would end it all. One little step, a brief, cosmic fall and—done. Finished. Over.

In my mind this had always been the coward's way out, but now my cousin Matt's voice is crying up from the pavement. It's not angry or vindictive; there's no I-told-you-so about it, although right now, Matthew Hunter would be justified. Toward that nineteen-year-old who'd swallowed a bottle of sleeping pills, I'd been ruthlessly unforgiving. I was a boy who'd lost his idol and the closest thing I'd ever known to a big brother.

There's no debate here. I'm not going to jump. But I stand on the ledge for twenty minutes before stepping down with heartbreak for my cousin and anyone else who's been pushed beyond the brink. Then I lower myself to my knees. I ask Matthew for forgiveness and beg God to please, somehow, someway, bail me out of this mess.

The next day, during my fourth-hour prep period, Melvin Jackson saunters into my classroom and hands me a slip of paper with a name and a phone number. "She's the best in town," he says, and walks out.

DELIVERANCE

Irene Shapiro is a middle-aged woman with the bawdy laugh and salty tongue of Joan Rivers. Three years ago, she and her orthopedic surgeon husband left their high-rise in Manhattan to live a slower, simpler life in the sticks. It was his dream, her nightmare, and she makes no bones about it. She spends the first five minutes of our meeting lamenting the fact there's not one decent seafood restaurant in town.

Her second-story office reeks of tobacco, and she hacks in between drags on her Virginia Slims, intermittently excusing herself: "Sorry about that. These damn things are killing me!"

She's not the cheapest attorney in town by a long shot—the $5,000 retainer is hardly chump change—but if it means a good night's sleep and no more jumping through the roof every time the phone rings, it will be money well spent.

I voice my deepest fear. "What if this goes to trial?"

Shapiro rolls her eyes and whistles, then crushes the stub of her cigarette into an ashtray and promptly lights up another. "We'll cross that bridge if and when. I can't guarantee anything, but it probably won't."

*   *   *

She doesn't waste time. Two days after I present her with a check, she calls me at home. Did you know the person accusing you of sexual misconduct is a female student who was in your fourth-period class in the fall of 1977? Alice Conway?

"You're joking?"

"Why? Have you got some dirt on little Alice?"

"Dirt?"

"Look, Todd, let's not be naïve. You're in a battle for your life. The cops haven't pressed charges yet, but they're building a doozy of a case. They're trying to lump abduction with sexual misconduct together as a motive for homicide. Serious shit, Todd. She's not some sweet teenager. She's the enemy. Now… have you got any dirt?"

I'm stunned. This is a foreign way of thinking: student as adversary, student as enemy, student as the guy or girl who slits your throat in your sleep. But my heart's racing, and the fog clears quickly.

"She was the only kid out of all my classes that got an F that semester. That's one out of a hundred and thirty-something."

"Why did she get an F and nobody else? Is she a minority? Black, Hispanic, Asian, any of that?"

"No."

"Thank God! I don't want anyone playing the race card. That's all we need to really muck things up. So, tell me—why the F?"

"Other than not turning in any assignments, failing every test and quiz, and refusing to do anything in class—nothing."

"Ah, sarcasm! I like that—a little sass, a little salsa. But if you ever use it in deposition, in an interview, or in front of a judge, I'll personally string you up by your testicles—got it?"

I nod, very slowly.

"Have you got any proof? About this deadbeat student?"

"My grade book. She pretty much got straight zeros."

"Did you pick on her in class? Call her names—Fat Alice, Dumb Alice, anything like that?"

"You're joking, aren't you?"

"Yes and no. You hear all kinds of stuff in this business, and I don't like surprises. Just doing my homework here. So—again—did you pick on her in class?"

"No."

"Good answer! It means we'll wrap this case up real fast."

"Seriously?"

"Oh, easy. There were no other witnesses. It's her word against yours. She's got motive: revenge. She was pissed off at you because she got an F. No one's going to believe that kid, especially if I get my hooks into her."

*   *   *

As it turns out, Irene is right. Alice Conway may go to her grave believing she saw Todd Hunter remove Jennifer Abernathy's dress on October 19 in the storage room of his biology classroom at Ponderosa Junior High School. But Alice, now a seventeen-year-old, will recant her previous statement. She will also write me a letter of apology, and the police will drop their investigation of me for sexual misconduct with a minor. In addition, any references to the incident will be purged from my personnel file—this, at Irene's insistence.

"One down, one to go," Irene says. The other investigation is far more complicated and will drag on for another five months. But my pit bull attorney is relentless. First, she goes after Detective Carlyle, accusing her of pursuing a personal vendetta.

"That's absurd! Why would I have anything against him? He's just a teacher!"

Irene jogs her memory: "Didn't you pull your kid out of my client's classroom? His first year on the job?"

"That was my husband's idea."

"Same difference."

"My *ex*-husband."

"Either way, there must have been some bad blood between you and my client. I'm just saying, it doesn't look good."

Carlyle backs off, but Detective Gruber remains relentless. Then one day, thirty months into the investigation, he makes the mistake of calling Irene's office while I'm present, and my attorney feels obliged to show me she's worth the money I spent. So she proceeds to put on a show.

"Look, you need to stop badgering my client!" she says. "No, you can't have another interview. I don't care if you've got new information. I've had enough of this. Either press charges or leave him the hell alone. Shit or get off the pot, Detective!" She crushes her smoldering Virginia Slims in the ash tray and winks at me. "Then we'll just call this case closed—at least for my client. If you badger him again, I'll file a harassment suit!"

Slamming the phone down for effect, she says, "We've got 'em!"

And she's mostly right. The case isn't closed but suspended.

"That means they've shelved it," Irene explains. "Waved the white flag."

"It's over?"

"As far as you're concerned it is. If they ever contact you again, call me—but they won't. Not unless they want to wrangle with me again."

I'm speechless a moment. Then, "Thank you." I want to take her hand and kiss it. "Thank you."

She smiles and winks. "My pleasure. Sweet dreams."

That's the end of it, technically speaking. I still call it "The Lost Years," 1977 to 1981. Very little progress on the pond. My body wasted, and my soul—who knows what happened to that. My students severely short-changed. My reputation shot to hell. Through it all, only Mark Fitzgerald has remained loyal to me; good old Fitz. But even he has reservations.

"Did you ever consider how that father must be feeling? His daughter suddenly gone? What kind of torment he must be going through?"

"Sure I have. No more punching bag for him. Some torment."

"You don't get it, do you? If that was your kid, you'd be madder than hell."

"If that was my kid, I wouldn't go around beating her up every morning before breakfast."

Fitz gets real quiet and looks at me suspiciously, as if I'm one of his high school students trying to cheat on an exam.

"Do you know something you're not telling the cops?"

I'm tempted to unload the whole miserable story on him, but instead I remain defiant and defensive. Even if I admit that I could have—should have—handled Jennifer's situation differently, I can't tell Fitz or anyone else. Ever. I've dug the hole too deep and I'm just now climbing out.

"You've got to trust me on this, Fitz."

"Is that a no?"

"Just trust me. Please."

* * *

It takes several months, but gradually—stick by stick, stone by stone—I feel the weight of the world lifting from my shoulders. Jennifer remains a permanent resident in my head and in my dreams and in my prayers, but life begins to get normal again. Even so, it's a full year before I sleep soundly through the night or eat a meal without fear of intestinal repercussions. And you're never completely OK. Something that traumatic changes you, for better and worse. I look at my students differently now, and people generally. And I'm always hearing footsteps.

MONKEY BUSINESS

It's a snow day, and schools are supposed to be empty. Yesterday, shortly before noon, a winter storm hit like a sneak attack, blackening the skies and dumping a relentless barrage of snow across the northern half of the state. By nightfall, the town looked like Ice Station Zebra, with no end in sight.

The snowplows worked through the night, but the job was for Sisyphus, not seasonal city employees. The instant a foot of pavement was cleared, the heavens ruthlessly whitewashed it. Customarily, the superintendent waited until five a.m. to call a snow day, but there was no reason to postpone the obvious: the interstate was closed, the town paralyzed, and school cancelled until further notice.

No one's going anywhere today unless they absolutely have to.

Or maybe not. At nine a.m., as snow continues falling like flour through a sifter, I grab a kitchen broom, trudge outside in my winter coat and boots, and knock down the two-foot shell of snow cocooning my pickup. After shoveling a narrow path to the street, I strap chains to the rear tires, fire up the engine, and drive toward school, where seventy-eight science projects wait to be graded.

* * *

This year, John Baxter and the rest of the Science Department proposed a school-wide science fair, requiring all students to submit a project worth 25 percent of their final grade. I argued that my biology students already do a group science project—the pond—but my colleagues insisted on an individual entry from each student, no exceptions. In short, I was outvoted.

That may explain why I haven't touched those projects since my students submitted them two weeks ago. Now the natives are getting restless. Jack Baldwin and his brat pack have been hounding me: "When do we get our projects back, Mr. Hunter? Have you graded our projects yet?"

A snow day seems the perfect opportunity to get butt-loads of work done in a short time, undisturbed by Melvin Jackson's voice booming over the intercom or colleagues dropping by to borrow a beaker or brainstorm a lesson. Peace. Quiet. Solitude.

At least, this is what I tell myself as I navigate a maze of snowbanks that make these city streets look like a bobsled run. In truth, I'm driving to the junior high because I've got nowhere else to go. The ski lifts are closed due to high winds and lack of visibility, and the town has shut down: no movies, no museums, no coffee shops. Even the fast-food joints have conceded defeat. Emergency services only is the order of the day.

At the school parking lot, my pickup explodes through a three-foot wall of snow, hydroplaning despite the valiant but futile efforts of the chains. I gun the engine and my truck bolts forward, plowing a path across the lot before stalling against a giant accordion of compressed snow.

Greeted by a warm gust of air when I step inside, I pause just long enough to confirm the silence—yes, I'm absolutely alone—and then plod down the dark hall, its industrial carpeting softening the thud of my boots. Scanning the empty stools spaced evenly around the eight lab tables of my classroom, I suffer a moment of loneliness—a quick dart to the heart that I pull out and toss aside, reminding myself that I've got work to do and this snow day is a rare gift, a freebie I can't squander on self-pity.

I reach into the cardboard box by my desk and remove the first report. Most of these will be handwritten on line-ruled paper in a barely legible hybrid of beginning D'Nealian and Egyptian hieroglyphics, the sheets secured by little silver brads in cheap, colored folders. A few kids will submit their reports in gaudy binders, each page encased in a plastic, see-through sleeve—the well-to-do sons and daughters of doctors and lawyers and university professors who don't have to choose between fancy packaging for a school project and Thursday night's meal. It's fine if they like window dressing, but I grade them on the stuff between the covers.

I'm pleasantly surprised by the title of this first one: *Are Dreams Arbitrary or Meaningful Constructs?* A psychological study! Something new. Not the same old same old: *Do Plants Grow Faster in Sand or Topsoil? Will a Nail Rust in Water? The Stages of a Butterfly.* Or worse, a homemade volcano.

This gem belongs to Tammy Henson, an honors student. No surprise there. She's also the star of my algebra class.

Every morning for two months, Tammy has faithfully recorded her dreams and then tried to find links between her unconscious narratives and events and images in her daily life. Insights and observations pepper the pages with a passion and professionalism that would make college professors drool. Included are footnoted references to Jung, Freud, and even the great dreamers and interpreters of dreams in the Bible. Tammy is halfway through eighth grade.

"Damn!" I say, turning the final page. "That's nice!"

I write a full page of comments followed by a colossal "A" with three pluses, three exclamation points, and a final message: *Outstanding work!*

That's the start I was hoping for. More of those, please!

But my euphoria is short-lived. The next several reports range from hastily scribbled one-page products submitted to avoid an F (I never fail them if they make an attempt) to paint-by-the-numbers products that include all the required components (hypothesis, explanation of the experiment, results, conclusions) but have as much flair as a phone directory. Some reports could be mass-marketed as insomnia cures. My one cardinal and unpardonable rule, other than submit something, is: "Don't bore me." This is science! We make artificial hearts and launch people into outer space! The grammar can be a train wreck, the rationale flawed, the experiment preposterous, but just please do not under any circumstances put me to sleep.

With a few exceptions like Tammy Henson, I'm talking to air.

I sigh and scribble a "C" with a circle around it. Then I reconsider. Billy Fremont probably stayed up till midnight rewriting his report because he'd misspelled a word here and there and didn't want to erase them or use whiteout because it would make the pages look messy. Do I punish the kid for not being as brilliant as Tammy? For not being a junior Galileo? He did everything I asked in a tidy, legible manner without skimping on length (seven to eight pages required, and he gave me nine). I apply liquid whiteout to the grade, blow on it to expedite the drying process, then write in a large and emphatic "B" and a note: *Very good effort!* Shaking my head, I drop the report in the "graded" pile—ten down. Sixty-eight to go.

Snow is falling vertically—a mesmerizing effect, like a waterfall. I could turn on the radio for company, but this will only slow me down. I'm not a kid anymore: I can't watch TV, listen to the Rolling Stones, and solve multivariate equations simultaneously. Maybe I never could. Multitasking's a myth unless you're doing mindless, repetitive work: folding clothes, shucking corn, punching holes in sheet metal. Back to work! Focus! I need to get these reports graded and get the hell out of here—and then what? Drive back to my grim trailer where I can shut the curtain on the day and eat another microwave meal while I search the cable networks for company? What's my hurry? I ain't got a hot date, that's for sure.

No, but I've got projects to grade and a free day to do it, so quit whining! Things could be worse. I'm not in jail, for starters. I can sleep through the night and eat a meal without wincing. And my new dream house is almost finished, and I'll be moving in a month.

*   *   *

I grade five more projects and then check the clock: half-past noon. The liquid breakfast I gulped down is a fleeting memory. The wolves are howling for something more substantial. I head down the hall to the faculty lounge, where I keep a microwave lunch in the refrigerator for unexpected occasions like this: stuck at school for whatever.

The door's locked, but I've got a key and when I push it open there's a swift, compressed, and awkward commotion on the carpeted floor. Before I can fully process the image, I pull the door shut with both hands. Shit! Shit! Shit! I step back, hyperventilating, and then I run. It's a split-second maneuver: open, gasp, shut, run. Sprint down the dark hallway, clodhopper boots pounding the carpet. Yank open the classroom door, toss the reports into their box, and then I'm running out the side exit, high-stepping through the snow like a drum major down the walkway and across the parking lot to my pickup truck, which has been re-buried under another half-foot of snow. Clearing the windshield with a sweep of the arm, just enough so I can peer through the periscope lens, I squeeze into the cab, switch on the ignition, and shove the stick into reverse. In a fury of spinning wheels and grinding gears, my truck whips in a half-circle, flinging a feathery arc across the lot. My foot slams the accelerator, powering hell-bent forward, oblivious to the possibility of a passing car or snowplow. Fishtailing down the street, truck flanks scraping the snow banks, I slide and glide through the labyrinth, never letting up on the gas. At the trailer park, I shut and deadbolt the door, then fling myself down on the Salvation Army sofa that was supposed to be temporary. For the first time since moving into the cramped quarters, I feel genuinely grateful to be home. That epiphany both comforts and depresses me.

For the next several minutes, as Tsegi does the happy dance around me, I stare at the blank TV screen, almost expecting it to turn on by itself and replay in living technicolor the scene I'd just witnessed in the teachers' lounge: the kneeling and naked backside of a fifty-something man (judging by the butt sag and the freckles and liver marks blighting his skin). Protruding on either side of him was a pair of bent legs, the naked kneecaps staring at me like eyeless, mouthless faces. Then a real face, a woman's, peering around the man's shoulder: the big, frizzy hair; the Egyptian eyebrows arching in disbelief; the violet eyes as big as saucers: the unmistakable face of Raquel Chamberlain, the second-year principal at Ponderosa Elementary School.

And then the face of the man as his freckled neck craned backward, blue eyes more perturbed than surprised. It only took a flash to recognize the fiery hair and impish grin of Superintendent of Schools Dale Hanagan.

I heard nothing. Saw no flurry of flesh, no embarrassing scramble for pants, shirts, blouses, underthings, coats, socks, sweaters. Maybe they just shrugged me off and jumped right back into action. Maybe they didn't recognize me; maybe my face was a blur they summarily dismissed?

Then why are my hands shaking? Why am I staring at that TV screen as if any moment the superintendent's face will materialize and order me to report to his office first thing tomorrow morning? Why did I hear an audible click when my eyes locked with theirs?

*   *   *

I don't know what to do, so I call Fitz, who teaches social studies at the high school.

"Man, you sound really stressed," he says. "What happened?"

"Nothing. I just need to talk."

"It's snowing pretty bad out there."

"I'll come to your place."

I brave the snow again and somehow negotiate the snot-slick roads to Fitz's ranch-style home on the east side. He has a steaming cup of coffee waiting for me, and his wife is conveniently occupied on the treadmill in the basement. He settles me into an easy chair, deposits his six-four frame in the rocker, and crosses his massive arms.

"What's going on?"

After all but extracting a blood oath that he will never, ever, ever repeat this to anyone, I spill my story… and Fitz throws back his head and laughs.

"What the hell's so funny? Don't you get it? I'm toast! I am toast!"

"Are you kidding me? He's not going to fire you. In fact, he's never going to hassle you again. You've got his balls in a ditty bag!"

"What?"

"Hell, you should be chugging down champagne or vodka to celebrate, not this watered-down rooster juice."

Fitz reaches for my coffee mug, but I pull it away. I hadn't considered the incident in that way. Too much adrenaline zipping through my veins. Too much shock and awe. I'd opened the door and—wham!—a two-by-four had smacked me across the face.

"No way in hell is Dale Hanagan going to say a word about this, and neither are you. You've got the ace of spades up your sleeve. You are in Fat City, my friend!"

I'm breathing easier now. Blood pressure down. Pulse stable. Hands still. Shoulders relaxed.

Fitz is right. I smile. "Think I'll take you up on those celebratory spirits."

"Jack Daniels?"

"Perfect."

* * *

Everything's good, for a while. Whenever I cross paths with Dale Hanagan, he briefly trades eyes and offers a curt but professional, "Good morning, Mr. Hunter," no doubt messaging me that he's not one bit intimidated; nothing unethical or out of the ordinary has occurred—in fact, nothing at all happened on the floor of the faculty lounge at the junior high on that snow day the sixteenth of February, and, most importantly, nothing has changed. He's still superintendent, and I'm still just a teacher he can dismiss at his pleasure. Yes, there are rules and regulations, policies and procedures, but if he truly wants to get rid of me, there's always some cloak-and-dagger way to make that happen.

As for Raquel Chamberlain, now that Amy is completely out of the picture, I almost never visit the elementary school. On those rare occasions when I do run into Raquel, she smiles at me in the most peculiar way, as if we had once been lovers but now she's moved on to greener pastures.

Everything is quite simpatico in my world until one day in mid-April, when Deborah Rhinehart calls from the district office and asks if I can meet with the superintendent at four p.m. today.

"In regard to what?"

"Don't know," the superintendent's secretary says.

"Don't know because you can't say, or don't know because you don't know?"

"Don't know because I don't."

I arrive five minutes early, waiting on the small sofa while Deb pecks away at her IBM Selectric II and ignores me. It's almost four-thirty when the door to the superintendent's office finally opens and the new chief of police steps out — a burly, balding man who looks like an ex-football coach. They shake hands, the two local power brokers smiling amiably, the chief giving me a courteous if condescending nod as he saunters by.

The superintendent's about to vanish back into his lair when Deb looks up from her typewriter.

"Dale." She motions to me, the after-thought sifting through the contaminated remains of the morning paper: "Your four o'clock."

"Oh, right!" the superintendent says, smacking the heel of his hand to his forehead as if to say, My life is so overflowing with important people that how could I ever possibly be expected to remember the lowly and insignificant likes of you? But come in anyway.

Mind games.

I step into his den — by far the biggest, fanciest office in the school district: a cherrywood desk the size of New Hampshire with a padded leather swivel chair befitting a monarch, a leather sofa, and a mahogany table long enough to host a Thanksgiving feast, although it's used mainly for meetings with the city elites (or maybe as a hardwood mattress for an elementary-school principal after hours).

He motions to one of the three leather chairs facing his mammoth desk and settles into his padded throne, leaning back, left ankle propped on right knee as if he were relaxing on his front porch for a neighborly chat. Any moment he's going to break out a jug of moonshine.

Directly behind him is a framed picture of the snow-capped peaks above a bank of winter mist. To the left is a plaque that reads:

"Here's one attaboy for a job well done. This doesn't make up for an aw shit if you screw up."

Two shelves are packed with the twenty-plus volumes of "West's Law Code." Framed diplomas and certificates verify his credentials: B.S. in Secondary Education; M.S. in Educational Administration; Superintendent's Certificate.

The first fifteen minutes are consumed by routine chatter.

"Did you get an elk tag?"

"Yes. Seven-A. You?"

"I missed out on elk, but I got drawn for javelina. How's Amy doing?"

"I really don't know."

"I thought I heard a rumor you two—"

"Nope."

"Well, I wish you the best. She's a great lady—and a great teacher."

"She certainly is."

"Looks like we're facing another round of budget cuts. It's getting to be the damn rule, you know, not the exception. Coffee?"

"No, thanks."

Rolling forward in his chair, he stands and pours himself a cup. "Say, do you remember a student named Jennifer Abernathy?" He gestures to me with the coffee pot and I shake my head. "So, you don't know her?"

"No, I was declining the coffee."

"Then you do know her?"

Of course I know her—and everyone in town knows I know her. It was plastered all over the papers for months. I wonder if he's rehearsed this interrogation to throw me off my game or if it just naturally rolls off his forked tongue. "I had her several years ago. She went missing. Why?"

"Oh, nothing." The superintendent eases back into his chair. "Her father's been making some noise—new police chief and all. You've probably heard this already, but he's thinking about reopening the case."

"No, I didn't know that."

He pauses just long enough to turn up the heat. "Yes, well—you know Craig Savage? The new chief?"

"Not personally."

"Craig wants to know if we've got any new information. There's a rumor floating around about some foul play. Do you know anything about that?"

I don't like the direction or the temperature of his interrogation. It's my turn to shift gears.

"Yes, I heard something like that."

Hanagan tilts forward and cups his hands on his desk: a snap-trap. He thinks he's got me. "Where?"

"From Raquel Chamberlain."

"Raquel?"

"Yes, the elementary-school principal. You know Raquel, don't you?"

The superintendent leans back and takes a long, slow sip from his mug. "Well, hell, yes. She's one of my principals. And a damn good one."

"Well, she told me."

Hanagan nods, sets his mug on the desk, and glances at his wristwatch. Subtext: We're done here.

"Let me know if you hear anything else," he says.

"About Raquel?"

The superintendent looks annoyed. I've outmaneuvered him, at least this round.

"Jennifer Abernathy," he corrects.

"I sure will."

He stands and I follow suit, accepting his freckled paw when he reaches across his desk. He smiles. "Happy hunting," he says, a delta of wrinkles radiating from the corner of each eye.

"You too."

CROSSROADS

It turns out to be a long and silent armistice. Dale Hanagan never says another word to me about Jennifer Abernathy, and I stay mum about his shenanigans with Raquel Chamberlain. But his tacit threat is a grim reminder of the thin ice underfoot. I can sleep at night, but one eye's always open. When the phone rings, my stomach still tightens.

But time marches on—five years, ten—thankfully, without any catastrophic trauma. The scales of life remain fairly balanced, giving a little here and taking a little there. Raquel accepts a position as an assistant superintendent at a school district in Phoenix, while Dale controls the school district's joysticks for another nine years before calling it quits. I move into Dream House II, a secluded log home where deer sneak down at twilight to sip from a nearby spring. Instead of bell-bottoms and tie-dye tank tops, the school rebels now wear dog collars and holocaust cloaks. Tsegi loses a step, then another, and one day I notice a lump on his furry chest that within a week grows to the size of a grapefruit. He survives two surgeries before the vet helps him make that final passage to the Great Bark Park in the Sky. Three months later, I go to the animal shelter and adopt a husky pup, a frisky, blue-eyed Tsegi look-alike. I call him Milo.

Life is busy in a good way. I've got my students and the pond, where the kids are planting an aspen grove, adding three stations to the fitness trail, and purging the north shore of old shrubs and invasive species. I also hunt, hike, bike, and ski in season, while lending a hand at the soup kitchen on weekends. I date occasionally, but nothing too serious. No more river trips—at least not as a guide. That's a young man's game, and I'm pushing forty-five. Mountain trails seem longer and steeper, and routine injuries take forever to heal. Minor viruses I used to shake off in two days now mutate into major sinus infections that make my head feel as if it's been squeezed into a fishbowl. I'm still a long way from the finish line, but I'm also equidistant from the brash thirty-year-old who ran across the Grand Canyon twice in a day.

*   *   *

This is my state of mind when, two weeks before the end of my twenty-third year in the classroom, the new superintendent calls me into his office, ostensibly for a friendly chat. A burly ex–football coach from Terra Haute, Indiana, Steve Walker has received mixed reviews in the faculty lounge, ranging from "he's a mover and shaker" to "he's a headhunter hell-bent on cleaning house."

Sitting in the waiting area outside Walker's office, I ask the one person who can give me the straight scoop: Deborah Rhinehart.

"How's he doing so far?"

Deb glances up from her computer just long enough to roll her eyes and smile. "He may look laid-back on the outside, but that guy's so busy he doesn't have time to wipe."

The first thing I notice upon entering Walker's office is the repositioning of the mammoth cherrywood desk. Instead of fronting the wall-size window, it's been moved into the corner, creating a well-defended triangle with the superintendent perched at its apex in a leather chair. The regal arrangement is at odds with his folksy, Will Rogers demeanor—sleepy brown eyes on a blocky if slightly sagging face. Unlike his predecessor, whose unruly stacks of documents and file folders created a sense of chaotic urgency, Walker's desk is stripped bare and freshly polished. The only thing blighting its glossy surface is a steaming mug of coffee.

After the standard handshake and niceties—have a seat; coffee? water then?—Walker settles his voluminous frame into what suddenly looks like a miniature chair.

"Well, Todd—it's all right if I call you Todd?"

I nod; he smiles. He's dressed like a super: pressed gray slacks, a purple shirt with a matching striped tie, a gray suit coat hanging on the rack.

"I got an elk tag for Six-A, but I'm still the new kid on the block here." He cups sun-tanned hands over a bulging belly. "Can you spare an old farm boy some advice?"

Internally I breathe a sigh of relief because, (1) I'm not in trouble, and (2) I'm not going to be asked to do anything substantial, like chair a district-wide committee or spearhead the annual United Way drive. So we talk hunting for an hour. I even draw a map showing the location of one of my old blinds. I'm about to stand up, shake hands, and hit the road when Walker's massive body tilts forward—dangerously so, like the *Titanic* listing. He exhales loudly, his linebacker shoulders collapsing.

"I know you're a great teacher and you love what you're doing in the classroom, but I really need someone to lead the charge with this new math program. We want to roll her out next fall, and the principals are getting a lot of pushback."

No surprise there. The new math books are big, unwieldy things with faddish, neon-blue covers that have already been purchased—against teacher protests!—thanks to a textbook adoption committee that was top-heavy with administrators.

"Todd," he says, "I'll get right to the point. I'd like you to be the new math and science supervisor for the district."

My first impulse is to laugh. I've never particularly liked administrators, and I certainly have no desire to become one.

"You're well respected in the district," Walker says. "You're a dynamite teacher—we all know that. But you're a great leader as well."

He mentions my work chairing the Secondary Science Curriculum Committee and the way I mobilized the community to support the Pond Project.

"You put this town on the map. You made this district a household name!"

Even though I know he's piling it on deep enough to bury me, I'm flattered.

My face and body language are saying, "Thanks but no thanks," but he's still selling. He sets his bifocals delicately on the desk, as if they're made of air.

"As a teacher," he says, "you impact—what? A hundred twenty, a hundred and thirty kids a year? But as an administrator, you'll impact thousands! Think about it: for every teacher you train and inspire and motivate, that's another hundred and fifty kids who'll reap the benefits. That's seventy-five-hundred kids a year who'll be getting a better education and a better shot at life because of your work behind the curtain."

I'm smiling, trying to be polite.

"Todd," he says, sensing the sale slipping through his fingers, "sometimes with people of your talent, you just have to sacrifice for the greater good. You're at a crossroads. You can continue to be a captain and a very good one, comfortable and successful in the classroom, or you can be a general and make history. We need you. What do you say? Will you join our team?"

I ask for twenty-four hours to think about it.

"Agreed," Walker says, smiling.

*   *   *

In the end, I don't need twenty-four hours and a sleepless night to make up my mind. For show, I'll wait until the next day to officially accept the position, but the decision's relatively easy, and it has nothing to do with relationships with my students or the kinetic energy of the classroom or the adrenal rush of teaching a mind-expanding lesson. It's got nothing to do with influencing hundreds of teachers who will influence thousands of students. It has nothing to do with making history. In the end, it comes down to simple mathematics.

As I'm leaving Walker's office, the superintendent plays his trump card. "Oh, and Todd? Did I mention this position makes about a third again your current salary?"

I stop.

Walker winks. "Just a little carrot," he says. "Otherwise none of us would ever leave the classroom."

"Good to know," I say as I saunter out the door, but once in private—I duck into the nearest men's room and gratefully find it vacant—I mentally calculate the numbers that will make my decision a no-brainer. I'm currently earning just over $40,000 a year. At the present rate, factoring in a modest salary step increase each year, by the time I retire my salary will be around $50,000. My annual pension, based on the average of my top three consecutive years of earnings, will be about 60 percent of that, or $30,000 a year.

Rough numbers, but they'll do for now. As a supervisor, I'd start at sixty grand a year and would retire making close to seventy, which would boost my annual pension to over $40,000. I've got my answer before I flush a urinal that doesn't need flushing. Mathematics. Economics. Money. Not gobs and gobs of it. Not the difference between owning two vacation homes or three. Just the difference between living or scrimping in my old age. The difference between taking an occasional Caribbean cruise or clipping discount coupons out of newspaper inserts to make ends meet.

NO MAN'S LAND

N ew job, new school year, and it takes me less than a day to acknowledge the obvious: I miss the back-to-school excitement and energy, where every young face is a fresh start, at least for the moment, and every new class full of promise, at least for the day.

Instead of standing in front of twenty-five slouching teenagers, I'm sitting at a desk in a honeycomb of claustrophobic cubicles in a Dilbert-land called "The Supervisors Center," wondering how I'm going to make a dent in the current state of science and math instruction without miming the nitpicking, browbeating trail bosses who preceded me. I share the second floor with five other supervisors, four program coordinators, and five secretaries. The ground floor belongs to the top administrators—the superintendent, two assistant supers, the business manager, the human resources director, and myriad secretaries and office aides.

As the year progresses, more and more I'll miss having daily contact with the students, and by Memorial Day I'll be aching for the good old days when I could submit final grades and be done for the summer. I'll miss the occasional snow days and the long vacations—two weeks in December, a week for spring break in March, and ten long, lovely weeks in the summer. (I work year-round now, with thirty vacation days to use at my discretion.) I'll miss the camaraderie of the faculty lounge much more than I'd expected—John Baxter's perpetual grousing, Wendy Wilson's juicy gossip, and Judy Macnamara's unbridled enthusiasm. I'll even miss Melvin Jackson's muggy voice over the intercom. And I'll miss that feeling of power you get commandeering your own classroom: captain of the ship, lord of the castle, pilot of the jumbo jet. But mostly I'll miss the whole notion of being a teacher, of standing at center stage each day and, for better or worse, impacting the lives and the futures of young students by the words I say, the things I do, the opinions I share, what I teach, and how I teach it. It's daunting and exhilarating, and I miss it deeply.

But there are some nice trade-offs. For instance: no more lesson planning, parent meetings, late-night grading marathons. No more report cards or hall passes or lunch, bus, or hall duty. No more eating on the run or torturing my bladder until the bell rings. No more chaperoning dances and after-school activities. I've got more autonomy, timewise and otherwise.

If I come to work a few minutes late, I'm not greeted by a cluster of surly teenagers waiting for me to unlock the door while the principal cuts me down with knife eyes. I've got standard work hours—eight a.m. to four p.m.—but I usually start at seven thirty and don't head home until six or seven, so if I roll in late one morning, no one calls the Timecard Police.

As a supervisor, I work until the job's done. Sounds easy, but I soon discover there's not one job but many, and there's no real end to them. The moment one project's completed—a curriculum written or a textbook adopted or a group of teachers trained—I have a dozen others in progress and more piling up. There's no end, just little end points. I work more hours in the long run, but flexibility's my reward: I can eat lunch at my desk or even pass an hour at a restaurant, anathema in the teaching world.

*   *   *

I'm pretty good at this new gig. I take new teachers under my wing, offering encouragement and showing them simple tricks of the trade that would have saved me hours of prep time as a rookie. I share my grading system, my discipline philosophy, even time-saving tips for taking daily attendance and writing report cards. Some teachers are receptive and grateful, while others tell me, in so many words, to buzz off. But I persevere, soliciting "Super Science Lessons" and "Marvelous Math Lessons" from my teachers and then organizing them by topic and grade level into classroom handbooks. And I get the new science curriculum written—or, more accurately, I organize and chair the committee and then rah-rah the team to get it done.

Overall, I'm enjoying my new job, except for two things. The first one is annoying, but the second is devastating, so I'll start with number one: a few resistant math and science teachers who want to continue using stone-age methodologies. Chief among them is a young fifth-year teacher who was originally hired to coach varsity wrestling and teach five sections of earth science—one prep, easy pickings. His name is Robert Brubaker, and our swords first cross when he refuses to serve on the Secondary Science Curriculum Committee, claiming "coach's immunity" from extracurricular activities.

That's not unusual—coaches have their hands full with after-school practices and games and not much monetary compensation to show for it. I get that.

What pops my cork is his response after I set up a mandatory training to introduce the new science curriculum. He's the only no-show. I send him an invitation to a makeup training, but once again he's AWOL. The next day, I visit his classroom after school as he's hastily erasing the scrawl from his whiteboard.

"You'd better talk fast," he says. "I've got to go."

"I thought wrestling season was over."

"I've got a meeting."

"All right, I'll make it quick. Why didn't you come to my training?"

Brubaker sets the eraser on the metal rail and turns around, squaring off with me like a bull elk preparing to defend his harem.

"I don't have to use your curriculum."

"It's not *my* curriculum," I explain. "It was developed by a committee representing the secondary schools. You could have been on the committee, but you chose not to—and that's fine. But this is the curriculum we're using. All of us." I sound like a robot, but I'm trying to be professional instead of telling him flat out that he's acting like an asshole.

Brubaker has a slightly out-of-whack mouth that translates into a permanent smirk. I want to reach out and wipe it off his face, but I know the score: athletic coaches are sacred in the district, especially if they're winning. He picks up a red marker, turns his back to me, and begins neatly printing an assignment on the whiteboard.

"You know," he says, "I don't have to do anything you say. You may be able to con the other teachers into doing your pet projects, or even intimidate them like you're trying to do now. But you know something"—he drops his writing hand and aims the red marker right between my eyes—"You have no authority over me. Zero. None."

I pause, debating my next move, and choose the high road, at least for now. "That curriculum's been approved by the school board," I say.

"Talk to my principal," Brubaker says. "I've gotta go." He grabs a backpack from his desk and blows by me into the hall, his voice trailing behind: "The door's locked, so pull it shut on your way out."

Brubaker's right. When I meet with his principal, Paul Weisman, he drops his shoulders apologetically and mumbles something about standing by his teacher. He doesn't appear to like the man any more than

I do, but Brubaker had just led a group of quasi-criminals and misfits nicknamed "The Dirty Dozen" to the state wrestling championship for the third consecutive year.

The win elicited positive local press and diverted attention from a massive demonstration in which over half the student body walked out of school at midday and marched to city hall to protest a new provision in the school dress code outlawing any gang-related attire, including ski caps. The next day, right before the final lunch bell, in a masterpiece of choreography, more than nine hundred students removed ski caps of various colors from their coats, backpacks, and book bags, pulled them over their heads, and made another mass exodus into the streets while poor Weisman impotently tried to deter them with a megaphone: "Students, you need to return to class… there will be serious consequences if you don't return to class right now… Students…"

*   *   *

Ironically, a month after my showdown with Brubaker, he's promoted to assistant principal, and a month after that, Paul Weisman is fired and Brubaker becomes his interim replacement. It's a role he will perfect over the next six years as he plays second fiddle to a cavalcade of principals—doomed experiments, in retrospect, some bold but tragically flawed, others comically incompetent. They have very different leadership styles and personalities but share one attribute: they're short-timers. None lasts more than two years, and some don't survive two months.

Every time one resigns or is fired, Robert Brubaker, the ever-faithful assistant, fills in as interim principal and later, when the job is posted, applies for the vacancy. Each time, he receives a conciliatory phone call from the superintendent, reassuring him that there were so many great applicants for the job, many of them—including Brubaker, of course— more than worthy of the position, which made it all the more difficult to make a decision. However, unfortunately, in the end… I'm so sorry.

Brubaker persists, and his fifth trip to the plate, he finally hits a home run (sort of), no thanks to me. For some reason, Superintendent Walker adds me to the selection committee. Despite my personal feelings about Brubaker, I try to remain objective, but after reviewing the files of fifty-three applicants, I find Brubaker sorely lacking and don't include him among my top ten candidates to be interviewed. I'm in the minority, and the other committee members want to know why.

"He's got no vision," I say. "He has no idea where he wants to take that school and how he'd get it there—especially compared to the other candidates. We can interview him, but it's a waste of his time and ours."

"But he's been assistant principal for like forever!" one committee member exclaims.

"This is the fifth time he's interviewed!"

"It would be so embarrassing if we turned him down again."

"An insult, I think."

I sit with my chin propped on joined fists, elbows forming an apex on the giant table in the windowless room, patiently listening as the others state their case for Brubaker. When the last one finishes, I take a long gulp of bottled water, set the container down, and say, "Why don't we get a bunch of poker chips."

"Poker chips? Why do we need—"

"I'll tell you why. We'll write a number on each one, one to fifty-three. Then we'll assign a number to each applicant. We'll dump the fifty-three chips into a hat and then we'll each pick out a chip and those will be the nine we interview. Don, you're the committee chair, so you can pick two chips and that'll give us an even ten, if you want that many."

There are a few smiles but mostly stern, reprimanding faces, especially from Pete Hawthorne.

"Come on, get serious," he says. "We've got a job to do here."

"Then let's do it right. Are we hiring a principal or choosing the prom queen?"

The debate seesaws back and forth between me and the other eight, but ultimately I lose the show-of-hands vote. Brubaker gets his interview and, by luck of the draw, I get to ask the most revealing question on the sheet: "Under your leadership, what will Ponderosa High School look like ten years from now?"

Brubaker's mouth opens, a giant hole waiting for him to stick his foot into it. After a minute of silence that seems like an hour, he offers up a cliché-ridden response about not fixing what ain't broken and keeping the machine tuned and well-oiled. Not much to arouse the snoozing troops there; not much to hang a war cry on.

The would-be emperor has been exposed in all his nakedness, and I assume this will disqualify him, but the other committee members disagree.

"I think he's steady." Hawthorne says, setting his pen on the table with finality.

"And proven," says another.

"Loyal," says a third.

I place my palms flat on the table, capitulating: "Well, he can probably play fetch, too, but do you really want him as your principal?"

Once again, I'm outvoted.

*   *   *

Selection committee proceedings are supposed to remain confidential, but somehow (via loose lips at a cocktail party or pillow talk—Hawthorne likes to make the rounds) juicy tidbits always filter into the district mainstream. In this case, the tidbit is my vehement objection to hiring Brubaker as principal.

By the time the rumors have traveled through the ranks, depending on who's telling the tale and to whom, I'm being portrayed as everything from a sleep-deprived martyr (think Jimmy Stewart in *Mr. Smith Goes to Washington*) valiantly but vainly filibustering against a mediocre candidate to a pulpit-pounding lunatic with a sociopathic vendetta against an aspiring administrator. Brubaker, I'm sure, gets an earful of the latter version.

None of which bothers me much at the time—there's no love lost between me and Brubaker, and I've got no control over the district gossips. In truth, I may even take a little pleasure in knowing my objections have gone public. And there's no question that I relish the fact that, as a principal, Brubaker has absolutely no authority over me—zero, none—but I have quite a bit of sway over his school's math and science programs. He needs to play nice, at least for now.

COSMIC JUSTICE

Working with a couple deadbeat teachers like Brubaker is irritating but manageable. However, the second thing I don't like about my new job cuts much deeper, and it has to do with the Pond Project. As an administrator, I'm no longer involved except as a "facilitator," which means I can only offer advice without intruding. This has been frustrating because my replacement at the junior high, an earnest young man from back East named Carson Stubblefield, doesn't buy into "the whole pond thing" (his words). He's more of a traditional prep-school teacher, who tells me frankly that he can't possibly cover all the material in the textbook if he's dragging his kids outside three or four days a week to "pull weeds and play in the dirt."

His first year, he goes through the motions, probably to keep me off his back, but by year two he's relegated the Pond Project to a once-a-month activity, and by the end of year three it's discontinued altogether. Trash appears at the far end of the pond and proliferates until it looks like a dumping ground. The word is out: the pond is back in the junkyard business. For several weekends, I take volunteer groups consisting of former students to tidy things up, but it seems hopeless. We can't keep up with the volume of rubbish that's being deposited daily on the north end.

Coincidentally about this time, the Arizona Department of Education launches a new campaign to emphasize instruction in the sciences. All students in grades 3, 5, 9, and 11 are given a standardized, multiple-choice test measuring basic skills in physical science, earth science, space science, and life science. On average, Carson Stubblefield's ninth graders score above the 70th percentile on all four sub-tests, the highest grade-level performance in the state. Shortly after, Stubblefield is named Arizona Science Teacher of the Year. He's a phenom now, untouchable and intractable. Who needs a damn Pond Project to teach science?

By my fifth year as a supervisor, the pond has gone to rack and ruin. Invasive plants, especially the notorious field bindweed, choke out the native species. The front end of the fishing dock sags into the water. After five hard winters without maintenance, the archeological dig and the other learning stations are barely recognizable, hidden in a weedy, jungled mess. A thick, green membrane of scum coats large sections of the pond. Meanwhile, Melvin Jackson sits back watching all this happen— and I swear I will never forgive him for it. Several times, I try to intervene, but as always, Jackson sides with his teacher—ironically, one of the traits I most admired about him when I was playing on *his* team.

On several occasions, Jackson and I exchange heated words, but always in private. Then one conversation spins out of control when he tells me, once again, the pond is no longer my baby.

"Todd, I love you for what you did. I love you and I'll always love you for that, but..."

When I protest, he reminds me that *I* was the one who chose to be an administrator; *I* was the one who abandoned the pond, not vice versa.

"You've got to let go and move on, son."

It's like watching him kill my only surviving child right before my eyes, and for some reason I think he's enjoying it. I blow up, and the fallout spills into the main office, where the two of us engage in a shouting match in front of horrified parents, students, and staff.

Afterward, I'm lucky to keep my job, but the formal reprimand that allows me to remain employed stipulates conditional banishment from the junior high school. I will only be allowed on campus with Melvin Jackson's pre-approval. I will have to sign in at the receptionist's desk and state where I'm going and who I will be interacting with and why. And under no circumstances will I be permitted to go outside anywhere near the pond. Ever.

For the next three years, I avoid the junior high altogether. If I need to train secondary science or math teachers, we meet at the Supervisors Center or another neutral site. People look at me differently now. They think I'm a smoking volcano, and they're probably right.

*   *   *

At the end of my eighth year as a supervisor, Superintendent Walker solemnly announces that an internal audit of the Business Office has revealed an accounting error resulting in a three-million-dollar budget shortfall. Every school and department in the district will have to tighten their belt to make up for the deficit, but none more so than the Supervisors Center, where two secretaries, all four program coordinators, and three supervisors will be axed, including me.

In public I act like it's no big deal, but privately I'm sweating bullets. The good news—for me at least—is that I've got thirty-one years of seniority, so I won't be tossed out on the street. I'll be transferred into a teaching position vacated by some poor first- or second-year teacher, who will get canned instead. I'll also be fifty-two, two years from retirement, and my pension will be based on my top salary for three consecutive years as a supervisor—so I can weather the pay cut of moving back to the classroom. But after almost a decade in the administrative ranks, it's a transition I'm not sure I can make. Am I really ready, willing, and able to do teenagers again? All that high hormonal drama and everything that comes with it: prepping lessons, grading papers, faculty and committee meetings, bus duty, lunch duty, parent conferences? I get PTSD just thinking about it.

The *coup de grace* is that I'm assigned to fill the only vacant science and math position in the district, which just happens to be at Ponderosa High—Robert Brubaker's school. It's either that or hit the bricks.

I could go hat in hand to Melvin Jackson and beg him to pull some strings to get me back to the junior high to resurrect the Pond Project, but my pride won't allow it. Besides, he's got his new golden boy now.

* * *

At least Brubaker's honest about my reversal of fortune, and his. The week before school starts, I stop by the main office at the high school to pick up my classroom keys from the receptionist. I'd hoped for a quick grab-and-go, but as I approach the receptionist's counter, Brubaker's voice calls through his open doorway.

"Mr. Hunter, you have a minute?"

I trudge into his office, where he's perched behind a massive desk half-buried under stacks of documents and file folders, three paper weights, and two overflowing wire in/out baskets.

"Close the door, please," he says, and I do.

"Have a seat." He gestures to a spartan-looking, hard-back chair stationed directly in front of him. As I sit down, he settles into his swivel chair, plucks a random document off his desk, and begins skimming it, signaling that he's a very busy man now and doesn't have time to waste on small fish like me, but nevertheless—sigh!—here we are. He continues reading for a good half minute before glancing up, acting surprised, as if he's just remembered I'm there.

"I just want you to know," he says, "that I don't want you here anymore than you want to be here."

His jowls suddenly look bloated, like a little reptile that puffs up its body to look more formidable so it won't be swallowed whole by a Komodo dragon.

"Fair enough. Can I have my keys?"

Apparently a simple declaration of hate isn't sufficient. Brubaker feels compelled to elaborate, in case I didn't get the message. "I don't like you," he says. "I don't like your sense of humor, I don't like your smart-ass anecdotes, and I don't like your uppity sense of superiority—your sense of… of… *entitlement!*"

He holds out a ring with two keys dangling from it, one to enter the building and the other to unlock my classroom, and waits for me to take it and quietly disappear. That is exactly what I should do, but once again, my uppity sense of entitlement gets the best of me.

"Bob, let me tell you something about people like you. You're like the guy who takes fruit on a backpacking trip, but he doesn't share it with anyone. And do you know what happens to that fruit after two or three days if he doesn't share it? It goes rotten. Something to think about."

With my thumb and forefinger, I gently tweezer the keys and remove them from Brubaker's hand. He watches my leisurely exit, no doubt smiling. I've just played a pair of threes, and he's holding four aces. But the game's just beginning.

To blow off steam, I head to the animal shelter. I lost Milo almost a year ago, and the silence in my house has grown progressively more deafening. Up until now I've managed to ignore it. Walking rows of cages stinking of animal feces and cleansing chemicals, I see the forlorn faces of abandoned dogs that look pretty much the way I'm feeling. Then I spot a frisky terrier-mix pup. "Duchess" quickly becomes the new love of my life.

BACK IN THE SADDLE

BIOLOGY 1

This class is designed to prepare students who might be interested in college entrance. Although many students might not major in science in college, biology is a lab science required at Arizona's three state universities. For that reason, we are asking for some extra work and responsibilities from our students.

This fall, we are working on local environmental materials that may not be found in the printed text. The outdoors has been our classroom and the ecology here in northern Arizona is the emphasis of our curriculum. This semester, we are studying life zones and plants associations. During the next few weeks, we will look at the major animals that use those associations.

As the weather turns cold, our labs will be indoors, where our job will be to investigate cells as they relate to the major plant kingdoms.
The grading system in this class consists of mastering cognitive material needed to understand our outside emphasis, as well as taking the material outside the classroom and into our daily lives. Many of our projects include a student's home life. We enjoy input from parents, so please don't hesitate to contact us regarding the daily class operation, as well as our long-term direction.

Todd Hunter, Biology Teacher

Fortunately, my classroom is located on the second floor of a renovated wing of the school, far from the snooping eyes of Robert Brubaker. Barring a fire or student riot, I could do just about anything in that room—show movies all day, peddle drugs—and Brubaker would be none the wiser. Also on the upside, my class sizes are manageable, ranging from twenty-three to twenty-five students. On the downside, in addition to three sections of biology, I'm also teaching a section each of chemistry and geometry. Three preps—Brubaker's first salvo.

For the most part, my transition back into the classroom goes smoothly. I no longer have the Pond Project—and I don't have the ambition or the energy to embark on another epic, cast-of-thousands undertaking at this stage of the game—but I try to keep my classes interesting, with outdoor activities and field trips. Over the years, I've stockpiled enough creative lessons to house a library, so preparation—at least for biology— is minimal. My workaday world has shrunk to a thirty- by fifty-foot room, but no more long, after-school trainings or late-night school board meetings; no more fretting over whether or not the math and science teachers have received their textbooks in time and are using them consistently; no more ponderous paperwork or grant-writing or report-making; no more refereeing or babysitting grown-ups; in short, no more administrative headaches.

And the biggest bonus: by the end of my first year back at the teacher's desk, I'll be eligible for full retirement. If I've got enough fuel in the tank to teach another three years, I'll have thirty-five service years and the maximum retirement benefit. And I'll only be fifty-six, with plenty of tread on my tires, God willing.

Four more years. That's the plan, but if at any time I get tired of the routine or Brubaker yanks my chain a bit too hard or my students get mouthy or I wake up one morning and say, "To hell with it! I'm done! I'm sailing to Bora-Bora," I can toss my keys on Brubaker's desk and walk out the door. There's something consoling in that.

*　*　*

Right now, I'm in it for the long haul, mainly because of the biggest upside to returning to the classroom: the kids. I realize this as the latest crop of summer-tanned students straggle into my first-period class and a Navajo girl with a pink stripe glowing down the center of her raven hair approaches me.

"My father says to say hello," she says.

"What's your name?"

Her smile summons up a pair of heartbreaking dimples. "Felicia Goldtooth," she says.

"Jimmy's daughter!"

She nods. "He told me to mind my p's and q's."

"Good advice. What's your dad doing these days?"

"He works at the tire shop on Paradise Road."

The news saddens me, but I try not to show it. Thirty-two years ago, Jimmy was a rising young star, the kid who would defy the odds and cure cancer or male-pattern baldness. I hope he's a manager or a supervisor, something that requires him to use that gifted brain.

"I think about your dad every day."

Felicia beams. "He says you're the best!"

"Tell him the check's in the mail."

Felicia's eyebrows squiggle. She's missed the joke.

"I pay him for those compliments."

"Oh," she says, smiling awkwardly. "I get it now."

*   *   *

The kids are all right. I've watched too many pass through the gauntlet to be fazed by frills in fashion or language. Hippies, goths, skaters, stoners, punk-rock wannabes, gang-bangers, jocks, preppies—kids masquerading in all kinds of disguises to grab attention in one way or another. The current shockers are nose rings, tongue rings, and tattoos on the face, the arms, the ankles, maybe the ass for all I know. The kids talk about bytes and video games and cyberspace. They carry pagers the size of cigarette packs in their hip pockets, and a few even have portable phones—"cell phones," they call them.

I gave up trying to keep pace with teenage trends years ago. I figure some things never go out of style: the scientific process; good teaching; the ability to think, create, experiment, analyze, synthesize. But within a few days, I realize something's different now. I'm missing the *a-ha!* moments—mouths opening with wonder, eyes lighting up with delight. My jokes clank like bad rim shots, and days that used to speed by now limp along on crutches. I've spent more time clock-watching the first week of school than I had in my previous two decades in the classroom.

I'm tempted to blame the students—they're smart enough, but dispassionate and lethargic about learning, with zilch curiosity or sense of humor—but I'm afraid I'll morph into a frumpy old fart like John Baxter: "I provide the information; it's the students' responsibility to learn it. If they don't, it's their fault." Classroom sin number one: blame the students for your ineptitude.

At the end of week three, I have a come-to-Jesus moment with myself. The simple truth is, deep down, I don't want to be here. I'm still angry at Steve Walker for zapping the supervisory position he'd all but begged me to accept. I'm rankled at Brubaker for his full-frontal attack on my character. And I want to deep fry Melvin Jackson's eyeballs for standing idly by while my brainchild died on the vine. As much as I've tried to leave those toxic thoughts in the hallway or in the outhouse where they belong, they still shadow me into my classroom. In particular, I'm in no mood for lukewarm bodies that do not under any circumstances want to be in school and obnoxiously announce the fact, verbally and via their body language, slouching in their desk chairs, hiding behind their hair, loudly smacking gum they aren't actually chewing, or, worst of all, trying to infect the rest of the class with their drooling indifference.

This is the case in my third-period class, where a girl who wears her jet-black hair in a pageboy likes to amuse her blonde, blue-jeaned sidekick by grunting, giggling, and intermittently grieving aloud: "This is so boring!" As I introduce my lesson on mitochondria, she lays her head sideways on her desk and begins snoring loudly. I stop, pick something off my desk, walk to the back of the class, and look down at her, waiting while the guffaws and giggles she's incited simmer down to hushed suspense.

After several moments of silence, she gazes up at me. "Uh, good night," she says and closes her eyes.

Laughter roller-coasters through the classroom.

I calmly wait for the chuckles to subside, then say softly: "Veronica, wake up. I have something to tell you."

Yawning, she stretches her arms like a lazy leopard. "Yeah?"

"Do you want out of this class?" My voice is gentle, grandfatherly.

She looks up curiously, and I hand her a hall pass, a block of wood cut in the shape of a key. I raise my fist, slowly curling and uncurling my fingers. "Bye-bye," I say.

It takes her a moment, but then she catches on. "Where do you want me to go?" she asks.

"Anywhere you want, Veronica."

"My name's not Veronica."

"Well, whatever your name is, go wherever you want to go—just stay out of my class." I smile when I say it, my voice never deviating from that soft, fireside tone.

First she sneers, then she scowls, and then she plucks her black bag off her desk and saunters out the door. "Screw you!" she snarls.

"Go anywhere you want, Veronica!" I call after her. Half the class is laughing and the other half whispering insurrection on behalf of their exiled friend. I remove my eyeglasses, blow on the lenses, and wipe them with a Kleenex. "Well," I say, scanning the rows, "anyone else want to take an F and check out?" I lock eyes with the blue-jeaned blonde. "What about you, Betty?"

"My name's not Betty," she says.

"Any takers? Last call! Going once, going twice?" Twenty-four teenagers stare at me like dumbfounded sheep. "All right then, let's get to work."

I don't encounter any more trouble, at least for the rest of the period, but at the end of the day, Brubaker's booming voice invades my classroom via the intercom: "Mr. Hunter, can I see you in my office." A pause, then with heat: "*Now!*"

* * *

Brubaker must be having a piss-poor day too. He doesn't even invite me to take a seat in the hard-back visitor's chair before unloading on me.

"What do you think you're doing, throwing a student out of class?" He's standing behind his gargantuan desk, hands on hips, the football coach chewing out his errant left tackle.

"My job," I say.

"You can't do that," he says. "You can't just kick a kid out of class."

I laugh. "Maybe I can't, but I did."

"You could get sued for that, you know."

"I'll take my chances," I say. "Anything else?"

Brubaker's bossy frame suddenly collapses into his padded swivel chair, legs splayed, head drooping, the fallen giant sulking in his corner. "Oh, shit," he mutters, and for a moment, I almost feel sorry for him. School administration can suck the living daylights out of you in a day.

He reaches for a yellow, legal-size tablet, grabs a pen out of the miniature Arizona Cardinals football helmet on his desk, and jots down the date. With a Paleolithic blend of grunt and sigh, he says, "Tell me what happened."

* * *

Two days later, Veronica trudges into class with an apology. It's half-hearted, but it's the best she can do. I've always been an advocate for second chances. She and Betty turn out to be fairly good students when they apply themselves, both earning solid B's in the course.

I'm less tolerant toward students who have been lavishly blessed with money or brains (or, as in Gabe Bronson's case, both) and choose to waste those gifts. Exceptionally bright, Gabe is also an arrogant lone wolf who objects to my unorthodox grading system in which exams and quizzes only count for 30 percent of the final grade. The rest is all touchy-feely Sesame Street stuff (except Gabe doesn't call it "stuff"): how well do I work with my classmates (10 percent), my attitude (20 percent), class participation (10 percent), class projects (20 percent), and a kiss-ass letter (his words) to the teacher, describing all the wonderful things you learned in class (10 percent).

I've been to this rodeo many times before with other Gabes of various sizes and persuasions. I don't mind discussing my grading policy publicly in front of the entire class or privately after school, but not publicly and belligerently as I'm passing out five-week progress reports.

"This sucks!" Gabe hisses as he slams the half-sheet of paper on his desk.

"Do you have a question, Mr. Bronson?" I ask.

To the novice, Gabe cuts an intimidating figure: a tall, bulky young man who shaves his pumpkin head to the skin and wears a silver-spiked dog collar around his throat. "I've gotten an A on every test and every quiz, and I'm getting a D! How's that fair?"

I briefly review the grading criteria, which evokes from Gabe a louder and more forceful, "Well that sucks! It really sucks! Half of this doesn't have squat to do with biology!"

A third of the class—mostly those who have aced their exams and would like them weighted more heavily—look sympathetic; the other two-thirds are squirming: my "multiple indicators" grading system has rescued a few of them from a semester-long sentence to the F list.

"There's a lot more to science and biology than tests and quizzes," I explain. "There's the ability to work with your colleagues, and—"

"Oh, bullshit!" Gabe shouts. "This is all bullshit!" He crushes the grade report into a ball and pitches it across the room. "You're such a freaking fascist!"

That's the wrong thing for Gabe to say to me: not "bullshit," which qualifies him for a trip to the principal's office but in the larger scheme of things is peanuts; typical fallout from a petulant teenager. It's the other word.

*   *   *

After my sophomore year of college, I took the summer off to travel around Europe on a shoestring. This was the mid-sixties, when the former Soviet Union controlled a fourth of Germany and the city of Berlin was divided by a wall topped with coils of razor-sharp concertina wire and patrolled from intermittent towers by armed guards. I'd traveled to the east side of the city, the Soviet side. After visiting all the government-sanctioned sites, I said to my amicable German guide—a proper and congenial fellow who looked like an old Swiss watchmaker—"This is great! Really interesting. But I'd like to see two more things: a church and a library." I said this with a little salsa. It was a challenge.

The guide nodded formally, like a man accepting an invitation to a duel.

He led me to an old stone building with a jagged peak on top, the remnants of a cross. Sheets of plywood had been nailed over the doors and windows. From a distance, the building looked like a face that had been blinded, gagged, and bandaged. The guide hesitated a moment before prying off the two sheets of plywood blocking the front doorway. I followed him in, stepping quietly and carefully through the wreckage: broken pieces of plaster, tipped altars, shattered glass, rows of crippled pews on cracked tiles; faded frescoes of Christ and his apostles, so riddled with bullets and graffiti that they looked like deformed dot-to-dot portrait puzzles.

Crossing through the nave into the transept, we stood for several moments, taking in a silence that was once holy.

What happened next was like the sudden lunge or the flashing knife blade and subsequent scream at the most intense moment of a horror movie, except the hair-raising culprit wasn't a serial killer but a single metallic click that echoed through the vaulted chamber like a gunshot. I jumped, but only slightly, then turned and saw a young soldier, a slender blond who without the military uniform would have made a perfect propaganda photo to promote Bavarian tourism. With the uniform, he looked like a poster child for Hitler's Youth, except his cap and shoulders bore the blood-red star of the Soviet Union. The loud click belonged to the rifle he had leveled fifteen feet from my face.

He was speaking in German, not loudly but firmly, and he was speaking to me, not my guide. My hands had gone up instinctively and remained there, even as my guide instructed me to leave quietly, now, which I did. Later, outside, when I asked what the uniformed young man had said, my guide hesitated. "Said?"

"Yes, what did the soldier say?"

"He said, 'I am eighteen years old and I do not want to kill you, but if you do not leave here right now, those are my orders, and I have to follow them.'"

*   *   *

Three and a half decades later, I turn to Gabe and speak to the young punk loudmouth in the same soft but firm voice of that Soviet soldier:

"Do you know what a fascist is? Because if you don't, we'll look it up together and you can stay in my class. But if you do know, then you're outta here!"

But Gabe has already driven off the cliff. "Well I do!" he snaps.

"You're outta here."

"But I'm getting A's on all my tests!"

"So what? You're outta here."

It's no surprise when, ten minutes later, Brubaker's voice interrupts over the intercom. "Mr. Hunter, come see me after school."

When I enter his office at three thirty, Brubaker doesn't stand, he doesn't extend his hand, he doesn't offer me a seat in a Spartan chair, and he certainly doesn't offer me a bottle of pure Rocky Mountain spring water from his mini-fridge. He tells me to be at school at seven thirty tomorrow morning for a meeting with Gabe Bronson's father.

"I won't be there," I say, "but my lawyer will."

"What are you talking about?"

"Well, Bob, it's like getting my transmission fixed. If my transmission's broken and I tear into it, it won't get fixed right. So I take it to a transmission shop. I want this thing with Gabe fixed, so I'm going to send my attorney tomorrow to fix it. Anything else?"

Brubaker sits at his desk, head down, his forefingers rubbing his temples.

"I didn't think so," I say.

*   *   *

For me, it's another brash exit and another long night wondering what the hell's going to happen tomorrow, because I'm 99 percent bluster and I know it. I don't have an attorney, and I'm not going to hire one—not at this stage of the game, anyway—but I'm not going to eat crow in front of Brubaker either. And no way am I going to apologize to the parents of an obnoxious, back-talking, entitled brat.

Fortunately for me, Brubaker's hanging onto his job by a thread. The latest debacle to hit the papers is a hazing incident involving the football team. Allegedly the equipment manager, a freshman special ed student, was roughed up by several players, making for an embarrassing front-page headline. Brubaker can't afford to call my bluff and lose, so he calls me at home instead. I've got caller I.D., so I don't answer, but I smile smugly as my nemesis leaves a message on the machine: "Mr. Hunter, I just wanted to let you know you don't need to come to the meeting tomorrow morning. Gabe will be coming to class, but he won't make any more trouble. He'd stopped taking his meds for a few days, if you need an explanation. We can talk more later."

"No, we can't, Bob," I say to the machine.

That night I sleep like a young man in the arms of his first love.

* * *

Gabe returns to class and is fine for about three weeks. Then he goes off track again. This time it's over a bad grade on a project he did solo when he was supposed to work as a team. When I return Gabe's report, placing it upside down on his desk so he has to turn back the corner to see the grade (a bright red C+), he flings the report across the room, pages fluttering like a wounded bird.

"I'm going to freaking shoot you!" he yells.

I stop distributing projects and stroll across the room until I'm standing over Gabe's desk. "What did you say?"

Gabe stands up—a brawny boy who could have played defensive tackle on the football team if he'd had an ounce of interest. He aims his index finger at my mouth, pulls the imaginary trigger, and says, "I'm going to shoot you. POW! You're dead."

"Come with me," I say and grab him by the arm. When he resists, I give him a good, hard yank. (A move like that today would probably land me in jail, but the world was more rough-and-tumble at the turn of the millennium.) I hustle Gabe out into the hall, poking my head into the room next door: "Dave, keep an eye on my class for me, please. We've got a date with the police."

"Police?" Gabe Bronson says. "We don't need no police!"

I drag him down the hall and into the main office, past the receptionist and Brubaker's secretary and two astonished counselors, finally depositing him in Brubaker's office, where the principal has the phone cradled between his jaw and shoulder as he scribbles on one of his infamous legal-size tablets. He looks up, visibly perturbed. "Steve, I've got a live one here," he whispers into the phone. "I'll call you right back."

I don't wait for him to hang up.

"This kid says he's going to shoot me," I say, "so I'm going to press charges."

Brubaker tells Gabe to wait outside for a few moments, then closes the door. "Why are you doing this, Todd? We can handle this in house."

"It's against the law for a student or a parent to threaten a teacher."

"I know, I know."

Then I unleash: "Why are you so damn obsessed with protecting this kid? To keep your enrollment numbers up? To get that forty-five-hundred dollars from the state? Is it money? I don't get it. How many times has this kid been suspended? How many more fire alarms does he have to pull? How many more windows does he have to break? Or are you going to just keep looking the other way until he does something really stupid and hurts somebody really bad?"

Brubaker runs a finger under his mustache and adjusts his Clark Kent glasses, but it's obvious no Superman is going to emerge from underneath his white shirt and tie.

Brubaker sighs. He looks exhausted, like a blow-up toy that's swiftly losing air. "Captain Walters from the police department says he wants this kid. He's been dealing drugs."

"Ask Captain Walters if he's eighteen."

Brubaker turns gray. "I'll call him back and check," he says. "He also said once they get him to the station they're going to strip search him."

"So? What's that got to do with me?"

"Just work with me this once, OK? We've got bigger fish to fry here."

"Your fish or mine?"

"Todd. Please?"

And for once I back down. Gabe is arrested that afternoon, not for threatening me but for drug trafficking. I never see him again in my classroom or at school. And I never lose a night's sleep over it. I believe in second, third, and even fourth chances, to a point. Kids selling drugs to kids? That crosses the line. Infection. Contagion. Cancer. Get rid of it.

*   *   *

My involuntary return to teaching is marred by incidents like this. I'd had my fair share of disciplinary issues in the past, but this is getting out of hand. A visit to Brubaker's office seems like a daily event. His hard-back guest chair has become a default friend.

More stuff, more folly. At midyear the superintendent announces another budget shortfall and Brubaker hits the panic button, instituting a school-wide paper-rationing policy. When I enter the copy room and ask Liz Machado, the office aide, for five sheets of paper, she backs away as if I've just asked for the keys to the money vault. Liz shakes her head vigorously: "I'm sorry, Mr. Hunter, but Mr. Brubaker says we're on a strict paper budget. We can only photocopy tests and quizzes."

I smile. "Liz, if I type up a test and give it to you, what will you do with it? You'll xerox it, right? So look at this." I hold up an invisible sheet of eight-and-a-half-by-eleven: "Now, you see this? This is my one-page exam. I put it on the Xerox machine like this…"

I lift the lid, place the imaginary exam on the glass, close the lid, and push the start button. The machine hums briefly and deposits a blank sheet of paper in the hopper.

"And—abracadabra!" I snatch the sheet of paper and wave it triumphantly. "There! A blank sheet of paper, just like I'd asked for in the first place! Now, just do that four more times and everybody's happy."

Liz is staring at the coffee stains on the industrial carpet. Timidly, she says, "But you asked for five sheets, Mr. Hunter."

I answer with a big, condescending smile. "Pretend it's a five-page exam."

I'm shooting the messenger, and I know it. Liz is in tears and two other aides are watching in shock. What the hell's wrong with me? Typically I treat the secretaries and office staff like royalty, bringing them treats on Halloween and chocolate hearts on Valentine's Day. I want to think this is an aberration, but episodes like this seem to be accumulating.

*   *   *

My return to the classroom isn't what I'd expected, or maybe I'd just forgotten the little pieces of shit sprinkled on the sunshine. Yes, Brubaker's a pain in the butt and the budget's always on the brink and there are some crazy parents and some sassy kids, but what's new? Welcome to public education! And for every one of them, I've got a hundred gems— kids who want to learn or are at least receptive enough to let me open up the lid and stir their brain a bit. And every once in a while, a kid like Janie Hawkins walks into the classroom, reminding me why I stubbornly remain in this profession.

An African-American girl who's five feet tall on tiptoes, she approaches me at the end of class in the second week of the spring semester, after the other students have exited, and says in a timid whisper: "Mr. Hunter, can I talk to you?"

I set down my dry-erase marker and turn away from the whiteboard. "Sure, Janie, what's up?"

She's staring down at the no-name sneakers she probably bought discount at Walmart. She wears faded jeans and a baggy sweatshirt with a hood. "Mr. Hunter, I really like your class," she says, "but I think I'm going to have to drop out."

I almost laugh. "Why, Janie? You're doing great. You aced the first test."

"I know, Mr. Hunter, but I gotta drop out because we have six field trips in this class and you said we gotta do all six of them."

"Yes, that's right. Is there some reason why you can't attend the field trips?"

Janie looks at me as if she's ordering a strawberry shake and says, "It's because I've got a baby at home. My mother works nights and sleeps during the day, so she can't watch my little girl."

I'm stumped and speechless. Janie's seventeen years old, although she looks even younger.

"How old is your baby?"

"Two years and two months," she says.

The mental math is swift and painful.

"You're not dropping out," I say.

"But I can't do those field trips," she says. "I take three classes in the morning and then I go home at lunch. Take care of my girl."

"Janie, you need this class to graduate."

"Yes, sir, I do," she says. "But I can't do those field trips."

"We'll work something out. OK? You just stay in school."

"Yes, sir, Mr. Hunter."

That afternoon I call Frank Waterson, the transportation director at the bus barn and an avid bow-hunter. We talk shop a bit—did you get drawn for elk this year? what unit? how'd you do?—and then without naming names I explain Janie's unusual circumstances.

"I think we can bend the rules a bit here," Frank says.

"You're awesome, Frank! I owe you, buddy."

The next day I tell Janie, with a caveat: "You know, this will only work if I tell the whole class."

"Yes, sir. I know that," Janie says.

I tell her not to come to class today—go to the library or something.

She nods solemnly. "Yes, sir, Mr. Hunter."

After the tardy bell rings and the students have plopped into their seats, I stand before them like an orator with stage fright. "We've got a girl who's doing really well in class," I say, "but she can't go on the field trips unless she brings her baby along. If you want to stop this right now, go tell the principal and that'll be the end of it. Otherwise, that little baby will be joining us on our field trips. What do you think? It has to be unanimous. How many say yes?"

Every student in my classroom raises a hand, some quite enthusiastically. Someone shouts: "Let's do it, Mr. Hunter!" I want to reach out and hug every last one of them. Even factoring in the many miracles of the Pond Project, I've never felt so proud as a teacher.

* * *

Janie and her baby attend every field trip, and the other students—especially the girls, but some of the guys too—fawn over that child as if she were their own. Janie finishes the class and graduates that spring. The last day of school, she gives me a thank-you card and a kiss on the cheek.

"Thank you, Mr. Hunter," she says, "for saving my life."

I blush. "Hardly," I say, "but I'll take whatever compliments I can get, however far-fetched. So what now?"

A glowing smile fills the lower half of her coffee-colored face. "College!" she says. "I got accepted at ASU!"

"That's great! You're going to be a Sun Devil! What are you going to major in?"

"Business administration."

"Super! They've got a good program for that. You're going to do great! You stay in touch."

"I will, Mr. Hunter. I promise!"

Then she twirls around like a little girl and darts out the door shouting gleefully, arms waving in the air. For a moment, I think she might start skipping down the hall. Six years later I'll receive a postcard featuring the Marriott Hotel in Hong Kong, where she's working as director of human resources.

* * *

That afternoon I go to Dr. Moss for a routine checkup. He's a grouchy old bear who's been monitoring my health for over thirty years. He's also prone to random philosophical meanderings, one of which he delivers while assessing the status of my lungs through a stethoscope.

"As a profession, medicine is kind of a downer," he says. "We're always dealing with death. People come to me because they're sick and they're going downhill. We deal with the present, which will soon be the past. But guys like you—teachers—you deal with life; you deal with the future."

I'm imagining a group photo of the three-thousand-odd teenagers I've taught over the years, with Janie Hawkins's face front and center smiling her half-moon smile, when I reply, "Yes, Dr. Moss, that's true. That's absolutely true."

REUNION

The rows of padded chairs are filling quickly as I lean into the podium and tap the microphone, inciting a trio of amplified echoes. The technology's cooperating—always a good sign. I give a thumbs-up to the uniformed woman in the back, who nods and disappears.

They've scheduled me in a mid-size conference room, which should be more than adequate given the ho-hum title of the presentation: "How to Energize Your Students AND Teach the State Standards." Its original title—"How to Teach the State Standards Without Putting Yourself and Your Students in a Level-Three Coma"—had been edited by the reps at the Department of Education to, in their words, "convey a more positive message about research-based, standards-driven education."

Those are the buzzwords my colleagues and I have been forced to ingest and digest, although I think the end product is mostly glorified waste matter—excrement artfully perfumed by politicians and policy makers for public consumption. (In fairness, the standards themselves aren't bad—they were written by fellow teachers—but the draconian way they've been shoved down our throats by self-serving non-educators in lofty offices has been a sore spot.)

Despite its doctored title, my presentation has generated ire or interest, because teachers wearing conference badges and lugging complimentary canvas tote bags keep pouring through the doorway. At this rate I'll soon be testing the room's capacity limits, set by the fire marshal at 150.

The accommodations are fine. Next to the podium, a stainless steel pitcher of water and three crystal glasses rest on a table draped with a linen cloth, plum-colored to match the padded chairs. A burlap-looking fabric covers walls bordered with a Native design, and an audiovisual screen forms a spacious white backdrop (although I have no PowerPoint or other jazzy bells and whistles).

My audience is an eclectic group: chatty packs of elementary teachers, a few sullen administrators, casually attired high-school teachers, and a smattering of overdressed men in suits and ties and women in pencil skirts and high heels who treat a teachers' conference like a night out.

A big-haired woman with padded shoulders approaches me and asks in a Bronx honk: "Do you have handouts?"

I shake my head. "Nope. Sorry."

She shrugs. "I guess I'll stay anyway."

As the last stragglers settle in, I begin to feel jittery. I haven't presented to a group this size for several years—and certainly not to so many young people. I'm concerned about the number of bent heads studying their cellphones as if searching for gold. The digital age has exploded in the twilight of my career, and I've been slow on the uptake. I use email and enter grades digitally and all that—I'm not a complete fossil. But these folks can design a theme park on their phones during a coffee break… or catch me in a brain fart and share my jackass moment with a worldwide audience. What can I possibly tell them that they can't tap-tap on their devices and summon a cyberspace genie to answer? I'm not only a small fish; I'm old news. National Science Teacher of the Year! That was a lifetime ago—two lifetimes. Suddenly I feel ridiculously, preposterously old.

*　　*　　*

In the front row, I notice three young teachers: a very pregnant Latina woman; a vivacious redhead who looks like the grownup version of Little Orphan Annie; and a sixties throwback who reminds me of a young Ali MacGraw: brunette hair falling straight to her waist, a light sprinkling of freckles, a paisley blouse, leather sandals, and a canary-yellow skirt.

As I size up my audience, my eyes linger for a moment on hers—a gemlike green—and during that split second, she flashes me a smile and a wink—was it a wink? Or just some inadvertent tic? No, she's still smiling at me, so I smile back then quickly move on, thinking life is a bit crazy. Or maybe just men are. Thirty seconds ago, I had two feet in the grave and was nailing shut the coffin. Now I'm remembering that I am unattached and available.

I don't make a habit of picking up women at conferences—I'm not a skirt-chaser like Dale Hanagan—but over the years, I've met a few women and felt a connection so strong and instantaneous that a transaction seemed inevitable. In the vernacular, sparks flew. It's happened twice in my career.

The first instance resulted in an enchanting weekend at a resort in the Catalina Mountains just north of Tucson. We forged a friendship that remains strong (and platonic—she's now happily married, with three grown children).

The second encounter was like Glenn Close in *Fatal Attraction* minus the dead rabbit in the Crock-Pot. Our first night together was fine, but when she started talking marriage at our morning-after breakfast, I pumped the brakes, perhaps too abruptly. She was hurt, then angry, then wounded again, then gentle and apologetic. I thought we'd mutually parted ways, but the following weekend when I returned home from a hunting trip, she'd set up house in my trailer. She even put her custom silk sheets on the bed. Don't ask me how she got in. I had to call one of my former students, now a local cop, to scare her off.

Both encounters were with women within a decade of my age, not a twenty-two-year-old. I remind myself of this, and also that, as a professional, I'd trained my eyes to skim over young women as if they were my daughters or cousins barely out of high school.

But there's a different vibe with this woman in the paisley blouse. I've registered the French braid that circles her crown and appears to secure her waterfall of hair; the turquoise and silver necklace resting just above a bit of cleavage; and the absence of any jewelry on her left ring finger, all in that split second.

* * *

"Well," I say, motioning to the wall clock, "we'd better get started. My name is Todd Hunter, and I've been asked to talk about how to energize your students and teach state standards at the same time. I'm supposed to say something about how you can transform your classrooms too. Is that right? Is that why you're all here?"

There are a few smiles and some nods. I feel an immediate bond with my audience. They're all teachers or former teachers turned administrators, all fighting the good fight. But morale is low. I can feel it in the air, a falsely sweetened sadness. Less than a week ago, the state Department of Education debuted its latest strategy to improve public education: a letter grade assigned to every school, based primarily on the results of a statewide test administered in the spring.

The results weren't pretty unless you taught at an elite school in an upscale, white-bread neighborhood. The others got mostly D's and F's, and the results appeared in every newspaper in the state and all over the internet. They were also mailed to the parents of every student in Arizona. So when Mrs. Jones or Mrs. Rivera or Mr. Todacheeny opened last Wednesday's mail, the first thing they read was: *Congratulations!*

Your son Johnny's being educated at a failing school, and you have the legal right to enroll him at another school of your choice. This wasn't just a casual criticism of Johnny's teacher but also a swift kick to the groin that said, in essence: You're not doing your job. You're failing our children and your country and community, along with mom, apple pie, and the Stars and Stripes forever.

Some of my peers have questioned the Department of Education's wisdom in scheduling their statewide teacher-education conference in the immediate aftermath of this academic bloodbath, but I call it a stroke of genius. What better opportunity to deliver the message, loud and clear, that what we're doing is obviously not working, so they are riding to the rescue with a new and better, research-based, standards-driven way. Come, they're saying, follow us to the Promised Land. The teachers should look beaten to a pulp. Instead, most of them are smiling, or trying to, despite the sledgehammer that's been smashed against their heads.

I've spent two weeks preparing my presentation, but I'm refusing to play the game. I'm going off script. "I've got a question," I say. "How many of you are getting paid to be here today? Raise your hands."

I cross my arms, waiting a good ten seconds for a hand to shoot up. None do.

"I don't see a single hand raised. That's called dedication. That's called commitment. That's called being a teacher. That's who we are, that's what we do. And you don't need me or anyone else telling you how to transform your classroom. If you did, you wouldn't be here right now. You'd be at the mall or the movies or a hundred other places instead of sitting in a crowded conference room on a Saturday hoping to get a few ideas to make you a better teacher. And that's what this is all about. Teachers, not systems. Teachers, not tests. Teachers, not politicians."

There are nods and smiles. Some people look serious, all seem engaged. Little Orphan Annie looks like she's about to break out into song. I think I see tears welling up in the eyes of a silver-haired woman, but it could just be allergies.

"Here's what I'll do," I say. "I'll tell you a few things that have worked for me in the classroom, and maybe they can make your jobs a bit easier. Does that sound all right?"

More nods, a few more smiles. These folks are hungry for good news, a pat on the back, reassurance—a little hope, dammit. So I start by talking about students—the single most important purpose of a teacher.

"Every kid's unique, so we need to approach each one differently. Some respond best to praise, others to humor, and others to a swift kick in the butt—metaphorically speaking. And we've got to show them—not just say it, but show it—that we give a damn. We're here to help them learn, and we'll stand on our heads and play chopsticks if that's what it takes."

I'm not telling them anything they don't already know, but there's more laughter, some scattered applause. I want to keep the ball rolling, but a hand goes up, the paisley-clad brunette's.

"This is really interesting," she says, "but I was wondering—could you tell us about the Pond Project?" Her smile is gone, replaced by a pensive double-dent where her forehead meets the bridge of her nose.

I look down, smiling at the irony of her question: in my mind, nothing seems more old-school and just plain old than the Pond Project. And yet I'm suddenly clutching the podium as if it might blast off. "You don't really want to hear about that."

But several others chime in: the lady with the Bronx honk, Little Orphan Annie, a goateed administrator, and dozens more, all urging me on: "No! No! We want to hear about the pond! The pond!"

I'm flattered, on the one hand, and astounded that anyone in this room still remembers anything about it.

"That's last year's news," I say. "Or more like last century's."

The brunette is leaning forward in her chair, palms pressed together like a child at prayer. She smiles and mouths one word: "Please?"

*　　*　　*

I start at the beginning: how, as a first-year teacher with four preps, I was staying up past midnight planning lessons from textbooks that put my students to sleep.

"I may as well have force-fed them Nyquil."

I describe the gimmicks I used to trick them into learning and keep them entertained—games, competitions, cutesy stuff. Junk food. Fluff.

"It was fun, amusing maybe, but it wasn't real science and I knew it, and so did they. Students can smell a fake a mile away, and once they do, you're dead in the water because you've lost their trust.

"Then one day I'm walking out back of the junior high and I'm staring at a god-awful eyesore of a junkyard. It's the old city dump and it's been there forever, but today I'm looking at it differently. Then the light clicks on! It wasn't a voice from heaven or anything like that, but a sudden thought: make it real. Give them real problems to solve using real science.

"The next day I took my first-period class outside and said, 'How do you like staring at this junkyard every time you look out the window?'

They said they didn't, so I said, 'What do you want to do about it?' And that's how the Pond Project got started."

I explain how the students came up with the idea, created the plan, and presented it to the city council; how they built the dam and removed invasive species and planted native trees and shrubs and eventually created an outdoor science learning center.

"It didn't happen overnight, but every day, every week, every year we did a little bit more. The kids did all that."

Another hand goes up, the woman with the Bronx honk: "I love what you did—I love it! The energy and enthusiasm! And I can just see my kids doing something like that. But with the new law, now we've gotta spend our time preparing our kids to take the ATBS test. There's no time for creative projects like this. I don't know—how did you avoid teaching the standards?"

"I didn't," I say. "I integrated standards into whatever we happened to be doing that day."

"But how did you do that if you're teaching seventh- and eighth-grade science where you're teaching a bit of everything? Astronomy, earth science, physics, chemistry. Not just biology."

"You'd be surprised how you can work all of that in," I say. "Think about the physics involved in moving heavy objects. We were always moving boulders and logs and refrigerators. Or think about the geology involved in pond formation and soil conservation. Think about the science standards. A lot of them deal with the scientific method. There are a million ways you can incorporate that into an outdoor project. It's not easy, but there's a way to do it. It takes time—no doubt about that. Hours and hours, and sometimes I dragged myself home from school so exhausted I didn't know how I could get up the next day and do it again. Weekends, holidays. It was a 24/7 project for me. It was the hardest thing I've ever done in my life, but it was also the most rewarding. I wouldn't trade a minute of it for anything."

There's an awkward pause as my voice catches so briefly my audience probably doesn't notice. In that instant, I travel back to those days when the Pond Project was the place where I'd disguised sorrow and loneliness as joy; my refuge from the ice cave that had become my home. I've caught myself in a half-lie. There was one thing I would have traded for those days… in a heartbeat.

Another hand goes up, from a middle linebacker in the third row. "If I did something like that, I'd get fired!"

"That may be true," I say. "A lot depends on where we are, who we work with, what the rules are, and how far you can bend them without getting your hand chopped off. The only reason I'm standing here and you're sitting there listening to me yap is because I happened to find some things that worked with my kids. I'm sure every one of you could get up here and tell us all something phenomenal you've done."

I scan the room for a moment, smiling. "The key is to find what works for your students in your circumstances, and then do it. You don't make excuses, and you never blame the kids. You know how I know when a teacher's finished? When he starts blaming his students. 'My first-hour class is awful! They're lazy, they misbehave, they don't respect me or the flag or their parents or their dog.' When a teacher starts talking like that, what he's really saying is, 'I can't reach these kids, and if I can't reach them, I can't teach them. I'm done.'"

I'm preaching to myself now, voicing grim reminders. It's a wake-up call, all this undeserved adulation.

"You make it work — we all make it work," I say. "Somehow, someway."

"I see what you're saying," Mr. Linebacker says, "but if these kids don't pass the ATBS test, they don't graduate. And once they get that test in their hands, they're on their own. We can't even look at them."

As if he had flipped a switch, I can feel the collective frustration rising. Even the brunette and her two sidekicks are grimly awaiting my response.

"I know what you're saying, believe me, and it really sucks. As teachers, we're not judged by how many students we save from illiteracy or the crack house, or by how many kids we inspire to pursue a career in medicine or law or business or the arts. Our total worth's been reduced to how well our kids perform on a winner-takes-all test at the end of the school year. And to make matters worse, it's a multiple-choice test designed by highly trained professionals who get paid big bucks to trick our students."

There's a smattering of applause; I can sense the pendulum swinging back in my favor. High-stakes, multiple-choice tests are an easy target, universally despised by teachers.

"Think about it. They pose a question and give you four possible answers. There's the correct answer, an almost correct answer rigged to trick you, a ridiculous answer, and a distractor designed to get you second-guessing yourself. And to cover their rear ends, they insert some mealy-mouthed disclaimer: "Choose the *best* possible answer."

I can see by the nodding that they're back on the bus and enjoying the ride. I give the podium a gentle but exclamatory rap with my knuckles, to show them I mean business.

"And just what the hell does multiple-choice have to do with science? Or any other discipline, for that matter? Science is all about questioning and hypothesizing and experimenting, not picking the best out of four predetermined answers. Science is about discovery; it's about asking the big questions, not nailing down small-minded answers. Multiple-choice tests pretty much force you to advise your students: don't think too much. Read the question and pick. Whatever you do, don't overthink! That's the exact opposite of the scientific mind, which is trained to consider all variables and possibilities. Can you imagine a detective approaching a case like that? First thought, best thought? First suspect, best suspect? That's the difference between Sherlock Holmes and the Keystone Cops."

* * *

The natives are restless and they're definitely aroused. I look to the back, where the lady in uniform nervously draws her forefinger across her throat, then points to the clock. A dozen arms are outstretched, yearning to be called upon.

"Hey, I'd love to answer all your questions, but they're giving me the heave-ho." I snatch a dry-erase marker and hastily print my information on the whiteboard. "Feel free to contact me if you've got any questions—by phone or email."

Gazing at their faces, I can see I've touched a chord. They want—and need—a little more.

"You know, what we do is part art and part science and a whole lot of guts, creativity, commitment, and perseverance, and a damn thick skin to withstand all the undeserved criticism heaped on us by politicians who know zilch about educating kids. *We're* the teachers, not them. We know what works; they don't. And I'll set my hair on fire before I turn my classroom into a drill-and-kill sweat shop just so my kids can pass a multiple-choice test to put a smile on the face of some fat-assed legislator!"

Like extras in a well-choreographed musical, they rise out of their seats as one, applauding with gusto. My heart soars as I scan the audience—Mr. Linebacker, Ms. Bronx Honk, Little Orphan Annie, and of course, the brunette, everyone clapping loudly. I'm enjoying the moment, but I feel guilty as well. They're cheering for an earlier version of myself. They're cheering for an idea more than an individual. They're cheering for hope.

And now my eyes begin tearing up as I repeatedly whisper "thank you" into the mic, nodding, smiling, nodding until the applause simmers to a hum as the participants begin gathering their tote bags and programs and squeezing through the exit like softly braying cattle moving through a chute. Several stay behind to ask questions, including the brunette. She's hanging back a bit, which means she wants to speak to me last, privately.

Mr. Linebacker squeezes my hand as if wringing juice out of it. "Great presentation!" he says. "I'm going to do something like that with my kids. Not sure what, but I'm going to do something!"

"Find what works for you," I say.

Ms. Bronx Honk gives my hand a vigorous shake. "I've gotta tell you—I loved your presentation! Loved it! I do a unit on hunger. My students do all kinds of research about food and nutrition and agriculture, then they do projects to help our local soup kitchen. It's a life changer! It's a-*ma*-zing!"

"That's fantastic," I say. "We need more teachers like you."

* * *

By the time the brunette with the emerald eyes steps up, the room is empty except for a few stragglers sitting at a table in the back whispering conspiratorially about lunch options. She takes my hand gently but firmly.

"I just wanted to tell you—your talk, it was totally awesome!" She smiles, her freckles all but leaping off her cheeks. She looks a bit older up close but not much: maybe mid-twenties, mature but a little giddy too.

"Thank you…" I glance down at her name tag. "Margo! And what do you teach?"

She beams. "Middle-school science!"

"Middle school. Well, there's a special place in heaven for you."

She laughs as she swats an imaginary fly away from her face. "I totally love middle-school kids. I know I'm like the exception—they're quirky and confused and think they want to be adults, but not really."

"I started my career at junior high and loved it. The kids aren't jaded yet."

"No," she says. "Not at all."

"Then they get to high school and we pound all that hope and optimism out of them." I smile extra big to make sure she knows I'm joking, but her brows are knitted, disturbed.

"I hope not," she says. "That would be so sad."

"I was kidding."

"Oh, of course," she says. "Hey, I was wondering if you have plans for lunch? I'd really like to pick your brain."

Throughout this brief exchange I've been second-guessing myself. The gap between me and her seems to grow wider and more comical by the second. I've got an easy out if I want to put a swift and merciful end to this right now. She's smiling again; those damn freckles.

"Sure! Whatever's left of it, you're more than welcome to it. Where would you like to go?"

"There's a great Thai restaurant just across the street."

"Thai it is!" I say, and as the two of us head toward the open double-doors, I notice that all of the lingerers are gone except for one, and she's now standing: tall and slender, with a full head of curly chestnut hair flecked silver-gray so it looks as if she's just walked in from a light snowfall, although it's triple digits outside. She's wearing a long, boho-style dress that slopes gracefully from her narrow shoulders to her delicate ankles, and even from afar I can see the cinnamon sprinkling of freckles on her heart-shaped face, and the crow's feet that angle out from the corners of her eyes as she smiles and lifts her hand in a modest half-wave.

"Are you OK?" Margo asks.

I've stopped in mid-stride to stare at the last loiterer with shock that almost instantaneously shifts to confusion, and then to unmitigated joy.

* * *

"Amy," I whisper.

"No, Margo," Margo says. "Are you all right?"

I turn to her and suddenly—no, not suddenly at all, but finally—acknowledge what I've known from the beginning: she looks so young and unblemished and… so young. A kid with her whole life ahead of her and the world waiting for her. She shouldn't complicate that life with a man who's already walked most of the road and is hobbling toward the end of it.

"Lunch?" she says. "Remember?" She smiles, and those perfectly white, evenly spaced, uncapped, uncrowned teeth almost melt my resolve. She steps toward the exit, but my feet are stuck in concrete. Amy is still smiling, shaking her head, gently pulling me the other direction while patiently waiting for me to decide: the lady or the tiger?

Margo lifts one beautiful, thick eyebrow. Well? she says without saying it. She glances at Amy, confused and perhaps insulted by her competition.

I want to say something clever and face-saving for both of us, but my tongue is Silly Putty. I wince stupidly and apologetically and finally mutter a feeble, "I'm sorry," but she's already halfway out the exit.

I turn back to Amy, who's still smiling but perplexed and perhaps a little sad.

"I hope I didn't interrupt anything," she says.

"No," I say. "She just wanted to pick my brain."

"Is that all she wanted to pick?"

"You mean my pocket too?"

"Among other things. Great presentation, by the way."

"You saw it?"

"Start to finish."

"I didn't see you."

"I was in the back."

She's still smiling. I want to reach out and touch her to make sure she's real and not just another phantom teasing me in my sleep.

"I'm famished," I say. "Have you had lunch? My treat."

AMOR

We walk two blocks to Red Robin instead of the Thai place, just in case Margo follows through on her original plan. Amy orders lentil soup with a side salad while I get the guacamole burger.

I lower my menu and look up at the spry young woman with orange, spiked hair and TIFFANY printed on her plastic name tag.

"Tiffany," I say, "can I sub sweet-potato fries for the regular fries?"

"Absolutely!" Tiffany says, scribbling on her notepad. "Anything else?"

"No, I think we're good."

"We'll have those out in a minute," Tiffany says and hustles off.

Amy's pencil-thin eyebrows arch. "That's a switch."

"I'm trying to watch my blood-sugar levels," I say. "My A1C's borderline pre-diabetes, so I'm trying to control it with diet and exercise and all that good stuff."

"Like sweet-potato fries?"

"Actually, there's good science behind that."

"Of course there is."

"Seriously. Regular fries are like mainlining soda pop. The sugar goes straight to your bloodstream. Bam! But sweet potatoes are low on the glycemic index, so the sugar just moseys along through your system."

"Or I suppose you could substitute a salad?"

"Probably—but what's the fun in that? You look great, by the way."

"Oh, right!" Amy says, lowering her saucer eyes. I'd forgotten how large and expressive they are. "I was going to say the same about you."

"Me?" I pat my modest paunch. "I picked this up just last month."

"The lecture circuit will do that to you."

"Circuit? I'm a one-hit wonder. Did you really see my whole presentation?"

"Start to finish," Amy says. "It was inspiring." She leans forward, resting her elbows on the edge of the table. "Really."

227

"I didn't see you."

She smiles mischievously. "You mean you didn't *notice* me—apparently because you were checking out the younger models."

I tilt back in my chair, creating a little distance. "Come on, Amy. That's not me."

She looks embarrassed for having brought it up. "So what have you been up to, Todd?"

It's the first time that she's called me by name, and there's a nice, familiar ring to it, unique to her voice. I can't quite put my finger on it now, but later that night, when I'm alone again, I'll recognize it as the voice of love.

"Same old, same old."

"You're still doing the pond?"

"No. Ten years ago they talked me into administration, so I became the math and science supervisor."

"I'll bet you were a good one. Did you like it?"

"Yes and no. I liked the extra money. I liked the flexibility. And I liked being able to help teachers really up their game, which in turn helped students…"

She smiles. "But?"

"I missed the kids. I missed the classroom."

"Did you go back?"

I laugh loudly. "I didn't have a choice. The budget got tight and they cut the fat—I guess supervisors are considered adipose positions. So I'm back in the classroom—at the high school."

"Do you like that?"

I could give a far more nuanced answer—yes, no, and maybe, depending upon the day, the hour, the students, the situation—but instead I keep it simple: "It's like coming home."

*   *   *

She smiles, and for a moment I survey the lines and blemishes that have taken up residence on her face since I last saw her: the wrinkled deltas at the far edge of each eye; the twin vertical lines that had once been cute dimples on her cheeks; the crepe texturing on her eyelids and along her upper lip; the once-dainty freckles that had converged to form a few cornflake-size patches. It's certainly not the face I said farewell to twenty-eight years ago, and yet in its own seasoned way it looks more beautiful than ever.

"It's your calling," she says. "It always has been."

I wonder what she's thinking, gazing into my weathered old mug, mostly unwrinkled but patchy pink from a recent acid wash to stave off the cancer cells that have been trying to plant a flag in my face. My jawline beard has the frosty tint of an old Civil War general's, and my once sky-blue eyes have faded to milky turquoise.

"I don't know," I say. "I still think back to those first god-awful few weeks, how badly I wanted to quit."

She reaches across the table, sliding her hand over mine and giving it a gentle squeeze. "You just had to find your footing, that's all."

"I've got you to thank for that." As I look at her now, any lingering animosity seems to evaporate. What had finally brought us to that breaking point of no return? We'd lost children and potential children, but we still had each other. Was it the chilly reception every time I entered the house? The slow withdrawal of life, love, and affection? Or the relentless cold war that finally thawed into nasty mudslinging, name-calling, heart-scratching fights? And how much of that was on me, going ice age in my own way? Playing the affable ghost? Looking at her now—the radiant eyes, her beaming smile, even the lines in her faces like etches of wisdom—it all seems so foolish and so impossibly long ago.

"So what have *you* been up to?" I ask.

Her head snaps back with a bawdy laugh. "Oh, you don't want to hear my long, sad story!"

"No, I do!" I say. "I really do. Please."

A young man sidles up to the table with Tiffany in tow and sets the soup and salad in front of Amy and the guacamole burger in front of me.

"Those are bottomless fries," Tiffany reminds me.

"Terrific," I say. Amy looks down, smiling.

"Anything else I can get you?" Tiffany asks.

I smile. "No, I think we're—" I catch myself. "I'm good—how about you, Amy?"

"I'm fine."

"Well, if there's anything else I can do…" Tiffany vanishes like smoke.

*   *   *

I unfold the paper napkin swaddling my silverware before carefully slicing my burger in two equal parts. A long, slow bite. "Oh, that's good!" I say, eyes closed, savoring. Then, as if I've suddenly awakened from a trance: "So I moved out of the house on Shadow Mountain and into a trailer. You stayed in town until the house was sold and moved to Phoenix. Then what?"

Amy forks a few leaves of lettuce into her mouth, then dabs at her lips with her napkin.

"I was pretty messed up, if you recall."

"It was a tough time for everybody, but especially for you."

"I wanted a fresh start—somewhere no one knew me and I didn't know them. So I went to Yuma."

"Good gosh. The armpit of Arizona!"

"It wasn't so bad."

"If you like living in a blast furnace."

"I had A/C—down there everyone does. I got a job teaching ESL. Nine out of ten kids speak Spanish, and I don't mean as a second language. But the people were sweet. Really friendly."

Amy resumes working on her salad and motions to the hamburger lying dormant on my plate. "I'm not talking till you start eating."

I take another bite. "And then?"

"There's not that much to say. I piddled around for a few years working nickel-and-dime jobs—"

"I thought you said you taught ESL?"

"Eventually. But I wasn't ready to get back in the classroom. I wanted to keep a low profile awhile. When you're a teacher, suddenly the whole community knows you, and there you are at Walmart and the movies and Safeway and one of your students is tugging his mom's skirt, pointing at you, telling the world, 'Look! There's Mrs. Hunter!' Yes, who's got no husband and even though it's nobody's business, somehow it always ends up being everybody's. No thanks. I was a receptionist at a dental office; I worked in the shoe department at Dillard's. I even worked the graveyard shift at a Circle K."

"A jack-of-all-trades!" I smile but it saddens me to think of her quilting together a life way below her capabilities, that brilliant young mind shuffling through files in a cramped office.

"It paid the bills. I had my split from selling the house, so I had enough to get by. But after a couple years, I just got the itch to teach again. Every time I saw a school bus or drove by a school and saw kids out at recess running around, I always said to myself, 'Why are you here when you know you should be in there?'"

"So one day you waltzed into the school and they hired you—and wisely so!"

"Not hardly. I didn't want all the pressure, you know? I wasn't ready for that yet. Prepping lessons, parent-teacher conferences, after-school meetings, report cards, blah-blah-blah. You know how it is. When you're a teacher, your life's not yours. If you're not teaching a lesson, you're prepping one in your mind. I wanted an easy, eight-to-three job, so I was hired as a classroom aide. You come to school in the morning, you do what the teacher says, and when you go home in the afternoon, the rest of the day is yours. No fuss, no muss, no burning the midnight oil cutting out a hundred paper circles and squares for the penguin unit."

"I can see that. In fact, it sounds pretty damn good right now."

Amy sighs. "To a point, yes. I did that for a year and a half, and I liked it. I mean, I really loved being back in school—the morning bell calling everyone to class, announcements over the intercom, the pledge, the fussy parents and the negligent ones too, the funky fundraisers and silly slogans and the smell of cafeteria food. The student assemblies and motivational charts and stickers and student work plastering the walls and cartoon colors everywhere. And the kids, of course—I'd forgotten how much I loved working with kids. All that crazy, restless energy and enthusiasm—every day's an adventure, you know? And they say the damndest, sweetest, funniest things. This is elementary school I'm talking about, not those full-grown thugs you get in high school."

"Hey! Those are *my* babies you're talking about."

"Oh, yes, your unblemished little brutes. Anyway, halfway through my second year, the ESL teacher goes on maternity leave and never comes back. So just like that, we're down an ESL teacher. Our principal's a second-year kid who's still wearing braces, you know, and he hits the panic button. We've got four hundred ESL kids in a school of six hundred, and the state department's coming in a month to monitor our program. He tries advertising the position, but it's midyear and anyone worth their salt's already working. We've got three other ESL teachers, each teaching a hundred kids a day, and he knows if he tries to slough the extra hundred off on them, he'll have a full-scale mutiny. So one day at a faculty meeting, in a total act of desperation, he asks if anyone knows anybody with ESL experience. 'If so, contact me like yesterday!' His exact words."

"Amy to the rescue!"

"Pretty much. That afternoon, after the buses pull out and the kids are gone, I knock on the principal's door. 'What can I do you for?' he says. When I tell him I've got ESL experience, he catapults out of his chair, scoots around the desk, and grabs me by both hands. 'You're kidding?' he says. 'We can get you emergency certification.' When I tell him I'm already certified, I think he's going to kiss my feet. 'Bless you!' he says. 'Bless you!'"

"And the rest is history."

"I was hired, yes. Full time with benefits. Overnight I was making three times what I made as an aide. It still wasn't much—instead of eight dollars an hour, I got twenty-three. But I was back in my element. Like you said, I was home."

* * *

"Are you still teaching?" I ask. It's a rush, listening to her voice, like riding whitewater. I don't want her to stop.

"I taught at Desert View for ten years, then moved to Phoenix and taught for twelve years at one school before transferring to Woodcrest where I've been for the past three years."

Amy tips her head back and laughs—a new affectation that seems to suit her present state of mind. "Oh, yeah. I can't afford not to. Every year I say, 'This is it! This is it!' but I just keep coming back. It's that masochistic streak, I guess. Or old habits die hard."

"I'm sure it's more than that."

"It's in the blood, I think." She points to my barely nibbled burger. "You promised me you'd eat if I started yakety-yakking."

"Sorry," I say and take a gargantuan bite out of my burger. "Did you—did you ever... meet anyone?"

"No, no. I told you mine; you tell me yours. What have you been up to, besides making megabucks on the lecture circuit?"

"Megabucks? You mean the free tote bag and complimentary conference badge?"

"Come on, fess up!"

So I tell her the *Reader's Digest* condensed version of the last thirty years of my life—minus the Jennifer Abernathy part.

"I'm sorry to hear about the pond," she says.

I shrug. "Easy come, easy go."

"I wouldn't call that easy."

"No, it wasn't. Coming or going." I take another mammoth bite out of my burger, chewing slowly, stalling. "So, did you meet someone?"

"Oh, sure. Life goes on, you know. I married him, too—poor dumb me!" She smacks the side of her head with her hand. "What's that old saying? Fool me once, shame on you. Fool me twice, I'm an imbecile. Something like that. If I had an ounce of brains, I'd have married rich, but no—I married a teacher! A charismatic, fast-talking P.E. teacher who should have been selling used cars or drugs for a living."

I'm shaking my head as she tells the story.

"He had the gift of gab, I'll give him that," she says. "He was always tinkering with some get-rich-quick scheme that inevitably blew up in his face. His last big plan involved a process that supposedly increased the fertility of chickens. It cost thirty grand to buy in, with promises of a 50 percent return the first year and double that after—some preposterous number. There was a glossy brochure with a prospectus and all that. I told him I smelled a rat, but he emptied my savings on the sly and that was that. We lasted two years that seemed like an eternity before I pulled the plug. What can I say? The grass was never greener or anything like that. The only good thing that came out of that little catastrophe was Ramon."

"Ramon?"

She laughs, arching her elegant, needle-thin eyebrows. *"Rrrrra-món!"* she says in a deep voice, rolling the R. "He was one of my ESL kids. His family moved to the U.S. when he was six—undocumented, illegal, whatever you call it. Shortly after, his father ran off with who-knows-who and the mother was snatched up by the *migra* when she was returning from her night shift at the Super 8. She got deported, along with three of her kids. Somehow Ramon got left behind. He was spending the night at a friend's house. He goes home the next day and everybody's gone. The poor boy thinks they all got up and left, like his father.

"Long story short, Ramon's six years old with nowhere to go, so I took him home with me. I know! It was utterly insane behavior on my part, from a legal-slash-professional perspective, but what was I supposed to do? Take him to ICE so they can scare him to death and then send him back to a home he hasn't got anymore? You're not eating."

"What can I say? I'm... fascinated!" I take another monster bite. "I can see exactly why you did that—especially you. How couldn't you?"

"Thanks—because after that, there were plenty of people who wanted me certified and I don't mean for teaching. The first night, I fed him and put him in my spare bedroom. He only spoke a few words of English, and I'm fumbling along with whatever I remember from ninth-grade Spanish, but somehow we meet halfway and make it work. I tuck him into my soft guest bed, but the next morning when I go in to wake him, he's curled up on the hardwood floor. Later I find out he'd been sleeping on dirt floors for the first six years of his life in Chiapas and now he was continuing the tradition in the good old USA.

"Ramon lived with me for a year and a half and with a little—well, actually a whole helluva lot of help from an attorney friend and a ton of red tape, I adopted him."

"No!"

Amy's beaming. She takes a sip of ice water with a wedge of lemon, tearing up. "He's the love of my life," she says as she ferrets through her macramé shoulder purse to hand me a thumbnail photo of a devilishly handsome young man with jet-black hair and chiseled cheekbones.

"He looks like a movie star!" I say. "Like a young Antonio Banderas."

"Much handsomer than Antonio Banderas," Amy says. "He's a junior."

"In college?"

"No, silly. High school."

"He looks older than that—more mature."

"Oh, he is. It scares me sometimes, he's so serious. He says he wants to go to med school so he can work in disadvantaged communities— those are his words, not mine."

"He's got his mother's heart," I say.

"I don't know. I never met his mother." Amy takes another sip of water and resumes working on the salad she's been neglecting.

"No," I say, more slowly and emphatically this time, pointing at her chest to remove any ambiguity: "He's got his mother's heart."

Amy looks down, sniffling a bit as her hand gropes through her purse for a tissue to dab at her eyes. "I guess I am," she says. "You'll have to meet him sometime."

"I'd like that very much."

"He really loves science—he always has. I've told him all about you."

"Not the stuff on the wanted poster?"

She smiles, still sniffling. "No. Just the good stuff."

I set down my half-eaten burger. "Did you tell him about us?"

* * *

Amy looks down at her still-untouched bowl of lentil soup and begins fiddling with the package of saltine crackers. A tear dislodges from one eye and leaves a glossy trail down her cheek. The other eye follows suit. Tiffany swoops by the table and places the check gently on the edge, as if it were a motion-activated bomb. Sensing a private moment, she whispers, "Any time you're ready."

I look up and mouth a perfunctory "thank you," but I want her to instantly disappear.

"When he was a little boy," Amy says, "he used to ask me, '*Mamacita*, were you ever in love?' I told him, 'Yes, I was in love once.' 'Like in the movies?' he said. And I thought about it for a moment, and I said, 'Oh, better than the movies.' And then I thought about it some more, and I said, 'Much better.' When he asked what happened, I said, 'I left him.' He said, 'But why, *Mamacita*? If you loved him even better than the movies?' And I said, 'Because I was young and sad and very foolish.'"

I reach across the table and clasp her hand, which is clutching a soup spoon. She's staring down at the pebbled pool of lentils, and her hand remains firm around the spoon.

"You were young and you were sad," I say, "understandably—but you were never foolish."

In the long silence that follows, she continues staring at her lentils and I continue staring at her clenched hand. All four TV monitors placed strategically around the room feature the same Arizona Diamondbacks pitcher winding up and delivering the same wicked curveball to the same befuddled Los Angeles Dodger, who swings vainly at the phantom ball and then slams his bat on home plate like an enraged caveman. But that is the outside world, and this is a delicate moment in time, like the thinnest membrane of water, and I don't want to do anything that might disturb the unspoken feelings binding the two of us so perfectly back together. And a single word—the wrong word—could break the magic spell and send us both back home, alone.

BLISS

Under any other circumstances I might have called it a bad omen—three bad omens, to be honest, starting with an early morning flat tire midway between the Marble Canyon Trading Post and Jacob Lake. Fortunately, I was able to steer my pickup onto the sandy shoulder without incident and change the tire solo while Duchess watched curiously from the cab. With no cell service, I couldn't have called a tow truck even if there had been an available provider within a hundred miles. So no harm, no foul.

My do-it-yourself job cost me half an hour, and although I'd taken precautions—removing my tie, rolling up my sleeves, placing an old blanket on the ground to kneel on—I noticed dust stains on my black dress pants (easily wiped away) and some less-forgiving smudges that now looked like cigarette burns on my white Sunday shirt.

At least the scenery was nice; actually, it was downright stunning as the sun crowned the mesa, setting fire to a seemingly never-ending wall of vermilion cliffs. Barren desert beauty. Quiet, solitary, enchantingly spooky. Sunrise on the planet Mars.

*　　*　　*

Amy and Ramon had spent the night at the Grand Canyon Lodge on the North Rim and were probably enjoying a leisurely breakfast about now: Spanish omelets and a spectacular view of the world's most famous canyon. I could have joined them and made the process much less complicated, but I'm old-fashioned, and superstitious too: what future misfortunes was I courting if I glimpsed the bride prematurely on her wedding day? Or shared a bed with her the night before? And had sex the morning of?

So this was my reward for chivalry and virtue: a blown-out tire in the middle of nowhere.

From the lodge, Amy and Ramon had a one-hour drive to the wedding site. I, on the other hand, had chosen to make a five-hour journey that would start at four a.m. and include multiple stops in the Kaibab National Forest to post way-finding signs for the thirty-eight guests traveling to the one o'clock ceremony. Even with the flat tire, I had more than ample time to set up signs, unfold chairs, and arrange the refreshment table, if not for bad omen number two.

Five miles after gassing up in Jacob Lake, I was cruising down the paved highway, blissfully admiring the fall colors—a confetti-like explosion of red, green, and gold—when out of the corner of my eye I noticed a light-brown blur. In the instant it took to divert my eyes from left to right, a deer flashed across the highway in three bounding leaps that seemed like one. I didn't have time to wince or curse or slam on the brakes. All I remember was the blur and the sickening thud that registered on my left-front bumper.

I crushed the brake pedal, propelling Duchess against the dashboard, but the damage was done. In my rear-view mirror I watched the buckskin ghost vanish into the forest, most likely to die from internal bleeding as soon as the shock wore off and the animal realized it had been fatally clobbered by a moving machine.

I coasted to a stop on the shoulder and tried to elbow the door open, but the force of the blow had jammed it shut. Folding myself like a contortionist, I eased across the bench seat, reached around Duchess, and pushed the passenger door open, freeing the two of us.

The left-front bumper looked as if it had been ripped away by the Incredible Hulk during a hissy fit. A few fiberglass threads clung desperately to the main body. Half the grill was smashed in: it looked like three rows of hillbilly teeth. The headlamp was a giant eyeball hanging from its socket by a single wire. In a split-second, my stout Dodge pickup had been transformed into a mutant, space-age cyclops. The good news? I wasn't hurt (patting myself, double-checking to make sure: no cuts, no broken bones, no bruises—yet!) and neither was Duchess. I popped the hood, relieved to see the engine intact. The radiator was a slightly dented but not leaking fluid. And I had one functioning headlight.

I retrieved my toolkit and some rope from the truck bed, laid out the old blanket for kneeling purposes, and set to work. An hour later I had tied up all the dangling parts so they didn't interfere with the motor or with free movement of a tire. I was back on the road at ten a.m.; plenty of time still, provided there were no more surprises.

* * *

The paved highway divided a vast, green meadow where deer would sneak down to feast on the grass at night or to play stupid suicide games with passing vehicles by day. At the DeMotte intersection, I pulled off on the road heading west, removed one of four signs wedged into the jam-packed bed of my truck, and staked it into the ground: TODD AND AMY HUNTER WEDDING.

I could have had a simple gathering at any number of churches in town and made the whole affair much easier on everyone—me, Amy, Ramon, the minister, the guests. But Amy and I had gone bare bones the first time, a five-minute ceremony before a justice of the peace that was over before it started. Sixties iconoclasts, we didn't want a church wedding with all the trappings. Too commercial, gaudy, and predictable. And too damn expensive. So *ex post facto*, we'd mailed family and friends a simple announcement with no photo. In retrospect, it was a slap in the face, though not an intentional one.

Amy had always insisted she preferred it that way—simple, no fanfare, a handful of very close friends, not armies of strangers with onion breath. But I'd always wondered if she regretted that anonymity on what for many people is the biggest event of their lives. Was there a Disney princess secretly lurking in her heart, yearning to be the belle of the ball? At least for this one moment? Life, too, is cluttered with good intentions. You don't get many second chances, so this time around we would do it right: traditional in format but with a touch of the unconventional that she'd never forget.

"If unforgettable's the goal, then mission accomplished!" I grumble to Duchess as my pickup rattles down the washboard road. "Isn't that right, girl? We've had all the unforgettable we need for one day."

I stop at a three-way fork in the road, pound in another sign, and continue driving deeper into the labyrinth of twisting paths, all hemmed in by towering pines and groves of gloriously golden aspens. When the slightest breeze passes, their coin-sized leaves flutter like schools of goldfish. Every cluster of red ferns looks like Moses's burning bush. To my left, a small flock of wild turkeys struts around a fallen pine. Still un-nipped by October frost, wildflowers cover the earth like a coat of many colors.

I smile. One good omen easily erases the other two.

I drive on, admiring the colors, soaking in the day, humming an old Beatles song: "If I fell in love with you/would you promise to be true..." All's right with the world until three miles from my destination, when

I encounter omen number three. My fist hammers against the dash: "Dammit to hell!"

A week ago when I scouted this road, it was clean and clear. Now a ponderosa pine's fallen across it, exclaiming, in essence: THOU SHALT NOT PASS! Because it's not a measly sapling; this is one of the grand patriarchs, its roots finally shriveled to the point where a stiff wind had knocked it down. With a wall of aspens on one side of the road and a village of dog pines cluttering the other, there's no detouring around the obstacle. My pickup bed and back seat are stuffed with two long tables, forty folding chairs, and two gargantuan ice chests packed with drinks and refreshments. In other words, I've got no chain saw, no dynamite, no magic wand.

"Hell's freaking bells!" I holler, scaring a nearby squirrel that scurries up a tree. Accustomed to my occasional tantrums, Duchess gazes out the window like a world-weary wife.

I want to throw something, break something, anything. Climbing out of the truck, I slam the door. I want to take a running kick at the stupid log, but I'll scuff up my new Doc Martens. Instead I follow Amy's counsel and close my eyes for a deep, cleansing breath, counting four on the exhale. And another-two-three-four. And another-two-three-four. When I open my eyes, Duchess is calmly relieving herself while the squirrel perches on the fallen log, staring at me.

"What are you looking at?" I bark. "You probably think this is funny, don't you?"

The squirrel doesn't budge. Duchess seems oblivious to everything.

I may not have a chain saw or dynamite, but I do have an ax. So I remove my white shirt and undershirt—rip them off, is more like it—grab the ax from the cab, and in the speckled sun and shade of the quickly expiring morning, I begin chopping.

I'm so angry and fed up with stupid, idiotic omens that each swing of the blade takes a carnivorous bite out of the log. But it's a mammoth piece of timber, the very reason why chain saws were invented. With no other options, I keep swinging: chop chop chop, the sweat soon lacquering my back and chest and dripping down my face. At first I'm chopping in a blind fury, but as my muscles tire and my rage abates, my strokes become more focused and productive. I settle into a slow but efficient rhythm, assuming that if I can sever one good-size section, I might be able to roll it far enough off the road for cars to pass.

I glare at my squirrel friend, still quietly observing, then at Duchess, wondering why she hasn't chased the varmint away. Normally a squirrel sighting sets off Duchess's internal fire alarm. Apparently—today at least—she finds my boiling frustration far more entertaining than some random forest rodent.

"Where the hell's the Forest Service when you need them?" I grunt. "Isn't that a good question, Duchess? What about you, squirrel? What's your take on the situation? Don't just sit there like a lump. Run up a tree, fly, tell a joke!"

The squirrel remains inert, as does Duchess.

An hour later, soaked with sweat, exhausted, I've chopped a wedge so deep that only a stubborn fragment of wood unites the longer section to the shorter one. With a little pressure from my foot, the fragment snaps.

"There now!" I proclaim to my audience of two. "How do you like that?"

I toss the ax aside and take a long drink from the thermos I brought for the post-nuptial celebration. Even that brief buzz of alcohol feels heavenly. I remove two water bottles from the ice chest and empty one into a bowl that Duchess laps up before I can lift the other bottle to my lips.

Lowering my shoulder and engaging every muscle in my legs, glutes, back, chest, and arms, I push. Nothing. I dig two small holes for my feet for extra leverage, squat lower for more thrust, and with a berserk cry that could gain me instant entry to Valhalla, I push again. Nope. I may as well try to move a dump truck.

"Dammit dammit dammit all!" I fling the empty water bottle against a tree.

Then I get another idea, no thanks to my squirrel friend, who looks bored with my antics. I grab a coil of rope and use the ax to dig a shallow hole under one end of the shorter section of timber. Running the rope under the log and securing one end tightly, I tie the other end to the back of my truck, shift it into four-wheel drive, climb into the cab (followed by Duchess), and say a short but heartfelt prayer. "Dear God, please do whatever You need to do to get this log out of the road and out of my hair and out of my life. Thank you, amen."

When I depress the accelerator, the engine purrs and whines as the heavy-duty Michelin tires spin fruitlessly in the dirt. I shift into reverse, backing up almost to the log; then, shifting into the lowest gear, I begin driving forward, slowly but forcefully gathering momentum until I feel a slight tug on the rope. My foot stomps on the gas and the engine roars as the tires bite deep into the dirt, and slowly, steadily, the truck inches forward. "Yes!" I yell, slapping the dash. "Yes!"

The log slowly straightens out behind me as the truck crawls along. I drag it until I find a small clearing just off the shoulder. There I leave it, out of sight, out of mind.

"Good freaking riddance!" I shout, and drive on.

* * *

By the time I arrive at Locust Point, it's just after noon, which means guests will be arriving—well, any moment. My bare chest is still soaked with sweat, my Doc Martens look like used hiking boots, and my dress pants appear more brown than black. I wipe my face, back, and chest with a hand towel, then squirt a few drops of hand sanitizer in my palm and go after my armpits. I take a quick look in my side mirror and groan: "I look like the damn Prisoner of Zenda!"

No time to pretty up. I begin hauling the folding chairs two hundred yards down a narrow trail to a rocky isthmus that juts out over the canyon—forty chairs divided by four chairs per trip equals ten trips. More sweat and grime, but I get it done. Solo. Two sections with an aisle down the middle, four rows of five chairs to a section. Neat. Orderly. Symmetrical.

Next I set up two folding tables at the head of the trail, near the parking area, and lay out wine, soft drinks, and bottled water from the ice chest. Working fast, working crazy. Checking my watch: twelve thirty. Amy's sister is bringing the postnuptial feast, build-your-own sandwiches: ciabatta rolls, pickles and olives, platters of ham and cheese, mayo and mustard, macaroni salad, potato salad, and petits fours frosted with rose instead of a traditional wedding cake. Thank goodness I don't have to worry about all of that. Or do I? Arlene, who teaches math at a community college in southern California, can sometimes play the absent-minded professor. That's all on Amy, I'm thinking. Come what may.

I run the hand towel over my back, chest, and shoulders again, but sweat instantly reappears. My head and face are budding with the stuff. A dozen friends had offered to help set up, but I'd waved them off. "No, no, it's fine. Just come and enjoy! It's a long trip. We're going to make it real simple, you know."

Now cursing silly pride and self-reliance, I pull on my undershirt and button up my white dress shirt, trying to ignore the sweat sticking like adhesive to the fabric. I fuss a bit with the chairs, straightening rows here and there. And then, at a quarter-to-one, I stand by the split-rail fence sectioning off the dirt parking lot, and I wait.

Charley Gibbs, the minister, is the first to arrive, a goateed fellow who's wearing his casual-Sunday best: jeans, cowboy boots, and a black shirt with a white ministerial collar. One of my students from the early years, Charley had enthusiastically accepted my invitation to perform the ceremony. He offers his hand and I give him a warm embrace. He asks if he can help with anything.

"No, we've got it all under control. Thanks for being here. It means the world to us."

"Wouldn't miss it for anything," he says. He mentions the log that almost blocked the road.

"It's a good thing the Forest Service took care of that."

"Yes," I say. "A really good thing."

More guests arrive in SUVs and sedans and pickup trucks, and one couple cruises up in a Hummer that probably could have rolled right over that fallen log. School people, hunting buddies, Amy's book-club friends. Fitz and Sally. My childhood friend Stan and his wife Liz have come all the way from Maryland. I'm touched, flattered. I shake his hand slowly and deliberately, looking into his watery brown eyes: "Thank you so much for coming." I kiss Liz on the cheek.

"I've heard so much about you," she says. "And some of it's even good."

I laugh. A sense of humor. I always like that. Good. Good. Everything's good now.

A Cadillac Seville rolls up and a withered old woman with a beehive of white hair slowly emerges in a blue dress suit. Amy's mother! From San Dimas, California. She's accompanied by a very proper-looking old gentleman in an outdated tux. I greet them affectionately, then offer drinks to them and everyone else.

"Drinks are on the table! Help yourselves!"

A battered old van pulls up and four twenty-somethings climb out—a young man with hair to his waist holding a guitar, a male and a female dressed in neo-hippy attire, each carrying a violin, and a preppy-looking lady lugging a cello. All former students. I shake their hands, thanking them profusely for coming all this way. I can feel my emotions breaking off the leash, running helter-skelter right over the edge of the canyon, and I try to rein them in, but tears are coming. I turn away abruptly: get a grip, man. Keep it together.

* * *

The guests are helping themselves to water and soda and wine, moseying down the rocky trail to the point, and taking their seats. I continue making the rounds, shaking hands, expressing thanks, inquiring about their drive and their lives and their plans for the future.

Up until this moment I've been too preoccupied to appreciate the splendor of the setting, but now that the guests have safely arrived and the dust has settled, literally, I gaze beyond the rocky point where the guests are settling in and remember why we chose this particular spot for our nuptials. On the far side of the mile-wide chasm, a massive sandstone wall twists from east to west as far as the eye can see. Below it, an endless mirage of walls within walls within walls, striped sedimentary layers of red, tan, yellow, and white; some sections as smooth as glass, others like a painstakingly pieced mosaic.

It's a vast mural in stone, a timeless museum of thrones, alcoves, ramparts, obelisks, and cathedrals, intricately chiseled or roughly jackhammered out of rock. I'm thinking, This is the place where, on the seventh day, God turned his royal stone-cutters loose to play, and here is the result. No matter how many times I've stood on this ledge, it still looks too majestic to be real. It's like some ocular illusion designed to inspire head-scratching, mind-boggling human awe. And yet there it is, dwarfing the stately ponderosa pines and the mighty Colorado River that twists through its sheer corridors en route to watering half the state of California.

Two ravens glide and dive playfully in the void separating the North and South Rims. I almost think I could take a running leap into that turquoise expanse and soar alongside them.

An old Toyota Tercel with rust along the wheel wells and the original scarlet paint faded to a murky pink pulls into the parking area, interrupting my reverie. The driver's door opens and a handsome young man with a head of black, slicked-back hair steps out. He's wearing a dark sport coat, a purple shirt, and shiny two-tone shoes: Ramon. He hustles around to the passenger side and, with a tender touch of Old World gallantry, pulls the door open as if for the arrival of the queen. For a moment, I think he might even bow.

Her hair appears first, a shoulder-length shawl of silver-flecked, chestnut curls circled on top with a wreath of tiny flowers. As she straightens to full height, I see a bit more—her shoulders, her upper back—but the rest remains hidden behind the car. She hooks her arm around Ramon's and together they step around the vehicle where I see her, finally, in her fullness: tall and slender in a pale-blue Gunne Sax dress with white boots on her feet and a bouquet of wildflowers in her hands.

From a distance, she could be twenty, the vivacious young flower child I'd met and married thirty-five years ago, except today she looks grim, pensive. Is she having second thoughts? Getting cold feet? Her eyes drift past me and rest on the majestic canyon, holding it a moment before returning to the crowd. And then with a jolt, the dreamer awakens. She thrusts the bouquet into the sky like Lady Liberty and begins waving back and forth, shouting out to me: "Hey, stranger! You made it!" At that moment she looks so damn happy I think she might kick off her white boots, lift her skirt a bit, and come running full throttle into my arms.

"Yes," I deadpan. "I did."

"It's beautiful," she shouts, turning a full circle to take it all in.

I holler back: "Yes! Beautiful!"

She shakes her bouquet at the trail. "Hey, you're supposed to be down there! Bad luck to see the bride!"

"I've already had enough of that."

She cups a hand over her ear. "What? You've had enough of me already today? I just got here!"

I laugh. "Never mind," I say, and I turn and begin the second-longest journey of my life, with Duchess nipping at my heels.

*　*　*

I don't remember much after that—what the musicians play or how Amy ambles down the rocky aisle or what the guests are wearing as the two of us stand shoulder-to-shoulder facing them or the red and gold flowers polka-dotting the point or the minister's brief sermon on the sanctity of marriage or his standard recitation of the wedding vows or our double "I do's" or any lingering regrets about the decades lost and the what-might-have-beens when the two of us were wandering solo. The moment our lips touch, officially sealing the union—or reunion—everyone and everything else vanishes—the musicians, the guests, the minister, the eavesdropping ravens, the pungent flowers, the golden aspens, the canyon's majestic and impenetrable walls—and it's just the two of us, all alone on a narrow outcrop of rock that has become a magic carpet hovering above a bottomless abyss at the fringes of our new life together. Again.

VALEDICTION

Fitz plunks down in the padded booth at Keri's Cafe where I've been waiting, head bowed, brow knitted, trying to make heads or tails of my new cell phone.

"Hey, there you are!" I say, hiding my shiny toy—mostly out of embarrassment, because I'm a bumbling novice while Fitz is a tech savant, especially for our generation.

Fitz glances left, right, then leans forward with a clandestine look, as if he's about to offer his last confession.

"I turned fifty-five yesterday," he whispers.

"Congratulations—but why all the hush-hush, Deep Throat stuff?"

"You know what happens when you turn fifty-five?"

Actually I do. Been there, done that a year ago, but I play along.

"What happens?"

Fitz looks remarkably youthful today—there's not a wrinkle on his cherub cheeks or a fleck of gray in his bristly, brown hair. By contrast, the threads of gray in my beard have turned winter white.

Fitz smiles, his blue eyes as cool as poker chips. "When you turn fifty-five," he says, "sex is like playing pool with a piece of string."

He laughs, and normally I would too, but not today.

"The maintenance guys at the high school split a gut when I told them that," Fitz says. "They said, 'Come on over and we'll shoot it with some lock-freeze!'"

He laughs again, waiting for me to do the same, and I halfheartedly oblige.

"You all right?" he asks.

"I'm fine."

"You don't look fine. You look like you're going to the electric chair, not like someone who's retiring in a week. You having second thoughts?"

"No, no, it's definitely time."

"Is it Amy?"

246 | *Just a Teacher*

"She's good."

"I know she's good—she's great. But how does she feel about you riding off into the sunset while she's still slaving away in the classroom?"

"She's excited for me—at least that's what she says. She has three more years till retirement, but she'll probably work another twenty. She loves those kids. She just doesn't want me to turn into a retirement zombie—you know, wandering aimlessly around the house all day looking for crumbs in the corner, rearranging socks in the drawer."

The waitress—a ponytailed thirty-something with a cheerful smile—glides up to our table and asks us how we're doing this morning. I order the California Special—eggs benedict on sourdough bread with avocado slices and other California things—while Fitz opts for the lumberjack deluxe, a heart-clogging conglomerate of eggs, bacon, sausage, hash browns, and pancakes slathered with butter and maple syrup.

"This is on me," I say, smiling, but my eyes are darting from the Southwest kitsch decorating the north wall to the window to the east where tourists in summer attire are sauntering by.

"So what are you going to do with all that spare time?" Fitz asks.

"Lots of stuff—projects and stuff. No worries there."

"How are you feeling—about retirement and all that?"

I take a packet of fake sugar, tear off the corner, and pour the granules into my steaming mug of coffee, stirring it vigorously. I usually take it straight black, maybe with a few drops of cream. Twenty seconds pass.

"Todd?"

*　　*　　*

Our orders arrive, sparing me from giving an immediate response. Instead of consuming my meal like a hungry bear with a healthy appetite, I nibble around the edges, eventually devouring it by a thousand tiny cuts and bites.

An hour will pass before the entire meal is transferred from the porcelain plate to my belly. During that time, I'll talk about my sister, Dottie, the elementary teacher who retired after four decades of loyal service with a hero's sendoff that included gifts, cards, accolades, and a full-page write-up in the local newspaper. I'll speak about the swift kick-in-the-ass bon voyage I'm expecting from Robert Brubaker… but not too much. I'll say—twice—that I don't want to wallow in self-pity, although I'm doing exactly that. Eventually, however, I'll answer Fitz's question: "So how are you feeling?"

"Seriously? I feel like a World War II bomber pilot who just made his final run. I feel like I finished my last mission and escaped with my ass."

When Fitz asks, "Why do you say that?" I'll talk about another teacher, a woman in distress I met many years ago while working as a guide on the river. I'll tell him what a class act she was and all the things she'd done for so many people—kids, sure, but adults too; just a real salt-of-the-earth, give-you-the-shirt-off-her-back kind of lady. Underpaid—hell yes, underpaid, but she never complained about it. Never complained about anything except, briefly, about the husband she put through law school working double-shifts, just to be dumped for some California beach bunny. The only silver lining was a decent divorce settlement that enabled her to move to an obscure town in northern Montana where she changed her name, got a job at the local elementary school, and made a beautiful new life for herself.

During the telling of this tale, Fitz will listen intently, genuinely interested albeit confused as to what this has to do with me, a soon-to-be-retired teacher, or why I'm feeling like a bomber pilot who's just slithered through the jaws of death.

Eight days later I'll lock up my classroom and make the final walk to Brubaker's office. I'll listen to the ghost echoes of teenagers crowding the hallways, slamming lockers, hustling to class, and making out under the stairwell. I'll chat briefly with Lisa Marguiles and say a final adios to Bob Garcia the custodian. I'll hand my keys to Brubaker, who'll accept them as if I'm the random UPS man or the pizza delivery guy, minus the tip. Then as I'm walking out the door for the last time, a hundred steps from freedom and euphoria, he'll insert the knife, slowly, with a twist.

FLIGHT

Iglance up from the papers I'm grading and check the clock: 4:10. She's chickened out. The last of the buses pulled out forty minutes ago. She's on board, almost home by now. Maybe. Give her ten more minutes.

At the top of the paper, I print 15/20 in red ink, scribble "Good work!" and add a smiley face. I snatch another paper from the stack and begin to read, but my brain is galaxies removed from the mostly pedestrian meanderings of my ninth graders about the effects of invasive species on a riparian ecosystem. In fact, I'm mostly killing time. I check the clock again: five more minutes and I'm out of here.

Then I hear her voice—faint, weak, apologetic. Jennifer.

She's standing in the doorway, her willowy body filling a fourth of the frame. Arms crossed, pressing her notebook against her chest like a life jacket, her flimsy cotton dress drooping unfashionably to the bottoms of her knobby knees. Looking like she did earlier that morning except for a ghastly green sweater, unbuttoned in front, that has Salvation Army stamped all over it. Her ash-blonde hair is divided at the middle of her forehead, sloping either way to frame a delicately freckled face shaped like a heart that's been routinely broken.

"Jennifer!" I spring out of my chair, trying to appear calm, confident, and excited, although I've been second-guessing this all afternoon. Only now do I realize just how deeply relieved I would have been if the clock had struck four thirty and that doorway had remained empty. She looks so young and fragile and afraid.

I smile big, trying to reassure both of us.

"Does anyone know you're here?"

She replies with the inimitable Jennifer Abernathy head shake, a barely perceptible, five-degree rotation to the left and right.

"Did you tell anyone?"

Another head shake.

"Jennifer?"

"No," she whispers, a little annoyed.

Now look who's the chicken-shit. This was my idea, not hers. Pull it together, Todd. Put up or shut up.

I try another overbearing smile. "All right then, this is what I need you to do. I want you to turn left and walk straight down the hall and out the back exit. That'll put you in the parking lot. My vehicle's the root beer–colored truck. It's parked in the second row as you come outside. Most of the teachers should be gone by now, so it should be really easy to spot."

Jennifer's pale-blue eyes seem to glass over. She looks drugged.

"Jennifer, are you OK?"

She nods slowly. If I give her a choice now, she'll probably bail. I could drive her home before her father returns from work with strict instructions never to utter a word of this business to anyone, and we could both walk away unscathed. Then I look at those spindly shoulders and fragile bird bones that her father's grizzly-bear paws could crush like balsawood. Unscathed? Speak for yourself, Todd Hunter.

"Jennifer, I need you to listen to me very carefully. Will you?"

Her eyes narrow sharply as her head dips and lifts an inch.

"Go out to the parking lot like I said. Check around to make sure no one's there. It should be empty, but just in case. When nobody's watching, open the door of my truck and get inside and wait for me—can you do all that?"

She nods grimly. I may as well be giving her directions for jumping off a bridge.

"Good. What color's my truck?"

"Root beer," she says.

"Yep, root beer. When you get inside my truck, lie down on the seat, OK? Just lie down on the seat and wait for me. I'll be there in about ten or fifteen minutes."

"OK," she whispers.

"All right, go ahead. Down the hall and out the exit."

I linger in the doorway for a few seconds, watching her wraithlike body drift a dozen yards down the hall before ducking back inside. I'll give her fifteen minutes, just in case someone's within eyeshot of the parking lot.

I pluck another student analysis from the stack.

*   *   *

My eyes keep flitting back to the wall clock where the long, black minute hand seems permanently stuck. Come on, you bastard. Move! Move!

I re-read Tom Bauer's paper three times, but it still doesn't register because my mind is speeding through the horror house of possibilities, most of which could land me in jail. I've got no legal defense for what I'm doing.

"Mr. Hunter?"

My head jerks around and my hand—the one clutching the red pen—draws a nasty, blood-red scratch across Tom Morrison's over-simplified analysis. I'd recognize that groggy, baritone voice in a Category 5 hurricane. In the time it takes to set my pen on the desk, I wipe the worry from my face, replace it with a salesman's smile, and turn to greet my unexpected guest.

"Mr. Jackson!" I say, smiling too cheerfully for the occasion. Tone it down, Todd. Sherlock will start sniffing if you start playing too nice.

"I'm glad I caught you," Melvin Jackson says. "But it doesn't surprise me. You've never been a clock-watcher like some of these assholes."

That's about as close to a compliment as I'll get from Jackson, so I'm wondering what's up his sleeve.

"You got a minute?"

"Actually, I've got to go rob a bank!" I laugh and, fortunately, so does he. "What's going on?"

"Take a look at this!" Jackson strides across the room and slams a sheet of paper covered with official-looking print on my desk. I skim the document without touching it. I'm not sure why. Maybe I don't want to leave fingerprints. In some convoluted way, the document is now evidence.

It's a memo from the superintendent notifying principals and other administrators of a projected budget shortfall of $550,000. To make up the difference, effective immediately: all purchase orders have been suspended, as well as all travel unless personally approved by the superintendent. Each school is supposed to earmark cuts totaling 10 percent of the school's total budget. The memo concludes with five words: *WE ARE IN CRISIS MODE!!!!*

"What do you think?" Jackson says.

"I think it stinks," I say. "How did we suddenly come up half a million short? Whose mistake was that?"

"That's what I said!" he fumes, downshifting into his vernacular. "Why should we have to pay for his dumb-ass mistake?"

"What are you going to do?"

"Well, I've gotta talk to the faculty. Sooner rather than later, you know, before the shit hits the fan."

"I think that's probably already happened."

"I know, but I've got to break the fall, calm the troops—let them know everything's going to be all right."

I glance at the clock: 4:35. Cut to the chase, man, cut to the chase.

"How can I help?" I ask, almost wincing, fearing some three-hour project while Jennifer expires on the front seat of my truck.

"Thanks for asking," Jackson says as he slides onto a lab stool. He fans five sheets of line-ruled paper on the counter. Each sheet is covered with a frenetic blend of words, numbers, dollar signs, and lots of angry scribbles and exclamation points. As he walks me through each page of proposed cuts and subsequent savings, item by item, I keep checking the clock, where the minute hand hasn't just risen from the dead but also gulped a handful of amphetamines, tick-tick-ticking as if marking seconds rather than minutes. I mostly nod and uh-huh, uh-huh, occasionally asking an innocuous question to show him I'm still on the bus.

"Does anyone want a reduction in hours? I heard Mrs. Lucero was interested in going part-time?"

"Good! That's good!" Jackson says, but it's an hour before he finally gathers his papers, shakes my hand, and shows himself the door.

"I appreciate this, Todd," he says. "I really do! We may have our differences, but I respect your opinion. You think they'll be OK with this?"

"Of course they will! You've got a great staff—all of them, top to bottom."

"I do, don't I?"

"You bet."

Jackson's stuck in my doorway like a Christmas guest lingering into New Year's. "We're cleaning up the super's mess, you know?"

"I'm sure it is."

"You know what'll happen if this hits the paper?"

I swallow hard. "Oh, yes. Absolutely." Every word out of Jackson's mouth carries a self-inflicted irony.

"Better to get ahead of the story, you know."

I nod. The sterile face of the clock seems to mock me: twenty minutes to six. Good luck making it to Winslow unless I've got a rocket in my hip pocket.

"Thanks again, Todd. You really think this is good the way I've got it?"

"I think it's great! Right on the money!"

Jackson grimaces. "We'll find out tomorrow, won't we? The good news is, no one's getting canned. Not at my school. Not on my watch."

"No, sir. Not on your watch."

Jackson gives me a double thumbs-up and steps boldly into the hall. "I owe you one, Hunter!"

My voice chases after him: "Glad to help!"

*   *   *

I wait until the heavy footsteps have faded down the hall. Then I hastily gather the loose papers into a single stack, hit the lights, shut and lock the door, and beeline for the parking lot.

My truck's the only vehicle left except for Jackson's gleaming white Lincoln Continental harbored like a luxury yacht under a trio of security lights at the far end of the lot. The sun has just set, and night is settling in. As I approach my pickup, I mutter a muffled expletive because I can't see Jennifer's silhouette in the cab. I continue my string of soft expletives all the way to my vehicle, nursing the faintest hope that just maybe this fourteen-year-old kid followed my instructions and is curled up on the front seat patiently waiting for me. With the doors locked.

"Trust me, Jennifer," I whisper. "I'm coming. Trust me."

But as I near the driver's side, my heart sinks: No Jennifer. No notebook. No note. No nothing but an empty, super-size coffee cup.

"Dammit!" I bang my fist on the hood. "Fine then! Just fine!" I climb into the cab and yank the door shut, sending a shudder through the windshield. I fire up the engine and roll out of the parking lot and onto Elm Street. Now I've got a missing kid, and it's dark. What do I do? Go to the cops? Go back to school with my tail between my legs and throw myself at the mercy of Melvin Jackson? Confess the whole damn mess and then what? He could probably pull some strings to get me off the hook, but I'd be his bitch till doomsday. No, I'm too deep into it now. Too many arrangements, too many bridges already crossed and burned. Shit! Shit shit double-triple-quadruple shit!

Instead of turning right to head for the main highway, I head for home. At least there I can regroup, rethink, figure out something maybe. It's while I'm idling at the first traffic light that I notice an unusually large, smooth, and alien hump under the ragged horse blanket that usually rests in a jumbled heap in the bed of my truck. I flip on my blinker and pull off onto the first semi-deserted establishment in sight, which happens to be a bank. The bustling hive of activity by day looks like a cemetery now.

I drive around to the back and climb out. The hump is moving ever so slightly, a tiny bit up, a tiny bit down, almost mechanically.

"Jennifer?"

No response.

I pinch a corner of the blanket and slowly pull it back, revealing a head of ash-blonde hair tucked into a curled-up torso, like a giant seahorse.

"Jennifer, it's OK. You can come out now."

She lifts her head, bug-eyed, like a child seeing snow for the first time.

"Why didn't you just stay in the cab?"

"I had to use the bathroom," she says. "I guess I locked the door. It was an accident." She's looking down, ashamed, tilting back a bit, away from my hands which I promptly stuff inside my pockets. "When I got back, the door was locked. I'm sorry. It was an accident."

"It's all right."

Half-swaddled in the dirty blanket where I store my tools and hunting gear, she's crying. "I didn't mean to."

"It's OK. Come on—let's get you out of there."

Struggling to her feet, she looks so damn fragile. I lower the tailgate and help her down.

I check my watch: five fifty. "Climb in, kid! We've gotta make tracks!"

*   *   *

It takes ten minutes to drive across town, but soon we're flying east down Route 66. I instruct Jennifer to curl up on the bench seat and keep her head tucked, just in case. I can't risk any witnesses, and I don't want any messy explanations. The speed limit's fifty-five, and the highway patrol will usually gift you another five before flashing you down. But I'm doing a hair under eighty, racing double-deadlines: the bus leaves Winslow at seven and my alibi—a volleyball game back at the junior high—starts at eight. Winslow is fifty-seven miles from town. I can't get a speeding ticket, but I'm rolling the dice. If a cop pulls me over, there will be all kinds of nosey and incriminating questions about the girl and where I'm driving her like a bat out of hell. I may as well stick my hands out and say, "Cuff me, officer." Or: "Kick me, I'm stupid!"

I try to appear calm, but my armpits are soggy with sweat. Every time I pass a car, I wince in fear that the driver's snooping eyes might see something suspicious sitting next to me. The odds are slim to none, but my hands grip the steering wheel as if I'm trying to strangle it.

The tall ponderosas soon give way to scrub pine—pinyon and juniper; Cro-Magnon silhouettes crouching along the freeway. Within another ten miles, the trees disappear, and we're cruising an ocean of blackness blighted by a tiny oasis of lights: the cow town of Winslow.

As we approach the lights of Winslow, I review the plan one last time with Jennifer.

"You're going to Great Falls, Montana. There'll be lots of stops along the way, so plenty of breaks. Make sure that when you get off the bus for a break, you get back on the same bus. Remember your bus number, because they all look alike. When you arrive at Great Falls, wait at the station. It'll be late afternoon. A woman will meet you. She's fiftyish, kind of a cowgirl-looking lady. She'll be wearing blue jeans, a red-checkered shirt, and a cowboy hat. Her name's Claire. She's a good friend. Don't worry, she'll find you. She's going to ask you your name, and what will you say?"

"Connie," Jennifer says.

"Connie what?"

"Connie Altman."

"That's right, Connie Altman. That's your new name. If anybody ever asks, just tell them you're Claire's niece."

"For how long?"

"Forever," I say.

At five minutes to seven, we pull into the bus station—a modest building the size of a convenience store with a single row of plain, vinyl chairs and a scratched linoleum floor. I hustle Jennifer inside and invite her to take a seat. A Navajo woman in a bright red velveteen blouse and a squash blossom necklace occupies the chair at one end, and a young man in jeans and cowboy boots sits at the other end. Jennifer sits midway between them.

I go to the window and purchase a one-way ticket from a woman who yawns when she asks what I want and never looks me in the eye.

I hand Jennifer the ticket with a warning: "Guard that puppy with your life."

She nods.

"What's your name?"

"Connie Altman."

"Who are you looking for?"

"Claire."

"Where are you going?"

"Great Falls."

"What's my name?"

"Mr. Hunt—"

I wag my finger in her face. "What's my name?"

"I don't know. I've never seen you before."

I smile. "Good. Perfect."

Removing two twenties from my billfold, I clasp them in Jennifer's cupped hands. "This is for food and snacks and things."

The Navajo woman and the young man stand up and amble toward the glass door.

"Looks like your bus is ready," I say. "Are you all set?"

She nods.

"Scared?"

She shakes her head, but her lips are tense and her eyes are beginning to water.

"You'll like Claire. She's a lot of fun."

I smile, recollecting her cheerful belly-laugh on the phone. I'd asked for a big favor and she'd called it "manna from heaven." She'd always wanted to be a mom, and this was her chance. Too bad I'd never know the outcome.

"You can never contact me," I'd told Claire.

"Of course. I understand."

"I mean never."

"Then this is goodbye?" she'd asked.

"Yes. And Claire?" I'd paused to swallow the catch in my throat.

"Thank you."

*   *   *

Now *I'm* starting to tear up as I look at Jennifer, who's staring at the gum stains polka-dotting the linoleum floor. I want to wrap my arms around her and transfer whatever remains of my confidence, bravado, and wisdom to this frail little matchstick girl, but right now I'm running on empty. Instead, I hold her hand briefly, gently, and tell her everything's going to be fine. And as she passes through the door and takes her first bold step into her new life, I close my eyes and try my very best to believe it.

THE THINGS I TAUGHT

I taught them math and science. To be more exact: biology, life science, earth science, physics, chemistry, algebra, geometry, trigonometry, calculus, statistics. I taught them about life zones, plant associations, cells, tectonic plating, volcanism, alluvial fans, atomic weights, the elements. I taught them about fractions and integers, sines and cosines, algorithms, coefficients, the Pythagorean Theorem, geometric proofs. I taught them all the required stuff—the state standards, the district-adopted curriculum, and whatever else my higher-ups deemed essential for an educated young adult to know before we launched them out into the cold, cruel world. I taught them all of that, and I tried to teach them more. So much more.

I tried to teach them about the beauty and blind justice of numbers. Numbers are forever faithful. Numbers don't lie. Numbers don't cheat. Numbers don't stab you in the back. If they break your heart or neck or spirit, the numbers aren't the villain but some human act or natural event—betrayal, theft, assault, tornado, volcano, hurricane, typhoon. If your team loses 13–10, the fault, dear Brutus, isn't in the numbers. Score another touchdown and you win.

Don't blame your team's ineptness on the integers; blame their porous offensive line and lead-footed quarterback. Numbers are pure, constant, undeviating. If A=B and B=C, then A=C. Always and forever. No exceptions. But numbers can be manipulated. Ask Mark Twain: "There are lies, there are damn lies, and there are statistics." So I taught them about the laws of probability, how gambling in Vegas or Laughlin or any of the million roadside casinos that have sprung up like wildflowers all over the country is a losing proposition: you may get lucky for a moment, but in the end, the house always wins. And then I showed them why.

I tried to unmask the mysteries of planet Earth, how the great canyons, rivers, mountains, and oceans were forged by wind and rain and fire and time, for utility, yes, and Darwinian survivalist stuff, but for variety too. And beauty! Pure unadulterated beauty! Otherwise the entire planet might have looked like the Mojave Desert! For my religious students, the elements (wind, rain, fire, ice) were God's instruments to hone His handiwork. For nonbelievers, it was pure if random science. I closed no doors and left all the windows open, with screens to keep the pesky mosquitoes out. It had to make sense. It had to be verifiable. Provable. Science.

I taught them about the human body and its diverse and complex systems—digestive, circulatory, skeletal, cardiopulmonary—how they were all controlled and coordinated, voluntarily and involuntarily, by this remarkable computer permanently lodged between our ears called the brain, and how we only use a fraction of its capabilities. It's a computer with a million programs, but most of us only turn on a handful. I taught them about that relentless, never-vacationing, never-napping, never-stopping miracle machine, the human heart, how regardless of the weather or your mood or the size of your bank account it just keeps pumping and pumping and pumping. Gallons, buckets, barrels, an ocean of blood in your lifetime. As long as you take care of it and don't clog up the plumbing with French fries and bratwurst or, worse, street drugs that will turn it to tissue paper over time. Then one day, you'll blow a valve and end up in the hospital, if you even make it that far. Which is why you've got to take care of that baby: sleep, diet, exercise. The holy trinity of the human heart.

I taught them about phyla and kingdoms and species relationships and how all living things are interconnected. We're all in this together, cohabiting this little blue marble floating in outer space. I taught them how one person's careless discarding of a cigarette can burn a city or a forest to the ground, and then I took them up the mountain and showed them the blackened wasteland where it had actually happened, right in their own backyard. One stupid, careless kid with a cigarette. I didn't preach politics, but I taught facts and figures and explained why they mattered; why we really do need to give a damn about them because they all come back to us personally. We're all in this together, and it's our job to make this world a better place. Better than we found it. We all share the same space, and we can either make it a beautiful vacation resort or a brick shithouse. Our choice. Our call. Our bodies. Our lives. Our planet. Our home.

*   *   *

I had rules, and I made sure everyone knew what they were and just how far they could bend the rubber band before I snapped. And when I did, they all knew it. Sometimes it was humor, other times tough talk. But they listened to most everything I said, even if they didn't always get it. Even if they didn't—in their vernacular—give a rat's ass about the hypotenuse of a right triangle.

Some just wanted to know what they had to do to earn a passing grade, while others asked if it was going to be on the next test. And the most belligerent blocked fake yawns and groaned as if they were in an Inquisition chamber being stretched on the rack: "What does this have to do with the real world?" By "this," they meant just about anything presented in class. "When am I ever in a trillion years going to use any of this stuff?"

To which I would reply: "Well, Karl (or Bill or Susie or Betty or Jackie or whoever), I'm going to teach you everything you'll ever need to know for the rest of your working life. Then I'm going to write you a note excusing you from my class so you'll never have to come here and suffer again. Are you ready? Here you go: 'Do you want fries with that?' Can you say that? Because that's all you're ever going to need to know, where you're headed."

More student indignation. More huffing and puffing and bluffing: "I'm going to tell the principal!" Or the bolder, more privileged ones: "I'm going to tell my lawyer!"

* * *

I taught them. And every so often I'd see a special gleam in a kid's eyes, like gold dust on an otherwise bland and sandy bank. Because teaching was more than doling out information—a book can do that, or a well-trained parrot. Teaching was about lighting a fire—in their eyes, in their hearts, and, in some cases, under their asses. Most would earn a passing grade and hopefully recall enough basic math and science to navigate the day-to-day world and maybe even walk away with a few good memories, but that was gravy. But some—a few—truly caught the vision. They not only saw but embraced the bigger picture, how art and math and science can merge to make magic. To build steeples to the sun, or harvest jewels from the bottom of the sea. To send a voice across the world in the blink of an eye or store the Library of Congress on the head of a pin. To make a baby in a petri dish or put a man on the moon. To change the way we think, feel, talk, laugh, live, and die. That's math. That's science. Art. Poetry. Truth. Beauty. To change the world and then to save it too. Or in the wrong hands—in the hands of evil geniuses—to destroy it. So you need to gain knowledge; you need to learn this stuff. You need to get smart, and then you need to be the good guys, and then you need to take over.

I taught hundreds, thousands, diligently entering grades for each one in my spiral-bound book—grades for tests, quizzes, midterms, finals, projects, presentations. I totaled the points and printed the final grade on a progress report by hand, adding personal comments to each one, even after computer programs did the calculating and grade-entering and tried to completely usurp me and my fellow teachers with a dropdown menu of clichés: *You are a very good student. You make a good effort in class. Your work is unsatisfactory. You need to submit assignments on time.* Yawn. Sigh. Zzzzzzzzz.

I served on curriculum committees (with and without extra pay) and advisory boards. I sponsored a science club and coached the ski team. I chaperoned at school dances, ballgames, field trips, theater productions. On average, each week I spent thirty hours teaching; eight hours prepping; five hours counseling, mentoring, and otherwise trying to keep my students up to speed (academically) and out of jail (literally); five hours grading; three hours researching and keeping pace with my profession so I didn't turn into a dinosaur before my time; two hours in faculty and department meetings; one hour meeting with (usually irate) parents; and two hours monitoring students (in the lunch room, hallways, cafeteria, the bus drop-off and pickup; in good, bad, and absolutely nasty weather), for a grand total of fifty-seven hours a week.

But my best work never showed up on a report card or in a teacher evaluation or in a feature article in the newspaper. My very best work was never performed within the walls of my classroom. Neither was my most heartbreaking.

So I'll go to my grave remembering this: fall 1973, the start of my fifth year at the junior high. I'm a seasoned veteran now with good classes, good students. Things have even improved on the home front. Amy and I have moved into our Dream House and she's sleeping better now. There are fewer nights when I'm awakened by her footsteps pacing the wooden floorboards. The weekly chats with Dr. Knox have helped, and the meds seem to have stabilized her moods. No more exhilarating highs when she'd prance around the house like a wood nymph turned cheerleader, reveling over life's minutiae—the sun sparkling on the grass, hummingbirds orbiting around the feeder, fresh-squeezed orange juice—delighting me with morning kisses and mattress-crushing, midnight love, but I'll gladly lose all that in exchange for dumping the other: those dark spells that struck like a curse and laid her up in bed for a week or more, staring at the ceiling, inert, unresponsive, cloaked in gloom. Now she's more even-keel: no high-highs, but no low-lows either. We've also met with Dr. Knox together, pledging to move forward and not look back. Thus far we've both kept the ghosts and skeletons padlocked in a Houdini-proof trunk in the attic.

So life is good for now; school is good. Home is getting much better.

Then one afternoon the week before Thanksgiving, Melvin Jackson strolls into my classroom during my prep period, and I set down my steaming mug of coffee and close my grade book. He isn't sneering and he isn't smiling.

"I've got a problem," he says. "I've got this kid, a ninth grader—he's a real troublemaker. He's already been suspended twice for fighting and now we're looking at expulsion."

He stands with a neutral face, waiting. I know he doesn't want to ask me for another favor, but I also know *he* knows I'm one of his best teachers. I take a long, slow sip from my mug, set it down on the desk, and whisper, "Send him to me."

The next morning during my prep hour, a rangy kid with streaked blond surfer bangs slinks into my room. He stands with a bent head and fallen shoulders—a self-consciously skewed posture adopted by many junior-high kids who think the NBC Morning News has its full barrage of cameras aimed at the solitary whitehead that erupted on the tip of their nose in the stealth of night. He's wearing the conventional rags of the mid-seventies: faded blue bell-bottom jeans and a tank top. He clutches a wadded-up windbreaker in his left hand. He doesn't look like a fighter.

I'm sitting at my desk outlining a lesson on photosynthesis.

"You're Felix?" I ask without looking up.

He nods.

"Is that a yes?"

"Yes."

I extend my hand and shake his—soft, reluctant, the nails chewed to the cuticles. I push my chair back and stand up. "Follow me," I say, then point to his jacket: "You may want to put that on."

We follow the concrete walkway around to the gravel trail that slopes down to the large pond behind the school. It's sunny but chilly, and Felix finally heeds my advice and snakes his arms into the flimsy nylon sleeves of his windbreaker. A few ducks are cruising around the reeds and cattails, and the morning sun has spread a glossy gold lacquer across the water's surface. A layer of frost sugars the shrubs and grasses. For the next few moments, I stand there, hands on hips, like a monarch proudly surveying his kingdom. This is my legacy. This is my domain. He needs to know that.

"We need a water tank," I say, "for the animals to drink from. It looks like this." I draw a simple plan on my clipboard: a concrete apron in the shape of a fan sloping down into a tank the size of a large casket. "The water will run down the apron and into the tank," I explain. "You'll have to get the material, dig the pit, calculate the measurements—everything. What do you think?"

One thumb hooked in his belt loop, Felix stares at the reeds poking above the dark green water like a thousand periscopes.

"Well?"

He shrugs. He could be handsome, a real heartthrob with those incandescent blue eyes, if he straightened his shoulders and lifted his chin a bit. And maybe scored one iota of success, enough to put some spring in his step to replace that laggard, don't-give-a-damn shuffle. But he needs encouragement, a nudge. I've seen his type before.

"Let me help you with your decision. Can I help you? It's real simple, Felix. It's either this or expulsion. Take your pick."

He looks down, mumbling: "I guess."

I hate mumblers—so lukewarm wishy-washy. "You guess *what?*" I'm getting irritated. I'm the one giving this kid a chance, and I tell him so.

"I guess yes I'll try it," he says.

"Try it or do it?"

"I'll do it!" he snaps.

"Hey, don't do me any favors. If you want to be expelled—"

"I said I'd do it!" It's his turn to get testy, and I like that: a little fire in the belly; a little spirit. And resolve.

"Don't let me down," I say. "I'm putting my ass on the line here."

Yeah, yeah, yeah, his blue eyes reply.

He starts that afternoon in earnest, calling the city building department, half a dozen construction companies, and two funeral homes. By the end of the week, a cement crew foreman agrees to swing by the pond at the end of each day and dump his leftovers—fifteen cubic yards over a five-week period. By week three, Felix convinces the director of a funeral home to donate a casket liner. "You can't sell it!" Felix argues. "Take the tax write-off!" Day by day he grows more shrewd, tactful, and cunning in the workaday world.

And he digs. Pick and shovel work, two hours a day after school.

Occasionally I sneak out back to watch him laboring in the elements—wind, snow, sub-zero cold. His long, lean arms slowly raise the pick above his head, then slam it down swift and hard on the stubborn, frozen dirt, his slender body shivering a bit on contact. There's a split-second break, then he's lifting again. Lift-slam! Lift-slam! Lift-slam! Over and over and over. If he pauses to take a break or look around, I back away, out of eyeshot. This is his project, not mine.

Ten weeks later, the day before Valentine's Day, shortly after the final bell rings and the students have cleared the halls except for a few stragglers fetching odds and ends from their lockers, Felix slips quietly into my classroom. I'm entering daily points, but I sense his presence.

"Yes?" I say, my eyes glued to my grade book.

"I'm finished, Mr. Hunter," he says.

I rise slowly, plunk a porkpie cap on my head, reach for my winter coat, and say, "Let's go have a look."

Felix leads me out the side exit, around back, and down the snow-packed path dipping down to the concrete dam that doubles as a roadway. I follow him to the far side of the pond.

"There," he says, pointing with his chin—pointing with a dispassion I mistake for a mix of humility and fashionable nonchalance.

I shake my head slowly, muttering over and over: "It's beautiful. It's really, really beautiful. It's... beautiful!"

And it is: the concrete apron fans out from a small trickle of water with perfect symmetry, the lip curling down like a concrete tongue to lap water from the casket. With the white winter backdrop, it looks like a mystical construct in a fairy tale.

"Thank you, Mr. Hunter," he says.

"No, thank *you!* This is wonderful! This is beautiful! This is—" I wrap an arm around his bony shoulders and pull him in close, tight, like a proud father bonding with his son. I hold this pose a moment, as if he were my own now.

When I release him, I see that for the first time in that three-month process, Felix Dunaway is smiling. Not a big smile—it looks more like fishhooks have been inserted in the corners of his mouth and suddenly yanked, hard, revealing a flicker of white, but it's a start. It's progress. By all measures, it's a smile.

* * *

I drive home whistling a Bob Dylan song, euphoric. Felix trudges home, sticks a 30/30 in his mouth, and says goodbye the only way he knows how.

That night, I call Fitz and empty my heart. I can't tell Amy because, as good as things are going with her recovery, life's still too fragile. Fitz reassures me it wasn't my fault.

"You did everything you could," he says.

"I could have done more."

"Like what? What else could you have done?"

"I don't know—something. We're teachers. We're supposed to do something."

"We can't fix everything, Todd. I know you think differently, but some kids are just too broken to fix."

"I don't believe that. "

"I know you don't. But it's life. We do our best, but there's going to be casualties, especially in this business. Could you have done more? Maybe, maybe not. Either way, you did a helluva lot more than anyone else for that kid. And sometimes that has to be good enough. Don't ask me why—it just does."

TRANSITIONS

"**L**et it go," Amy says, and I know I should, but I can't. Not like this. Fifteen years have passed since I locked up my classroom and handed my keys to Robert Brubaker. During that time, I've kept busy with a truckload of projects and activities. I built a sauna in our backyard and doubled the size of our vegetable garden. With help from friends, I constructed a large shed to house my snowblower, dirt bike, street bike, and other toys. I set up an archery range at the junior high and supervised some student teachers for the university. I bought an annual pass and skied almost every morning, weather permitting, from December through mid-April. We drove down through Mexico and Central America to the Panama Canal and back, seventy-three-hundred miles round trip. I went bow-hunting in season: deer, elk, antelope, turkey, javelina. With more help from my friends, I replaced the eroding blacktop on my driveway with pavers. Every morning I do twenty minutes of aerobic exercise—just enough to keep my legs fit and my heart pumping—and every afternoon I shoot one hundred arrows at targets pinned to bales of hay in my yard. I accompany Amy to Bible study Wednesday nights and to the Lutheran church on Sundays.

Amy turned in her classroom keys two years after me but wasn't nearly as conflicted about it. She took up watercolor painting and pottery-making and discovered she had an aptitude for both. So now every morning, after a light breakfast of whole-grain toast and homemade yogurt, she slips inside the spare bedroom I converted into her private studio, shuts the door, and doesn't emerge until late afternoon with a canvas or vase completed and a summery smile on her face. For her, retirement has been a simple shift from one passion to another.

I had a much tougher transition. My first year of retirement, I was obsessed with staying busy busy busy all the time. I thought if I slowed down, I'd turn into a cheese-nacho-chewing Jabba the Hutt. So I volunteered for the county literacy program, the local search and rescue team, the national forest's trail maintenance crew, and on and on until my schedule was so jam-packed from dawn to dusk there was no time left for discretionary pursuits. Hobbies. Avocations. Fun.

But I finally learned the power of "no"—or, more gently, "no, thank you." And over time I've gotten used to the slower pace in this greener pasture, not needing to wring the bittersweet life out of every second of every day. Now there's time to sit down at lunch and actually taste the food instead of shoveling it down on the run, as if a lion were waiting to snatch my snack first and me second. If I feel hungry, I eat; if I feel tired, I take a nap. If Amy and I want to see a movie, we drive over to the theater by the mall. If we find an intriguing trip on the internet for a decent price, we book it without wincing or double-checking our bank accounts. We're not rich, but between the two of us there's sufficient to live comfortably and travel a bit without pinching pennies.

There are more family obligations now, but in a good way. Halfway through medical school, Ramon met and married Mandy Alexander, a blonde Valkyrie half a head taller than him, and now they're expecting in June. Our first grandchild—no, grand*children*. The ultrasound revealed twin girls. Amy's ecstatic. Somewhere during our long separation, she discovered Jesus and she thanks Him daily for her many, many blessings, the greatest of which, she insists—is me. I feel the same about her. And I thank God every day for just about everything: Amy, Ramon, my friends, health, home, the ponderosa pine forest that's my backyard and the blue sky above it, meaningful work in a meaningful world.

In mid-August, when the wildflowers bloom and the weedy green fields magically turn into shimmering oceans of gold, I no longer feel the bittersweet rush that signals summer's end and the beginning of a new school year. I no longer flee to the North Rim or some other wilderness to avoid the first-day blues triggered by the sudden appearance of school buses reminding me of the life I left behind. And I no longer feel a stab of pain as I watch the restless exodus of teenagers flood through the doors of the high school like a great dam breaking: youth, with all its eagerness and optimism and lofty aspirations complicated by an ill-timed but God-given hormonal overdose that makes the standard-bearers comic and tragic and everything imaginable in between. They're coming, with suntans and summer tales and plans to make a dent on the football field or the student council or the dating carousel, or a run for homecoming king or queen or the lead in the spring musical. Or maybe they are just trying to survive the day without getting their head shoved in the toilet or trying to do whatever to get enough D's on their report card to punch their ticket out of there. For some, it's trying to get high enough to make it through the day, without getting caught. And for a few, it's feeding a voracious appetite to discover what makes the world tick and why and how they can change it. Fix it. Or there's the rare genius kid who's just marking time, yawning in between watered-down explanations, or the closet dyslexic breaking his butt to fake it through another day.

No more of that in my new life. Not from the inside. I'm an observer now, peering through tinted glass, and that's OK. I toted the torch, and now it's someone else's turn. No more fretting. No more checking in at seven-thirty sharp and saluting sitcom clones like Brubaker. My life's in neutral although I'm busier now than when I was working full-time, the biggest difference being that I can pick and choose my projects, and if I get bored or hassled or fed up I can move on to something else. Life is good; life is great; life is awesome.

* * *

Or so I'd thought.

"Let it go!" Amy says, her voice rising to comic pitch as she rinses off the last of the dinner dishes and sets them on the sink to air dry: with just the two of us, it seems wasteful and silly to load the dishwasher for a handful of plates, so we take turns washing them by hand. Tonight is Amy's night, which means I get to sit back and grouse.

"I know," I say, rising to feed another juniper log into the woodstove. I lower my head near the opening and blow some life into the sleeping white embers, now glowing bright orange. I close the ceramic door, twist the latch shut, and sigh — resignation, surrender. "I know."

On the dining table sits a faux-parchment card cordially inviting me to the dedication of the Gordon K. McDowell Memorial Pond.

Looking at it, I'm reminded of a student teacher I supervised twelve years back. Ursula Schroeder had aspired to become a science teacher, so I'd told her how I tackled the job. When she seemed interested, I explained the history of the Pond Project. Her eyes lit up as I extolled how my students, especially those hardy ones who'd survived my first year as a teacher, proved you can learn science outdoors.

"That's so totally cool!" she'd said. But when I told her the Pond Project had faded while Carson Stubblefield was teaching at the junior high, she decided to go see for herself. Later, she'd asked, "How could they let it revert back to a junkyard? I don't get it!"

"It's a long story," I said. "And complicated."

When Ursula was hired to teach science at Ponderosa Junior High, she immediately resurrected the Pond Project, starting with a massive cleanup effort. It took a good ten years to fully restore the pond to its former state, with a new fishing dock and refurbished learning stations, but once it was completed, Ursula's students successfully petitioned the city council to designate the pond a municipal park, thus placing it under the city's maintenance and protection. In theory at least, the pond would never go to rack and ruin again.

*   *   *

"My pond," I mutter, returning to the present. "Named after Gordon McDowell, that self-serving son of a bitch…"

I've got no proof, but I'm pretty sure Melvin Jackson and Dale Hanagan lobbied to get the city council to christen the park in honor of the late, great war hero.

"That dick did everything he could to sabotage that pond," I say.

"That's true," Amy says, "but what's the important thing?"

"I know, I know. The kids, the community—all the people who ever have or ever will use that overgrown puddle of water."

Amy sets a glass of juice on the granite countertop where I'm now perched on a barstool brooding over the face-slapping news. "Here," she says. "Drown your sorrows in this."

"Pomegranate juice?"

"I can whip up a mean strawberry-banana smoothie if you'd like."

"I'll stick with this. Maybe it's fermented." I lift the glass and down it in one Viking gulp.

Amy's hand slides across my back as she settles onto the padded stool beside me. The floral cushion is one of the dozen projects she's fashioned by hand. Similar knickknacks decorate the house, adding a civilizing feminine touch to my once mountain-man quarters. Instead of the blank walls of bachelorhood, I'm surrounded by wall hangings, fresh fruit suspended in wire baskets, and mini-sermons hand-carved in matching blocks: EAT, PRAY, LOVE.

I lift my empty glass. "Can I get a shot of tequila with this?"

Amy laughs—a response that's instantly therapeutic because I remember all too well those dark days when I would have sold my home and my soul to see her laugh like that.

"You look like you'd need more than one," she says. "How about the whole bottle?"

"I won't say no."

"Look," she says. "It's your pond."

"No. There were lots of people involved. I know that. It's not mine and I don't know why—"

"Pull-leeez! Don't do the false modesty thing."

"It's not false—"

"Todd," she whispers as she takes my wrists and gives them a firm tug like she used to when commanding the undivided attention of an unruly student. "Listen to me," she says, forcing eye contact. "If there was no you, there'd be no pond. It's that simple. And they can call it the Cow Manure Pond or the J.T. Magillicutty Pond or the Holy Snot Pot Pond—it doesn't matter. It's yours, and it will always be yours. You know it, I know it, and everybody that had anything to do with it knows it."

"What about ten years from now, when the people who know me are all dead?"

"So what? Who cares? Fifty, a hundred, two hundred years from now—who cares? Kids will still be going to that pond to fish or stroll around or sit on a bench and watch the sunset or make out with their girlfriend. It's a beautiful place—a gift to this town and everyone in it."

"I guess."

"Good." Amy refills my glass. "Now drink your juice and stop feeling sorry for yourself!"

She's become a lot more like that—direct, unsentimental, pragmatic. A thicker skin too, much less likely to wilt under fire or to dole out false sympathy. Shake it off and get back in the saddle! Hot damn and hallelujah!

*   *   *

So on a warm afternoon in early April, Amy and I join thirty others who have gathered at the south end of the pond, near the dam. Spring leaves are just beginning to speckle the trees my students planted over four decades ago. A mother duck cruises across the glassy, green surface, trailed by eight obedient little ducklings that leave in their wake a replicating pattern of miniature V's. At the north end, a grandfather patiently baits a little boy's hook. Overhead, the sun flexes its muscles, squeezing tears of sap from the mighty trunks of the ponderosa pines.

The six dignitaries are standing with their backs to the pond, with me, Amy, and the other spectators forming a horseshoe facing them. I see familiar faces up front. Melvin Jackson has flown all the way from Florida and Dale Hanagan has descended from his mountain-view palace. The once-stalwart Jackson looks as if he's lugging a refrigerator on his shoulders. He moves with a slow, shuffling gait, and I detect a Parkinson's quiver he tries to conceal by stuffing his errant hand in his suit pocket. I feel a little sorry for him. Hanagan has aged better, although years of sun damage have finally wreaked havoc on his freckled face. His pudding jaw sags and his throat has gone iguana, but the feisty administrator still looks fit.

Jackson speaks eloquently if long-windedly about the pond and Gordon K. McDowell's vital role in making this dream come true. "Without Gordon," he says, "this pond would be nothing more than an idea gathering dust on a shelf."

Amy squeezes my hand as I swallow what otherwise would have been a loud and conspicuous cough.

Hanagan speaks next, extolling Gordon K. McDowell's service to his country and to the city. "We lost a great one," he slobbers, "but now his name will be remembered forever as future generations come to visit this little piece of paradise in the pines."

Then, like a sculptor unveiling his masterpiece, the mayor rips away the black cloth, revealing a bronze plaque embedded in a large cairn of malpais rock. There's a hearty round of applause with cell phones clicking photos as a local reporter scribbles notes.

With Amy leading the way, I shuffle by to shake hands with the big shots. The mayor thanks me for coming. Hanagan says long time no see and asks if I got drawn for elk. I pause to study the portrait embossed on the bronze plate—the broken grin on the rawhide face of the man who at age seventeen had survived one of the deadliest battles in military history. Some folks called him the meanest, greediest man in northern Arizona, but maybe the war did that to him, or maybe he needed that nasty grit all along to survive. I feel some peace and consolation knowing that the honor has been bestowed on a true war hero and not on Melvin Jackson. And yet even there, I experience a partial awakening.

I'd thought time couldn't heal certain wounds, but as I shake hands with Melvin and feel the expiration date in his feeble grip, the ancient hurts and injustices seem to shrivel in my mind. Yes, he sat on his hands while my pet project shriveled and died, but Melvin Jackson also committed his life to making the path brighter and easier for kids. And he'd defend them to the death—there was never any doubt about that. That was Jackson at his best, and there was probably a lot more of that in him than the bit I'd obsessed over. Yes, we'd disagreed over a thousand things—picayune stuff, in retrospect—but he'd supported the pond from the get-go and he'd fought the good fight for a common cause (children, kids, youth) against common enemies: ignorance, discrimination, prejudice, poverty, hunger. And on the big things he was golden. If I ever pitched an idea, however bold or outlandish, he always asked one question: "Is it good for kids? Then, let's do it!" So the Pond Project was born. He wasn't the mother, but he was certainly the midwife.

Melvin Jackson peers up at me now as if through frosted glass, the invisible refrigerator bearing down on his back, and smiles.

"Todd Hunter," he says. "Well, I'll be damned." He grabs me by the arm, pulls me in close, and, in classic Melvin Jackson fashion, he growls: "Your name should be on that damn plaque, not that racist prick."

That makes me smile. Later it will make me weep.

"Thanks, Melvin," I say. "You were the best."

Arriving home that afternoon, I idle at the top of our dirt driveway while Amy retrieves the mail from the box. Most of it is junk addressed to "current resident," mingled with a water bill, a graduation announcement from a neighbor's son, and an advertisement about cremation services. And one shocking surprise.

"Hey, you got a letter from…" Amy holds the envelope at arm's length, squinting; she's left her reading glasses at home again. "It looks like Luxembourg!"

"Who's it from?"

"Do you know a Connie Altman?"

I pull over. "Let me see that, please."

STATE OF THE UNION

Two weeks after the pond dedication I'm sitting in a town hall meeting in the grand ballroom of the Little America Hotel discussing Arizona's public education crisis. There are more than two hundred of us, including representatives from the state legislature and the Department of Education, all gathered around small tables to share our opinions.

Three hours later, I walk out with a feeling of utter futility. The recommendations we developed are fine: more support from the legislature; an increase in the state sales tax by one-half percent with all the revenue going to pre-K through grade 12 public education; an increase in teacher pay. La-de-da-de-da. But is there a single recommendation on that list that hasn't been suggested a thousand times before? Did we really need the charade of a town hall to state the obvious so that now the governor can pound the podium as if he really means it while dishing out more lip service about how children are our future and education must be our number one priority and the buck stops here right now with him, double thumbs to the chest! Meanwhile, he's signing one bill to divert more funds from public education via vouchers and another to eliminate teacher-certification requirements so schools can hire anyone off the street. You speak English? You wanna teach? Hired: honors English! You designed jet planes for Boeing? You wanna teach? Hired: ninth-grade science! You fought in the Vietnam War? You wanna teach? Hired: U.S. history! As if teaching's nothing more than pontificating from a pulpit. I talk, you shut up and listen. I talk, you regurgitate. I talk, and if you don't get it, that's your damn problem. Oh, and here's your big fat F and don't forget to shut the door on your way out. Next victim!

* * *

That sense of futility is exacerbated a few days later when Amy and I go to the wedding reception of a friend of a friend. It's a crowded affair

271

at the Marriott. On the far side of the refreshment table, where molten chocolate perpetually flows from a stainless-steel fountain, I notice two young women who I'm almost certain are former students. Both are dressed in mortician's colors—black slacks, black turtlenecks, black stiletto heels. Long, straight hair to their waists. One blonde, the other brunette. Betty and Veronica! Of course!

They're each holding a champagne glass in the manner of Manhattan sophisticates—too cool for words, let alone this plebian riffraff—and both are stealing glances at me as they whisper between themselves.

As they mature into adulthood, most of my former students see life through the glass more clearly and realize that many of the salvos fired between teacher and pupil were simply defense mechanisms that enabled both parties to survive: the stuff we do so we don't lose our minds and our souls. Nothing personal, on the one hand, and yet profoundly intimate on the other. As adults looking backward, most students better understand the follies of their youth and the methods behind my apparent madness. Exhibit A: Betty and Veronica. After some initial head-butting, they'd really come around, both earning solid B's in my course. In my mind they were success stories—good kids who could have dived off the deep end with no water in the pool but stayed on deck instead. And I like to think I had something to do with that. They were both heading for life sentences in detention when I got hold of them. That's my recollection, anyway.

Which makes what happens next so shocking, at least to me. I wave and smile at them like an old friend. Betty looks at Veronica, and Veronica looks at Betty, and in perfect synchronization, like a pair of well-trained Rockettes, they each raise a middle finger and answer me with an emphatic two-fingered salute.

I turn away, reminding myself that even the very best at their craft are far from perfect. Michael Jordan missed half his shots. Hank Aaron failed seven out of ten times at the plate. And I've seen enough of the unsavory side of humans to know that even the grand Creator of all things sometimes misses the mark. Still, Betty and Veronica's little demo hurts much more deeply than I want to admit. I'm left wondering how many more of my former students would react that way, given the opportunity for split-second revenge? The thought nags me for the rest of the night and through the weekend.

*   *   *

Monday morning, I run a few errands downtown. Then, on a whim, I detour through the university. I think I might stop by the biology building and say hello to some old friends, and maybe swing by the new aquatic center. My timing's good. It's almost midsemester, so the back-to-school hustle and bustle of late August has simmered to a businesslike migration of students marching from building to building.

But the intimate little campus that was once a teacher's college in a sleepy mountain town has burgeoned into a sprawling mass of multistory buildings and parking lots. The growth has occurred almost imperceptibly, a little here, a little there, twenty, thirty, forty years' worth, until one day—today—I stop and look and say, "What the hell?" The once-iconic view of the peaks has been completely obliterated by academic high-rise.

Change of plans. I park my truck in the lone visitor's space outside the College of Education and enter through the imposing front door, not one bit certain what I'm looking for. After the town hall charade and my encounter with Betty and Veronica, I've got an itch and I need to scratch it. That simple.

I'm surprised by the lack of activity at ten in the morning. The large, vaulted foyer is empty and silent, almost morgue-like except for the squeaking wheels of a custodian's cart. I pass quickly through the room and divert down one of two long hallways. Most of the faculty offices are closed. Posters advertising conferences or symposia plaster the walls and bulletin boards, with an occasional inspirational quote or a cartoon from the *New Yorker*. Through an open door I hear a Xerox machine laboring away. I saunter past a large board that displays, alphabetically, the smiling mug shots of the faculty and staff, about three-fourths of them female. Beside it stands a trophy case featuring books and articles recently published by faculty, ranging from the pragmatic ("The Efficacy of the Ravens Progressive Matrices as a Measure of Giftedness in Minority Populations") to the esoteric ("The Re-colonization of Second Generation Yaqui Children in a Southwest Border Town") to the seemingly absurd ("The Role of Finger-painting in the Accelerated Cognitive Development of Preschoolers").

I peek through an office door that's slightly ajar and spot a man having a stare-down with his computer monitor. He's dressed for casual Friday although it's Monday morning: jeans, an aqua-blue golf shirt, and New Balance sneakers.

"Excuse me," I say, rapping my knuckles lightly on the door.

He looks up, a bit irritated, as if he's on the verge of discovering the cure for adolescent apathy and I've just hijacked his Muse.

"My name's Todd Hunter. I'm a former science teacher for the school district. I was wondering if you had a minute?"

He nods politely. Plaques, diplomas, and framed certificates cover one wall of his cramped office; the opposite wall is a giant bookshelf stuffed with academic tomes. Squeezed in between the bookshelf and the vanity wall is a desk with a padded chair he currently occupies, and a small, hard-back chair.

"I'm really busy right now," he says, gesturing with both hands toward the computer monitor which, from a distance, appears to be displaying the front page of the local morning paper.

"I'm writing a book," I say, "about education."

"That's nice," he says. "Good luck with that."

Actually, I'd made the decision to write a book a year ago, when 40,000 teachers dressed in red T-shirts marched on the state capitol building to protest low wages and lack of adequate funding for K-12 education and got a slap in the face from several politicians, who called them selfish, self-serving agitators who were using children as hostages. "They just don't get it!" I'd thought. "They don't have a clue!"

So when the professor says, "I'm busy right now," it's a swift kick in my butt to get on it.

However, I don't want to be a nuisance or one of those has-beens who sits in a rocker scribbling angry letters to the editor and pining for the good old days. He's a working man; I'm retired. My time has come and gone; he's still swirling around in the whirlpool. I'm old news; he's making it. Or maybe not. Maybe he's just collecting a paycheck while reading the morning paper. I wrestle the empty chair out from the far side of the bookshelf and plunk myself down.

"Could you answer a few questions?" I ask. "I've got a few questions."

Actually, I do and I don't. I can certainly make some up. No notepad, no pencil, no tape recorder. Just me in all my blue-jeaned, flannel-shirted, just-got-back-from-Home Depot, quasi-lumberjack-looking glory. No wonder he doesn't want to give me the time of day. Maybe if I hold up a cardboard sign: WILL TEACH FOR FOOD.

"I'm really busy right now," he says. "Maybe later."

"Like in an hour or two?"

"No, I'm really busy today. Maybe in a few weeks."

"I'm writing a book."

"Yes, you already said that. Good luck."

"And you already said that."

"I'm really busy."

"And that too."

He gives me a martyr's smile, as if his best friend's just stabbed him in the back. "Well, good luck," he says. He rises, hand extended, directing me toward the door, but I remain seated.

"I'm sorry I can't help you," he says. He's standing beside me, waiting.

I stand and mash my porkpie cap back on my head. "I'm going to write a book," I say, "and you're going to be in it!"

"That's very nice," he says. He's treating me like a homeless person now. Any moment he's going to slip me a card with the name and address of the soup kitchen.

"Have a good day," he says. "And good luck with that book!"

*   *   *

I amble down the long hallway, through the eerily vacant foyer, and out into the open air. I stroll around to the sunny side of the building, sit down on a concrete bench, and let the sun work its autumn magic. For the first few minutes I simply admire the peaks where fall colors have interwoven arabesques of red and gold into the towering triangle of forest green.

But then I start pondering—who does that guy think he is, anyway? Doesn't he realize that no one in the state wants to be a teacher anymore? And if no one wants to be teacher, who needs a College of Education? Doesn't he get it? He's Nero, fiddling with his computer while public education goes up in flames! Where's the sense of urgency? That building's a damn ghost town!

I decide to do a bit of impromptu field research to prove my point. It's 10:35 when I start counting the students trickling in and out of the education building. By eleven, I've counted six going in, four coming out, data that tell me absolutely nothing. So I take a different tack and call out to a young man wearing a Pink Floyd T-shirt with a backpack slung over his shoulder and his nose in his iPhone.

"Hey, can I ask you something?"

He stops and lifts his head, confused and disoriented, as if someone's just pelted him with a snowball. He glances over at the concrete bench and sees an old-timer: irrelevant and innocuous.

"Sure," he says.

"What are you majoring in?"

"Secondary ed."

"That was my major. Can I ask why you chose it?"

He shrugs. "Well, I started out in poli-sci, but I know it's tough to get a job in that field. So I thought I'd take a few more classes and pick up a teaching certificate just in case—as a backup, you know."

I nod. "Well, good luck to you."

A few minutes later a young woman crosses the parking lot in a baggy sweatshirt and black leggings. I holler out to her: "Hey, can I ask you a question?"

She studies me through her glasses, then approaches warily, as if I'm a tiger in a cage. "OK," she says, keeping a safe distance.

"Are you an education major?"

She ponders this as if it's a trick question. Eventually, with indecision, she replies: "Well... yes."

"Elementary or secondary?"

"Secondary."

"Can I ask why?"

"I don't know. I really love history, but what do you do with a history major? I'm a junior and I figure I'm going to need a job." She shrugs. "So I might as well teach."

"Well, be a good one," I say.

Another ten minutes pass before a young man in a Phoenix Suns jersey and out-of-season sandals shuffles toward me, eyes frozen on his device.

"Careful," I say and he looks up just in time to avoid a collision.

"Oh, sorry," he says.

"No problem. Hey, are you an education major?"

"Yep! Elementary ed."

"Can I ask you why?"

Without hesitation, he replies, "Easy A's." Then he leans over a bit, man to man, adding: "And 90 percent of the students are girls. Not a bad ratio."

"No, not bad. Well, good luck."

I talk with several more students, but each interview reaps the same result: I need a fallback job; easy A's; I've got to pick something; I love... (fill in the blank: history, literature, art, science, etc.). So much for the field trip I'd hoped would lift my spirits.

"Let's get the hell out of here," I mumble to myself. Standing, I notice a young woman exiting from the east side of the building. She's bounding across the grassy quad as if she has springs on her feet. Any moment I expect her to drop her backpack and turn a cartwheel. I can't resist.

"Hey! Excuse me!"

She stops and flashes me a smile that belongs on the front of a Wheaties box.

I cup my hands around my mouth and shout as if into a raging storm: "Are you an education major?"

She nods enthusiastically.

"Why?"

She shouts back: "I love kids! They're the future!" And then she punches her fist through the autumn sky: "Education! Whoo-hoo!"

I have to smile. "Give 'em hell, kid," I whisper, and then I drive home.

JUST A TEACHER

When I trudge up the stairs from the garage and enter the great room, Amy's bustling around the kitchen as if it's Thanksgiving, checking the oven, tending three large pots simmering on the stove, chopping this, dicing that.

"What's going on?" I ask.

Amy looks up from the circle of pampered dough she's sculpting into a piecrust. "Ramon and Mandy are coming for dinner."

I groan, audibly.

"What's the matter? You look like someone stole your Tootsie Roll."

"Nothing," I grumble. "How can I help?"

"Turn that little frown upside down, for starters."

I answer with a shotgun-wedding smile.

Amy rolls her eyes. "That's a start, I guess." She aims her spatula at the cairn of potatoes filling the sink. "You can peel those for me."

"Are you feeding the five thousand?"

"Less talk, more action. They'll be here at five."

I pull a paring knife out of the drawer, grab a potato, and set to work.

Inhaling the medley of spices, sauces, and aromas that make our home smell part gingerbread house and part upscale restaurant, I smile. I can't help myself. It's one of Amy's many virtues—she's an exceptional chef.

"Is that salmon in the oven?"

"Yep." Amy pulls open the refrigerator door, removing three bottles of salad dressing and a half gallon of milk, then shuts the door with a swift thrust of her hip.

"Coconut-crusted?"

Pouring, stirring, sprinkling, stirring: "Yep."

"Is the Queen of England coming too?"

"Nope."

"Then what's the occasion?"

"I don't know. Ramon said he has an announcement for us—a surprise."

Normally, a visit from Ramon and Mandy is a cherry on an ice cream sundae day. Ramon's soft-spoken, respectful, intelligent, helpful around the house, and a good listener who laughs at my jokes and can give it back when I dish it out, although in a more subtle, deadpan fashion. Mandy's his equal: if you want to engage in verbal fisticuffs, she's not afraid to accommodate. And she has a good sense of humor about it; she knows when to jab, when to back off, and when to defuse. Ramon's majoring in premed and Mandy's studying law. The ultimate millennial power couple: a doctor and a lawyer.

"So she can defend all my malpractice suits," Ramon likes to say. "To keep me out of jail."

"No way, José!" Mandy counters. "I'd never have a break. You'd be a full-time job—my only client!"

I like that about them—the friendly banter, the give-and-take. Not like some young couples who seem to take offense at everything from a crossed eye to a slip of the tongue to a bad haircut or a bad joke about a bad haircut.

But tonight… I'm just not in the mood for banter or clever conversation or, quite frankly, surprises, especially if they require me to act joyful and oh so happy for them even if I think they're driving off a cliff. What's the point, anyway? What's the whole damn point of anything?

* * *

Mandy and Ramon arrive a little before five, casually dressed: jeans and a striped pullover for Ramon; for Mandy, a black dress that shows off her six-month baby bump.

We're eating out on the deck tonight. Amy carries a pan of baked salmon, followed by me balancing three bowls—mashed potatoes, mixed vegetables, and a Caesar salad. Ramon and Mandy bring up the rear with platters of fresh-baked dinner rolls, asparagus spears, and Jell-o walnut salad topped with whipped cream.

"*Mamacita*," Ramon gasps. "This is a feast!"

"Only the best for the best," Amy says.

"You shouldn't have gone to all this trouble," Mandy says.

"But she did," I say, "and I'm not complaining." As I reach for the dinner rolls, Amy's eye catches mine, her left eyebrow twitching ever so slightly.

I pull back, smiling. "I'll say grace." I bow my head and offer a short but heartfelt prayer, after which everyone shifts into dinner gear as a smooth and efficient ballet of hands and arms reaches and passes and, at times, intertwines around the little table. The remains of daylight darken and merge with the black silhouettes of the pines, and we can hear the rhythmic thunk-thunk-thunk of Phil Alvarez splitting firewood next door as the frontier fragrance of a woodstove wafts in from down the road. Elk begin picking their way through the woods like four-legged thieves en route to an early evening sip from Johnson's Spring.

After the usual small talk and catch-up, I mention my day at the College of Education.

"I don't know what's going on over there, but one thing's for sure: education's going down the toilet in this state and in this country."

I don't notice, but at that moment Mandy and Ramon trade a split-second look, something between a secret smile and a grimace.

"Did you see today's paper?" Amy says. "The superintendent's getting an 8 percent raise—him and all the other administrators."

"And they're freezing teacher salaries, I'll bet," I say.

"No," Amy says. "Teachers will get 3 percent, but there's a mountain of difference between eight and three."

"Three percent!" I grouse. "Throw the teachers a bone! That's so typical. No administrator should ever be paid more than a teacher." I hold up my fork, which has impaled a generous bite of coconut-crusted salmon, and give it a shake: "Ever!"

Ramon keeps his eyes on his plate like a paranoid inmate in the prison dining hall. Mandy, on the other hand, plucks another dinner roll from the platter, breaks it in two, slathers each half with butter, and takes a bold bite.

"I don't know if that's fair," she says.

Amy's inserting a forkful of salmon into her mouth when she freezes in mid-bite, her eyeballs rolling left to assess my reaction.

"Why do you say that?" I challenge.

"Well," Mandy says, taking another bite from her dinner roll, "if there's a shooting at school or there's a bus accident or some other catastrophe, who takes the heat? Who gets their name in the paper and their face on the news? Who has to answer all the questions and phone calls and deal with the lawsuits and backlash? Whose head's on the chopping block?"

"The building principal's," I concede. "Or the superintendent's."

"Or both," Amy says.

"Well, that's why administrators are paid more," Amy says. "More responsibility, more accountability."

Ramon stares at his plate, Amy holds her breath, and I look at Mandy as if she's just piddled on my newly refinished deck.

Mandy smiles and shrugs. "Just an opinion."

"I hadn't thought about it like that," I say. "Who has more ass on the line? That's a really good point. But I still don't think administrators should get 8 percent when teachers only get three."

I like her moxie—expressing her opinion, not backing down just because she's a guest and the wife and the in-law. She's going to be a go-for-the-jugular attorney.

"I think you're right about that," she says, "all things being equal. Amy, this salmon is to die for!"

And tactful too. That mix of sass and smile.

"Yes, *Mamacita*," Ramon agrees.

"Hey, what's this big surprise Amy's been talking about?" I ask.

Amy stands up and begins clearing the dishes. Mandy rises as well, but Amy motions for her to stay put.

"No, no," she says. "You keep Todd entertained. That's much easier than dish duty."

*   *   *

I manage a lemon-drop smile as Amy squeezes through the partially open sliding door with a stack of plates and silverware. She returns ten minutes later to absolute silence.

"What did I miss?' she asks. "Who died?"

"No one," I say.

"OK, then who's going to die? You three look like a funeral about to happen."

"It's Ramon," I say.

"Yes," Amy says. "What's the grand announcement?"

"He's joining the Army," I deadpan.

"You'd better not!" Amy says. "They'll send you to Afghanistan."

"Tell her," Mandy says.

"I've decided to change majors," Ramon says.

"Really? I thought you were going to med school," Amy says. "That's what you've wanted to do since you were a little boy—since the day I had the flu so bad I couldn't get out of bed. You put your hand on my head and said, 'Don't worry, *Mamacita*, someday I'm going to be a doctor and you'll never have to worry about being sick again.'"

Ramon looks down bashfully. "I was," he says, "but I've been doing some volunteer work—community service. For my major. We have to log so many hours a semester. Anyway, I've been helping out at the high school, kind of like an unpaid teacher's aide. Science classes, mostly. But the teacher—Mr. Nelson—he had this unit on anatomy and physiology. I had some ideas—you know, activities and things to make it interesting instead of the usual stuff, the kind of things that got me interested in medicine."

I nod, trying to show genuine interest. "Tell us what good old Mr. Nelson said."

Ramon smiles. "Actually, he's pretty young. But he—he said, Go for it! So I developed the unit and taught it and the kids really liked it and—well, so did I."

Ramon glances at Amy, then at me, then back down. Mandy's hand slides across the table, covering his.

"I mean, I really liked being up there teaching. There's just kind of a feeling—it's hard to describe. Kids—high-school kids with their hair in their face, acting like they'd rather stand in front of a firing squad than learn about the function of the left ventricle—but suddenly they're talking and asking questions and there's this connection between you and them—teacher and student, almost like you're teaching and learning from each other. So I'm standing in front of those kids and I'm thinking to myself, I love this! This is what I want to do for the rest of my life."

Mandy's smiling as she clutches Ramon's hand; Amy's dabbing her eyes with a paper napkin. I look like a poker player who's just asked for four new cards.

"We wanted to talk to you first," Mandy says. "I mean, I think it's great. If that's what he wants."

"You've got to follow your heart," Amy says. "Follow your dream."

"Yes," I say, "but some dreams pay a lot more than others."

"I know—I totally get that," Ramon says. "That's why we wanted to talk to you first. It's a major step, a big decision."

"What do you want to teach?" I ask.

"Science. High school. Like you."

I wipe my finger slowly across my lower lip, although there's nothing unwanted here. Night has filled in all the bare spots, transforming the forest into a black wall that seems to hold up the stars. An October chill had infiltrated the deck and everything around it. I stand.

"Well, let's go inside," I say. "It's getting cold."

*　　*　　*

As Ramon and Mandy sit on the leather sofa in the den, Amy lights a fire in the wood stove and I excuse myself, returning a few minutes later with three ten-by-twelve envelopes bloated to bursting. Strips of Scotch tape mend the split seams, and STUDENT STUFF is printed in black marker on each envelope.

I sit down on the ottoman and spend the next thirty minutes telling Ramon and Mandy all the reasons why he should no way, under any circumstances, pass up a career in medicine to become a teacher, starting with the horrendous pay.

"Money will always be tight. You're not going to starve, but you'll always fly coach. When you factor in all the hours of lesson prep, after-school meetings, parent-teacher conferences, and grading of exams, projects, homework, and reports, you'll be making five bucks an hour, if that. And you know all the hoopla about teachers getting ten weeks off in the summer? That really means ten weeks unemployed or else working a side job or teaching summer school."

Next, I attack the myth of adulation. "Everyone loves teachers, right? Sorry, Charley. No matter what you do and how well you do it, you'll have administrators, parents, the press, even your students chewing on your ass—not all of them, not even most of them, but enough of them to make your life miserable and to make you doubt what you're doing and why you're doing it. You'll stay up all night designing the coolest activity mankind ever imagined, and the next day your kids will·group-chant you out the door and into the parking lot. 'This is bo-ring! This is bo-ring! This is bo-ring!' You'll teach a concept twenty times, and half your class will fall asleep and the other half will stare at you as if you're speaking in tongues. You'll worship the voice on the phone on a cold winter morning that speaks the sweetest four words in the English language: SNOW DAY! No school!"

Finally, I go after job status and security. "Every year the budget axe will swing too close for comfort. And every year the newspaper will emblazon your school's test scores across the front page—READING, WRITING, MATH. Even though you don't teach those subjects, you and your colleagues will all be judged equally—all tossed into the same fiery pit or exalted on the same pedestal—depending upon how your students performed. And if you teach students who don't look, talk, walk, learn, or act quite like everyone else—students without an academic pedigree or students from the crack house or students who don't speak English—they'll lump them all together and slap a sticker on your chest: FAIL! FAILING! FAILURE! You'll always be damned by those damn standardized test scores. You'll be expected to do more teaching and testing and prepping and training and consulting and mentoring for less money every year. Your workdays will grow longer and public criticism louder. At parties and weddings and family reunions, when people are introduced and everyone else says: I'm a brain surgeon or an attorney or a movie star or an internet mogul or the CEO of Outer Space Enterprises, you'll lower your head and shrug and say, apologetically, "Me? I'm just a teacher."

When I finish my tirade, I expect Ramon to be staring at the carpet, ghost-white, a statue drained of all color and desire to do anything but vegetate until the apocalypse. Instead, he's leaning forward, elbows on his thighs, his chin resting on the apex formed by his twin fists, his dark brown eyes boring into mine, unflinching. A good sign. And an even better sign: Mandy is clasping his hand, smiling.

I reach into one of the envelopes, remove a random item and hand it to Ramon.

"Here, take a look at this."

It's a postcard featuring a dramatic color photo of Griffith Park Observatory in a lightning storm: blinding white pitchforks violating the night sky, their crooked tines impaling the great white dome. Ramon flips the card over and reads aloud:

> Dear Mr. Hunter,
> Greetings from L.A.! I'm visiting my cousin. Today we took a field trip to guess where? Not Disneyland but even better. I should send this to my science teacher for next year but you'll understand. You're the best!
> *Tanya*

"Ninth-grade science," I say. "She was the biggest pain in the ass, and then one day we started the astronomy unit and she fell in love with the stars."

I sift through several other postcards and letters until I locate a letter-size envelope with a cancelled foreign stamp.

"This is my favorite," I say, handing Ramon two sheets of four- by eight-and-a-half-inch stationery, folded into thirds. The first page is covered with cursive and the second displays an impressive black-and-white print of kid art across the top, more cursive in the middle, and a caption on the bottom: *Original Art Work by Marlene Keller Grade 2, "Luxembourg through my eyes."* Ramon flips back to page one and begins reading silently:

Dear Mr. Hunter,

This is LONG OVERDUE! A <u>thank you</u> for all you did to help me become a contributing member of our world. I have been a science teacher for 28 years. I have worked all over the world helping students understand science and inspiring some to enter the field of science and teaching science.

Just to review some of the things you taught me...
-science is a process that is organic, a constant exploration and revision of ideas
-science requires constant reflection
-science can make the world a better place
*And there is always the "boat" to go to if you get tired of what you are doing! (Your sailboat picture near your desk).

You were the first teacher to encourage me to teach, without saying a word about teaching. It took a while for that to sink in, but eventually I got it.

I have been using journaling in my classrooms for 28 years, because you used journals and helped us to "see" science around us. You taught me to be a kind, compassionate educator that cares more about teaching people and less about teaching a curriculum.

Thank you so much for being so inspiring! Your influence carries on, and really is making the world a better place.

And one more thing. All these years I've kept my promise to you and to Claire, but I have to tell you this too. After you put me on the bus, Claire finished out the school year and then we moved to Ammon, Idaho. (It's tiny—you can barely find it on a map.) She thought that was the only way to avoid too many questions. Anyway, five years ago I heard through the grapevine that my father passed away, and we lost our sweet Claire shortly after New Year's. So I think it's safe now. Thank you, Todd Hunter, for saving my life.

Sincerely,

Connie Altman-Keller (aka "Jennifer")

*   *   *

Ramon folds the two sheets into thirds and hands them back to me.

"That's beautiful," he says.

I slip the letter and postcard back into the envelope and set it aside. Then I lean forward, forearms braced across thighs, hands cupped together, my blue eyes like flames fully ignited for this come-to-Jesus moment.

"And that's why you do it," I say. "Not for the money. Not for headlines. Not for the trophy or the certificate or the polished piece of petrified wood with your name on it when you finally call it quits. Not to feed your ego. You do it for the postcard. You do it for the letter. You do it for the kid who some day's going to be teaching villagers how to dry-farm in Uganda or managing a restaurant in San Francisco or raising four kids in Nebraska. You do it to make their lives better, richer, a little more joyful and enlightened. And then you hope to God they take any good thing you teach them and pass it on to the next guy."

I stare into Ramon's eyes and see nothing weak or faint-hearted.

"It's a helluva job—a helluva hard job! But I'll tell you this: getting a letter or postcard like that—it's better than drugs, better than alcohol—so damn much better than self-pity. You read one of those and you're thinking, I've got to get my act together. I don't have time for this, sitting here sulking and what-iffing. Some of those kids are hungry, some are happy, some are born with SUCCESS stamped on their foreheads, others with REJECT red-inked on their ass; some come smiling, others look beaten up and thrown down the stairs. It doesn't matter what's going on in your life—marriage crumbling, sky falling, alien invaders vaporizing the planet. It doesn't matter. You've got to suit up and show up. You're the teacher, so it's all on you. Don't fail them. Don't blame them. Don't bore them. And never ever make them feel less than what they are. And if you can do that—if you want to do that—then by all means, be a teacher, and be a good one. But if you can't, then stay the hell out. We've got enough of those already. I love you, Ramon, you know that. But this is straight talk—no sugar-coating."

I sit up, lean back, and I wait.

Ramon looks as if he's been sucker-punched in the gut. His movie-star eyes are scouring the rugged carpet as if surveying a relief map of his future, with one road leading to the prestigious and more lucrative world of medicine and the other winding in the opposite direction.

"Well," I say, "did I scare you off?"

"No," Ramon says. Looking up, he smiles and whispers the reply I've been hoping to hear, "*Hell*, no."

EPILOGUE

I started writing this book in anger, but I finished in humility and awe. I was humbled by the immense faith and trust parents place in teachers every day as they send their children off to school to be cared for by someone else, a surrogate legally defined as *in loco parentis* but known by the simple title "teacher." I was humbled by the responsibility we assume and the influence we wield over the minds and feelings of impressionable young learners, how we set the tone not just for the day or for the school year but sometimes for an entire life. I was awed by our power and potential to make or break lives; how the seeds we plant, for better or worse, can blossom into mighty oaks and towering redwoods or wither on the vine; how with a look or a word or the stroke of a red pen we can inspire or expunge the hopes, dreams, and aspirations of a lifetime. And I was awed, not by anything I had done personally but by what teachers throughout our nation do every school day, answering the call to uphold that bold, outrageous public-school mantra that unapologetically thunders: *in the United States of America, we teach every child!* Yes, every child, regardless of race, color, creed, religion, sexual preference, culture, native language, or physical, mental, or social disability. It doesn't matter if the kid is Pollyanna or Charles Manson in embryo; Frankenstein's daughter or the next Mother Teresa; charismatic, gifted, obedient, obnoxious, dour, depressed, gleeful, honest, kind, mean, smart-mouthed, compliant, or a natural born hell-raiser. We get them; we teach them. It's that simple. *Give us your tired, your poor, your huddled masses yearning to breathe free. And everyone else, too!* Nothing is more American. Nothing is more human. Teachers don't just touch the future; we shape it, groom it, induce and provoke it. Doctors don't become doctors without teachers. Auto mechanics don't become auto mechanics, presidents don't become presidents. In fact, no one becomes much of anything in this world without teachers. At our worst, we sow the seeds of bigotry, hate, narrow-mindedness, discord, greed, selfishness, and fear of the unfamiliar. But at our best, we cultivate hope, compassion, curiosity, respect, wisdom, generosity, and the relentless pursuit of the impossible dream. And when we do it right, it's one helluva ride.

ACKNOWLEDGMENTS

The authors would like to thank the following individuals who were indispensable to the creation of this book: Rebecca Fillerup, who tirelessly edited the many preliminary drafts and gave the authors encouragement and the book focus and heart; Caryl David, who quietly calmed the storms and provided moral, emotional, and financial support; Julie Hammonds, editor extraordinaire, who asked the tough questions and pruned the wild bush without severing a single limb; and, finally, all the dedicated individuals—from teachers, parents, students, and administrators to cafeteria workers, custodians, bus drivers, and other staff—who make the miracle of public education a daily reality.

ABOUT THE AUTHORS

JIM DAVID

A former National Biology Teacher of the Year, Jim David served 27 years as a secondary math/science teacher and supervisor. An environmentalist with a passion for the outdoors, he founded the Resource Center for Environmental Education (now called Willow Bend Environmental Education Center) in Flagstaff, Arizona. He has assisted the U.S. Geological Survey with endangered species projects in the Grand Canyon and spent twenty summers safely guiding patrons through its majestic corridors via the Colorado River. His long-standing love affair with the canyon continues to this day. He is an avid hunter, skier, archer, cyclist, and storyteller. In 2015, the *Arizona Daily Sun* awarded him Citizen of the Year for his exemplary contributions to the Flagstaff community. He and his wife, Caryl, live in Flagstaff.

*   *   *

MICHAEL FILLERUP

Michael Fillerup is the prizewinning author of numerous short stories, a short story collection (*Visions and Other Stories*), two novels (*Beyond the River* and *Go in Beauty*), and several children's books and published several articles on indigenous language preservation. During his thirty-four-year career in public education, he developed and supervised programs for Native American, Hispanic, and other language-minority children. In addition, he designed and directed two Navajo language revitalization programs and is the founder and former director of Puente de Hózhó Tri-lingual School in Flagstaff, Arizona. He has two passions: writing and saving languages. His hobbies include hiking, cross-country skiing, swimming, kayaking, and theater. He lives in northern Arizona with his wife, Rebecca. Learn more at www.michaelfillerup.com.

ABOUT THE PUBLISHER

Soulstice Publishing took root between the ponderosa pines at the base of the San Francisco Peaks. Our community of Flagstaff, Arizona, is home to Lowell Observatory, Northern Arizona University, the Museum of Northern Arizona, and so much more. This mountain town abounds with scientists, artists, athletes, and many other people who love the outdoors. It's quite an inspiring place to live. Considering the dearth of oxygen at our 7,000-foot elevation, you might say it leaves us breathless. Soulstice was founded by professional editors who enjoy working together and with authors and potential authors whose stories intrigue and move us. We're experienced project managers who love to see good ideas—stories with soul—become quality books.

*   *   *

Soulstice Stories fulfills that same vision for authors and readers of fiction. To "look west" is to dare to explore beyond the horizon. When you look west with Soulstice Stories, you enter creative worlds in which memorable characters face adventures and challenges on their own frontiers.